Praise for the Deep in the Heart of
Texas Series

TROUBLE IN TEXAS

"This trip to Bramble, Texas, brings a close to the mystery of the Cates Curse with humor, romance, heartwarming affection, and some mighty intriguing characters. Readers are in store for some fine surprises and a glimpse at stories yet to be told."   —*RT Book Reviews*

"Katie Lane is a talented writer, who can add humor to her pages...Elizabeth and Brant are interesting characters and there is genuine chemistry. However, the real star of this novel is Brant's brother Beau, and I'm thrilled that he will get his own story."   —NightOwlReviews.com

"Katie Lane writes books that are hotter than Texas in July, and every reader always prays that they will keep on coming."

—The Reading Reviewer
(MaryGramlich.blogspot.com)

"I really enjoyed reading *Trouble in Texas*...The small town feeling with its grudges, history, and eccentric residents was a blast. I spent a lot of my time giggling and wondering what the henhouse ladies were going to do next...Lane has made me very curious about the previous three books, and I want to know what happens next in this series."   —TheBookPushers.com

CATCH ME A COWBOY

MAKE MINE A BAD BOY

"If you're looking for a romance true to its Texas setting, this is the one for you. I simply couldn't put it down."
—TheSeasonforRomance.com

"I absolutely loved Colt! I mean, who doesn't like a bad boy? Katie Lane is truly a breath of fresh air. Her stories are unique and wonderfully written...Lane, you have me hooked." —LushBookReviews.blogspot.com

"Another fun read and just as good as [*Going Cowboy Crazy*]...a perfect example of small town living and the strange charm it has. I really enjoyed reading this one and hope that Katie Lane is writing a third."
—SaveySpender.com

"It will make you laugh, and then make you sigh contentedly. *Make Mine a Bad Boy* is a highly entertaining ride."
—RomanceNovelNews.com

GOING COWBOY CRAZY

"Romance, heated exchanges, and misunderstandings, combined with the secondary characters (the whole town of Bramble), who are hilarious...This is the perfect summer read. Katie Lane has a winner on her hands; she is now my new favorite author!"
—TheRomanceReadersConnection.com

"Entertaining...[with] a likable and strong heroine."
—RT Book Reviews

"Ah, I want my own cowboy, tall, dark, and handsome, but alas he is only between the pages of the book, a good book at that. Katie Lane knows how to heat the pages and keep you burning for more. Romance, steamy love scenes, humor, witty conversation with a twang, all help the pages keep turning. I'm looking forward to reading other books written by Katie Lane."

—BookLoons.com

"An enjoyable romp...a fun, down-home read."
—*All About Romance* (LikesBooks.com)

"I enjoyed this book quite a bit. It really reminded me of an early Rachel Gibson...or early Susan Elizabeth Phillips. Faith became a sassy, intriguing heroine...The chemistry between these two ratchets up to white-hot in no time." —TheSeasonforRomance.com

"Frequently amusing...The lead couple is a wonderful pairing while the third wheel hopefully gets her own tale." —*Midwest Book Review*

Flirting with Texas

Also by Katie Lane

Flirting with
Texas

KATIE LANE

FOREVER

NEW YORK   BOSTON

Forever
Hachette Book Group
237 Park Avenue
New York, NY 10017

www.HachetteBookGroup.com

Printed in the United States of America

First Edition: July 2013
10 9 8 7 6 5 4 3 2 1

Forever is an imprint of Grand Central Publishing.
The Forever name and logo are trademarks of Hachette Book Group, Inc.

The Hachette Speakers Bureau provides a wide range of authors for speaking events. To find out more, go to www.hachettespeakersbureau.com or call (866) 376-6591.

The publisher is not responsible for websites (or their content) that are not owned by the publisher.

*To Joseph Abner—a farm boy,
a soldier, and my daddy*

Chapter One

"EXCUSE ME, BUT AREN'T YOU supposed to be naked?"

Beauregard Cates pushed up his Stetson and squinted at the middle-aged woman who stood in the pool of light from the streetlamp. She wore one of those touristy t-shirts that vendors hawked on every corner and a bright orange visor that would work real well on an elk hunt. She did seem to be hunting for something. Beau just wasn't quite sure for what. He'd been propositioned before—more times than he could count—just not when the woman's husband stood right next to her. A husband who looked as interested in the answer to the question as his wife seemed to be.

"Maybe you have to pay him to take his clothes off." The man held up his digital camera and clicked off a few pictures, the flash momentarily blinding Beau. "Hell, we've had to pay for everything else in this friggin' town."

The woman shot her husband an annoyed look before holding out her hand. "Give me a twenty, Marty. Joan got a picture with the Naked Cowboy, and I'm not leaving New York City until I get one."

It looked as if Marty might argue, but then he stuffed the camera into the bag hooked over his shoulder and pulled his wallet from the back pocket of his high-waisted khaki shorts. "I swear, Laurie," he grumbled. "You'd buy a dog turd if that crazy neighbor of ours brought one back from vacation."

Not denying it, his wife snatched the twenty out of his hand and waved it at Beau. "And could you hurry? We want to get to the Empire State Building before it closes."

Beau had done a lot of crazy things in his life, and regretted very few, but somehow he couldn't bring himself to stand in his underwear in the middle of Central Park while a tourist snapped pictures that would no doubt end up on Facebook. And after the incident in New Zealand, Beau's mama had threatened to yank a knot in his tail if he ever ended up naked on the Internet again. But before he could decline the offer, the woman that he had been following came out of the bathroom.

Except she didn't look like the same woman who'd gone in. The ponytailed blond hair had been tucked beneath a sleek black wig, and her waitressing outfit had been exchanged for a tiny white top and a skirt that showed off a good ninety percent of her mile-long legs. Not that Beau was a leg man. He was breast fed and proud of it. Still, he couldn't help but enjoy the toned calves and smooth thighs. But it wasn't her legs that gave the woman's disguise away. It was the determined tilt of her chin—and the "Think-Green" tote bag slung over her shoulder.

He tried to remember the name he'd been given. *Janine? Jennifer?*

A thump pulled his attention away from his thoughts,

and he turned in time to see Marty rubbing his chest above the thick black strap of his camera bag.

"What?" He glared at his wife. "You're going to get a picture with some naked guy, and I can't even sneak a peek at a streetwalker."

"She's not the Naked Cowboy," Laurie huffed.

"About that picture," Beau said as he uncrossed his boots and rolled up from the park bench, "I'm afraid I'm going to have to give you a rain check." His gaze returned to the woman in the black wig who appeared to be having a hard time walking in her sky-high heels. As she headed down the path toward Central Park South, she wobbled more than Beau's one-year-old nephew, Bobby.

"A rain check?" Laurie sounded thoroughly disappointed. "But we're only here until Monday."

Beau turned to her and pinned on his most brilliant smile. A smile that had gotten him out of more bad situations than he could count. "I'll tell you what. Since you're going to be here this weekend, what about if I leave you a couple tickets for the bull-riding competition at the ticket window of Madison Square Garden?" He glanced over at Marty. "Then you can take dozens of pictures of different cowboys—a few who won't mind at all getting naked for you."

"You ride bulls?" Marty asked.

"Yep."

Marty perked up. "No kiddin'? I didn't figure you for a real cowboy. I just figured that you ran around naked in a hat and boots for the money."

"All part of the illusion that's New York City." Beau tipped his hat at them. "Y'all enjoy your vacation now."

It didn't take him long to catch up with the woman.

She moved a lot slower in the heels than she had in the black running shoes she'd worn when she came out of the restaurant. More than a few times, she stopped to catch her balance and adjust the straps of the shoes. Pointy-heeled shoes that made her legs look twice as long.

As he slowed his pace to keep a few yards behind her, Beau had to admit he was a little confused. Why would a waitress walk to Central Park and change clothes in the bathroom? If she was meeting friends after work, why hadn't she changed at the restaurant? Or why hadn't she just gone home like any normal person would've done after working all day on their feet? It would've made Beau's job a lot simpler. If she had gone home, he would now have her address and would be on his way back to his hotel to cuddle up with the sweet little stock contractor he'd met that afternoon. Not only did Peggy Sue own some damned fine bulls, she filled out her western shirt to mouthwatering proportions.

The thought of Peggy Sue and her abundant twins had Beau tiring of his detective work. He hadn't minded sitting in the bar across the street from the restaurant, shooting the shit with the bartender and eating a double cheeseburger, while he waited for "a tall, skinny gal with blond hair down to her butt" to get off work. But he wasn't about to spend the rest of the night playing Dick Tracy when he had a better offer waiting for him back at the hotel. He had promised that he would get the woman's address, and he would, just not at the expense of his sex life. Especially when his sex life wasn't exactly going as well as he would like.

Of course, it was nothing to worry about. Just a little hitch in his giddyup. A hitch Peggy Sue just might be able to help him with.

On that thought, Beau started to turn around when the waitress suddenly veered off the main path and headed into the thicker foliage.

Well, damn. He didn't know a lot about Central Park, but he didn't think that any park was safe for a lone woman to be wandering around at night. So he mentally said good-bye to Peggy Sue and headed into the trees.

The trail was narrow and much darker than the paved path. In fact, he couldn't see more than a few feet in front of him. The waitress was nowhere in sight. He started to get concerned when a tree branch popped out and struck him in the chest. He stumbled back just as something hit him in the calves, knocking his feet out from under him and sending him to the ground. His shoulder hit first. The same shoulder he'd dislocated a few months earlier while kite surfing in Belize. Gritting his teeth against the pain, he rolled to his back and glared up at the woman who stood over him. From this position, her legs looked like they extended all the way up to the quarter moon that hung in the dark sky.

"Why are you followin' me?" she asked, her Texas twang twice as thick as the stick she poked in his chest. No doubt, the same stick that had his calves throbbing. "Did Alejandro send you to scare me? Well, it's not going to work." She pointed the stick at his nose. "Now, you listen and listen carefully. You go back to your boss and tell him that I'm not going to be intimidated. Especially not by some old, gray-haired cowboy who can't even fend off a girl."

Tossing the stick away, she adjusted her tote bag and wobbled back down the trail.

Beau lay there for a few minutes, staring up at the stars.

Old, gray-haired cowboy?

He sat up and rubbed his shoulder. It hurt like a sonofabitch, but it was nothing compared to his wounded pride. Not that he had anything to be ashamed of. The woman had caught him off guard, is all. Or not a woman as much as some kind of freakish mutant that was a cross between Gwyneth Paltrow and Jean-Claude Van Damme.

It took a while to locate his Stetson. He slapped it against his leg and placed it back on his head. He walked down the trail with every intention of hailing a cab and heading straight to the hotel and Peggy Sue. As far as he was concerned, his detective days were over. But when he reached the paved path, he couldn't help glancing in both directions.

He didn't see the waitress, but a group of kids raced by, four boys in baggy shorts and flip-flops. One passed off a handful of firecrackers to the kid who ran next to him. Beau grinned. Having grown up with four brothers, he knew how much fun firecrackers could be. And how much trouble they could get you into.

Beau's brow knotted. Speaking of trouble, what kind of trouble was the waitress involved in? Who was this Alejandro? And why would he send someone to intimidate a woman? Her aggressive behavior was more than a little annoying, but that didn't give a man the right to bully her. And maybe that was why she'd been so hostile. She was scared.

The thought had Beau turning in the same direction the waitress had been headed. As he walked, he tried to remember her name.

Joyce? Jeanette? No, it was two j names. Jilly June? Jeannie Joy?

Before he could think of her name, he found her. She stood by one of the horse-drawn carriages that were parked next to the curb, talking with a driver who wore one of those ridiculous top hats. Or not talking as much as flirting. She was laying it on thick, giggling and touching the man's arm.

Maybe Marty was right. Maybe the woman did a little streetwalking on the side to supplement her waitressing income. It made sense considering the disguise and revealing clothing—and who she was related to.

Beau probably should've left her to her business. It didn't look like the woman was in any kind of imminent danger. Still, he couldn't bring himself to leave until he was sure. He walked around the back of the line of carriages and slipped up on the other side. As he drew closer, he could hear the waitress talking.

"...hope you don't mind if I get a picture of you to show all my friends back home," she said in a voice with no twang whatsoever, "but you're just so cute. And I bet you have to be strong to handle a horse that big."

Beau peeked around the side of the carriage at the man's skinny arms and figured the woman could whip the driver's ass with one hand tied behind her back.

"Well, draft horses are pretty hard to handle," the driver's voice beamed with pride. "And Lightning is as stubborn as they come. If he doesn't watch himself, he won't be pulling a carriage for much longer."

"Really?" She held the camera higher. If she was taking pictures, she was doing it through video. The green record light was on. "What happens to stubborn horses when they can no longer pull a carriage?"

"They usually find themselves—" The driver stopped

and pointed a finger at the camera. "Hey, don't I know you? You're the blonde that was here last week asking questions and taking pictures." He stepped closer, his voice angry. "You almost lost me my job when my boss saw that video on YouTube."

"I don't know what you're talking about." The woman started to back away, but the driver grabbed her arm and pulled off her wig. The blond ponytail spilled out.

"You don't, huh?" He dropped the wig and made a grab for the phone. "Hand over the phone, Blondie."

Beau had seen about as much manhandling as he could take. Opening the door of the carriage, he climbed in with the intent of climbing out the other side and helping to even the odds. But before he could do more than open the opposite door, Blondie proved him right. The driver was no match for the skinny girl. She threw an elbow-shot into the man's stomach that had Beau sucking in his breath. The driver released her, but before she could make a run for it, a swarm of other carriage drivers came running. With all exits blocked, most people would've given up. Blondie wasn't even fazed. She vaulted up into the driver's seat of the carriage, took the reins, and shouted a deep-throated "hah!"

Beau braced to be thrown on his ass.

Instead, nothing happened.

"Hah!" Blondie continued to slap the reins. But the only movement it generated from Lightning was a flick of his tail.

Her shoulders drooped, and Beau figured she was about to accept defeat when the four boys in baggy shorts raced past. The scent of burning fuses warned Beau, but not quickly enough. The staccato pops of firecrackers

went off right next to the horse's front hooves. The draft
horse reared, and Beau was thrown back against the seat.
By the time he sat up, the horse was at a full run. Carefully, Beau made his way to the driver's seat. Blondie
wasn't quite as sassy anymore. She had lost the reins and
was hanging on to the side rail for dear life.

Without any guidance, the horse chose his own path.
Fortunately for the pedestrians, it was a less populated
route. Unfortunately for Beau and Blondie, it wasn't really
a route.

Shrubs and low-hanging branches whacked them in
the faces and scratched their arms as the horse charged
down a narrow trail. Figuring that the back was safer than
the front, Beau lifted the woman off the seat and pulled
her down to the cushioned red leather. It didn't surprise
him that she wasn't exactly happy about being protected.
She fought worse than a lassoed steer. Still, after being
bested earlier, Beau wasn't about to let her get the upper
hand again. And since he didn't want to hurt her, it turned
into something of a wrestling match.

The woman knew her moves. She tried headlocks, cra-
dles, and Half Nelsons. But Beau hadn't wrestled in high
school for nothing. After only a few moments, he ended
up on top with her legs pinned beneath him and her arms
held over her head.

The fight fizzled out of her just as the carriage came to
a stop. Beau's hat had come off, and his face was inches
from hers. So close, he could see the freckles that sprinkled the bridge of her nose. So close, he could see the star-
bursts of deep blue in her irises. Her hair had come out of
the ponytail and framed her face in long, wheat-colored
waves. He had always preferred dark-haired girls, but the

cloud of gold looked so soft that he couldn't help leaning down to rub his cheek against the silky strands. A scent drifted up. A scent he had no trouble distinguishing.

Cherry pie.

Homemade cherry pie piping hot from the oven.

Suddenly, Beau was hungry.

And not for food.

Like a lightning bolt straight from heaven, desire sizzled through him and settled in a hard knot beneath the fly of his jeans. The unexpected sensation had him pulling back in surprise, and the spitfire didn't waste any time taking advantage of the opportunity. She gave him a hard shove and rolled out from beneath him. Still stunned, he could only watch as she grabbed her tote bag and jumped down from the carriage.

The slamming door brought Beau out of his daze, and his gaze moved down to the hardened swell beneath his zipper. A smile spread across his face. Not the smile he gave to most folks, but a real smile that came directly from the relief that flooded his body.

Up ahead, he could see the woman hobbling down the path in only one high heel, her golden hair glistening in the moonlight. After an entire night's contemplation, a name popped into his head.

Jenna Jay.

Chapter Two

"SO YOU STOLE A CENTRAL PARK CARRIAGE?"

Jenna Jay Scroggs finished pouring milk over her Honey-Combs before turning to answer the question. Her neighbor, Sophia Caruso, sat at the small kitchen table with the morning newspaper spread out in front of her.

"I didn't steal it," Jenna said as she moved over and sat down in the chair opposite Sophia. She had already read the newspaper article, but couldn't help leaning over to take another look. "I just borrowed it to escape the lunatic driver."

Sophia glanced up from reading the article. "Let's define lunatic. A carriage driver who is trying to save his job? Or a woman who thinks she can save the world?"

Jenna spooned a bite of cereal into her mouth and munched on it. "I'm not trying to save the world. I'm just trying to bring people's attention to injustices."

"Don't get me wrong," Sophia said. "I think it's great that you organized all the apartment building tenants and convinced the landlord to fix the things in the building that have needed to be fixed for years. And I'm

all for pitching in on a bake sale to do away with childhood hunger and participating in a walkathon to Save the
Tigers. But when you start picketing the corner market
because their produce is overpriced and slipping around
in disguises to get videos of overworked carriage horses,
I think you've gone a little off your rocker." She tapped
on the newspaper. "You're lucky you didn't wind up in
jail."

"Why should I go to jail when the driver was the one
who attacked me?" Jenna said. "I only jumped up into the
carriage to escape him and his friends."

Sophia continued reading. "Well, either the driver was
worried you were going to press charges or he didn't want
any more publicity about the horses. He calls what happened 'an unfortunate accident' and doesn't say a word
about the YouTube videos or you trying to steal his carriage. The entire article seems to be about this cute cowboy and his 'near-brush with death.'" She held up the
newspaper to show Jenna the picture on the front. A picture of a grinning idiot sitting in the driver's seat of the
carriage with the reins held loosely in one hand while he
tipped his black Stetson with the other.

"I wouldn't call an old, gray-haired cowboy cute,"
Jenna mumbled and shoved in another bite of cereal.

Sophia took the newspaper back and studied the picture. "He has gray hair?"

*Silver hair. Thick silver hair that glistened like a shiny
new dime in the moonlight.* Not exactly sure where the
thought had come from, Jenna shook her head to clear the
image. "Do you recognize him? Do you think he's one of
Alejandro's thugs sent to snuff me out?"

Sophia laughed. "Snuff you out? You and your wild

imagination, Jenna. I seriously doubt that the Mexican Cartel would hire a rodeo cowboy to kill you just because you've decided to champion one of the neighborhood kids they hired to deal their drugs."

"Miguel doesn't deal drugs anymore," Jenna stated. "After I got him a job busing tables at Herbs and Spices, he promised me that he's sold his last hit of cocaine."

"I hope you're right, but kids who are involved with gangs and drugs don't just give it up overnight." She studied the picture. "So this cowboy was following you?"

"I veered off the path to make sure, and he followed right behind me."

"Well, he doesn't look like a mugger," Sophia said. "Maybe he just thought you were pretty and wanted to get your number."

It was possible, especially when he hadn't made one attempt to harm her. Even when they wrestled, Jenna had felt as if he held back. His holds were firm, but not bruising. And when he finally succeeded in pinning her, there was a moment when his thumbs had actually caressed the pulse points of her wrists.

Just the thought of his warm, gentle fingers had Jenna's stomach fluttering, and she ignored the last Honey-Comb and got up to carry her bowl to the sink.

"I better get going. I'm taking over Anna's shift this morning." Jenna rinsed out her bowl and placed it in the dishwasher. "You want to come over after I get off work? We can get take-out and watch a movie." She turned around and flashed a hopeful smile. "Or we could picket Fresh Mart and see if we can't get them to give us the same price on peaches as they give their Jersey customers."

Sophia got to her feet. "No, thanks. I'll leave price-slashing and saving the world to the superheroes. Besides, I'm still returning wedding presents. Which is exactly what I deserve for not cancelling the wedding before my big, fat Italian family sent gifts."

Jenna laughed and followed Sophia to the door. "I'll pick up take-out and meet you at your place to help. But be warned, my handwriting is atrocious." She held on to the door as Sophia stepped out into the hallway. "And I'm not bringing any of the healthy crap from Herbs and Spices. I've been craving a couple cheeseburgers with extra crispy fries."

"Get me a chicken sandwich," Sophia said. "I've put on ten pounds since becoming your friend. You might be one of those people who can eat whatever they want and never gain a pound, but that doesn't mean you're not clogging your arteries with all that fat."

Jenna shrugged. "Superheroes need at least one weakness, don't they?"

Before Sophia could reply, a high-pitched, whiny voice drifted up the stairs. Both women turned and watched as a tattooed rocker appeared. He held a guitar case in one hand and used the other to push back the wild mane of black hair that fell over his face. Hair that always looked like it had been through a tsunami. In college, it had been unique and sexy. Now it just made Jenna want to pull out a pair of electric clippers.

Davy stopped in mid-lyric when he rounded the corner and saw them. His smile drooped. "Hey, babe. I thought you'd be at work already." He walked over and gave Jenna a quick kiss that tasted of cigarettes and stale beer. Her annoyance must've shown in her eyes because he quickly tried to explain.

"I just had a couple beers with the guys—just to loosen up the creative juices. You'll be happy to hear that we got a gig."

"Wow," Sophia's voice was thick with sarcasm, "two gigs in a year. Before you know it, your picture will be on the cover of *Rolling Stone*."

With all the hair, it was hard to tell what kind of look Davy shot her, but his words were sharp. "And I'll try not to forget all the little people." He turned and ambled into the apartment.

When he was gone, Sophia quickly apologized. "I'm sorry. I shouldn't have been so mean. It's just that I don't get why you put up with the guy. In case you haven't figured this out, he's a deadbeat."

Stepping out into the hallway, Jenna closed the door behind her. "You sound exactly like my parents. Just because Davy has long hair and tattoos doesn't make him a deadbeat."

"No, but living off his girlfriend for the last year does." Sophia sighed. "Look, I wasn't going to say anything. But you saved me from making a bad mistake with Brian, and I think it's only fair that I try to save you. I realize you think you're in love with Davy. But are you in love with him or is he just another one of your causes?"

There were very few times in her life when Jenna had been struck speechless. This was one of them. She was shocked at how completely wrong Sophia was. Jenna loved Davy. That's why she put up with his hair, his loud music, his joblessness, and his cigarette smoking and drinking. That was why she had gotten in a fight with her family and hadn't talked with them for close to a year. Why she had moved from a state that she loved to a big city with buildings so tall she couldn't see where the earth met the sky.

"Okay," Sophia held up a hand, "that's the last time I'll bring it up. I'll see you later at my place?"

With her mind still a little stunned, Jenna only nodded before she turned and went back into her apartment. Davy was standing at the kitchen counter, pouring himself a glass of orange juice. For a moment, she studied him. Studied his mussed mop of hair and the too small t-shirt that clung to his thin torso. The miles of tattoos that covered his arms and the studded belt that hung on the hips of his skinny jeans.

"We're out of OJ," he said as he poured the last of it in his glass. "And can you spare a twenty? I need some new guitar strings—"

"I love you," Jenna blurted out.

There was a strained moment where Davy's shoulders tightened before he answered. "Yeah, I love you too, babe."

Relief flooded Jenna, and she walked over and gave him a hug from behind. He didn't turn and hug her back, but Davy had never been the affectionate type. Instead, he took a drink of his orange juice and pulled a cheese Danish out of a bag as if his girlfriend wasn't clinging to his back like a baby chimpanzee. The pastry smelled delicious, and she leaned up for a bite, but he pulled it away before she could get one and headed to the bedroom.

"Just leave the twenty on the dresser."

After he went to bed, Jenna got in the shower. While she stood under the hot spray of water, she went over all the reasons that she loved Davy. There had to be a million. So many that she was still at it when she walked into the bedroom to get dressed. Davy was sound asleep, his mouth drooling on the embroidered pillowcases her Aunt Lucinda had made for her. She suddenly remembered the twenty that he'd asked for and went in search of her tote bag.

She found her bag in the corner of the living room where she'd tossed it the night before. Along with one silver high heel. Just the sight of the lone shoe ticked her off, and she kicked it out of the way and grabbed her bag. She went to pull her wallet out when she noticed the side pocket where she kept her cell phone.

It was empty.

After dumping the entire contents of her tote out on the floor, she soon realized that a shoe wasn't the only thing she had lost the night before. She tried not to panic, but it wasn't easy. Not when it would take money to replace her phone, and when she didn't know who was in possession of all her pictures, videos, and Internet passwords.

Jenna thought back to the night before. The last time she'd had the phone was when the driver had grabbed her. Once she'd elbowed him in the stomach, she'd slipped the phone in her tote bag. Which meant that she'd lost it in the carriage. No doubt, while wrestling with the cowboy.

Did he have her cell phone? Or had the driver discovered it later?

There was only one way to find out.

Dropping the empty tote, she hurried back into the bedroom. Davy's jeans were on the floor where he'd left them. She pulled the cell phone from his back pocket. A text message came up on the screen—*Miss you already.* Since Davy's band members were always screwing around with him, she ignored it and dialed her number.

The phone rang a good six times before it was picked up. The thick country twang that came through the receiver made Jenna instantly annoyed.

"Beauregard Cates speakin'."

"I want my phone back," she said.

"Hey there, Blondie." His voice dripped with country boy charm. "I was wonderin' when you would get around to callin'."

Jenna could almost picture the smug smile on his face, and she gritted her teeth and repeated herself. "I want my phone back."

"Of course you do," he said. "And I'd like about two hours of my life back from the NYPD and that nosy reporter, but I don't think that's going to happen."

"The cops arrested you?"

"No, they just questioned me and the carriage driver, who seemed to forget most of the details, including you trying to steal his carriage. What were you doing there, anyway? It wouldn't have to do with the videos I found on your phone, would it? Are you one of those crazy animal activists?"

Jenna's eyes narrowed. "You went through my phone?"

"Of course." He didn't sound the least bit sorry. "How else would I locate the owner? I thoroughly enjoyed the pictures of Coney Island, but I've got to tell you that the pictures you took of your girlfriend in her underwear were flat-out scary."

Jenna went through her mind, trying to remember when she had taken pictures of Sophia in her under-wear, and what other pictures and videos she had on the phone. It was disconcerting to think that some stranger was getting to view her private life without her consent.

Suddenly, another thought popped into her head that was even more alarming.

"I didn't lose my phone, did I?" she said. "You stole it out of my purse on purpose. Who sent you to harass me? Is it Alejandro? Bruno, the owner of the Fresh Market? My landlord? The carriage driver's boss?"

"Hold up there. I didn't steal anything," he said. "And just how many enemies do you have?"

She ignored the question, probably because she didn't really want to know the total. With as many causes as she had gotten involved with since arriving in New York, the number could be staggering.

"That's not important," she said. "The only thing that you need to know is I'm not the type of woman who is going to be easily intimidated."

He laughed. "I think I've figured that out already, and my calves have the bruises to prove it."

"Well, you shouldn't have been following me."

"Who said I was following you? I just happened to be headed in the same direction as you were. When you slipped into the trees, I got worried that something might happen to a woman alone in a dark park. Obviously, I was mistaken. It's the men who need to worry."

Jenna sat down on the edge of the bed. Could he be telling the truth? After her last run-in with Alejandro where he threatened to fit her with a pair of cement shoes, she had become a little paranoid. But if he hadn't been following her, then how had he ended up in the carriage?

There was a rustling noise before a groggy woman's voice came through the receiver.

"Good mornin', sugar."

"Good mornin', yourself," Beau said with so much

sweetness that Jenna felt her stomach heave. The feeling intensified when the silence that followed was punctuated with a feminine groan of pleasure.

"Ohh, Beau."

Jenna rolled her eyes. Everything made perfect sense now. The snug jeans and black Stetson. The flirty smiles and aw-shucks country boy charm. The exaggerated drawl and arrogant strut. Beauregard Cates was like every other horny cowboy Jenna had met in her lifetime. A horny cowboy who was a long way from home and hoping to get lucky in the Big Apple.

And it appeared as if he had.

Jenna heaved an annoyed sigh. "Look, since the newspaper said you were here for the rodeo, I figure you're staying at a hotel. So just leave my phone at the front desk, and I'll pick it up."

When Beau came back on he sounded a little out of breath. "Didn't your mama ever teach you the magic word, Blondie?"

Jenna's mama had taught her the word. She just wasn't good at using it. But if it got her phone back, she was willing to make the effort.

"Could you please tell me where you're staying so I could come get my phone?" The words came out a little bitchier than she had intended, and he laughed. For some reason that she couldn't explain, the deep, husky sound brought up images of wide-open spaces and horizons that stretched to eternity.

"You don't like to give an inch, do you?" he said. "You remind me of this bull I once rode. Pissed Off was the stubbornest critter you'd ever want to meet."

A bull? He'd just compared her to a bull? It was truly

amazing how angry the man could make her. "Just give me my doggone phone back!" she snapped.

There was a long pause before his twangy voice came back on.

"I'll think on it."

He hung up on her.

Chapter Three

BEAU FLIPPED THE MENU CLOSED and tossed it down on the table. For once, he didn't feel much like eating. His shoulder still ached. His calves were sore. And he hadn't gotten nearly enough sleep the night before. Not only because Peggy Sue snored like a sawmill, but also because his giddyup still had a hitch and he stayed up half the night mentally cussing out the woman who was to blame.

Jenna Jay.

His gaze narrowed on the skinny blond waitress who hustled from table to table, ignoring the fact that he'd been sitting there for a good thirty minutes. He realized it was probably payback for him hanging up on her and refusing to answer her calls. But the woman really rubbed him the wrong way—something very few women did—and her defiant tone this morning had been the final straw.

Okay, so maybe she wasn't entirely to blame for his malfunction with Peggy Sue. But if she hadn't stuck him with returning the carriage and dealing with her mess, he might've gotten back to the hotel room with enough of a hard-on to properly give Peggy a run for her money. As it was, he was forced to use the "sex is bad for athletes" excuse and keep Peggy Sue happy with a little touch and tickle.

Fed up with sitting there twiddling his thumbs while he waited for Jenna Jay to notice him, he reached out and stopped the dark-haired waitress who passed by his table.

"Excuse me, ma'am," he flashed her a smile, "but do you think you could get my waitress's attention? I'm about to expire from hunger." The woman only stared at him, forcing him to repeat the question. "My waitress?"

She blinked, then blushed a bright red. "Oh. Of course; I'll just go get her."

Beau watched as she turned and hurried over to Jenna, who was chatting it up with the little gangster-looking busboy who had broken more dishes than he'd cleared. The waitress whispered something in her ear, then pointed over at Beau. Jenna's gaze pinned him, and he smiled and waved. A look entered her eyes that reflected the exact annoyance coursing through Beau's body. He was just better at hiding it. With a grumbled reply to the waitress, she headed over.

In the sunlight that shone in through the window, the freckles on her nose were even more noticeable. And if it weren't for those cold glacier eyes, she would resemble a ponytailed teenager in her lime green t-shirt and black pants.

"I'm assuming you found me from the work schedule on my phone," she said.

"Something like that." He held out the menu. "I'll take the chicken sandwich minus the frou-frou sauce. And I'll have French fries instead of apple slaw—whatever that is."

She jerked the menu from his hand. "We don't have fries. And I'd like my phone back ... please."

He had planned on giving her phone back. That was the reason he was at the restaurant and subjecting himself to her abrasive personality. But, for some reason, now he wasn't in any hurry.

"Apple slaw it is," he said. "And one of those strawberry smoothies."

She strode off. For a skinny thing, she had more than a little wiggle in her strut. Too bad skinny women had never appealed to him. He was now convinced that his hard-on was due to the thrill of the runaway carriage ride more than the thrill of having a tomboy blonde in his arms.

This theory was confirmed when she continued to irritate the hell out of him.

Jenna seemed to give everyone else in the place great service, but him. She refused to bring him water. It took a good forty minutes to get his food. And when she did flip the plate and glass down in front of him, his sandwich was cold and his smoothie runny. He thought about sending it back and raising some hell with the management, but then he figured he didn't need the aggravation. As much as the woman needed someone to put her in her place, it wasn't going to be him. He didn't have the patience or the desire.

Reaching into his front pocket, he pulled out her cell phone. Since she refused to glance his way, he nabbed another waitress and gave it to her to give to Jenna. Then he had the cashier total up his bill and paid with his credit card, flat refusing to tip for the bad service.

Once outside, his spirits lifted considerably. Having spent the day at the arena, he had the rest of the evening and night to do what he wanted. Maybe he would check out Times Square. Or do what Marty and Laurie had done and head on over to the Empire State Building.

"Hey, wait up!"

He might've stopped, if not for the Texas drawl that accompanied the words. He picked up his pace, but the annoying woman ran as well as she fought. Within seconds, Jenna Jay was next to him, her long-legged strides matching his.

"You didn't finish your dinner." She held out a sack and a paper cup with a lid and straw. When he ignored it and kept walking, she sighed. "Fine. I apologize for the way I treated you in the restaurant, but you could've told me that you planned to return my phone, instead of being such a jerk."

"Who is the jerk?" He stopped and turned to her. "You attacked me in the park, took me for a joyride in a carriage and left me to explain to the police, and then called and accused me of stealing your phone. If this is the hospitality New Yorkers show visitors, then I want no part of this city." He turned and headed up the street. Only a few seconds later, she followed.

"Where are you from in Texas?" she asked before taking a long sip of the smoothie. His smoothie.

"Don't you have to get back to work?" He pulled his gaze away from the sight of her full, pink lips puckered around the straw.

"I'm done for the day." She had no trouble keeping up with his quick stride. "I'd say east Texas by your accent. I used to live in west Texas in a little town called Bramble. My family still lives there."

Now would've been the time to mention that he'd been to Bramble. In fact, he had lived there for a few months. And his brother, Billy, still did. But since the Cates brothers had been plotting the demise of the town at one time, he figured it was best if he kept that piece of information to himself.

"How old are you?" Jenna asked.

The question had him glancing over at her. She was studying him, her eyes direct and rather disconcerting.

"Twenty-eight," he said as he watched her take another sip from the straw. She sucked so hard that her cheeks dimpled in. A swirl of heat settled in his stomach, and he quickly reached out and took the cup away from her.

She swallowed and released a low whistle through her teeth. "Wow, you are premature."

"What?"

"Your hair," she clarified. "I've never seen someone so young with silver hair."

If there was something that Beau was sensitive about, it was his hair. He had tried dyeing it once, but it grew out so fast that it hadn't been worth the effort. Ignoring her comment, he tugged his hat lower and took a sip of the smoothie. And damned if it tasted nothing like strawberries, and just like cherries.

"Well, I better get home," she said as she handed him the bag. "I'm Jenna, by the way."

"Beauregard."

She smiled. It was the first time he'd seen her smile. There was nothing special about it. No dimples. No flash of teeth. Just a simple smile that made her blue eyes sparkle with a contagious mischief. "Nice to meet you, Beauregard. I hope you enjoy your stay in New York."

"Thank you, Jenna. If I can steer clear of Central Park, I'm sure I will."

She laughed as she headed back the way they had come. After tossing the bag and cup in the trash, Beau kept walking in the opposite direction. He'd gone no more than five steps when he glanced over his shoulder. As it turned out, at that very second, Jenna was doing the same thing. Their eyes met and held before they both turned back around.

Keep right on walking, Cates. The woman is nothing but trouble with a capital "T."

Beau's thoughts turned out to be prophetic when, a few seconds later, he heard Jenna's loud bellow.

"Get your hands off me!"

Beau turned to find Jenna a half a block away, struggling with a mountain of a man who was trying to pull her toward a black limo parked by the curb. Beau took off at a sprint. Before he could reach Jenna, she kicked the guy in the knee and gained her release. The guy hobbled back to the car, and it squealed away from the curb. Beau arrived just as the little gangster busboy came running out of the restaurant.

"You okay, Jenna?" the kid asked before Beau could. "Who was that guy, anyway? You want me to have Alejandro take him out for you?"

Jenna pulled her gaze from the disappearing limo, and her eyes narrowed on the kid, whose pants hung so low they were in danger of falling off. "I thought you told me that you didn't work for Alejandro anymore."

"I don't." The kid stared back at Jenna for only a second before his eyes skittered away. If that wasn't a sure sign that he was lying through his teeth, the quick subject change was. "Who's the Yippee-kai-yay mofo?"

"He's a friend of mine." Jenna pointed a finger at the kid. "And watch your mouth. If your mama heard you, she'd warm your butt." Her expression softened. "How is she doing?"

The kid shrugged. "Her back's still messed up. And the as—buttholes at her job are late again with the workman's comp. Even though their stupid heavy boxes were the reason she hurt her back in the first place."

If Jenna's determined look was any indication, Beau figured that the kid's mom would have a check within the next couple days. If not, Beau would write her one himself. He had always been a sucker for a sob story.

Jenna dug around in her tote bag. "Here, Miguel." She held out a twenty-dollar bill, but Miguel shook his head.

"I got some money saved up."

This time, Jenna didn't believe him and stuffed the money in his front pocket. "Stay away from Alejandro and his thugs."

The kid nodded and then strutted back to the restaurant.

Jenna waited until he got inside before she turned and headed down the street as if fighting off giants and saving kids was something she did every day. Beau had started to wonder if maybe it wasn't.

"Aren't you going to call the police?" he asked as he fell into step next to her.

She shook her head. "I might've overreacted a little bit. The guy just wanted to drive me to Jersey to talk with his boss, who is a little upset about me picketing his grocery stores and scaring away business." She glanced over at him. "Thanks for coming to my rescue, but you don't need to follow me home. I can take care of myself."

"I don't doubt that for a second." He shoved his hands in his pockets and glanced up at the tall buildings. "And who says I'm following you home? Maybe I'm just taking in the sights of the city."

Jenna picked up her pace. "Suit yourself, Cowboy."

* * *

Beau had never been much for strenuous exercise. So he was more than a little winded after speed-walking home with Jenna and climbing the four flights of stairs to her apartment. Something Jenna didn't hesitate to take note of.

"You would think that a big stud bull rider would be in better shape," she said as she dug through her tote bag.

"I only have to last eight seconds." He stopped and leaned on the banister.

She glanced up, and a smile played with her lips. "Eight seconds? Is that all you last?"

He squinted. "Are we talking bull riding? Because if we're talking about something else, the proof is in the puddin'." He stepped closer. "And I've never minded sharing my puddin', sweetheart."

"I'm sure you haven't." She shot him a wide-eyed innocent look before speaking in a high voice. "Ohhh, Beau."

Beau grinned. "Heard that, did ya?"

"It was hard not to. The woman has a voice as loud as my sister's. And Hope won Miss Hogcaller of Haskin County five years running."

"No kiddin'?" He propped a shoulder on the wall. "Did you ever try your hand at it—or should I say your vocal cords?"

"No. I was more athlete than hog caller."

"Let me guess, state champion wrestler?"

She laughed. "No. But I wanted to go out for wrestling. My daddy wouldn't let me. I think it had to do with all those boys mauling me."

Beau understood exactly what she was talking about. Suddenly, he had the strongest urge for a repeat performance of their wrestling match—minus the part where she left him. But it didn't look like he was going to get it. The way she hesitated with her hand on the doorknob made it obvious that she had no intention of inviting him in. And it was for the best. She wasn't his type. Not his type at all.

"Well," she lifted her shoulders in a slight shrug, "I guess I'll see you around."

"Yeah." Beau sent her a smile before tipping his hat and backing down the hallway. If she had opened the door and gone inside, he could've easily walked down the stairs and never looked back. But instead, she stood there watching him, her hair straggling down from her ponytail and freckles covering her nose like little chocolate sprinkles. She watched him with eyes the same deep blue as a lake he'd once fished at in Canada.

"Y'all take care now," she whispered.

The typical Texas good-bye was Beau's undoing. In three long strides, he had her in his arms and pushed up against the door.

"What are you doing?" she breathed.

"Just testing something out," he said before lowering his mouth to hers. She didn't taste like cherries. She tasted like heaven. Her lips were warm and soft and opened without hesitation, allowing him full access to her mouth. Her hands came up and ran through his hair, knocking his hat to the floor and tugging him closer. Close enough to realize that her long legs were perfectly matched to his. He flexed his hips, and blue jean fly brushed against black cotton fly. Just that quickly, desire flooded his body, giving him a hard-on that was easily detected.

Jenna's hands dropped from his hair, and she pulled away. Her eyes looked as confused as Beau felt. He released her and took a step back just as the door was pulled open. Her friend stood there in the same baggy printed boxers she'd worn in the phone photos. Except on closer examination, Beau realized that the wild hair, skinny arms, and nipple rings belonged to a man, not a woman.

"Hey, babe," the man said before he reached out and hooked a tattooed arm around Jenna's shoulders. "Did you bring home some OJ?"

Without waiting for an introduction, Beau turned on his boot heel and headed for the stairs. He didn't realize that he'd left his hat until he stepped out of the apartment building. But damned if he was going back for it. He felt like a big enough idiot.

I just want to test something out.

Well, he'd tested something out all right. And he'd gotten his results. It seemed he was now turned on by skinny, aggressive blondes with girly, tattooed boyfriends. He shook his head. What a pathetic state of affairs.

On the way down the front steps, his cell phone rang. He thought about ignoring it, but then figured he could use the distraction. He realized his mistake when he heard the raspy woman's voice on the other line.

It seemed that today was Beau's day for having to deal with ornery, cantankerous women.

Chapter Four

MILLICENT LADUE, or Minnie as her friends called her, adjusted the bright yellow phone receiver to her ear. "Speak up, boy. I think we got us a bad connection. I asked if you found her." She pushed the button on the arm of her battery-operated wheelchair and zipped back over to the kitchen table, stretching the twisted phone cord to its limit.

A heavy sigh came through the receiver. "Yes, I found her."

"So the information I got was right. She is working at that restaurant." Minnie held the phone with her shoulder while she dealt out three cards, flipping the third one face up. "Did you follow her? Were you able to get her address?"

Beau paused for a second before answering. "Yes. But I've got to tell you, Minnie, I think you've made a mistake. This woman is about as far as you can get from being hen material. I can't see her catering to men as much as annoying the hell out of them."

Minnie's hand paused over a row of cards for only a

second before she recovered. "You met her? I thought I told you that we didn't want her knowing she was being checked up on."

"She doesn't know anything," he said. "She just thinks our meeting was accidental."

An accidental meeting? Now that sounded intriguing, as did the part about Beau being annoyed as hell. Beau was the type of man who let few things annoy him. Especially not women. Of course, how could a man be annoyed with women when they flocked to him like geese to a summer pond? Unless this was one woman who didn't flock to him.

Interesting. Very interesting.

Minnie placed two fingers to her lips and inhaled deeply, longing for nicotine-infused smoke instead of the clean air that filled her lungs. Smoking was just another thing that had changed since the Cates brothers had taken over. Or since Brant Cates had taken over. Beauregard might be one of the owners, but he rarely showed up at Miss Hattie's. And Minnie figured it was about time for that to change.

"Since you're in the neighborhood," she said, "I expect a visit."

Beau laughed. "I wouldn't exactly call New York City in the neighborhood."

She continued playing her game of solitaire that was spread out on the kitchen table. "If you can travel all over the world, you can travel to Texas for a few days."

There was another long pause. "I'll try, Minnie, but I can't make any promises."

"I've never put much store in promises," she said. "You either do something or you don't." She placed a four

of clubs on a five of diamonds before reaching in the side
pocket of her wheelchair for a pen and paper. "Now give
me Jenna's address."

Beau complied, but not without a warning. "Be careful, Minnie. Brant loves you, but if you push him too far,
he might just send you off to that old folks' home he likes
to threaten you with. And I'd say that inviting women to
Miss Hattie's to train them to become prostitutes is pushing him too far."

"Prostitutes!" She yelled so loudly that Baby came
running into the room, her high-heel shoes clicking
against the linoleum and her eyes wide behind her thick
glasses. Minnie flapped a hand at the hen who was the
spitting image of Marilyn Monroe—give or take thirty
years—and continued her phone conversation. "Why, I'm
ashamed of you, Beauregard Cates. I thought you knew
better than that. Hens have never been prostitutes."

"I just think you need to be careful what you do. This
isn't the eighteen hundreds when Miss Hattie's was at its
prime."

That was really too bad, Minnie thought. But she
couldn't turn back the hands of time. Besides, Miss Hattie's was still in operation. Just not the kind of operation
it had been for close to a hundred years. Now it was a
respectable bed and breakfast. The perfect front for what
Minnie had in mind.

"Well, I appreciate you worrying about me, Beauregard," Minnie said, "but I think I've got things under control. Now take care of yourself."

After hanging up with Beau, Minnie turned to Baby,
who still stood in the kitchen with a concerned look on
her face.

"Maybe Beau has a right to worry, Min," she said. "Maybe what we're doing is wrong. Most of the hens you want to contact don't even know who their ancestors are, and maybe it's best if we keep it that way."

Minnie rolled back to the table. "My intent is not to ruin their lives, but to enhance them. If I think that they are happy where they are or unable to benefit from what the henhouse has to offer, I'll keep my beak shut and let them live their lives without knowing their connection to Miss Hattie's. But you should know better than anyone, Baby, that sometimes a person needs to know where they came from before they can figure out where they're going."

At that exact moment, the doorbell chimed out the sweet melody of "Deep in the Heart of Texas" as if God was seconding Minnie's words. At least, that's the way Minnie chose to see it. She pressed the button on her chair and rolled closer to Baby, holding out the piece of paper she'd written Jenna's address on.

"Send out an invitation," Minnie said. "ASAP."

Marcy Henderson removed her finger from the doorbell and felt another wave of nervous jitters. Miss Hattie's Henhouse wasn't at all what she had expected. She didn't know what a whorehouse should look like, but she hadn't thought it would look like a pretty farmhouse with a bright red roof, deep green shutters, and a wraparound porch that belonged in some country home and garden magazine.

The huge front door opened, causing Marcy to jump. But she collected herself quickly enough and did what she always did when she was scared—became aggressive and belligerent.

"Jesus!" She held a hand to her abundant breasts and glared at the young woman who stood in the doorway. "Why don't you scare the crap out of me?"

The smile on the chubby woman's face melted. "Oh, I'm so sorry." She fussed with the ugly rose pinned to the waist of her formal. A formal that was almost as tight as the dresses Marcy wore. "I thought you were my piano teacher."

"Nope," Marcy said. "Never played anything but the kazoo." She shoved her hands in the back pockets of her Wranglers to still the shaking. "I'm here about the job."

The woman looked confused. "What job?"

"I'll take it from here, Starlet," a raspy voice said. Starlet stepped aside, and an old woman in a wheelchair and a really bad wig rolled into view.

"I'm Miss Minnie Ladue, the proprietor of Miss Hattie's. And you must be Marcy Henderson. Moses Tate told me that you seemed interested in the job." She waved a hand. "Well, come on in, child. We're lettin' all the cool air out."

Marcy hesitated. Once she stepped over the threshold there was no going back. Of course, there was no going back anyway. Her fate had been decided a long time ago. She was just following the path set out for her. Lifting her chin, she stepped into the house.

The inside was less country and more snooty. Everything, from the chandeliers to the *Gone With the Wind* staircase, looked old and expensive. Marcy clutched her hands in front of her and tried not to touch anything.

"Right this way," Miss Ladue said as she rolled toward a set of double doors. Starlet raced to open them for her, sort of like a puppy that wanted to please. Marcy had once been that girl, but when she'd discovered there was no pleasing her parents, she had taken a different route to get attention.

"Did you want me to get you some lemonade, Minnie?" the young woman asked.

"Thank you, Starlet, but I'll take care of the refreshments." Miss Ladue rolled into a room that was filled with bookshelves. "Did you get Miss Hattie's room cleaned?"

Starlet's face turned the color of Marcy's shirt. "No, ma'am. The Birminghams haven't been out of it all day."

Miss Ladue smiled as she wheeled her chair around behind the large desk. "I'm glad to hear that Miss Hattie's room is being used the way it should be. Better have Sunshine take a tray of food up. Sounds like they'll need the nourishment." She waved a hand at Marcy. "Don't just stand there lookin' stupid."

The words had Marcy bristling, and she strode into the room and flopped down in one of the chairs that sat in front of the desk. It was about the softest chair Marcy had ever sat in, but she didn't allow herself to relax back in the cushions. Instead, she got right to the point of her visit.

"I'm not one to beat around the bush, Miss Ladue—"

"Minnie," the old woman cut in. "Everyone calls me Minnie." Her crinkled-up eyes were direct. "And it's nice to know that you don't beat around the bush. I never cared much for it myself." She opened a desk drawer and pulled out a bottle. "Brandy?"

Marcy could've really used a drink about then, but after spending the majority of her twenties more drunk than sober, she'd sworn off hard liquor. She shook her head. "No thanks. About that job . . ."

"I guess I need to give you the details, don't I?" Minnie

said. "It only pays five dollars an hour, but that includes room and board. You'll be assigned certain rooms to clean upstairs and downstairs, besides helping with meals and running errands." She splashed the amber liquid in a glass and downed the entire contents before heaving a sigh and sitting back in her chair.

Marcy stared at her. "You mean to tell me that the job that Moses told me about really is for a maid?"

Minnie cocked her head to one side and arched an eyebrow. "What did you think it was for?"

Now more flabbergasted than nervous, Marcy flapped a hand around the room. "I thought what any intelligent person would think when told that Miss Hattie's had a job opening. I thought you were looking for hookers! Not some servant to do your bidding for a measly five dollars an hour. Hell, I can make more than that workin' tables at Bootlegger's Bar."

The old woman's other eyebrow joined the first. "And you think you'd make a good...hooker, do ya?"

"Just ask anyone in Bramble." Marcy got to her feet. "Sorry for the misunderstanding, but I need a job that pays more than five dollars an hour." She was almost to the door when Minnie laughed. It was a raspy laugh that sounded like some tortured animal rather than an amused old woman. And if Marcy hated anything, it was being laughed at.

She whirled back around. "And just what's so funny, old woman?"

Minnie took her good, sweet time answering. She wiped the tears of amusement from her eyes and then blew her nose on a flowered hankie she pulled from between her saggy boobs. "Life is funny, Marcy. Something I don't think you've learned. Now come back and sit down."

It was more of an order than a request. As far as Marcy was concerned, orders ranked right up there with people laughing at her. She remained where she was while Minnie opened another drawer and searched through it.

"You wouldn't have a cigarette on you?" the old woman asked. When Marcy shook her head, she shrugged and pulled a Dum-dum sucker out and unwrapped it. "It's probably for the best. Brant isn't around, but that wouldn't stop the hens from tattling on me. And that stubborn man can be a real pain in the butt when he wants to be." She popped the sucker in her mouth and looked back at Marcy.

"You're right, of course. A hooker is exactly what we need here at the henhouse." Minnie smiled slyly. "But we have to keep up appearances, you know. We wouldn't want word getting out to the wrong people."

The news that Miss Hattie's was a working whorehouse should've made Marcy happy. She needed money—lots of money—and since the bank had declined her loan, this was the only way she had come up with to get it. But she didn't feel happy. She just felt kind of woozy and sick to her stomach. Worried that her legs might give out, she moved over to the chair and sat down.

"What percentage would I get?" she asked.

Minnie's smile widened. "Here at Miss Hattie's, we believe in giving people a hundred percent of what they deserve."

A hundred percent? Marcy tried not to show surprise. It was much more than she expected. Of course, maybe they expected more than she was willing to give.

"I don't go for that kinky stuff," she blurted out.

Minnie stopped sucking her lollipop. "Of course not. But there will be some training involved, and during the day, you'll need to help with the bed and breakfast." She winked.

Marcy didn't mind helping out as long as it paid off in the end. Still, it took her a while before she could get the words out.

"I'll do it."

A look entered Minnie's eyes, and she studied her in a way that made Marcy extremely uncomfortable. Finally, she nodded her head and pulled a piece of paper out of the drawer. Rolling around the desk, she handed it to Marcy. Marcy had barely gotten a chance to read the heading— Henhouse Rules—when Minnie reached out and pulled her into her arms.

Marcy wasn't used to hugs. Her parents had been too busy fighting to show their children physical affection. Because of this, she stiffened up and tried to pull away. But Minnie was having none of it. With a strength that surprised Marcy, she held tight and thumped her on the back.

"Welcome to Miss Hattie's, Marcy. I think you found us just in time."

Chapter Five

THE HAT WAS JUST AN ordinary black Stetson. Very similar to all the other Stetsons Jenna had grown up with. And maybe that was why she couldn't keep her gaze from traveling over to the table where it sat. Her daddy had worn a hat almost identical to this one. Every day when he got home from work, her sisters Hope and Tessa, and her brother, Dallas, met him at the door and begged to wear it. Jenna had wanted to wear it too, but had refused to beg. Just like she'd refused to pick up the hat after Beau had left.

It was Davy who had walked into the hallway and picked it up, not at all concerned to find her with a strange cowboy. She should be glad that he trusted her. Instead, she felt a little disappointed that he hadn't been more jealous. Of course, there was nothing to be jealous about. Beau was gone. And if he hadn't come back for his hat in two days, he wasn't going to.

A knock at the door snapped her out of her hat-gazing. Signing out of her bank account website, she set her laptop down on the coffee table and got up to answer the door.

Miguel stood on the other side, the hood of his sweatshirt shadowing his face.

"My mom signed for this while you were at work." He held out a lavender envelope.

Jenna was more concerned with Miguel's new high-topped Nikes than she was with the letter. "Where did you get those shoes?"

His shoulders stiffened. "I bought them."

"With what? Joseph told me you quit Herbs and Spices this morning and didn't even wait around to be paid."

"I don't need that asshole's money," he said belligerently. "Especially when he takes most of it out for broken dishes."

She poked a finger in his chest. "So help me God, Miguel, if you're selling drugs again, I'm going to turn you in myself."

He stepped out of her reach. "Just because you got me a dumb job doesn't mean you got the right to tell me what to do." He stuffed his hand into his jean pocket and pulled out a twenty. "I don't need charity from you or nobody. I can take care of my mom all by myself." Before she could say anything, he flipped the money at her and raced down the stairs.

Jenna picked up the crumpled bill before going back inside. She was so concerned with Miguel selling drugs again that she barely glanced at the envelope. Her heart skipped a beat when she saw her full name scrawled over the front. No one but her family and the folks of Bramble used her middle name. And only because she had been named after her mother and it kept people from getting confused. Her mama was Jenna, and she was Jenna Jay.

Using the edge of her thumbnail, Jenna tore open the

envelope. A floral scent drifted up as she pulled the pretty cardstock out and read the printed script.

> *You are cordially invited to Miss Hattie's Henhouse*
> *where you will have the honor of being inducted as*
> *a hen as soon as you complete the proper training*
> *and pass the final exams. Please read the enclosed*
> *henhouse rules thoroughly.*
> > *We look forward to meeting you,*
> > *Millicent Ladue, proprietor.*

Jenna flipped the card over, but there was nothing on the back. She pulled out the enclosed sheet of paper and read the first rule:

> *Henhouse Rule #1: Always give a man the kind of*
> *welcome he won't forget.*

She laughed. This had to be some kind of promotional gimmick. The last time Jenna had been in Bramble, gossip had been flying about Miss Hattie's Henhouse, the infamous nineteenth-century whorehouse that had been turned into a bed and breakfast. But how had they gotten her address?

A website at the very bottom of the card caught her attention, and she walked back to her laptop. The front page of the website had a picture of a sprawling mansion surrounded by cottonwoods, along with a brief history of the house of ill repute that had been started in 1890 by a Miss Harriett Ladue.

Jenna clicked on "Accommodations" and scrolled through pictures of bedrooms that looked like they came right out of a history book. Each room was filled with beautiful antiques and named after the women who had worked there. Sassy Kate. Daring Delilah. Sweet Starlet. And the biggest and most expensive room—Miss Hattie's.

The website was professionally done and further supported Jenna's belief that the invitation was all part of a publicity stunt. Maybe some online company she'd purchased from had sold her address to Miss Hattie's, along with thousands of other names. She lifted the envelope and looked at the perfect writing. A tingle of apprehension tiptoed up her spine. But would they fill out each one by hand and then send it via registered mail?

Knowing she wouldn't be able to sleep until she had some answers, she reached for her cell phone. But while looking for a contact number on the website, she discovered something else.

The name of the owner.

Jenna probably should've changed before jumping in a cab. Leggings, a Saggio's Pizza t-shirt, and flip-flops weren't exactly appropriate clothing for a bull-riding competition. But then again, she didn't plan on staying long. Just long enough to squeeze some information out of a sneaky cowboy.

It was a lot easier to get tickets at the box office window than it was to get back to the bull riders. It seemed that numerous female New Yorkers wanted a chance to talk with a "real cowboy," forcing Jenna to lie through her teeth. The story she invented worked well on the arena employees, but not so good on the cowboys in the matching black shirts that guarded the chutes and holding pens.

"Who did you say your husband was?" the short cowboy with the beer belly asked.

"Beauregard Cates," Jenna said with a big smile. She held up the Stetson and laid on the Texas accent. "He forgot his lucky hat in the trailer, and Lord only knows what could happen if he doesn't have it on." She brushed at the corners of her eyes and sniffed. "And I just don't know what me and the kids would do without Beau."

The short cowboy exchanged a confused look with his friend. "Did you know that Beau was married?"

"Nope," the tall cowboy said. He looked back at Jenna. "What's your name?"

"Jenna Jay, but Beau likes to call me Blondie."

Jenna thought it was a nice touch, but the men still didn't look convinced. She was about to give up when a big-busted cowgirl came strutting up.

"Did you say Blondie?" the woman said. When Jenna nodded, the woman's eyes narrowed. "Why that good-for-nothing, manure-tossing cow-wrangler." She pushed her way between the two men and grabbed Jenna's hand. "Come on, honey. Let's go set some things straight with that no-account husband of yours.

"The name's Peggy Sue," the woman said as she pulled Jenna around a pen of bulls that didn't look the least bit vicious. Two were munching on hay, and another was licking his friend's ear. "And I want you to know that I had no idea that Beau was married before I slept with him," she continued. "He told me that you were just some woman who lost her phone. Of course, it explains a lot. Guilt can keep a man from doin' things he has no business doin'. And here I was thinkin' that his lack of enthusiasm had to do with me." She pushed out her big boobs. "As if."

Jenna had just started to piece together what Peggy Sue

was talking about when they came through an opening and out into the arena. It was only a few minutes before the show started, and the seats were filled to capacity. The bull riders sat on the railing or strutted around the chutes and holding pens with hats pulled low and chaps flapping.

For a moment, Jenna felt like she was back in high school, surrounded by arrogant cowboys who thought that women should kiss their dung-covered boots. It should've annoyed her. Instead, a nostalgic feeling came out of nowhere and brought a lump to the back of her throat. She barely had time to swallow it down when she was being hauled over to three bull riders who sat along the railing. They were all handsome and rugged. But only one was hatless with hair that gleamed silver in the bright stadium lights.

The lack of a hat didn't make Beau look any less of a rodeo star. Tan leather chaps encased his thighs and flared out from his bent knees, the red fringe hanging to the boot heels hooked on the rail. He wore a blue-plaid western shirt beneath a black Kevlar vest, and one glove hung over the silver buckle of his belt. He was laughing at something the cowboy on his right had said, and his eyes were still twinkling when they shifted over to Peggy Sue.

"Hey, darlin'." He jumped down to the hard-packed dirt. "I've been meanin' to call you, but—" His gaze finally drifted over to Jenna, and his eyes widened.

"But you got tied up with your wife and kids?" Peggy Sue delivered a slap to Beau's cheek that had Jenna cringing. "Shame on you, Beauregard Cates." She tugged Jenna closer. "Your poor wife stuck in the trailer with your kids while you're livin' it up at the Holiday Inn. And here I thought you were one of the good guys."

Only a slight tightening in Beau's jaw showed his

irritation. Instead of explaining things to Peggy, he turned to Jenna. "Honey, I thought I told you to never bother me at work."

As mad as she was at the man, Jenna couldn't help but be amused. She bit back her smile. "I know you did, su-ugar," she stretched out the endearment. "But I didn't want you to go without your lucky hat." She set the Stetson on his head and jerked it down so far it bent the tops of his ears. "There. Now ain't that better?"

"Much," he said between his teeth before he glanced over at Peggy Sue. "If you'll excuse us, I need to have a word with my ... wife." He latched on to Jenna's arm and dragged her back the way she'd come.

They ended up in a corridor that smelled of manure and popcorn.

"What the hell do you think you're doing running around telling people that we're married?" He dropped her arm and glared down at her.

For some reason, she couldn't help adjusting the hat on his head and smoothing out the brim. "It was the only story I could think of to get back to see you."

Beau blinked, and his shoulders relaxed as a smile tipped the corners of his mouth. "You made up that tall tale just to see me? Did you break it off with your nipple-ringed boyfriend?"

She rolled her eyes. "Don't get a big head, Cowboy. I didn't come to stroke your ego." She dug around in her tote and pulled out the lavender invitation. "I came to ask you about this."

It only took one glance for Beau to whip off his hat and slap it against his thigh. "Damn it, Minnie."

"Minnie? Who is Minnie? And how did she get my

address?" She stepped closer. "You gave it to her, didn't you? That was why you were following me." His mute-ness confirmed her suspicions, and her anger deflated, replaced with bewilderment. "But why?"

Beau combed his fingers through his hair and blew out his breath. "I did it as a favor for Minnie, who manages the henhouse for me."

"So you're saying you knew nothing about this?" She flapped the invitation in his face.

Before he could answer the announcer's voice echoed down the corridor. "Welcome to Madison Square Garden and the fifth annual bull ridin' ..."

"Look, Jenna," Beau said as he pulled his hat back on. "If I was you, I'd just ignore it. Minnie's old and delu-sional." He turned and walked back the way they'd come, his boots clicking on the cement floor and his chaps flapping against his legs.

Jenna looked down at the invitation.

Ignore it?

Not likely.

Being Mrs. Beauregard Cates earned her the right to sit in the box seats with a bunch of beautiful women, who did happen to be married to bull riders, and a couple from Idaho who seemed to be waiting for the cowboys to strip off their clothes. At least, the woman was.

"...my friend, Urlene, got a picture with The Naked Cowboy, but he wasn't nearly as cute as him." She jabbed a long nail in the direction of Beau, who had pulled off his hat and placed it over his chest as a rider with the United States flag entered the arena. The woman leaned closer and whispered in an overly loud voice. "Don't tell Marty, but that cowboy makes my panties do the cha-cha-cha."

Jenna wished she didn't know what the woman was talking about. Unfortunately, her panties did more than the cha-cha-cha when Beau had kissed her. They almost incinerated. And it was wrong. So wrong. She loved Davy. She didn't want a man who strutted around to the screams and sighs of the rodeo "buckle bunnies" like the cock of the walk. A man whose forearms below the rolled-up sleeves of his western shirt were as big as Davy's calves. A man who didn't hesitate to position himself over the back of a two-thousand-pound bull who was already slamming into the railing of the holding pen like the Tasmanian Devil.

Switchback seemed to be a favorite of the crowd. The roar was deafening when the announcer said the bull's name. It was Jenna's experience that rodeo crowds liked the bulls tossing off the rider more than they liked the rider staying on. And if they loved Switchback, it could only mean one thing.

"...so I told Marty," the woman next to her continued to ramble as Beau eased down on the back of the bull and secured his gloved hand beneath the rope, "retirement is for enjoying life. Not sitting around watching *The Price Is Right*. That's why we bought my cousin's Winni-bago. We plan on traveling all over the country this summer." She leaned down and picked something up off the floor by Jenna's feet. "Here, sweetie, you dropped this."

But Jenna didn't reach for the invitation. Her gaze was pinned on Beau. It would serve him right if he got his butt tossed to the ground. Which didn't explain why her stomach clenched when the gate swung open and beast and cowboy whirled out.

Beau hung on, his hand posed behind him and his legs

hugging the animal's sides. He had almost stayed on for the full eight seconds when the bull switched directions and did a high kick. Beau went sailing. Unfortunately, his hand remained firmly tucked beneath the bull rope.

Jenna came to her feet as his body flopped alongside the still-bucking animal. After what felt like an eternity, he finally freed his hand and landed on his feet, racing over to the railing as the bullfighters corralled the bull back toward the chute.

"The Henhouse?"

Jenna looked down to find the woman reading the invitation, completely unconcerned with what had taken place in the arena.

"Marty," she jabbed her husband in the ribs, "we need to check this place out. I bet Urlene hasn't been here."

Her husband rolled his eyes. "Before or after your picture with The Naked Cowboy? Although it doesn't look like you're gonna be gettin' that." He pointed his camera and snapped off a shot. "That's a dislocated shoulder if ever I saw one."

Chapter Six

BEAU'S SHOULDER THROBBED LIKE A SONOFABITCH. And to make matters worse he was stuck in a cab with Nurse Ratched, who didn't seem to understand that when a man was hurt he wanted to be left the hell alone.

"You should've taken a painkiller like the doctor said." Jenna picked up the blue ice bag that he'd hooked over his knee and pressed it to his shoulder. "And keep the ice on it."

"I don't need a painkiller or friggin' ice," he snapped as he tossed the bag to the floor of the cab.

"My, for such a happy cowboy, you sure are a surly patient." She sent him a know-it-all look that really got on his last nerve. For a second, he thought about showing her how surly he could be and tossing her ass out of the cab. But then he remembered how well she wrestled, and he figured that with a bum shoulder he'd more than likely lose.

And he'd already lost once that night.

He leaned his head back against the seat and sulked.

Damn the woman for showing up and making him lose

his concentration while riding Switchback. And damn her for realizing he was injured. And really damn her for bringing everyone's attention to it by climbing over the railing and jumping down from the box seats like some kind of television cop. After completely stunning the crowd, she'd started issuing orders like a marine sergeant with new recruits. The other riders had rushed to do her bidding, going for the rodeo doc and helping Beau down from the rail whether he wanted to be helped or not.

Beau hadn't wanted the help. He preferred to suffer in private.

He glared out the window. He hated being sick or injured. Hated it with a passion. It was a cruel reminder that, no matter how fast he ran, the grim reaper was just a step behind him.

The buildings outside the window finally drew his attention, and he sat up.

"Just where the hell are we going?"

Jenna lounged back in the seat, casually leafing through the program she'd gotten at the competition. "To my apartment."

"Oh no, I'm not." The last thing Beau wanted was to spend the night with Jenna and her nipple-ringed boyfriend. He leaned up to tell the driver to take him to his hotel when a sharp pain shot through his shoulder and forced him to sit back.

"You don't have a choice." Jenna reached down, picked up the ice bag, and handed it to him. "Since you refuse to go to the hospital, and the doctor at the arena said that you shouldn't be alone, I'm your only option."

"You wouldn't be if you hadn't made up that story." Beau pressed the ice bag to his shoulder. "If you hadn't convinced everyone there that you were my loving wife, I could've found someone else to nurse me back to health."

"Like Peggy Sue-per Boobs."

Beau forced a smile as his gaze slid down to her chest. "I can see where you'd be jealous."

"Not in the least," Jenna said. "I wouldn't lug those things around on a bet. And as for making up the story, I wouldn't have had to make up anything if you had been truthful with me from the beginning. Which is the other reason that you're spending the night at my apartment. I want the truth about the invitation."

The truth. Beau wasn't so sure he knew what the truth was. Was Minnie actually thinking about starting up a house of ill repute? Beau refused to believe it. Still, why else would Minnie be searching for long-lost hens?

The taxi pulled up to the curb, and Jenna got out. Beau might've remained right where he was if she hadn't reached in and grabbed his black backpack. He traveled light, but what he did carry he cherished.

With a mumbled curse, he got out of the cab. Jenna was already searching through his pack to pay the cab driver. She pulled out one silver high heel and shot Beau a questioning look. Okay, so maybe he didn't cherish everything in his backpack. The shoe he had tossed in on a whim.

She had just finished paying the cab driver when something down the street caught her attention. She dropped his backpack and her shoe and took off like a shot, leaving Beau standing in front of her apartment. Her target was a slick blue Mercedes that had just pulled up to the curb. She barely waited for the man in the gray suit to step out before she started yelling.

"I'm through with you terrorizing this neighborhood,

Alejandro! I told you to leave Miguel alone. Since you refuse to listen, I'm going to make your life a living hell. Every time I see you, I'm calling the cops." She pulled out her cell phone.

The man only smiled. He was a creepy-looking dude with shoulder-length black hair and a pockmarked face.

"Now, chica, why would you want to go and do that? I'm just trying to earn a living."

"By ruining people's lives with drugs." She poked his chest with a finger as if the five thugs that had gotten out of the car with the man weren't towering over her.

Well, damn. Beau tossed the ice bag down to his backpack.

Fortunately, before he could intervene and get his ass whupped, a police squad car came around the corner. Alejandro's smile dropped, and he motioned for his posse. Like cockroaches, they all disappeared inside the building where the Mercedes was parked.

"Do you always make friends so easily?" Beau asked when Jenna came striding back over and picked up his backpack, her shoe, and the ice bag.

She tucked a shoulder under his arm and pulled him up the front steps. "I guess I'm just personable."

Moments later, Beau stood in the small living room of Jenna's apartment.

"You can have the bedroom." She led him into the next room. "Davy works nights, and I don't have a problem sleeping on the couch."

Beau might've argued if the couch hadn't been the size of a saddle blanket. The bed wasn't much bigger. Still, he sighed with relief when he sank down into the saggy mattress. Jenna didn't waste any time straddling each leg and pulling off his boots. Even as tired as he was, he couldn't help noticing her butt. It wasn't really a butt. More like an extension of her mile-long legs. Beau preferred lush, round bottoms with enough junk in the trunk to hold on to.

Which didn't explain the spiral of heat that settled in his crotch.

Thankfully, once his boots were off, she left him to finish getting undressed. It wasn't easy with one hand and a sling to contend with. After the hassle of getting his shirt off, he decided to leave his jeans on and climbed into bed. He had just punched down the pillow when he heard the shower, followed by Jenna singing. And the woman was no Carrie Underwood. Still, the night's events caught up with him, and Beau dozed off before she got to the part about digging a key into the paint of some poor guy's truck. He didn't know how long he slept. He woke to a dark room and a cool hand pressed to his brow.

"I brought you some water and your pain pills," Jenna said as she clicked on a small lamp. The light had Beau squinting for a few seconds before his vision cleared.

Jenna sat on the edge of the bed in a tiny little white tank that clung to her small, high breasts like a second skin and a pair of plaid boxers with the baggy legs riding high on firm thighs.

"How are you feeling?" She handed him the water, but he refused the pills. He'd rather have pain than numbness.

He took a sip of water and flexed his shoulder. It still hurt like hell, but not as bad as before. "Better." He handed her back the glass. Their fingers brushed, and with the contact came a swift bolt of desire.

It made no damned sense. She wasn't even close to the

type of woman he preferred. She was too skinny. Too flat chested. And way too involved with another man. Which was why he'd spent the last few days trying to put her out of his mind. It hadn't been easy. The kiss they had shared slipped in when he least expected it. And if he were truthful, he would have to admit that a part of him had been overjoyed to see her at Madison Square Garden. The part that couldn't seem to take his eyes off the tiny little nubs poking through her white top.

"You're certainly in a better humor," she said.

Beau lifted his gaze. "I'm sorry about that. I'm a pretty shitty patient." He leaned back on the pillows. "So why did you do it? Why would you bring home a stranger? And don't give me that bit about the invitation."

She set the glass of water down on the nightstand and got up and walked over to the window. She bent to tug it open, making him realize that she had a butt after all. Two smooth cheeks peeked out from beneath the hem of her boxers, forcing Beau to rearrange the sheet over his lap.

"You're not a stranger." She pulled up the window and turned around, her eyes direct and serious. "You're a Texan."

He didn't know why his throat suddenly felt dry and clogged with emotion. Maybe because he'd lost the right to call himself a Texan. Now he was more of a drifter who avoided Texas like the plague. Or maybe what he avoided the most was his family. A family who reminded him of what he could never have.

Sitting up, he reached for the glass of water and downed it in three big gulps. It didn't help. Now the raw emotion seemed to have settled in his stomach. It grew bigger as Jenna continued.

"You know what I miss the most?" she said as she walked over to the dresser. The top was cluttered with all kinds of crap, but her hand unerringly found the silver frame. From that distance, all he could tell was that it was a picture of a group of people. A family as big as his own. "I miss knowing the names of every person in town. I miss living within walking distance of the elementary school where I learned to read. And the church where I was baptized. I miss walking down the street and having folks ask about my mama." She set the picture down as if she couldn't stand to look at it anymore and returned to the window.

Beau knew how she felt. Lately, his homesickness had become a gnawing ache that nothing could soothe. Suddenly, he realized what attracted him to Jenna Jay. It wasn't her slim, athletic body. Or her pretty, long hair. Or the freckles that sprinkled her nose. It was the place she hailed from. The place she called home.

Texas.

"So why did you leave?" he asked as he came up from the bed. "Davy?"

"That was part of it," she said. "And maybe I left because I wanted to see who I am outside my large, over-achieving family. In Texas, I'm just a Scroggs. Here, I'm my own person." She paused. "Still, I miss it."

Trying to lighten the mood, he moved up behind her. "So how's your mama?" he said with the thickest twang he could muster.

She didn't turn around, and when she spoke, her voice was soft and hollow. "I don't know. I haven't talked with her."

If Beau had learned anything about women over the

years, he'd learned that they didn't always want a man to ask a lot of questions and try to fix things. Most of the time they just wanted you to shut up and hold them. Beau figured this was one of those times. So he slipped his arm around her waist and pulled her back against him. Her muscles tensed for a second before she relaxed. Her ponytail brushed his nose, and he breathed deeply. Tonight she didn't smell like cherries. She smelled like lemons. The kind his Aunt Tess used every summer in her fresh-squeezed lemonade.

"You could call her, you know?" he said as he fought the strong desire to lean over and brush his lips along her neck to see if she tasted sour or sweet.

She glanced over her shoulder. "It's not that easy."

Beau understood. He talked to his mother at least twice a week, but it never got any easier. She wanted him to come home. Something Beau couldn't bring himself to do. Not now. And maybe not ever.

A piece of Jenna's hair had come undone from her ponytail, and Beau reached out and smoothed it back behind her small, shell-shaped ear. "My mama's hair used to be this exact color. Of course, she dyes it a different color every other week so she was bound to stumble on yours eventually."

Jenna smiled and turned to face him. "My mama has never colored her hair. It's as brown as a sable mink, just like my sisters'. I'm the only one in the family with hair this blond." She reached up and gently rested her hand on his shoulder. "You should be in bed with ice on this."

"It doesn't hurt that much anymore."

"Why bulls?" she asked. "Do you have some kind of a death wish?"

"Not even close." He lifted her hand from his shoulder and examined the palm, running his thumb along the crisscrossed lines. "In fact, I have more of a life wish." He drew a finger down the center. "I want to live. Not forever, but just until I do everything I want to do. Experience everything I want to experience." He brought her palm to his lips and kissed it. "Taste everything I want to taste."

"I don't think this is a good idea," she said rather breathlessly.

"But that's the funny thing about ideas." He nibbled on the tip of her index finger before running it along the bottom edge of his teeth. "Sometimes bad ideas can lead to really good times. Example—riding a bull with a dislocated shoulder led to me being here with you." He kissed his way to her wrist. He tested the pulse that throbbed there with his tongue before looking up at her. "You want to see where another bad idea will lead? Because I sure as hell do, sweetheart."

He didn't wait for her reply. Instead, he released her hand and leaned down to kiss her softly parted lips. The desire that had been simmering since he'd first met her caught fire, and he lost himself in the heat of her mouth.

Unfortunately, she stopped him before he could get his fill.

"No." She stepped back. "I can't—"

"Jenna?"

They both turned. Her boyfriend stood in the doorway. He looked shocked, but instead of yelling or throwing a few punches, he just turned and walked out.

Jenna quickly followed, closing the door behind her. Figuring that was his cue to leave, Beau walked over and picked up his shirt off the chair. Rather than take time to get it and his boots on, he stuffed them in his backpack. Since he wasn't about to walk through the apartment and cause more problems, he headed to the window. He had just stepped out onto the fire escape when he heard Jenna's voice coming out of the open window next to him. She was rambling, spilling much more than Beau thought was necessary.

"... he was hurt and didn't have anyone to take care of him so I didn't think you'd mind if I brought him home. And I was just giving him some more painkillers because everyone knows that you have to stay ahead of the pain. Then we got to talking about Texas—because like I told you the other day that's where he's from—but nothing happened. I mean, nothing more than that stupid kiss."

Stupid kiss? Beau moved closer to the window.

"I'm not mad, Jenna," Davy said. "In fact, if you want the truth, I'm relieved that you found someone else."

"What do you mean?" Jenna's voice sounded strained. "I didn't find anyone else. That cowboy means nothing to me."

Beau's brow knotted.

"It doesn't matter," Davy said. "It's just not working out, babe. We're two different people. I'm laid back, and you are ... in some crazy hyper-drive. It worked out okay in college, but that kind of intensity doesn't work for an artist. It smothers creative juices."

Smothers creative juices? What an asshole.

Beau heard a door open, and Jenna's voice came from the bedroom window.

"See. He's gone. And I promise he won't be back." There was the sound of a drawer being opened. "What are you doing? You can't leave me. I need you."

Davy laughed. "You are the one person in the world who doesn't need anyone." There was a long silence that had Beau leaning over to peek into the window. Jenna stood in the middle of the room, watching as Davy shoveled most of the hair care products off the dresser and into a duffel bag. Once he had it zipped, he walked over and gave Jenna a brief kiss.

"See ya around, babe."

Now Beau wasn't a man who rejoiced in other people's tribulations. Nor was he the type of man who looked a gift horse in the mouth. For some reason, fate had given him the hots for a skinny tomboy and then offered her up on a silver platter. And Beau wasn't about to ignore the offering.

Of course, he would need to give her a little time to grieve the loss of the nipple-ringed dude. But since Beau was out of the bull-riding competition, he had nothing but time. He turned to head down the stairs when he ran smack dab into a hooded figure.

"Shit!" the boy yelped and threw a punch at Beau. He missed and hit the backpack, knocking it out of Beau's hand and sending it sailing over the rail of the fire escape. Before he could correct his aim, Beau grabbed his sweatshirt and shoved the kid against the living room window.

"Beau?" Jenna's head appeared. Her gaze ran over him before moving to his assailant. "Miguel? What are you doing out there?" She climbed out the window. "Does your mother know you're up this late?"

"Let me go, Mofo!" The kid squirmed and tried to get away from Beau.

"I knew it," Jenna said. "You're dealing drugs, aren't you?"

"No," the kid said belligerently.

"Shall we find out?" Beau slipped the black backpack off the kid's shoulder and tossed it to Jenna. For an athletic girl, she sucked at catch. Or maybe her reaction time was slow due to her depression over losing Davy. Either way, she missed, and the pack went sailing over the railing to join Beau's.

That seemed to send the kid over the edge. He twisted inside his sweatshirt and fought like a little demon. Beau might've been able to hang on to him if he hadn't hit him in the sore shoulder. Once Miguel was free, he raced down the stairs in a clatter of feet.

Beau would've let him go if Jenna hadn't charged after Miguel. She couldn't catch, but she could run. She was already racing toward the street by the time Beau jumped down from the fire escape ladder. Figuring Jenna could handle the kid, Beau searched around for his backpack. He found the kid's, but not his. He had just picked it up when Jenna's voice rang out.

"Can't you get it through your heads? I'm not going with you!"

Beau came around the corner to find Jenna fighting with two men in cowboy hats and...John Wayne masks? Damn, the woman was more trouble than she was worth. Beau dropped the backpack and drove into the mountainous John Wayne. It was like running into a brick wall. The man just wrapped his tree-trunk arms around Beau and squeezed. Pain shot through Beau's shoulder, and he groaned. The next thing he knew Jenna was hanging from the huge man's back like a monkey.

"You leave him alone, you big ox!" She wrapped her arms around his thick neck in a death lock. He released

Beau, and once he was free, Beau stepped back and threw a punch at John Wayne's big rubber chin. Unfortunately, the man twisted at the last second, and instead of Beau's fist connecting with his jaw, it connected with Jenna's.

Like a tranquilized calf, she slipped from the man's back and landed in a puddle at his boots. Before Beau could do more than blink, a fist the size of a dinner plate came at him.

There was an explosion of pain, followed by complete darkness.

Chapter Seven

"JENNA? WAKE UP, SWEETHEART."

The word "sweetheart" had a warm, contented feeling settling in Jenna's stomach. She tried to go back to sleep, but the person who had called her a sweetheart wouldn't let her. He gently shook her until she opened her eyes.

Darkness greeted her before a flash of light illuminated Beau's concerned face.

"Are you okay?" he asked as he reached out and cradled her chin, brushing his thumb over a very tender spot.

The light faded, throwing the room into darkness again. Jenna tried to get her brain to work. What was she doing in the dark with Beauregard Cates? Hadn't she already decided that being alone with Beau was a bad idea? Except it didn't feel like a bad idea. With his jeaned legs pressed against hers and his warm hand cradling her jaw, it just felt right.

Lights flashed again. They looked to be coming from the window above Beau's head. A tiny window that Jenna didn't recognize. Nor did she recognize the dingy curtains that swayed from the skinny rod. Before things could register, a loud horn blasted, causing Jenna to sit straight up and crack her head on the low ceiling.

"Dang it!" She fell back down to Beau's chest and grabbed her head, but she must've hit his sore shoulder because he released a pain-filled groan. She scooted over only to come in contact with a wall. "Where are we?" she asked.

"We're in a camper," Beau stated. "Similar to the one my Uncle Jasper used to take me fishing in when I was a kid. Which might explain why I remember the bed being a lot bigger."

"A camper?" Jenna carefully lifted her head and looked around as the next set of headlights flashed through the window. "What are we doing in a camper?"

"I've been waiting to ask you the same thing," he said. "I only came to a couple minutes before you did. I'm assuming we have one of your many enemies to thank for this camping vacation."

Suddenly, everything that happened that night came back to her. Beau's kiss. Davy breaking up with her. Chasing after Miguel. Two masked men waiting outside her apartment building. The fight that ensued. Her getting hit in the jaw by . . .

"You hit me!" She slugged Beau in the shoulder, realizing too late that it was the injured one.

His breath hissed out before he grabbed her fist. "Shit, woman, calm down. I didn't exactly do it on purpose. The idiot you were choking moved at the last second."

"I would've been able to bring him down with the chokehold if you hadn't interfered."

"Remind me not to come to your rescue again." He released her hand and flopped back on the pillow.

"Especially when all you've done is cause me trouble. I would be sleeping soundly in my hotel room right now if not for your interference."

"No doubt cuddled up next to Peggy's super boobs," she huffed as she climbed over him and jumped down to the floor. It didn't take her long to locate a light switch. She flicked it on, and a dull overhead light came on. The camper wasn't big, or particularly well cared for. The material on the small table's bench seats was worn and stained. The paneling on the walls was scratched and peeling away from the metal frame. And the entire place reeked of beer and fish.

There was one door and two windows. The windows were small and covered on the outside with some kind of metal. The door was locked and wouldn't budge. Even when Jenna tried to kick it open. With pain shooting up her leg, she sat down on one of the bench seats at the table and rubbed the sole of her bare foot.

"You planning on diving out while traveling over sixty miles per hour?"

Jenna glanced up at Beau, who was peeking over the edge of the mattress. His hair was mussed and his jaw twice as bruised as hers. He was right. If it hadn't been for her, he wouldn't be in this mess.

"Look, I'm sorry about getting you involved in this," she said.

"So who do you think it is?"

"Probably Bruno Sawyer, who owns the Fresh Marts I've been picketing. He's the only one who employs a goon the size of Andre the Giant. Although I can't see Bruno's guys wearing masks or sneaking around in the dark."

Beau jumped down from the bunk, and Jenna had a hard time keeping her gaze off his bare chest. He didn't have bulging muscles, just long, lean ones that washed down his stomach in smooth ripples. And every ripple was tanned a toasty brown.

She had noticed his muscles and tan the night before. What she hadn't noticed was the small tattoo on his chest. Since it was partially covered by his sling, she couldn't tell what it was. But it looked like some kind of Japanese writing. She got a closer look when he leaned over her to test the strength of the metal on the window.

"Well, whoever it is," he said, "he's worked hard to make sure we can't escape." He brushed by her and checked the door before looking in all the cabinets. When he reached the small door next to the bunk, he opened it and sighed with relief. "Thank God."

Jenna sat up. "What is it? Did you find a way out?"

He stepped in and closed the door behind him. The steady splash, followed with the whoosh of a flush, answered Jenna's questions. Beau stepped out and climbed up the short ladder to the bunk.

"What are you doing?" she asked.

"I'm going to get some sleep." He stuffed a pillow under his head.

"But we need to find a way out of here."

"I problem solve better after a few hours of sleep. Wake me if we stop." He stretched his stocking feet over the edge.

There was a hole in one sock, and his big toe stuck out.

Not wanting to spend her time staring at Beau's toe, she got up and searched through the drawers and cabinets. The only useful thing she found was a butter knife that she bent trying to pry open the door. The camper seemed to be going faster now. Since the only windows she could see out of were in the bunk, she shut off the light and climbed up the ladder.

"Scoot over." She pushed at Beau's feet. He grumbled before inching over just enough for her to get up on the small bed. In order not to touch him, she had to scoot as close to the window as she could get. She couldn't see anything, just the glow of taillights and the occasional flash of headlights. She tried to keep her eyes open by imagining what she was going to do to Bruno when he released them, but soon the gentle rocking of the cab lulled her to sleep.

Jenna woke from a very pleasant dream. Pressing her face into the pillow, she tried to recapture the image. But it was too late. Reality slipped in, and she started to notice things. Like the rocking of the bed. The soreness of her jaw. And the fact that the pillow she rested against wasn't a pillow but a warm chest that held the scent of spicy soap and...cow?

She opened her eyes to bright sunlight and the slightly whiskered jaw of the man who was stretched out beneath her. A man that didn't smell like cigarettes, stale beer, and hair products. And he didn't feel like skin and bones. This man felt like muscles. Warm, defined muscles that seemed all tight and flexed.

Slowly, she lifted her head.

Beau was watching her, the sapphire of his eyes peeking through the dark fringe of his lashes. A warning signal went off in her head, but before she could take heed and move away, he tipped his head to the side and captured her mouth with his. The signal cut off in mid-warning as every thought in her head dissolved beneath the scorching kiss. He kissed like he smiled, teasing and sizzling hot. His tongue brushed against hers and coaxed it into his mouth where he gently sucked on it until she moaned.

While he kissed her with a skill that no boyfriend had ever had, his hand slid up her bare thigh to the edge of her boxers. His fingers slipped under the fabric and caressed her butt cheek, sending a line of heat straight to the spot between her legs. She clamped them together, but it only intensified the sensation. He seemed to understand her dilemma, because his callused hand didn't stop at her cheek. It dipped beneath her panties, the tips of his fingers brushing the crack of her flexed butt.

With a swirl of tongue and heated suction, he pulled back from the kiss and nibbled his way over to her ear. "Easy, sweetheart. Just relax. I'm not going to do anything you don't want me to."

That was the problem. Jenna couldn't think of a thing she didn't want him to do.

His tongue flicked out against her earlobe. "Lean up just a little," he whispered. "Just enough that I can get to those sweet breasts of yours."

Probably for the first time in her life, Jenna obeyed without question. She pressed her hands to the mattress on either side of his head and held herself up so her breasts were inches from his mouth.

He looked at her, his eyes hot and his lips without a hint of smile. "Do you know how long I've been wanting to do this?" He leaned up and captured a nipple in his mouth. Moisture saturated the fabric of her shirt. "It feels like forever."

Jenna was so caught up in what his mouth was doing she didn't even pay attention to his hand until it settled over her butt cheeks and pressed her firmly against the rock-hard bulge beneath his jeans. She moaned at the intense feeling of being held tightly in Beau's hand on one side and pressed against his hardness on the other. She adjusted her hips, settling his rigid length between her legs. Consequently, the movement allowed his fingers deeper access. Her eyes widened as he dipped into her wet heat.

"Sweet." His mouth moved over to her other breast. "I knew you would taste sweet."

As his fingers thrust, his mouth manipulated her nipple through her shirt, the pull of his lips perfectly synchronized to every stroke of his fingers. Her orgasm burst upon her with a suddenness that took her by surprise.

As the intense feelings crested, Beau's fingers deepened, and he bit down gently on her nipple, prolonging the intense sensations coursing through her body. When it was over, she slumped down to his bare chest, careful not to rest on the arm in the sling. She would've gone back to sleep if he hadn't spoken.

"You're going to have to help me with these jeans, sweetheart." When she didn't move or say anything, he shifted her to one side. Transfixed by the play of sunlight on the muscles of his abdomen, all she could do was watch as he unsnapped his pants and pulled down the zipper. She had just gotten a peek of navy boxer briefs when he froze.

"Sonofabitch." He flopped an arm over his eyes.

"What happened? Is it your shoulder?"

He peeked out from under his arm. "I don't have a condom."

The word "condom" brought Jenna out of her sexual haze and back to reality.

"Oh my god." She scooted as far away from Beau's hard body as she could get. "What am I doing?"

Beau lowered his arm and looked at her. "I think it's called sex, but if you'd like to refer to it as making love, I don't have a problem with that."

"No!" She sat up, cracked her head on the ceiling, and then flopped back down.

"Obviously a slow learner," Beau said as he reached over to rub her head. She ducked away.

"There was no making love," she stated. "It was sex. Just sex."

Beau tipped his head. "Okay with me. Now can we get back to the 'just sex' because, if my memory serves me, I haven't had my turn?"

Jenna's mouth opened, and when not one word showed up, she snapped it shut.

There were about a million things she could've said, but not one of them made any sense. Probably because she couldn't make sense of what had just taken place. As it turned out, Beau didn't have any such problem.

"Oh, I get it. Now that you've used me to take care of your physical needs, you're suddenly feeling guilty about cheating on Davy. But if I remember correctly, didn't he walk out on you?"

"Because of you," she snapped. She didn't know why she was suddenly so angry. Maybe because the truth hurt. She had used Beau to take care of her physical needs. And Davy had walked out on her. And she'd let him.

"Now I don't think you can blame me for that." Beau readjusted the pillow behind his head. "According to what

I heard, he left because you emasculated him. You took on the male role, leaving him to be the woman."

Jenna pulled her gaze from his belly button in the sea of ripped muscles. "Well, you must have a hearing problem because that's not what he said at all. He did not leave me because I was too manly." She stared up at the ceiling, trying to remember the conversation. "He left because he..."

"Didn't feel needed," Beau finished for her.

Since that was exactly what Davy had said, she couldn't deny it. She also couldn't let Beau have the last word.

"He loves me, and I love him."

"I don't doubt it in the least. But we're not talking about love. We're talking about need. And need is a much stronger emotion than love. We need things we can't live without—air, water, food." He glanced over at the tiny kitchen. "Speaking of which, I wonder if the fridge has milk to go with those boxes of cereal—"

"Well, I need Davy," she cut him off.

He looked back at her. "For what?"

Jenna scrambled through her mind, but not one thing popped into her head. She could make a mile-long list of why she loved him, but not one reason why she needed him. Not to pay her bills. Or pick up dinner or groceries. Or fix things around the apartment.

Or give her orgasms.

"It's nothing to get too upset about, sweetheart," Beau said. "It's not easy finding a person you love and need. It will happen, just give it time." He squinted up at the window. "Do you think you could close those curtains? For early morning, that sun is blinding."

With her mind consumed with finding something she needed Davy for, Jenna followed his direction without argument. The sun *was* bright. And for the first time since waking up, she wondered what time it was. Certainly, they would've gotten to Jersey by now. Pressing her head against the glass, she tried to see where the sun was in the sky. Before she could, Beau's hand settled on her thigh, his fingers skating up toward her butt.

"I was wondering if there's any possibility that we could get back to the 'just sex.'"

Before she could smack his hand away and explain that she had no intentions of making the same mistake twice, a road sign out the window caught her attention. A sign that had her eyes widening and her heart pounding. She forgot all about Beau and Davy and everything else but the white reflective words and numbers.

NASHVILLE 248 MILES.

Chapter Eight

THE TOWN OF BRAMBLE, Texas, was ready for summer and the patriotic holidays the season brought with it. Red, white, and blue bunting was draped across Main Street, where it would remain until after Labor Day, and American flags filled shop windows and flapped over every doorway, commercial or residential.

Marcy Henderson paid little attention to the decorations as she pulled her Pinto into the first empty parking space she came to. Her mind was preoccupied with other things—mainly with becoming a hooker.

The hens had turned out to be a sweet group of old ladies, but either they had forgotten everything they learned about prostitution or they didn't want to teach it to Marcy. Sunshine had taught her how to make a bed you could bounce a quarter off of. Baby had taught her how to make chicken and dumplings and a delicious apple pie. And Minnie had talked her ear off about the history of the henhouse. But when Marcy asked questions about "the business," the hens looked at her as if she was speaking a foreign language.

Maybe Minnie thought Marcy knew everything she needed to know about sex. It wasn't like Marcy hadn't had sex before. Her teenage years had been filled with enough sexual experimentation to earn her the title of town slut. And in the years that followed, she hadn't had a problem feeding into the gossip. She had chased after men like a trailer-park dog after cars. Her sister, Samantha, thought Marcy's preoccupation with men had to do with the lack of love she'd gotten from their daddy. Sam was probably right. No matter how many men Marcy had slept with, she could never seem to fill the hole inside her heart.

But the epiphany had come a little late.

Or maybe it came just in time. A hooker didn't need a heart. What she did need was a little more information than she was getting about how to turn sex into a lucrative business.

Marcy climbed out of her car and stepped up on the curb. Across the street, Moses Tate was snoozing on the bench in front of Sutter's Pharmacy. So far, Moses was the only male customer who had been out to Miss Hattie's. Marcy might need the money, but she was happy the old, wrinkled guy had a thing for Minnie.

After adjusting the straps of her high heels, Marcy strutted past the bright pink caboose that served as Josephine's Diner. On a Saturday morning, it was jam-packed with people, a few spilling over into the parking lot as they waited for a table.

"Hey, Hot Mama! You lookin' for a little Johnnycakes?"

Marcy wanted to ignore the man who yelled, but Johnny Reardon wasn't the type of man who liked to be ignored. She had made the mistake of having sex with him one night when she'd had a little too much to drink, and she'd had to endure his bullying and asinine pickup lines ever since.

"Hey, yourself," she called and kept right on walking. "I'm late for an appointment, Johnny, but I'll catch you later at Bootlegger's."

Fortunately, Johnny was too lazy to try and catch up with her, and she continued down the street toward the public library.

Most folks would be surprised to find out that the library was Marcy's favorite place in town. Growing up in a house with arguing parents, it had been the only place she could find peace and quiet. But it wasn't peace and quiet that greeted her when she pulled open the door. It was the strong smell of permanent solution and nonstop chatter that she recognized immediately.

"... so I told Kenny Gene that if he don't poop or get off the pot that this girl is goin' huntin' for a different feller. I won't waste any more years of my life, not when my bi-oh-logical clock is tickin'."

Marcy stepped around the corner to discover Twyla had set up her beauty salon behind the circular counter of Ms. Murphy's desk. Hairbrushes, combs, and bowls of dye littered the top, while Darla sat in the caster chair with a plastic cape fastened around her neck and her hair twigged up in bright pink permanent rods.

"I don't know what you're complainin' about, Twyla," Darla said as she continued to work on the blanket she was crocheting. "The man gave you a diamond engagement ring that is almost as big as the one Lyle Dalton gave Shirlene. He's probably waitin' to marry you until he pays the thing off."

Twyla snapped in another rod. "Well, if that's the

reason, he can have it back. A diamond is not worth a two-year wait to have me another weddin'—" She glanced up. "Well, hey, Marcy. I haven't seen you around in a couple days. I thought you'd run back off to Fort Worth without sayin' good-bye."

Marcy waved a hand around at the clutter. "What in the world is going on here?"

Twyla was more than happy to explain. "Well, you know that Ms. Murphy up and married that hot Brant Cates, leavin' us without a librarian. We tried takin' applications. Even had a few bites." Her face scrunched up in confusion. "But after being interviewed by our selection committee—Mayor Sutter, Kenny Gene, Rye Pickett, and myself—the applicants didn't seem in such a hurry to take the job." She waved a comb at Marcy. "I think we asked them too many tough questions. I did the personality questions myself—like if you had five dollars what would you spend it on at Sutter's Pharmacy?"

"That is a tough one," Darla said. "Yesterday, I couldn't even decide between yarn, pipe cleaners, or sequins."

"See what I mean?" Twyla continued. "'Course, now I'm thinkin' I should've made them easier. Without a librarian, people are stuck volunteerin'. And some of us have to make a livin'." She frowned. "Especially when our boyfriends won't marry us and help pay the rent."

Realizing that Twyla was about to go on a tangent, Marcy quickly made her escape. "I'm just going to check out some books," she said as she headed over to the computers that sat on a side table.

"Help yourself," Twyla said, "but don't expect me to know how to check them out for you. I'm a hair stylist, not some computer whiz."

Marcy figured that was probably an overstatement. Twyla didn't fix hair as much as ruin it.

It didn't take Marcy long to pull up some books on the computer that might be useful. Since she couldn't find a pencil in the little basket on the side, she took note of the area the books were in and headed toward the back of the library. There were quite a few books written about sex, even one by a former prostitute. Marcy took the book from the shelf before heading around the corner to see what was on the other side.

With her attention on the upper shelf, she didn't see the man crouched down looking at the books on the lower shelf until she ran into him. He fell back, and in her slick-bottomed high heels, she fell forward, and they ended up sandwiched between the two shelves in a tangle of legs and arms.

It wasn't the first time this had happened to Marcy. And now that she worked at the henhouse, it certainly wouldn't be the last. Minnie might not have given her any instructions on sex, but she'd given her the Henhouse Rules. And rule number forty-four stated, "Don't give away the cart unless you've sold the horse." Which Marcy took to mean, no sex without first seeing the money.

Of course, perhaps this man had the money. He certainly had the desire. Marcy could feel it pressing against her leg. But just the thought of sex with some strange man for money had a sick feeling welling up inside her, and for a moment, she actually thought she was going to throw up.

She swallowed hard as she tried to untangle her legs from the man's. A man who wore a bright Hawaiian shirt, baggy shorts, and flip-flops. And the only person in Bramble who dressed like a surfer dude was...

"Pastor Robbins?" She stopped moving and stared

down at the man, who was looking at her as if she was his worst nightmare. Of course, given that he was a man of God and she a soon-to-be hooker, she probably was. But she had to give it to him. He recovered quickly.

"Well, hello, Miss Henderson." His gaze flickered down for a second before flickering back up with even more alarm reflected in the deep green of his eyes.

Marcy glanced down and immediately understood why. Her boobs had almost come out of her lacy Wal-Mart bra and were smashed against his chest like two over-filled water balloons. She tried to get up, but her high heel seemed to be stuck in one of the metal bookends. And her attempt to yank it out almost ended up changing Pastor Robbins's voice by three octaves.

He flinched, and she settled back against him. The hardness pressing into her leg was still there. And since he was a preacher, she had to wonder if he was packing a pistol. The old pastor had carried a Glock, but only after he'd tried to close down Bootlegger's and started receiving death threats.

"Just give me a second, Preacher," she said. "I think if you can slide over a few inches, I can get my shoe unhooked."

His gaze flickered back down before he slammed his eyes closed and nodded. Once he'd moved over, Marcy was able to pull her shoe free and climb off him. Within seconds, he followed her up. Although he kept his back to her for so long that she wondered if she hadn't kneed him in the balls after all.

"You okay?" she asked.

"Of course." He turned back around, his face still a little flushed. "How are you, Miss Henderson? I had heard you were back from Fort Worth. How is your mother?"

"Not so good. She had almost recovered from the first stroke when the second one hit. Now she can't even ask for a drink of water. But hopefully this new place we have her in will help." She reached down to pick up the books she'd dropped when she noticed that one had fallen open. An illustration of some Asian guy having sex with some fat Asian woman had her eyes almost popping out of her head. She was about to slam the book closed and save them both some major embarrassment when Pastor Robbins snatched it up and slipped it into the empty space on the lower shelf.

The same shelf that he'd been looking at.

Curious, she leaned closer to read the title, but the pastor stepped in front of her.

"So you were telling me about your mother, Miss Henderson. I was sorry to hear about her most recent stroke, but your sister said that your mother was very fortunate that you were there when it happened."

"I didn't do all that much, but call the ambulance," Marcy said absently, her mind still trying to piece things together.

"Somehow I doubt that," Pastor Robbins said. "You took care of her after the first stroke for two years. Most people wouldn't have lasted a month."

It had been a long time, but seeing as Marcy hadn't had anything better to do, it wasn't that big of a deal. At least, not as big of a deal as finding the pastor of her hometown looking at...

She leaned down and reached behind the pastor's legs, pulling the book back off the shelf. She looked at the title, and a smile lit her face, followed by a bubble of laughter. It had been so long since she'd had anything to laugh about, she gave herself up to it, leaning back against the shelf of books and holding her sides in glee.

The preacher didn't find it quite so amusing. He stood there watching her with a deep scowl on his tanned face.

"Hey!" Twyla's voice rang out, "this here is a library. So keep it down."

Marcy's laughter subsided, but her smile remained.

So did Pastor Robbins's scowl.

"I was doing research," he stated.

She glanced back at the book. "On the Kama Sutra? I haven't been to The First Baptist in years, but if that's what you're teachin' now, Pastor, I'll see you on Sunday."

Suddenly, the scowl disappeared to be replaced by a smile. Since Marcy tried to keep her distance from anything to do with church, it was the first time she'd really looked at the pastor. And she had to admit that he was a good-looking man, in a surfer dude kind of way. He had curly hair and pretty green eyes and a pair of shoulders that seemed wasted on a preacher.

As she examined their width, they lifted in a slight shrug. "I guess I'm busted."

"I guess you are," she said. "By the way, do you own a gun?"

He tipped his head. "Excuse me?"

She smiled even brighter. "Never mind." She went to hand him the book, but he shook his head.

"I think I've given in to my carnal flesh enough for one day."

Without hesitation, Marcy added the book to the stack in her arms. "Well, that's where we differ, Preacher Man. I can't seem to give in to mine enough."

The smile slipped, and he looked away. "Well, I guess

I should head on back to the church. It was nice seeing you, Miss Henderson." He turned and walked down the aisle.

When he was gone, Marcy was mad at herself for teasing him so much that he left. She probably would never get a chance to talk to him again. A preacher and a hooker had no business talking.

The front desk was empty when she got there so she opened up the little gate and stepped behind the counter. She had helped Ms. Murphy on occasion and knew how to use the scanner. Once she checked out her books, she noticed the full return bin and started checking those books back in. She had just loaded them onto a caster rack to return to the shelves when Twyla and Darla came out of the bathroom. Darla's hair was so tightly kinked she looked like Rachel Dean's toy poodle.

"Thanks, honey," Twyla said as she and Darla came back around the counter. "With three cuts, a dye, and a perm, I just haven't had time to get to the books."

"It's no problem." Marcy stacked the books on the cart. "I like to do this."

Twyla stopped fluffing Darla's curls, and her eyes lit up. "You do? Because I sure could use someone to take over my volunteer shift on Saturdays." When Marcy started to shake her head, Twyla's voice became pleading. "Please, honey, I'll give you a free haircut once a month and a dye if you can just help me out."

A haircut and dye from Twyla was the last thing Marcy wanted, but the thought of spending a couple hours in the library appealed to her. Certainly, she could squeeze in a little library time between her hooker duties.

"Fine," she said, "but only Saturdays."

Twyla whooped with delight and ran over to give her a hug. When she pulled back, she looked around. "What happened to Pastor Robbins? Is he still back there lookin' at bibles?"

"Nope." Marcy sent her an innocent look. "I think he's all through looking at books for the day. What's his story, anyway? Why doesn't he have a wife or a girlfriend?"

After covering Darla's hair in a cloud of Aqua-Net that had all three women coughing, Twyla answered. "Because some men are too holy to think about women and sex. And Pastor Robbins is one of those men."

Marcy glanced over at the Kama Sutra and smiled. "You don't say."

Chapter Nine

THE NIGHTMARE WAS ALWAYS THE SAME. It started with a dark, cloaked figure standing at the foot of Beau's bed and ended with Beau lying in a small, wooden box six feet under. In the dream, he didn't scream or try to get out of the coffin. He just lay there, counting his breaths until they finally drifted away to nothingness. But no matter how calm and accepting of his fate he was in the dream, he always came awake with his heart pounding against his ribcage and sweat beading his forehead.

Beau opened his eyes prepared to see the generic furnishings of a hotel room. Instead, he *did* find himself in a box. A brightly lit, metal box with a low ceiling and hard mattress. It only took a couple blinks to figure out where he was. The wall of the tiny bathroom kept him from seeing more than just the scarred wood cabinets and tiny kitchenette, but the steady sawing noise told him that his camping buddy was still with him and working hard to escape.

He flexed his shoulder. It was tender, but the sharp pain was gone. He removed the sling and tossed it into one corner of the bunk before placing a hand over the right side of his chest and tracing along his ribcage. It was a ritual he had performed every day of his life since getting the results of the CT scan. Of course, he couldn't feel the cancer growing inside his lung.

Just like he hadn't felt it growing inside him the first time.

There had been no lumps or obvious signs. He had gone in for a routine checkup and had come out with a life sentence. The lymphoma diagnosis had completely blindsided him. He had been a naïve kid fresh out of college who had never even considered death. His mind had been too consumed with living. His brothers, Brant and Billy, had wanted him to help with the family business, but Beau wasn't interested in the running of a big corporation. His dreams had been smaller. He wanted to live in his hometown of Dogwood and raise a passel of kids.

He had clung to that dream all through the radiation and chemotherapy. Had held fast to it even after his fiancé, Cari Anne, had given him back his ring and broken his heart. But the dream had been shattered forever when the doctor had called after his last checkup to tell him that now there was a suspicious spot on his lung scan.

Suspicious?

Suspicious was the unidentifiable veggie in your dinner salad. The Twitter account with no followers. The guy who lurks around a debit machine. It wasn't a fuzzy blob on an x-ray. That wasn't suspicious; that was out-and-out terrifying. Especially when Beau knew what it meant. He knew what his chances were if his cancer came back within a year. He also knew what his options were. And he wasn't willing to go through even more intense chemotherapy, stem cell transplants, and transfusions when the odds were stacked against him.

Instead, he had chosen to live what was left of his life on his terms. Cancer had already taken a huge chunk of his life. He wasn't willing to give it more than the routine morning check. After that, the day was his...until the nightmares returned.

Sliding to the edge of the paper-thin mattress, Beau jumped down from the bunk. Jenna was sitting on the bench seat at the table. She glanced up for only a second before going back to carving on the metal that covered the window. She had succeeded in making a small circle, which wasn't that great a feat considering the fact that she'd been at it off and on for the last five states.

"Give it a rest, MacGyver," Beau said as he walked over to the mini-fridge and opened it. The cool air felt so good he thought about shoving his head inside. With only one vent in the ceiling, the camper was like a prison hot box. Which explained why he was strutting around in nothing but his boxer briefs. That, and he wanted to fluster Jenna. Unfortunately, she didn't seem to care one way or the other.

He shot her an annoyed look before he took out the milk and a can of Hawaiian Punch. After setting the items on the counter, he lifted the box of Honey-Combs and poured it into the bowl he'd left there earlier. He preferred Cocoa Krispies, but whoever had stocked the cupboards had done so with only one cereal choice. They had also stocked them with enough bread, peanut butter, and jelly to feed an entire preschool for a month.

Beau hated peanut butter. Or anything that stuck around for too long.

He poured milk on his cereal and glanced over his shoulder. "Still planning on diving out of a moving vehicle?" He pressed the cereal pieces down in the bowl with his spoon to help them absorb more milk, then picked up the bowl and can of punch and moved over to the bench opposite Jenna.

"No, but I can signal someone for help." She continued to saw with her bent butter knife. She had pulled all that wheat-colored hair up on top of her head with some rubber bands she'd found in the drawer, exposing a neck that seemed to go on forever. A bead of sweat trickled down it, and Beau had the strongest urge to lean over and kiss it off. He resisted the temptation. Mostly because he didn't want to get punched in the head.

Being held captive did not agree with Jenna Jay.

Trying to cool his thoughts down, Beau popped open the can and took a deep drink. "Sort of like you signaling that trucker from the little window in the bunk? All that got you was a…" He held up a fist and tugged it twice. "Beep. Beep."

Jenna tossed the knife to the table where it knocked over the rooster saltshaker. "At least I'm making an effort to get us out of here. You, on the other hand, couldn't even be bothered to help me kick in the door the last time we stopped."

"Because I'm more brain than brawn." He took a heaping bite of cereal. The slight crunch had him setting his spoon back down.

Jenna snorted. "Are you trying to tell me that you're working on a plan?"

Beau was working on a plan. Just not a plan to escape. At their very first stop, while Jenna had been kicking at the door, Beau had been looking out the bunk window. What he saw had alleviated any concerns he might've had about being kidnapped by someone who planned on harming them. And since God had seen fit to give him this opportunity, he wasn't about to waste it on escape plans. Instead, he was working on getting Jenna back in bed.

And failing miserably.

Since she had discovered that Bruno wasn't taking them to Jersey, her mind had been consumed with two things: escape, and nailing the responsible parties' balls to the wall. If he could only figure out how to get all Jenna's fire focused on sex, he'd have it made. Of course, without a condom, he couldn't have intercourse with her, but he could think of about a million other things he wanted to do with her sweet body.

If his mileage calculations were correct, he only had one more night. The night before, she'd figured out how to make the table into a bed and left him in the bunk all alone with his fantasies. He didn't intend to let that happen again.

"And just when do you plan on implementing this great plan?" she asked. "You've done nothing for the last day and a half but sleep, eat, and run around in your underwear." She picked up his spoon and helped herself to a bite of his cereal.

If Beau had learned anything while traveling with her, it was that Jenna loved to eat almost as much as he did and was much happier when she had a full belly. Which was why he decided to share.

"You can't expect a man to wear clothes when it's hotter than blue blazes in this tin can. And as for the food and sleep, I'm just building up my strength." He lifted his uninjured arm and flexed. She gave his bicep one unimpressed glance before taking another bite.

Beau lowered his arm and tried not to feel deflated. It was getting harder and harder. If the trip lasted much longer, he wouldn't have any self-esteem left at all.

"It's almost like you're enjoying this," she said.

"It's not that bad." He sent her one of his best smiles. "Don't you like to camp?"

"This isn't exactly what I'd call camping. We're hostages, for God's sake."

"It's all in the way you want to look at it. I prefer to look at it as just another adventure."

"Well, unlike wealthy business owners," she said over another mouthful of cereal, "I don't have time for adventures. I have rent to pay."

"I wouldn't call myself a wealthy business owner. I'm more of a drifter."

She quirked an eyebrow. "A drifter whose family owns most of Texas." When he lifted his own eyebrow, she smiled. "Before I stopped talking with my family, I got an earful about the Cates brothers. My mama just failed to mention the youngest one."

"Younger," he corrected. "Beckett is the youngest boy."

"Does he get a kick out of riding bulls and buying whorehouses, too?"

He smiled at the thought of his bookish little brother on a bull or in a whorehouse. "No. He's gotten a little citified since college."

She finished off the last of his cereal before she set the spoon down and studied him. "So what's up with the invitation, Beau?"

It wasn't exactly the topic he wanted to talk about. He

would've much rather talked about something more entertaining, like the way her nipples pressed against the cotton of her white top. But the mulish look on her face said that she wasn't up for a topic change. And he figured he'd put the truth off long enough.

"Believe me, it wasn't my idea," he said as he reached over and grabbed the box of cereal, hoping she'd left him enough milk for soaking. "Minnie's an eccentric old gal who has a mind of her own. She sends out the invitations in hopes that the henhouse will return to its former glory."

"But hasn't it already been restored? It looks like a nineteenth-century mansion to me."

He poured more cereal into the bowl, and when she reached out and nabbed a Honey-Comb off the top, he pulled the box in between her and his bowl. "She doesn't just want it to *look* like Miss Hattie's. She wants it to *be* Miss Hattie's, complete with new hens."

Jenna stopped crunching. "Hens as in prostitutes?"

Since Beau had never thought of the hens like that, it took a moment for him to answer. During which time, Jenna choked on her bite of cereal. He reached out to thump her on the back, but she shoved his hand away and picked up his can of Hawaiian punch. It took more than a few swallows before she could talk.

"Are you saying that Minnie wants me to be a prostitute?"

Beau shrugged. "I'm still trying to figure that one out. The only woman to take her up on an invitation is about as far from being a prostitute as you can get. So I'm hoping that the old gals just want a little female company in their old age."

"But why me?"

He took a deep breath and released it, figuring that his

chance for sex with Jenna was just about to fly right out the window. "Because they think you're related to a hen."

Her eyes widened. "But that's crazy. I know for a fact that the only job my mama's ever had in her life is at The Feed and Seed. And my grandmas were all churchgoing housewives."

Beau held up his hands. "I tried to explain to Minnie that she got the wrong girl, but once she gets something in her head, it's hard to get it out. For some reason, she's convinced that you're the descendant of a hen." He laughed. "Obviously, she hasn't met you."

Jenna's brow knotted. "Are you saying that I wouldn't make a good prostitute?"

He stopped with the can of fruit punch halfway to his mouth. Before he could figure out how to answer the no-win question, she continued.

"I suppose this has to do with you not getting an orgasm."

It really didn't, but now that she brought it up...

"You do owe me." He tipped up the can and took a deep drink. It ended up spilling down his chest when she jumped to her feet and jarred the table.

"I don't owe you anything!" She thumped herself in the chest. "And I'm good in bed. In fact, I'm great in bed." Before he could suggest that she prove it, she did a complete one-eighty. "Okay, so maybe lately I've had a little bit of a slow spell, but everyone has bad months." She pointed at him. "Even world-traveling playboys."

"Hey," he held up a hand, "don't bring me into your duel-personality tirade. Up until I met you, my sex life has been just fine."

"Really?" She stared at him. "If that's so, then why couldn't you get it up with Peggy Super Boobs?"

He slammed down the can and got up. "And just who told you that?"

"Straight from the horse's mouth." Jenna smiled smugly. "Of course, Peggy thought it had to do with your concern over cheating on your dear, sweet wife." The smile slipped, and she looked slightly confused. "Why couldn't you get it up with her?" Her gaze dropped to his boxers. "Because you don't seem to have any problem getting it up with..." Her eyes widened. "Oh. It's more a problem of completing the act."

It was the final straw. The woman had taken him for an unwanted ride in a carriage, lost him a bull-riding championship, and gotten him knocked out and kidnapped. And now she was going to question his virility.

Like hell.

He reached out and pulled her against him. "Shall I prove it?"

The smug smile returned. "Sorry, but no condom, remember?"

Any charm he'd ever possessed had been snuffed out by two days spent with her sassy ass, and he dropped his charm and went straight to obnoxious.

"I'm not looking for the works, sweetheart. A hand job will do."

Her eyes widened, and her mouth flapped for a few seconds before she could get any words out. "You've got cabin fever if you think that I'm going to give you a hand job." She shoved past him, but he wasn't quite done yet.

He followed her to the tiny sink and moved behind her, pressing her up against the counter with his hips. "Oh, come on, sweetheart. I promise it won't take long. Five minutes tops."

He curled his fingers around her waist right before he dipped his head to nibble on her shoulder. She tasted of salt and something much more erotic. Something he couldn't seem to get enough of as he kissed his way up her long neck. He thought she would've slugged him by now, but instead she just stood there, her hands gripping the counter and her breath softly rushing out. He made a pit stop at her earlobe and pulled it into his mouth for a gentle suck.

"Just touch it, Jen," he whispered. "Just a little, sweetheart." Except he wasn't trying to piss her off anymore. He wanted her to touch him. To slip those cool fingers into his boxers and stroke the length of him. A length that was growing by the second.

He nipped at the spot behind her ear. "Pretty please."

Jenna turned toward him, her head tilting up and her lips reaching for a kiss. He gave it to her. Gave her the kind of kiss that he'd wanted to give her since wrestling with her in the back of the carriage. Deep. Wet. No holds barred.

She responded immediately, her hands sliding into his hair and manipulating his head so she could devour him at will. Then after she had deep-fried his brain, she did something that totally shocked him.

One hand slipped down to his throbbing penis.

Another thing he'd learned about Jenna was when she decided to do something she didn't beat around the bush. Without hesitation, she firmly took him in hand. Then with a stroke that had his knees almost buckling, she gave him what he'd asked for.

Except he didn't expect to like it so much. While hand jobs were nice, they had never been his preferred technique for reaching orgasm. He liked oral. Loved intercourse. But hand jobs were just foreplay, a mildly fun interlude on the way to the grand finale.

Jenna changed his mind. There was something about being in her hand that excited him more than he thought possible. Maybe it was her enthusiasm. Or her strength. Or her rhythm. Whatever it was, he liked it. A helluva lot. In fact, so much that he closed his eyes, tipped back his head, and waited for nirvana.

It didn't come. Correction: he didn't come. Right when he was about to reach the summit, she stopped. Thinking she just needed a breather, he waited. While he waited, he noticed a few things.

The camper wasn't moving.

And someone was unlocking the door.

Beau barely had time to remove Jenna's hand and snap the elastic of his boxer briefs back in place before the door was being swung open. He expected to see a grinning cowboy. Instead, he saw an entire town. An entire town of folks who started out smiling, but then looked a little stunned.

"Lord have mercy," Rachel Dean fanned a large hand in front of her face, "whoever said that size don't matter ain't seen Beau's."

Chapter Ten

JENNA LOOKED OUT THE DOOR of the camper and couldn't quite believe her eyes. She'd been prepared for Bruno's goons or a bunch of Mexican drug lords. What she wasn't prepared for were the townsfolk of Bramble, Texas. Townsfolk who appeared to have gotten over their shock and were now grinning like they had just been given the best birthday present ever. Of course, the women's eyes all seemed to be plastered on Beau.

And not his face.

Annoyance bubbled up in Jenna. She tried to push her way by him, but he was too big and the space too little. They ended up pressed together like two slices of bread in a peanut butter sandwich. Crunchy peanut butter since there was no hiding the fact that Beau hadn't cooled off just yet.

"Would you get dressed for God's sake!" she hissed under her breath.

Beau shot her a heavy-lidded look that made heat flood her entire body. "Yes ma'am." The hard length of him brushed against her as he ambled to the back of the camper.

Jenna took a deep, calming breath before she turned

to the open door. The townsfolk had moved closer as if watching Dallas Cowboys football on the big screen television at Bootlegger's Bar.

Mayor Harley Sutter was the first one to separate from the group. He hitched his pants up over his big beer belly, and his handlebar mustache twitched with a broad smile.

"Welcome home, Jenna Jay."

The mayor's greeting caused the crowd to snap out of it, and they all started talking at once.

"We shore missed yew."

"It ain't been the same without yew."

"New York might be nice, but this here is your home."

"Hell yeah, it is!"

Lord only knew how long they would've continued their chorus of greetings if Jenna hadn't placed two fingers in her mouth and shrilly whistled. Everyone shut up and exchanged proud smiles, as if she'd just accomplished a great feat.

Jenna's gaze pinned the mayor. "Uncle Harley, do you mind telling me what's going on?"

His huge mustache twitched, but before he could say anything, a cowboy stepped out from around the side of the camper and pushed back his cowboy hat. His dark skin was mottled with bruises, but that didn't stop him from smiling brightly.

"Hey, Jenna Jay," Kenny Gene said. "I shore hope you ain't mad at me for comin' to get you." He touched the bump beneath his eye. "Although I think you should've gone out for boxin' instead of volleyball. That right hook of yours shore rattled my brains."

Jenna frowned. "You kidnapped me, Kenny Gene?"

"Now, 'kidnap' is a mighty harsh word," Mayor Sutter

said. "We just brought you home so you could mend the fences between you and your mama."

Most people would be completely mind-boggled by the fact that a town would actually plot a kidnapping. But Jenna had grown up in Bramble and knew how crazy the townsfolk could be. No, she wasn't mind-boggled. Just angry that they had come up with such a loony idea. Wondering if her family had been behind it, she quickly scanned the crowd. But she didn't see her mama. Or her daddy. Or her brother or sisters.

"They ain't here, honey," Rachel Dean said. "Your folks and your siblings all went to the NASCAR races for Memorial Day. That's why we figured it would be a perfect time to go get you so we could surprise them when they get back next Tuesday."

Jenna's eyes widened. *Next Tuesday?* That was a week away. She started to protest when Rachel Dean held up a large hand and flapped it.

"Come on out, Bear."

A man moved out from the other side of the camper. A man as big as, if not bigger than, Bruno's goon.

"You remember Bear, don't you, Jenna?" Harley said. "He's the bounty hunter who helped us find your sister's baby's daddy. Although it turned out the daddy was right in our own backyard and we didn't need Bear after all." Harley thumped the man on the back. "You did a real good job, son. But what I can't figure out is why you brought Beauregard Cates along with Jenna Jay."

Jenna wasn't surprised that the townsfolk knew Beau. It made sense given that he owned the henhouse that was only a hop, skip, and a jump away from Bramble, and his brothers were both married to Bramble women.

"We couldn't just leave him passed out in the middle of the street, Harley," Kenny Gene said. "Besides, I've missed fishin' with Beau."

Twyla stepped up and ducked her head, trying to see between Jenna's legs. "What I'd like to know is what Beau was doin' with Jenna Jay in the first place. I thought her boyfriend was some scrawny dude from Minni-soda. There's nothing scrawny on Beau. Especially his—"

"Why, thank you, Twyla."

Jenna glanced back to see Beau standing right behind her. Thankfully, for the sake of the sex-starved female population of Bramble, he had on his jeans. The women still looked awestruck. Something that really bothered Jenna. But no more than Beau's cavalier attitude. He didn't seem surprised at all to be back in Bramble.

He flashed a smile that had the women in the crowd sighing. With a slight shove, he moved Jenna out of the way and jumped down from the camper. "No man likes to be thought of as scrawny." He slapped Kenny Gene on the back. "And I like to go fishin' with you, too." He glanced at Bear. "I guess you're the one who knocked me out cold."

"I wouldn't have knocked you out," Bear said, "if you hadn't of hit the little missy."

"You hit Jenna Jay?" Uncle Harley's eyes narrowed. "Now, we shore like you, son. But if you've hurt our little Jenna Jay, there'll be hell to pay."

For a second, Jenna considered letting them make Beau pay. It wasn't like he didn't deserve it. Not so much for hitting her as for spending the last couple days driving her crazy. When he wasn't annoying her, he was tempting her to do things she had no business doing.

A hand job? What had she been thinking?

She hopped down from the camper. "It was an accident. And an easy one to make, considering it was dark and we were being attacked by two yahoos in John Wayne masks."

Kenny beamed. "That was my idea."

"But I still don't get what Beau was doin' at Jenna Jay's apartment," Twyla said.

Darla stepped up, her knitting needles clicking like a telegraph machine as she worked on what looked to be a pair of adult-sized booties. "Probably the same thing he was plannin' on doin' when we interrupted him. I don't think I've ever seen a man more rarin' to go in my life. It reminded me of the time my daddy let me watch his stud horse—"

"Well, this turned out better than we thought," Rachel Dean said. "Now there's no reason for Jenna Jay and her mama to be fightin'. Jenna Jay has done got herself a Texas cowboy."

Beau laughed. But Jenna knew this was no laughing matter. When the town started assuming things, it could turn ugly quick.

"Beau is not my boyfriend," she said. "He was only at my apartment because he'd been thrown off a bull and hurt his shoulder."

There was a moment of stunned silence before everyone burst out in laughter.

"Bulls in New York City." Mayor Sutter chortled and pointed a finger at Jenna. "You'll have to come up with a better one than that, Jenna Jay. 'Course, you never was a good liar. Remember that time that you and Dallas got caught shoe polishin' Sheriff Winslow's squad—"

"I'm not lying," Jenna said, but no one seemed to be listening to her. Before she knew it, they all started reminiscing about her childhood days. And Beau wasn't the least bit of help. He just stood there with his shoulder propped against the camper and a stupid smile on his face. Realizing that there was no use in trying to explain, she gave up and pushed her way through the crowd.

"Where are you goin', Jenna Jay?" Twyla fell in step next to her, as did the rest of the town. The only one who didn't follow her was Beau. And that suited her just fine.

"I'm going to my parents' house to get some clothes and a car," she stated as she hopped up on the sidewalk that ran in front of Sutter's Pharmacy. Moses Tate was sitting on the bench napping. He didn't budge as she and the entire town swept past him.

"And then what?" Darla hurried along next to her, knitting needles still clicking. "You goin' over to Josephine's Diner for dinner? Tuesdays are meatloaf with mashed potatoes and green beans. Or are you headed over to Bootlegger's for a cold—"

"No," Jenna interrupted, "I'm not going to Josephine's. Or Bootlegger's Bar. I'm going to Lubbock where I plan to catch the first flight home to New York City."

Her words seemed to throw a wrench into whatever craziness the townsfolk had come up with. Their steps faltered, and suddenly Jenna was walking alone. She glanced back to find them all standing on the corner in front of the First Bank of Bramble with stunned looks on their faces.

"But, Jenna Jay," Kenny Gene said, "Bramble is your home."

It was a struggle to keep walking. Jenna didn't like

hurting people's feelings. Especially people she had grown up with and loved. But she knew from experience that if she gave the townsfolk an inch, they would take a good twenty miles. They needed to realize that they couldn't run her life. She had a job to get back to. Not to mention a boyfriend.

In the last few days, when she hadn't been fighting against her weird physical attraction for Beau, she'd been thinking about Davy. And she had come to the conclusion that Davy had been hiding his true emotions behind the entire "we don't suit" argument. He was no doubt devastated at finding her with another man. Who wouldn't be?

And maybe Beau was right. Maybe she hadn't done a good enough job of making Davy feel needed. She had been so busy trying to save the world that she'd neglected the man she loved. But now she had a new goal, and she was going to achieve it. She would save her relationship with Davy come hell or high water.

Or crazy townsfolk.

Rounding the huge cottonwood tree, she stepped onto the acre lot of her childhood home. It looked exactly like it had a year earlier. A cinder-block garage sat off to one side while the other was filled with a beat-up pickup, a couple dented Cadillacs, and an open-bed trailer. The house was single-story with a wide front porch that held a swing that conjured up memories of hanging out with her family on hot summer nights, eating Popsicles or scoops of homemade ice cream.

In front of the porch was her daddy's flower garden. It still amazed her that a man as big and tough as Burl Scroggs could grow dahlias the size of hubcaps. She stopped to smell a pretty white and pink one before she climbed the porch steps. Since no one in Bramble locked their doors, she walked right into the house.

The curtains had been closed and the air conditioner turned off so the house was hot and muggy. It smelled like her mama's fried chicken and her daddy's shaving cream. On her way back to the bedroom she'd shared with her sister Tessa, Jenna couldn't help stopping to look at the pictures that lined the walls.

The photos were separated by gender. Dallas's pictures were on the left side of the hallway, while the girls' were on the right. There were numerous pictures of Hope and Tessa in homecoming gowns and cheerleading uniforms, and a couple pictures of Hope's twin sister, Faith, on her wedding day and receiving her teaching diploma. In her volleyball uniform with sweat-drenched hair, Jenna stood out like an ostrich at a duck farm. All three of her sisters were dark and petite like their mama. The complete opposite of Jenna, who hadn't been a cheerleader, or a homecoming queen, or a student who graduated with honors.

Jenna had hated college and only attended because it meant so much to her parents. Tests freaked her out and teachers intimidated her, no doubt a direct result of being diagnosed with a learning disability in elementary school. She overcame the disability. She did not overcome her fear of being made fun of by the other kids. And maybe that was why she always fought for the underdog. And why she'd never felt like she belonged in a family of overachievers.

Even Dallas was an exceptional student. Football was his main love, but academics came in a close second. She studied the picture of him in his Bramble High football uniform. Of all her siblings, she and Dallas were the closest. Her brother was the only one who hadn't gotten on her case about Davy. So why had she stopped texting him and started cutting their phone conversations short so that he finally stopped calling altogether?

Unwilling to give in to the melancholy feelings the family pictures evoked, she turned and walked to her bedroom. The room looked the same. The walls were still the color of mint green she and Tessa had painted them in high school, and the double bed was still covered in the pink polka-dotted bedspread she had bought with tips she had made from working at Josephine's Diner.

After two days without more than a sponge bath, she headed straight to the bathroom. The hot shower felt wonderful. While she scrubbed and conditioned her hair, she started to feel guilty about the way she had treated the townsfolk. True, it was a crazy plan, but they had only done it because they missed her. Thinking of their warm greetings, she had to admit that she missed them, too.

What would it hurt if she stayed a couple nights in Bramble? She had taken shifts for numerous people at work, and she was sure she could get them to cover for her for a few days. As for Davy, maybe time apart was a good thing. Her mama had always said that absence makes the heart grow fonder. Maybe by the time she got back to New York, she wouldn't have to do more than step into Davy's arms.

After blowing out her hair, Jenna went in search of clothing. She would've liked shorts and a tank top. Instead, she found a pair of wranglers, a sleeveless blouse, and her old roper boots.

Since she couldn't fit in her mama's bras and wasn't about to wear granny panties, she went without underwear.

Once she was dressed, she stepped in front of the full-length mirror on the closet door. A country girl looked back at her. A country girl she'd almost forgotten existed. It was like she was looking at one of the photographs in the hallway. A person she'd once been, but was no more.

For some reason, it made her as sad as looking at the photographs. She had just started to turn away from her reflection when something caught her attention out the window. She walked over just in time to see Kenny Gene slamming down the hood of her daddy's old pickup. In his hand was a black rubber radiator hose.

"Oh no you don't!" Jenna yelled as she grabbed the cowboy hat off the corner of the mirror and headed for the door. But by the time she got outside, all that was left of Kenny Gene was a billow of dust. It didn't take an academic genius to figure out what Kenny had been up to. Still, she checked every engine to make sure. They were all missing one hose or another.

Tugging her hat down, Jenna started for town. Unfortunately, by the time she got there, Bramble had turned into a ghost town. All the businesses were closed up tight, and the only person in sight was Moses Tate, who still sawed logs on the bench in front of Sutter's Pharmacy.

Jenna walked over and flopped down next to him. "Why those wily coyotes," she muttered.

" 'Wily' ain't the word I'd use," Moses Tate said, causing Jenna to jump. He tipped his hat up, blinking in the bright sun. "Blame fools is more like it. They never did know how to use the old noggin."

"Do you think I could borrow your truck, Moses?" she asked.

"You in a hurry to leave town, Jenna Jay?"

"After Kenny's stunt, I should be. But I think I'll stick around for a couple days. I just wanted to take a little drive."

"Any place in particular?"

Jenna did have somewhere in particular in mind. She just didn't think Moses needed that information. "Just a drive."

Moses nodded. "Welp, I wish I could help you out, but I already loaned out my truck."

A loud grinding of gears had both of them looking down the street. A beat-up Ford pickup headed toward them, jerking and sputtering like a cat coughing up a hairball. With sunlight reflecting off the windshield, Jenna couldn't tell who drove the truck until it was almost to them. She released her breath in a groan as the truck pulled up to the curb.

Resting an arm on the open window, Beau gave Jenna a twinkly-eyed once-over.

"Care for a ride, Cowgirl?"

Chapter Eleven

PASTOR SEAN ROBBINS STOOD AT the window of his office and watched as Jenna Jay Scroggs climbed into Moses Tate's truck. He was curious about why Beauregard Cates was driving the truck, but his curiosity was dimmed by his joy at seeing Jenna Jay home. Her mother had talked to Sean about their falling out and he hoped that Jenna Jay's appearance meant their disagreement had been resolved. He had done everything he could to try to soothe Jenna's fears about her daughter marrying a tattooed band member, including giving more than a few sermons on accepting the differences in others.

Turning from the window, Sean sat back down at his desk. Unfortunately, there was nothing there to occupy his mind. Tuesdays were the slowest day of the week. Technically, it should be his day off, but there was little to do in the small town except hang out at the house the townsfolk had provided for him. And he didn't like being home. It was too lonely. The large family room, country kitchen, and big bedrooms all called out for a horde of children and a wife.

None of which Sean had.

Although more and more lately, his mind had been filled with thoughts about marriage and starting a family. He just wasn't about to find a wife in Bramble. Not when he had no intention of remaining in Texas. He had learned a lot from pastoring the small church and had come to love his congregation. But he was a California boy, born and raised, and he couldn't wait for God to send him back to the West Coast.

Sean had to admit that the Lord was taking His good sweet time. Sean had put in for a transfer months ago and had yet to hear a thing. Searching for guidance, he reached for his worn-out bible that sat on the corner of the desk and flipped it open. He glanced down, and a verse in Hebrews jumped out at him. *"That ye be not slothful, but followers of them who through faith and patience inherit the promises."*

Sean glanced up and smiled. "Thank you, Lord. It looks like my Sunday sermon is going to be on faith and patience."

For the next couple hours, he worked on his sermon. He had just finished searching online for a clever anecdote that went with the subject of patience when he heard the squeak of the front door. The large wooden doors had needed oiling for months. And since it was probably the custodian, Mr. Sims, it was a perfect time to bring it up. Besides, helping the older man would give Sean something to do.

Except it wasn't a gray-haired man who stood in the foyer, studying the picture above the event bulletin board. It was a woman Sean would just as soon never see again. For a second, he thought about slipping back into his office and pretending he hadn't seen her. Unfortunately, the door wasn't the only thing that made noise. He took a step back, and the wooden floor creaked beneath his Reef flip-flop, pulling the woman's gaze over to him.

"Hey, Preacher Man." Marcy Henderson smiled a smile that said she knew every carnal thought that had ever crossed his mind. And recently there had been plenty. Since looking at the illustrations of the Kama Sutra, he'd had a hard time keeping the images from filtering into his brain. And it wasn't just images of the drawings. It was images of him and this woman in the same positions.

A part of him wanted to blame her. Any woman who paraded around in a shirt so tight and low that her bosom was practically falling out was asking for lustful thoughts. But the other part of him knew he was the one to blame. Marcy hadn't done anything but catch him red-handed doing something that he had no business doing. And a part of him hated the fact that she had witnessed his human frailty.

"Hello, Miss Henderson," he said. Normally, he took the hand of the people he greeted, but he figured he'd touched Marcy quite enough. "What brings you here on a Tuesday afternoon?"

Instead of answering, she nodded at the painting. "What does the ocean have to do with church?"

"To some people, the ocean is a church," he said. "But this is a picture of the Sea of Galilee. The same sea that Jesus walked upon."

"It looks a little too rough to walk on if you ask me— even for the Son of God."

Sean took another step back. "It's nice to hear that you believe Jesus is the Son of God, Miss Henderson."

She continued to look at the painting. "Just because I don't come to church doesn't mean I don't believe." She glanced at him. "And the name is Marcy. Do you have a first name, Preacher Man?"

The knowing smile was back, but he chose to ignore it. He also chose to ignore her question. And the way the sunlight shining through the stained glass window reflected in her dark eyes.

"Is there a reason you're here, Miss Henderson? Because I've got a sermon to finish."

The smile faded. "Are you kicking me out of church? That doesn't seem very Christian-like."

He took a deep breath to try and calm his nerves, but all he succeeded in doing was inhaling the scent of her. It was a clean, fresh scent that had him closing his eyes and listening for the sound of ocean waves crashing over a vast expanse of sparkling sand. A soft touch on his wrist brought him out of the daydream and, just that quickly, pulled him into a fantasy that involved her soft, gentle fingers doing all kinds of wicked things.

"I'm sorry," she said, completely unaware of the effect her touch had on him. "I'll stop teasing and get to the point of my visit." She glanced around, for the first time, looking nervous and uncomfortable. "But do you think we could go for a walk?"

Since Sean was willing to do just about anything to get her to stop touching him, he quickly nodded and stepped away.

The afternoon was hot and humid as they made their way down the street. Which might explain why the town seemed to be deserted. The only person around was Moses Tate, who slept on a bench a little farther down the street. It was wrong, but Sean couldn't help saying a prayer of thanks that no one in town was around to witness his stroll with the notorious Marcy Henderson.

"I'm going to volunteer here on Saturdays," Marcy said as they walked past the library. "So if you should want any more—" She bit down on her lip as if to keep from finishing the sentence. It was very disconcerting. Not the fact that she was about to mention his interest in erotica, but the sight of her teeth nibbling the plumpness of her bottom lip. A bottom lip that was stained a deep scarlet red.

He looked away and concentrated on the cracks in the sidewalk. "That's very charitable of you. Most of the patrons on Saturday will be relieved not to have to smell Twyla's toxic fumes while perusing the shelves."

"Perusing? So that's what you were doing?" Without waiting for a reply, she cut across the sparse grass of the park to the children's playground. By the time he caught up with her, she had her high heels off and was sitting in a swing. Her skirt had hiked up, showing off so much thigh that Sean felt himself blush.

"Come on, Preacher Man," she said as she wiggled her bare toes above the rutted hole beneath the swing, "give a girl a push."

Sean glanced around before he shook his head. "I don't think that's appropriate."

Her head tipped. "Why? You got a girlfriend that the town don't know about?"

"No, but I am the pastor."

"So that means you can't have any fun?" She sent him a smile, but this one was different from the others. It held no hidden meaning. "It's just a push, Preacher Man."

As much as he shouldn't, Sean moved around the A-shaped poles of the swing set and stood behind Marcy. At least, on this side, he couldn't see her bare legs. All he could see were the waves of brown hair that hung down her back. Not wanting to touch her, he grabbed onto the chains of the swing and pushed her forward. But when she came back, he couldn't help but reach out and place a hand on her back. Her hair was as silky as it looked.

"See? That wasn't so hard," she said as she soared up, sticking her legs out in front of her. Her toes were painted the same scarlet as her lips.

"So is this why you came to the church?" he asked. "You couldn't find anyone else to give you a push?"

She giggled again as he shoved her even higher. "Nope. Although I could get used to this. I've never had a man push me in a swing before."

"Considering how many men you've been with, I find that hard to believe." The words came out without thought, and he tried to take them back. "What I meant was—"

"I know what you meant," she said without a trace of anger. "And you're right, I have been with a lot of men, but not one of them gave me a push in a swing. Not even my daddy pushed me. He was always too busy fighting with my mama to care about taking me and my sister to the park."

Sean had heard about how neglectful Samantha Henderson's parents had been. But for some reason, he hadn't been able to connect Sam with her sister, Marcy. Maybe because the two were such complete opposites. Samantha was a sweet veterinarian who married a farmer and helped out in Sunday school. And Marcy was...the town slut.

It was wrong for him to even think it, but he couldn't deny that it was the truth. Not only had he overheard it from the townsfolk, but also he'd witnessed her promiscuous behavior himself before she'd left town.

Marcy loved men—all men.

He stopped pushing her and stepped back.

After a few swings, she glanced over her shoulder. "So I guess the fun and games are over." When he didn't say anything, she turned away. "Time to get on with business." But she didn't stop pumping; she just kept on swinging as if the back-and-forth motion helped her to get the words out.

"I have a proposition for you. One I'm sure is going to shock that silly shirt and them baggy shorts right off you. But before you give me an answer, you better think real hard on it. Because, here in Bramble, you won't be gettin' one like it any time soon. And if I learned anything in the library the other day, it's that you're a man just like any other man. A man with needs that can't be taken care of by what's in a leather-bound book—or the Kama Sutra, for that matter."

Sean bristled at her brutal honesty. He was about to turn and leave when she continued.

"I know that you're not supposed to give in to your physical needs. But if that's so, then why did God give us bodies that need water, food, air…and sex? Why didn't he just make us like ghosts, floating around the surface of the earth? I figure it's because he wanted us to enjoy things. Like the smell of fresh country air early in the morning. The taste of a summer tomato straight off the vine. The sound of children's laughter. And the feel of someone's arms around you—" she hesitated, "even if they don't love you. Even if you're just there to fulfill their fleshly needs."

Marcy stopped pumping, and the swing slowed to a gentle sway. "As much as you might want to deny it, you need a woman. I'm willing to be that woman. I won't tell a soul anything about what takes place between us. The only thing I'll want from you is money. And not a lot. Just enough to get me used to the idea."

Shocked, Sean reached out and grabbed the chains, stopping the swing and twisting it until she faced him. "What are you talking about? You're wanting to prostitute yourself to me?"

There were tears in her eyes. Big, watery tears that made her eyes look twice as big. "Minnie doesn't refer to it as prostitution."

"Minnie?" It took a moment for the name to register. "Are you talking about the woman who runs Miss Hattie's Henhouse? Are you telling me that she hired you to work as a prostitute?" His only answer was a tear trickling down her cheek before she pushed him back and stood. She took his hand and pressed a piece of paper into his palm, closing his fingers around it.

"This is my cell number. Just call when you're ready." Then before he could utter a word, she walked away. Halfway across the park, she turned and sent him the cocky smile. "Thanks for the push, Preacher Man."

Sean didn't know how long he stood there. By the time he finally snapped out of his daze, the sun had moved farther toward the horizon and the townsfolk had reappeared. As he tried to orient his world, his gaze wandered down to the pair of red high heels that Marcy had tossed into the grass. He walked over and picked them up.

They weren't new, or even expensive. The straps were some kind of synthetic leather that had ripped on one shoe. A piece of red electrical tape had been used to fix the tear. It was an ingenious fix. The tape not only strengthened the strap, but also blended so well with it that only close scrutiny would be able to detect the flaw.

Just like Marcy.

Sean didn't know if the voice came from God or just his head, but he listened. He listened and, for the first time since meeting her, thought of Marcy as something more than a temptation he needed to avoid. He realized that like the shoe, she was hiding a broken soul that needed healing. And not just by a superficial piece of tape.

He had preached about accepting people for their differences, but he obviously hadn't listened to his sermons. Just because Marcy was different didn't mean she should be shunned or avoided. In fact, the outcasts were the ones who needed love and guidance the most.

Sean gently ran a finger over the torn strap of the shoe.

And what good was a preacher man if he couldn't bring a lost sheep back to the fold?

Chapter Twelve

MISS HATTIE'S HENHOUSE LOOKED LIKE it belonged in the rolling hills of Kentucky rather than in the middle of the barren landscape of west Texas. Not only was Jenna surprised by the grandeur of the rambling house, but by the trees that surrounded it. Trees were a rarity in west Texas, and Jenna counted at least three huge cottonwoods on the property, their gnarled branches stretching out in cool billows of green.

"It's pretty amazing, isn't it?" Beau said.

She glanced over to find him slouched down in the seat, watching her—something he'd been doing for most of the hour-long trip. Jenna figured it was the western wear and hat. They were a big change from her city clothes. Still, it was very disconcerting. Especially when he seemed in no hurry to look away.

One of the front tires bounced down into a rut, and Jenna tightened her hold on the steering wheel and returned her eyes to the road. It had been like pulling teeth to get Beau to let her drive. Despite his carefree smile, he had a macho thing going on and a stubborn streak a mile wide. But he didn't have much of a choice. Moses's truck was a stick shift with the stick on the side of Beau's injured arm. Still, it had taken a jerky ride down the entire length of Main Street before he had finally pulled over to the curb and let her take the wheel.

Beau sat up and pointed. "Just turn in here."

She turned into the circular, brick driveway and parked in front of the porch steps. "Are you responsible for the renovations?"

"I helped with the planning, but it was Minnie and her granddaughter, Elizabeth, who completed it."

On the way out to Miss Hattie's, Beau had explained how he had ended up owning the henhouse, and how Elizabeth Murphy, Bramble's librarian, was related to a hen. And not just any hen, but Miss Hattie herself. Jenna still couldn't quite believe it. Ms. Murphy had always been considered the town's old maid. Not that she was that old. She was just so straitlaced and... boring. But according to Beau, Ms. Murphy wasn't as straitlaced as Jenna had thought. She had led Beau's brother a merry chase and now had a little boy and another child on the way.

Jenna put the truck in park and turned to Beau. "So these women—these hens—aren't going to handcuff me to the bed like Ms. Murphy did with your brother, are they?"

Beau's eyes were direct and serious. "If there's any handcuffing done, I promise it will only be done by me."

"Don't get your hopes up," she said, "I won't be staying that long."

"That makes two of us." He reached across his body with his good hand and pulled up the door handle. It seemed to be stuck, and Jenna didn't hesitate to jump out and run around to his side to help him out. Except when she finally got the door opened, he looked a little annoyed.

"What?" she asked.

"Nothing," he grumbled. When he got out she noticed his stocking feet, which made her feel a little guilty for not inviting him to her house so he could clean up. His feet looked big enough to fit in her daddy's boots.

"So why don't you plan on staying long?" she said as they headed to the front porch. "You didn't seem all that upset when the camper door opened." She followed him up the steps, doing a double take at the large sign that stuck out of the flowerbed:

TRESPASSERS WILL BE PROSTITUTED.

"Because, during my many travels, I've come to realize that anger is a wasted emotion." Beau pressed the doorbell. A rendition of "Deep in the Heart of Texas" chimed out.

"Spoken like a true spoiled playboy," Jenna said. "I assume you feel differently about lust."

He sent her a look that left her a little breathless. "Lust is never wasted. Not as long as there's an opportunity for it to come to fruition—"

A pretty, dark-haired girl flung the massive door open. She took one look at Beau, and her brown eyes became the definition of lust.

"Beau!" She launched her ample body straight at him.

Pain tightened Beau's features as the girl hit his injured shoulder with the force of a linebacker. He stumbled back, and they both would've tumbled right off the front steps if Jenna hadn't reached out and grabbed the girl's ugly satin dress and held her back long enough for Beau to catch his balance. Unfortunately, Jenna might've tugged a little too hard. There was a loud rip, and she ended up with a strip of purple satin in her hand and the dark-haired girl at her feet.

"Geez, Jenna," Beau hurried over and helped the stunned girl up, "do you always have to be so rough?" He tipped up the girl's chin and smiled at her. "You okay, Starlet?"

Starlet didn't answer. She just stood there staring at Beau as if he was the second coming.

Jenna rolled her eyes and tossed the piece of material down to one of the wicker rockers. "I'm not about to let you fall on your butt and dislocate your shoulder all over again. Not when you're the worst patient this side of the Pecos."

Beau's smile dimmed. "You try being thrown from a bull and see how you feel."

"I wasn't thrown off a bull, but once I was thrown off a bronco, and it wasn't that bad—"

Beau slapped a hand over her mouth. "Do you have any idea how you emasculate a man?"

Jenna glared at him while Starlet reached out and touched Beau's shoulder. "You got thrown off a bull, Beau?"

"And it looks like trampled as well."

Both Jenna and Beau turned to the doorway, where a scary-looking old lady in a maroon wig, red negligee, and more makeup than Twyla sat in a battery-powered wheelchair. Two women stood behind her. One with long, braided gray hair and dressed in bohemian-styled jeans and a peasant blouse. One who, despite the thick glasses, resembled Marilyn Monroe in heels, cropped jeans, and a midriff top.

"It's about time you got yourself home, Beauregard

Cates," the woman in the wheelchair said as she motored out onto the porch.

Beau smiled. It wasn't as bright as his usual smiles, but somehow Jenna liked it much better. This smile seemed more genuine and sincere.

"You told me to come for a visit, Minnie." He held out his arm. "So here I am."

"Don't give me that crap," Minnie said. "I heard about what happened. And if it wasn't for the crazy folks in Bramble, you wouldn't be here." She glanced over at Jenna. "Although I can't seem to figure out how you became part of Jenna's kidnapping."

"Jenna was just giving me a little TLC after I got thrown from the bull," Beau said.

"So she's your girlfriend?" Starlet asked.

"No!" Jenna clarified. "I have a boyfriend."

"Complete with nipple rings and hair as wild as Minnie's," Beau added.

The announcement had Starlet beaming, and Minnie cackling like a madwoman.

"So that's how it is," the old woman said before turning to Beau. "Were you raised in a barn, Beauregard? Introduce us to this young lady."

"This is Jenna Jay Scroggs," Beau said. "Jenna, this is Starlet Brubaker. Minnie Ladue." He smiled at the Marilyn Monroe lookalike. "Baby Evans." He winked at the hippie woman in her jeans. "And Sunshine."

Sunshine beamed back at Beau before studying Jenna with eyes that looked more than a little vacant. "You remind me of someone." She reached out and stroked Jenna's hair as if she was a prize pet. "Pretty hair. Could I braid it?"

"Maybe later, Sunshine." Baby removed her hand from Jenna's hair and held it in her own. "Welcome to Miss Hattie's, Jenna," she said in a breathy voice.

Jenna nodded at the women. "It's nice to meet y'all. I hope I'm not imposing."

"Not at all," Minnie backed up the wheelchair. "We've been expecting you." Before Jenna could get answers to all the questions that had been nagging her since receiving the invitation, Minnie zipped around and started issuing orders. "Sunshine, make sure Miss Hattie's room has fresh towels. Beau looks like he could use a nice, hot bath. Starlet, see if you can find him some clean clothes and boots. I think Brant left some last time he was here. And Baby, set two more places for supper. Beau's favorite of chicken and dumplin's will be appreciated." She glanced back at Jenna, who still stood on the porch. "Jenna, you come with me. I'd like to show you around the henhouse."

The henhouse was even more impressive in real life than it had been on the website. On the main floor, there was a grand salon, ballroom, dining room, billiard room, library, and kitchen. Off the kitchen were the servant quarters where the hens lived. There were seven bedrooms upstairs, but since Beau was in Miss Hattie's and three others were occupied with guests, Jenna only got to see three. They were all beautifully furnished with private bathrooms and views of the gardens that surrounded the house.

The tour ended in the basement, a huge room Minnie referred to as The Jungle Room. To Jenna, it looked more like The Austin Powers Room. Purple shag carpeting covered half the floor while the other half was some kind of a disco dance floor, complete with a mirrored ball hanging overhead and rows of strobe lights. There was a chrome and leather bar in one corner and a blue grand piano in another. And on the walls were frameless canvases covered with bright splashes of color.

"After the fire, we had to have it completely redone," Minnie said as she rolled next to a big, fuzzy orange chair. "Lucky for me, I have a photographic memory so we were able to duplicate the décor exactly as it had been." She waved a hand at an abstract painting on the wall. "Except for my Warhol paintin'. That I couldn't replace so I had to settle for some new artist out of Houston. But it isn't even close to the same." She pointed to a zebra-print couch. "Sit down, Jenna Jay, you're makin' my neck hurt."

Jenna took a seat. The zebra skin was stiff and made her feel very uncomfortable. But then again, so did Minnie's intense gaze.

"So I hear that you aren't plannin' on stayin' long." Minnie popped the arm of the wheelchair down and maneuvered over to the orange chair. Jenna got to her feet to help, but one warning look from Minnie had her sitting back down.

"No more than a few days," Jenna said. "I have responsibilities in New York." She cleared her throat and decided to get straight to the point. "I think you've made a serious mistake, ma'am."

"Just Minnie." Minnie pulled a sucker out of the side pocket of her wheelchair. One of those Dum-dum suckers that Jenna had loved as a kid. "Sucker?"

Jenna studied the wrapper. "It's not the mystery flavor, is it?"

"Not one who likes surprises, I take it." She unwrapped

the sucker and popped it into her mouth. "That's a shame. Surprises are the best part of life." She searched for another sucker in the pocket and handed it to Jenna. "So what kind of mistake have I made this time, Jenna Jay?"

Jenna unwrapped the sucker and placed it in her mouth. The cherry lollipop was as good as she had remembered and brought back memories of going to Sutter's Pharmacy with her sisters and brother. As she savored the flavor, she answered Minnie.

"The mistake of thinking I'm related to a hen."

Minnie's penciled-in eyebrows shot up. "And just who told you that?"

"Beau." She took the sucker out. "Is he wrong? Why else would you send me an invitation?"

Minnie studied her with her intense, beady eyes as she sucked on the lollipop. "This boyfriend of yours. Is he the same boyfriend who caused the tiff between you and your parents?"

Did the entire state know about her fight with her mama?

She nodded. "One and the same. Now about the invitation—"

"You love him?"

"Yes," Jenna answered without hesitation.

Minnie pulled the sucker out of her mouth. "So you gave up Texas for love. That seems like a fair trade. Although it must be hard to love a man your family doesn't approve of. 'Course, I didn't have to worry about my parents' approval. My mama and daddy didn't care enough to approve or disapprove. My mama worked here at Miss Hattie's, and my daddy was an oilman who had a family of his own."

Jenna settled back on the couch. "So you lived here?"

"I lived with distant cousins of my mama's. Aunt Lula and Uncle Joe were good folks, but I never did fit into their family."

"I know what you mean," Jenna said. "I'm sort of the black sheep in my family, too. Which is why it wasn't that hard for me to move to New York with Davy."

"So you fit better there than here?"

Jenna had never given it much thought. New York City had been terrifying at first. Now she was used to the tall buildings and the crowds of people. But did she fit in New York? And could she see herself living there the rest of her life?

Minnie took her silence as affirmation. "So if you're happy in New York City, why haven't you married this man? It seems to me that it would be the quickest way to get your family to accept him. You can dislike a boyfriend, but it's a lot harder to dislike the husband of your daughter or the father of your grandkids."

It was a good question. Why hadn't she married Davy? They had been going together for three years and had never even talked about marriage.

"I guess I hadn't thought about it," she whispered more to herself than to Minnie. "But you're right; marriage would fix things. Once I'm married to Davy, my folks would have to accept him." Of course, she couldn't bring up marriage now. But it gave her another goal to work toward. She bit down on her sucker and finished it off, then wrapped the stick back up in the paper wrapper. "Can I use your phone?"

A frown added even more wrinkles to Minnie's forehead. "I'm afraid the phone lines have been down for the last couple days. The wind, you know. And cell reception out here is so bad that we don't even waste our time buying them. But it sounds like you'll be back in New York City before you know it, and you'll have plenty of time to get hitched to that man of your dreams." She maneuvered herself back into the wheelchair. "For now, why don't you help yourself to a cold drink from the fridge behind the bar and take a stroll through the garden? It's got a real nice hammock for napping."

Since Jenna had gotten very little sleep in the last few days, it wasn't a half bad idea.

"I might do that," she said.

Minnie smiled her approval before zipping toward the elevators. It took the doors closing for Jenna to realize that she hadn't gotten one direct answer from the wily woman about the invitation. She might've followed after her if she hadn't been intrigued by the thought of being alone in the hen sanctuary. She got up from the couch and wandered around the room, plunking out "Chopsticks" on the piano before opening up two huge feather fans she found in a vase and swirling them around. After almost choking to death on a loose feather, she moved over to the bookshelf and pulled out one of the photo albums.

It was filled with pictures of women dressed in bell-bottom jeans and loose tops similar to Sunshine's. She didn't find a picture of Sunshine, but she found one of Minnie and Baby. Minus her glasses, Baby looked exactly like Marilyn as she blew a kiss at the camera, her arm hooked over Minnie who stood next to her, kicking up a shapely leg.

The thought of the woman in the picture now confined to a wheelchair made Jenna sad, and she put the photo album away and walked over to the bar. She opened the

small refrigerator and pulled out a can of Mountain Dew.
As she popped the top, she noticed the cordless phone on
the end of the bar. Even though Minnie had told her that
the phones were dead, she couldn't help picking it up and
pressing the talk button.

She didn't hear a dial tone.

Instead, she heard a man's voice that she recognized
instantly.

"...so you're gonna continue to lie to her?" Moses
Tate asked.

"Not lie," Minnie said. "Just avoid the truth. She has
her mind made up about what she wants to do, and it will
only make things worse."

"I don't know if I agree," Moses said. "A person needs
to know about their heritage."

There was a stretch of silence before Minnie spoke.
"She already feels like she doesn't belong, Moses. What
do you think will happen when she finds out she was
adopted and her mama worked at Miss Hattie's Henhouse? It will only confirm her worst fears."

"You might be right," Moses conceded.

"So let's keep it to ourselves," Minnie said. "There's
no tellin' what would happen if word got out. I'm just
hopin' I can talk her into stayin' long enough to get in
touch with her hen-ness."

"If anyone can do it, you can, Min."

"Thank you, Moses. I'll keep you posted."

The phone clicked twice as the can slipped from Jenna's hand. It hit the carpet with a muffled thump too soft
to be heard over the cracking of Jenna's world.

Chapter Thirteen

BEAU SANK DOWN INTO THE huge bear claw tub and released a sigh. The warmth eased the soreness in his shoulder and had him resting his head back against the rim and closing his eyes. He had wanted to get into the bath sooner, but the hens had kept him from it. Baby had brought up chocolate chip cookies and milk. Sunshine had wanted to rub some herbal ointment on his shoulder. And Starlet had continued to look at him with those big, brown eyes as if he was the most wonderful thing on the face of the earth. Their attention should've made him feel loved and special. Instead, it just made him feel guilty that he hadn't been back sooner.

And if the hens were this happy to see him, there was no telling how happy his family would be if he stopped by. Which made him feel even guiltier, because he had absolutely no intention of doing so. He knew he was being immature. A bigger man would be happy that his brothers had found good women to love and now had families of their own. And Beau was happy for Billy and Brant. He had no problem talking about their wives and kids on the phone. And he liked the pictures and videos they sent. He just didn't think he could witness their happiness up close and personal.

Not when they were living out his dream. A dream he could never achieve.

He reached an arm out of the tub and felt around for the glass of brandy he'd brought into the bathroom. He had just downed the last of it when there was a commotion outside the bathroom door. Before he could do more than sit up, the door flew open, and Jenna stepped in. Starlet was standing behind her, her eyes pinned on Beau and her face a bright red.

"What the hell!" The glass slipped from Beau's hand and hit the water, splashing him in the face.

"If you'll excuse us," Jenna said to Starlet, "I need to talk with Beau." Before Starlet could say a word, Jenna slammed the door and locked it.

She turned, and her gaze slid over his body, hesitating on the water that lapped against his waist. Damned if Beau didn't turn as hard as a stone. He blamed it on the western wear. Jenna in boxers and a tiny top was bad enough, but Jenna in cowboy boots and tight jeans that made her legs look longer than a stretch of highway was more than a man could take. Not to mention the hat. He had always had a thing for a girl in a cowboy hat. The entire ride from Bramble, he'd been tongue-tied and turned on. It annoyed him so much that he couldn't help but be a smartass.

"You ready to finish that hand job, Blondie?" He pulled the glass from the water and forced himself to relax back in the tub, even though there wasn't a relaxed bone in his body. And hadn't been since he'd met her. Obviously, he needed to make another trip to his Chinese Taoist master.

Her gaze lifted from the water, and she cocked an eyebrow. "No, but I'm sure Starlet wouldn't mind giving you one, seeing as how she likes to watch you take a bath."

It didn't surprise Beau. There were all kinds of secret passages in the old house that Starlet knew about. While living at the henhouse, he had woken up numerous times to find her in his room. Of course, this time, he had made it easy on her by not locking the bathroom door. Next time, he'd be more careful. There were way too many aggressive women in the house.

"At least she doesn't interrupt a man's bath," he said as he reached for the soap. "So if you're not going to make me happy, what do you want?"

She moved over to the toilet and sat down as if it was something she did every day. Of course, it probably was. She lived with a guy. Beau didn't know why, but the thought of Jenna sitting on the toilet talking to Davy really pissed him off. He tried taking a deep, even breath, but it got stuck in his lungs at her next words.

"I'm a hen."

Beau stopped lathering his arm and stared at her. "As in, Minnie made you an honorary hen?"

She shook her head. "As in, my mama was a prostitute."

The soap slipped from his hand and plopped down in the water. "But I thought you told me that your mama worked at the Seed and Feed?"

"Feed and Seed. And Jenna Scroggs does." Her shoulders drooped. "But my real mama—the one who put me up for adoption—worked here." Her eyes widened. "Unless she still works here."

"Minnie told you that?"

"Not me exactly." Jenna leaned up and dipped her

hand into the water. Her fingers brushed over his thigh. Before he could do more than suck wind, her hand resurfaced with the soap.

Beau stared at the soap and tried to catch his breath. Did the woman have no idea what turned a man on? He thought he'd been hard before; now he was like granite.

"I overheard her talking to Moses on the phone." She reached for the washcloth on the side of the tub.

Beau watched her lather the washcloth, and his mouth had trouble forming his next words. "Maybe she wasn't talking about you."

"So you think she was talking about Starlet? I thought Starlet knew she was a hen."

He tried to think, but it was hard when soap bubbles oozed through her fingers. "Maybe she knew you were listening and was just kidding around."

"She didn't sound like she was kidding." Jenna set the soap back in the dish. "And when I tried to get information out of her about the invitation, she hedged—like she was hiding something." She tapped him on the shoulder. "Sit up."

"What?"

"Sit up and I'll scrub your back."

His cock grew another inch. "You're not scrubbing my back."

She squeezed the washcloth, and bubbles dripped from her hand. "Suit yourself, but there's no way you can scrub up properly with a hurt shoulder."

There was a moment when he actually thought about grabbing the washcloth and tossing her ass out. The moment before his brain kicked in. What was the matter with him? He had a pretty woman offering to scrub his back and he was going to decline? Not likely.

He sat up. "So you think your mother has lied to you all these years? But I thought you had other siblings." He almost moaned out loud when the washcloth came in contact with the center of his back. The moment was fleeting. Jenna scrubbed backs like she did everything else in her life. Half his skin was rubbed off before he could stop her.

"Geez, woman!" He whipped around and grabbed the washcloth.

She shrugged. "See, I'm much rougher than any of my sisters. And I'm the only one in the family with blond hair—well, Dallas has blond hair, but it's not as blond as mine. And I'm the only girl who wasn't a cheerleader or homecoming queen. I'm not as smart as any of my siblings. And I have this really weird little birthmark on my right breast."

Shit. Beau tried to keep his eyes above her neck and his throbbing penis below the surface of the water.

She reached for the bottle of shampoo on the towel stand next to the tub. "Not to mention what happened to my sister, Faith. My mama got pregnant with her when she was young and decided to put Faith up for adoption. It makes perfect sense that my mama and daddy would want to alleviate their guilt by adopting me."

It didn't make sense to Beau, but at this moment, nothing did. Especially his sexual reaction to the skinny tomboy in front of him.

"So why don't you confront Minnie about it?" he said.

"Because for some reason she wants to keep it a secret." She poured the shampoo in her hand and started lathering his hair.

Since Beau was partial to his hair, he tried to push her hands away and do it himself. But it turned out that rough shampooing felt better than rough back scrubbing. Her strong fingers worked through his scalp, causing him to moan out loud.

"Lean back," she ordered. He listened, and she moved behind the tub. "And I don't want you telling Minnie that I overheard her conversation. Once she knows that I know, she might work harder to keep the truth from me. And I want to do a little investigating to make sure before I confront Minnie and my mother."

He cracked open an eye. She was kneeling over him. "Investigating? I thought you were headed back to New York City to make up with Davy."

"I am, but I can't just leave without getting answers. I called Sophia and she's taking care of things at my apartment, and then I called my boss and explained that I had a family crisis. He has no trouble with me taking a couple days off, which should be plenty of time for you and me to get things figured out."

Both of Beau's eyes came open, but when soap got in them and stung like hell, he slammed them closed again. "Oh no. I'm not getting involved in this. I'm heading out tomorrow."

"For where? You can't ride bulls with a screwed-up shoulder."

"No, but there's a beach in Mexico with my name on it."

"Don't be ridiculous. Mexico can wait." She pushed his head under water before he'd even taken a breath. Water burned up his nose. It was the final straw. He had been putting up with the woman's aggressive behavior for days, and he'd had it. All he wanted was a peaceful bath, and all he'd gotten was a raw back, soap in his eyes, and a hard-on that could jack up a semi. Well, it was too late to fix two of those things. But he'd be damned if he wouldn't fix the other.

Coming up out of the tub like Shamu at Sea World, he made a grab for Jenna and pulled her in with him—boots and all.

"You idiot! What—"

Beau covered her mouth with his. She caught his bottom lip between her teeth, and he glared back at her, daring her to bite him. She did. But the slight amount of pain he experienced was followed by a jolt of pleasure when she then released his lip and licked it better. Since she sat on his lap, he had little doubt that she felt his desire. He didn't care.

"I want you," he whispered against her lips. "I want to peel those wet clothes off your body and lick every square inch of your skin." Her breath escaped in a puff of warm heat, and his hand tightened on her wet, blue-jeaned hip. "And then I want to slip inside of you—deep inside of you." He nipped at her. "Do you want that, Jen? Do you want to feel me deep inside you?"

All the defiance melted from her eyes, and they turned a smoky blue. The hand she'd been pushing him away with slid up his chest and curled around his neck. Her lips opened, and she pulled him into the hot, wet recesses of her mouth. The kiss was as rough and demanding as Jenna. Her fingers bit into his scalp, and she tugged him closer, shaping and reshaping his lips as her tongue teased his.

She reminded him of a wild mustang he'd once seen in the hills of Wyoming. The cowboys he'd been with had fantasized about catching the horse, saddle-breaking it, and making it their own. Beau's fantasy had been much different. He hadn't wanted to break the horse's spirit—to turn it into just another saddle horse that was content to munch hay and bed down in a stall. All he wanted was to experience that wildness one time. Just one bareback ride across Wyoming before the horse rejoined his herd and Beau went back to his life.

And that's all he wanted from Jenna.

Just one wild ride.

Just one ride that would appease the desire that ached deep down inside him and get his libido back on the right track.

And it looked like Jenna was going to give it to him.

She shifted on his lap, and her hand slipped down in the water to encase him in a tight fist. He groaned as his head dropped back. Since Beau had suffered through foreplay for the last three days, he was locked and loaded. It only took a couple of strokes to have him ready to fire. He pulled back from her hot kisses and stopped her hand mid-stroke. If this was a one-time ride, he wanted to spend the entire time in the saddle.

"Easy there," he said. "Let's slow things down a bit." He lifted her hand and kissed the palm. "Why don't we get you a little more comfortable." He settled her hand on his chest, then shifted her around until he could get to the front of her shirt. It was a snap-down, and Beau couldn't help but smile at his good fortune. All it took was a slight tug for the snaps to pop. He separated the wet material and sucked in his breath at the two small, bare breasts that peeked back at him.

"Lord have mercy," he breathed.

"Okay, so they're little." She tried to tug the edges of the shirt from Beau's hands and cover herself, but his fingers had a death grip on the wet material. She gave up and let her hands fall back into the water. "All women can't have boobs like Peggy Sue. Although I doubt if hers are even real. And as far as I'm concerned, those plastic surgeons who prey on women's inferiority complexes should be hung up by their balls—"

Beau released the edges of her shirt and placed a hand over her mouth. "Shhh, when I'm looking at a work of art, I like complete silence." His other hand came up and fingered the shirt out of the way so he could capture one breast in his hand. It fit perfectly in his palm, like his old Spalding baseball. Except it was warmer and much softer. He brushed his thumb over the pert little nipple, and Jenna moaned against his hand.

"It's the color of flowers they have in the front of the Taj Mahal," he said as he bent his head to the treasure he cradled in his hand. "Not ruby," he breathed against the tip and it puckered prettily. "And not pale pink." He kissed the soft spot above her nipple. "More of a mix between the two. A dusty rose, perhaps."

She mumbled something behind his hand, but he ignored her and pulled her nipple between his lips for a thorough taste. Her hands came up and cradled his head, pulling him closer. He dropped his hand from her mouth, and her moans filled the room, along with his own. She tasted as good as she smelled, and he couldn't seem to get enough. Once he had feasted on one pert breast, he moved to the next. This was the one with the mole right above it, and he kissed it before moving on to the sweet center.

"Beau!" she gasped his name when his teeth scraped across her nipple. She wiggled against his hard-on. While the friction of the wet jeans felt nice, it wasn't nearly good enough. He slid a hand down under the water to the button of her jeans. The zipper proved to be more difficult. And the wet denim impossible. She helped by tugging off her boots and standing up, but even with both of them pulling, they could only get her jeans down to mid-thigh. Still, that was enough to distract Beau from the task at hand.

Jenna's hair below the waist was as sun-kissed as the hair above. And the way it nestled between those long legs was just about the prettiest thing Beau had ever seen.

"Would you quit gawking and help," Jenna fumed.

"In a minute." He leaned over and kissed the nest of curls. And for a few seconds, she didn't say a word while he learned the taste of her. But when her knees started to buckle, he accepted the fact that they would need to get her pants off if they wanted to proceed.

Beau got to his feet. "Sit down and give me your legs."

She followed his instruction, but not without putting in her two cents. "I don't think this is a good idea, not with your hurt shoulder. Maybe we should—"

He grabbed each leg of her pants and tugged. Her jeans didn't budge. Still, he wasn't about to give up. Not when he was so close. So hurt shoulder or not, he tightened his grip and pulled for all he was worth. The pants came off so suddenly that he lost his balance. He dropped the jeans and made a grab for the towel rack. It held him only long enough to break his fall before the screws gave way and it ripped out of the wall.

Beau landed on the floor with a jarring thump, his feet still in the tub and the towel rack in hand. Jenna resurfaced from the water, her hair plastered over her face. She barely had time to push the strands back and glare at Beau before the lock clicked and the door was thrown open.

Beau's back was to the door, but he didn't need to turn around to know who had come into the bathroom without invitation. The hum of a battery-powered engine told him everything he needed to know.

"I don't mind a little fun at bath time, Beauregard," Minnie said, "but Miss Hattie's doesn't go in for that S & M shenanigans. So put the bar down and step away from the tub."

Beau turned and stared at the woman in disbelief. "Doesn't anyone in this house knock?"

Minnie jangled the key ring full of keys at him. "I did knock, but you two were making so much racket you couldn't hear me. And I wouldn't have bothered you at all if we didn't have a visitor."

Beau cringed. "Brant? Or Billy?"

Minnie smiled. "Sheriff Hicks. And I don't think he's here to say 'howdy.'"

Chapter Fourteen

IT TOOK JENNA A LOT LONGER TO recover from Minnie's untimely arrival than it did Beau. Once he heard who was downstairs, a different person took over the body of the good ol' cowboy. This man had a determined look and wasted no time getting to his feet, whipping a towel around his waist, and leaving the bathroom.

But not before Jenna and Minnie had gotten an eyeful.

"I don't think Davy's got one of those," Minnie said as she turned her wheelchair around and followed Beau out of the room.

The mention of Davy had Jenna feeling instantly guilty. What had she been thinking barging in on Beau's bath? Scrubbing his back and washing his hair? She had never done anything like that in her life. Not even with Davy. Of course, Davy was very modest about his body. Something Beau didn't seem to be. He had traipsed around the camper in his underwear without the least bit of embarrassment. And maybe that was why she felt comfortable enough with him to intrude on his bath.

She had spent two solid days with him in close quarters.

She knew his habits almost better than she knew Davy's. She knew that he liked his cereal soggy, hated peanut butter, and slept on his back with one knee bent and an arm flung over his head.

Wasn't there a syndrome that people got when they were held captive with someone—some psychological thing that happened when they were forced into another person's company? That had to be it. There was no other explanation for what she had allowed to happen in the bathtub. Or her sudden need to keep him here with her while she investigated what she'd overheard.

After talking things over with Beau, Jenna was more convinced than ever that her mother was a hen. All the pieces of the puzzle fell together. She wasn't an oddball in a family of overachievers. She was just an ordinary duck in a family of swans.

She wrung out her soaking wet hair and wrapped it in a towel before putting on one of the robes that hung on the back of the door. She cleaned up the mess in the bathroom as best she could, mopping up the water on the floor and placing her shirt, jeans, and socks on the other towel rack that Beau hadn't pulled out of the wall.

Beau and Minnie were gone by the time Jenna walked into the bedroom. Her mama—or her adopted mama—had always said that Jenna had killed more than a few cats with her curiosity, and Jenna was about to kill one more. There was no way that she could remain upstairs when the sheriff was there.

Since she couldn't go downstairs in a bathrobe, Jenna searched through the huge walk-in closet for something to wear. It took longer than she thought. The clothes weren't as skimpy as they were out-of-date and completely unsuitable for west Texas heat. She finally settled on a pair of orange short shorts with an attached wide belt, the matching striped midriff top, and white boots. She figured if nothing else, her sixties-style outfit would go nicely in The Jungle Room.

When she got downstairs, Jenna found Baby, Sunshine, and Starlet clustered around the door of the library.

"What's going on?" she asked.

Baby turned and held a finger to her red lips. "We're trying to figure out why Sheriff Hicks is here," she whispered.

"Maybe he just came to play cards," Sunshine said with her wide-eyed vacant look, and Jenna had to wonder if the woman wasn't suffering from a little bit of dementia. "He used to do that a lot before Brant and Beau showed up."

"It's not cards." Starlet pulled her ear away from the door she'd had it pressed against. "He just said something about prostitution." She glanced over at Jenna, and her face became extremely unfriendly. "I thought you said you had a boyfriend."

Jenna tried to keep her gaze direct. "I do."

"So why did you lock yourself in the bathroom with Beau?"

Realizing there was no way to explain her behavior, she tried to go back to the previous subject. "So why don't you go in there and find out what he wants? Aren't you part of the henhouse too? How long have you been here, Baby?"

"Forty-three years," she cooed.

"And Sunshine?"

Sunshine looked thoroughly confused so Baby answered for her.

"Thirty-five."

"See," Jenna said. "You've got just as much right to hear what is going on as Minnie and Beau do."

"Aren't you going to ask me how long I've been here?" Starlet grumbled. Before Jenna could ask, she answered. "Over two years, which is much longer than you've known Beau."

"Right," Jenna said, not wanting to fight with the girl. "So you should be in there as well."

Starlet didn't look any happier. And Baby and Sunshine didn't look convinced.

"I don't know," Baby said. "We might make things worse."

"Nonsense." Jenna tapped on the door. "There is strength in numbers. One for all and all for one—" The door was thrown open, and the three women behind her scattered like a bunch of chickens from a fox.

A silver fox in pressed jeans and a sky blue western shirt that did really great things to his eyes. Although once those eyes settled on her, they didn't look all that happy.

"What?" he snapped.

Jenna smiled brightly. "The hens would like to be in on the conversation with the sheriff seeing as how what he has to say might affect them as well."

"The hens?" He glanced behind her, and his brow arched. His gaze returned to her and slid slowly down her body, stopping at her exposed stomach before lifting back up to her eyes. "Sorry, but you'll have to take that up with the go-go dancers' union."

"Very funny," she whispered, "especially since you're the reason I had to borrow clothes from Miss Hattie's closet in the first place."

A look entered Beau's eyes that was heat and annoyance mixed together. "Thanks for reminding me."

"Is that the new girl you hired?" a deep, masculine voice came from behind Beau. "Because I'd like to talk with her."

The irritation in Beau's eyes won out, and he stepped back.

"Jenna," he said, "this is Sheriff Hicks. Sheriff, this is Jenna Jay Scroggs." He paused for only a heartbeat before adding, "She's a guest at the henhouse and a close personal friend."

Jenna was so busy getting over the "close personal friend" thing that she barely paid attention to the man who got to his feet.

"Jenna?"

She stopped staring at Beau and looked at the sheriff. Recognition was instant. "Dusty?" She hurried across the room and flung her arms around the tall cowboy, squashing his hat in between them.

Dusty pulled back, looking thoroughly confused. "Please don't tell me you work here."

She took his hat from his hand and reshaped it. "I'm just visiting. And what are you doing here? I thought you were going to Houston to fight crime."

His smile slipped. "I guess I got sick of the fighting. What about you? You still inciting riots?" He glanced down at her exposed stomach. "I figure you could incite a few in that get-up."

She laughed, but it was cut short when Beau's fingers curled around her waist and pulled her out of Dusty's arms. His smile was as bright as always, but his eyes didn't look friendly at all.

"So I guess introductions weren't necessary," he said. "How do you two know each other?"

Dusty winked at her, and Beau's fingers tightened. "We met during a protest at Texas Tech. I was the one sent to keep things peaceful and had the job of dealing with a pain-in-the-butt blonde who was not satisfied until the dean agreed to change the menu in the campus cafeteria."

"All I wanted was chicken fried steak," she said. "Was that too much to ask for?"

"I guess not," Dusty said. "You ended up getting it. So how did you meet the owner of Miss Hattie's?"

Jenna opened her mouth to answer, but Beau cut her off.

"On a carriage ride in Central Park." He tugged her close, completely ignoring the elbow she shoved in his stomach. "She's taken me for quite a ride ever since."

Minnie cackled, drawing everyone's attention. She sat in one corner of the room, looking as pleased as punch. "So as you can see, Sheriff, there's nothing shady going on at Miss Hattie's. It's just a bunch of everyday people going about their everyday lives."

The smile dropped from Dusty's face and was replaced with a more intense look. "I hope so, Miz Minnie. I would hate to have to close you down." He smoothed out the brim of his hat and placed it on his head. "Because if I find out differently, that's exactly what I'm going to do." He turned his attention to Beau. "And as the owner, Mr. Cates, you'll be the one spending time behind bars."

Beau's smile remained intact, but there was an edge to his eyes that didn't look so cordial. "I'll remember that, sheriff."

Dusty nodded before he moved toward the door.

"Wait, Dusty," Jenna said, "I'll walk you out."

Beau's hand tightened on her waist, but released after only a second. "Don't be long, sweetheart."

Once they were out on the front porch, Dusty glanced over at her. "So what happened to the tattooed rocker dude that kept you from going out with me?"

Jenna could've explained her relationship with Beau to Dusty. They had become close friends after the protest, meeting for coffee on the nights that Davy had gigs, and Dusty had always been easy to talk with. But for some reason, she kept it simple.

"We broke up."

He nodded. "Davy always seemed like a self-centered deadbeat to me. Not to say that people with as much money as the Cateses can't be assholes. I still don't understand their interest in Miss Hattie's."

"So what's going on, Dusty?" she asked as she followed him out to his squad car. "You can't seriously think that Beau and a bunch of old women are into prostitution."

He pulled a pair of aviator sunglasses out of the breast pocket of his uniform and put them on. Jenna had to admit he was one fine-looking cowboy. Not as fine as some cowboys, but still handsome enough for a girl to notice.

"No," he said. "But I have to check out all complaints. Especially when they come from upstanding citizens."

"Perhaps they're just making an assumption based on what Miss Hattie's was before."

"Maybe." Dusty shook his head. "But this person claimed that Minnie had invited a new girl to the henhouse for that exact reason."

Jenna lowered her eyes to hide her reaction. Is that why Minnie had sent her the invitation? She wanted Jenna to become a prostitute like her mother? It didn't seem likely. When talking with Moses, Minnie hadn't acted like she was interested in prostituting Jenna. In fact, she had acted like she just wanted to help her. Because of that, Jenna wasn't yet ready to tell Dusty everything she knew.

Jenna shook her head. "I don't know anything about a new girl."

Dusty paused with his hand on the door handle. "But you'll call me if you hear something, right?"

"Of course."

He nodded. "I'd give you a hug, but I'd say that your boyfriend has had about all he can handle." He looked at the house, and Jenna turned to find Beau standing on the porch, his shoulder resting against a post.

"Be sure to stop back by again, Sheriff," he called. "Miss Hattie's always welcomes law enforcement officers."

Jenna waited for Dusty's car to pull around the circular drive before she turned and walked to the bottom of the steps.

"Do you want to explain what that was all about?" she asked.

"What? Your college boyfriend didn't tell you about our conversation?" He pushed away from the post and walked over to the swing and sat down. The chains rattled as he plopped a pillow in one corner and stretched out.

"I wasn't talking about his reason for being here." She climbed up the steps and stood in front of the swing. "I'm talking about you making him think that I'm your girlfriend."

Beau set the swing into motion with his foot and shrugged. "I wanted to get his mind off the entire prostitution thing, and it seemed like a good way to explain your presence at the henhouse. Did you have another explanation?"

"How about the truth?" She leaned back on the railing.

Beau laughed. "That we were kidnapped by two country bumpkins and brought all the way here from New York so you could make up with your parents? Your college sweetheart doesn't look like the type of man who would believe a hokey story like that."

It was really hard to concede a point to Beau, but she had to give him this one. She walked over to the swing and knocked his boot off the arm so she could sit down. "Okay, so what's going on? And please don't tell me that you're the owner of a house of ill repute."

"Of course not. Even if Minnie might be trying to change that." Beau replaced his foot on the arm of the swing and crossed his other boot over it, trapping her with his blue-jeaned legs. "Although it is an intriguing thought. You mind giving us a push?"

She rolled her eyes and pushed the swing back and forth with the toe of her go-go boot. "So who do you think sent him?"

"That's a good question. The sheriff wouldn't say, but I got the feeling it was someone who has more than a little pull. What I can't figure out is where this person got their information. According to Minnie, just the hens knew about the invitation they sent you."

"And Minnie hasn't hired anyone else?"

"Just some woman from Bramble to help with the cooking and cleaning."

Jenna continued to push the swing. She couldn't remember the last time she'd sat on a porch swing. Or the last time she was able to see the endless view of the horizon. A feeling of contentment settled deep down inside her, and she sighed and settled back.

"Well, it's probably nothing to worry about. Dusty seemed to be satisfied that nothing unlawful was going on."

"Only because he has the hots for you."

Jenna's gaze swept over to Beau. His eyes were closed, and one arm was tucked beneath his head while the other rested on his chest.

"Dusty doesn't have the hots for me," she said. "We haven't seen each other since college." Her gaze settled on the rolled-up sleeves of his shirt and the dark hair on his forearms. "Why isn't the hair on your arms gray?"

"I guess I'm just a freak of nature. And time doesn't make a difference to a guy. Once in heat for a girl, always in heat."

"You should talk about being in heat. You are the horniest man I've ever met. I'm surprised you haven't already found your way into Starlet's bed. I'm sure you'd be welcome."

Just the thought of Beau with Starlet ruined her contented feeling. She tried to push his legs off the arm of the swing so she could get up, but the toes of his boots got caught in the chain. She might've continued to struggle with his big feet if his next words hadn't stopped her cold.

He opened his eyes, and they seemed to drill right through her. "I'm not interested in Starlet."

Heat swirled up from some unknown place, spreading through her body and settling in the polyester crotch of her shorts. And it took a real effort not to crawl right on top of the man and take him up on what his intense gaze offered.

"I can't." The words came out in a breathy whisper. "I'm sorry, but what happened in the bathtub was a mistake."

Beau stared at her for only a moment more before he untangled his feet from the chains of the swing. Dropping his boots to the porch, he stood and walked to the railing. When he finally turned back around, his signature smile was in place, but his eyes held not one glimmer of heat. In fact, they were as cold as a New York City winter.

"Then I suggest you stay away from my bath time. Or on second thought, maybe it would be best if you stayed away from me altogether."

Chapter Fifteen

THE HENS WERE ALL CLUSTERED around the kitchen table having some kind of a powwow when Marcy walked in the back door. It must've been a private meeting because as soon as she entered, they all shut up. It wasn't a big deal. Marcy had never been part of the "in" crowd—or any crowd for that matter—nor did she want to be. She had been a loner all her life, and she preferred things that way.

"Hi, Marcy," Baby said. "Did you get the butter I asked you to get at the grocery store?"

Damn. Marcy had forgotten all about Baby's butter. She'd been so upset after talking with Pastor Robbins that she had forgotten about everything else, including her shoes. When she had looked behind her to see Pastor Robbins picking them up, she had been so worried that he would follow her to give them back that she'd slipped into the library to hide. There she had found a flustered Mayor Sutter surrounded by students from Bramble Elementary. Since the mayor didn't know the first thing about checking out books or locating the proper reading level for each child, Marcy took over for him. Dealing with the hyped-up children had helped to take her mind off her conversation with Pastor Robbins. But the ride out to the henhouse had brought it all back.

Was she crazy? Had she actually propositioned a man of God? She was lucky God hadn't struck her dead right there in Confederate Park. Of course, that didn't stop her from lying through her teeth now.

"The Fresh Mart was closed," she said. "Something about Ed's cousin being sick."

Minnie lifted an eyebrow. "Well, I'm sure Baby will get by until tomorrow. For now, there's something I'd like to talk with you about in the library."

Since Minnie only conducted business in the library, Marcy got a little nervous. She covered her reaction with belligerence. As soon as she walked through the library door, she snapped at Minnie.

"So are you gonna fire me for not getting Baby's butter? Well, go right ahead. I've done everything you asked me to do—including scrub out the toilets. Even though I can't see how that is going to get me ready for becoming a hooker. Or making beds. Or scrubbing dishes. What kind of man wants a woman touching him with dishpan hands?"

"I've known a few who don't mind at all," Minnie said as she rolled around the desk. "But I didn't call you in here to fire you, Marcy. In fact, I'm very proud of the job you've been doing at the henhouse." She smiled. "And for volunteering at the Bramble library. A good hen always does her civic duty."

It was the first time Minnie had referred to Marcy as a hen. And she didn't know if it made her happy or scared shitless.

"I don't know anything about civic duty." Marcy closed the door. "I just like the peace and quiet." She stared at the old woman as a thought struck her. "How did you know about that, anyway?"

"I've got my ways." Minnie took a sucker from the side pocket on her wheelchair, but then seemed to change her mind and put it back. "But that isn't the reason I wanted to talk with you. We had a visitor today." Her gaze settled on Marcy. "A male visitor."

Fear swelled up inside Marcy. A male visitor at the henhouse could only mean one thing. It was time for her to start her job. She glanced up at the ceiling. Was he up there now? Waiting for her? Just the thought of going to bed with a stranger sent a wave of dizziness washing over her. She swayed on her feet and barely made it to the chair.

"Are you okay?" Minnie asked, her voice concerned.

Marcy couldn't answer, not when she was fighting to keep from throwing up or passing out—or possibly both. She felt worse than the time she drank an entire bottle of elderberry wine. She placed her head between her knees and took huge gulps of air. She didn't know how long she remained there before a cool hand rested on the back of her neck.

"Slow and steady breaths, Marcy," Minnie said as she stroked her hair.

No one had ever touched Marcy like that. Mostly because she never let them. She didn't like to be touched, which was odd for a girl who'd had sex with as many men as Marcy had, but she was too busy trying to keep from passing out to stop the woman. Besides, the gentle strokes were soothing and seemed to work. After only a few moments, Marcy was able to lift her head.

Minnie held out a glass of amber liquid. "Drink it down fast. It will help."

She didn't have to tell Marcy twice. Marcy downed the brandy in one gulp. The fire of the alcohol brought a warmth to her stomach and a clarity to her head.

"I can't do it," she said as she handed Minnie back the glass. "At least, not yet. And not with some stranger." When Minnie looked confused, Marcy continued. "Please don't fire me. I really need the money. I just need to ease into it. I need to start with someone that I know and trust. I had someone in mind, but he's not interested. But I'm sure I can find someone else."

Minnie studied her. It always made Marcy extremely uncomfortable. The old woman's beady eyes pierced right through her like the creepy fortune-teller at the county fair.

"So you've already spoken with someone about your new profession?" Minnie asked.

Marcy thought about lying, but then figured that nothing got past the woman's eagle eyes. "Yes, but you don't have to worry about this man saying anything. I know something about him that he wouldn't want his congrega—other people to know."

If Minnie had caught her slip, she didn't let on. She only nodded and took the empty glass back. "So is this man your boyfriend?"

Marcy shook her head. "Not hardly. We could never be that. It would just be about sex. That's why I thought it would work."

"And why this man?"

It was a good question. Why had she chosen Pastor Robbins to initiate her into a life of prostitution? Did she think having sex with a preacher would exonerate her from her life of sin? She *was* crazy. Even if Pastor Robbins agreed to her harebrained idea, it wouldn't change what she was. In fact, she'd have the added guilt of corrupting a saint.

"I guess I just wanted my first time as a hooker to be with a good man," she said. "A good, kind man who wouldn't treat me like a prostitute." She slumped down in the chair. "But I guess it doesn't matter, does it? It doesn't matter if my first time is with a good man or a good-for-nothing criminal. A whore is a whore."

The slap that Minnie gave her had Marcy's head snapping back and her ears ringing.

" 'Whore' is a man's cockamamie word," Minnie said. "I won't have you using it in this house, and I sure won't have you using it to describe yourself. You've still got a lot to learn." Her eyes narrowed in thought. "And now I'm wonderin' if maybe I'll need a little help to fix all the damage."

Marcy didn't know what damage the old woman was talking about. The only damage she could think about was the damage Minnie's slap had done to her face. Her cheek stung like hell.

She rubbed it as she glared at Minnie. "You don't have to fix anything. I plan on pulling my weight here. And I will." She swallowed hard and got up from her chair. "If this customer upstairs wants company, I'll be more than happy to give—"

The library door opened, and a man stepped in. A tall cowboy in pressed jeans and a hat that cast a shadow over most of his face. There was something familiar about him, but Marcy didn't take the time to figure it out. The sick feeling was back and worse than ever. And no matter what she had just told Minnie, she didn't wait around for the introductions. With a hand clamped over her mouth, she headed to the door and brushed right by the man.

"Wasn't that Marcy Henderson?" Beau asked, once Marcy had left.

"One and the same." Minnie rolled back over to the desk and placed the empty glass on the tray. After talking with Moses, she'd been worried about Marcy. Now she wasn't so worried anymore. The girl still needed some work, but her fear of becoming a prostitute proved that she was headed in the right direction. Now all Minnie needed to do was help Marcy to discover her worth. Of course, she wasn't the only woman at the henhouse who needed to discover that.

Minnie smiled. It was going to be a long, busy summer.

"She's the girl I was telling you about," Minnie said. "The one I hired to help with the cooking and cleaning."

"You think that's a good idea?" Beau pulled off his cowboy hat and sent it sailing across the room. It hit the leather chair by the fireplace with the accuracy of a Frisbee. "From what I hear, she's not the trustworthy type."

"I never put much store in gossip," Minnie said. "If I did, Miss Hattie's would be nothing more than a house of ill repute."

Beau flopped down in the chair across from the desk. "Well, we should be glad that Sheriff Hicks doesn't either. Or we could have a big problem on our hands. Who do you think made the complaint?"

Minnie didn't know, but after talking with Moses Tate

and then Marcy, she had a good idea. Still, she wasn't
ready to let Beau in on that. Not until she found out what
Beau's plans were.

"Couldn't say," she said, "but lucky for us that Jenna
showed up and got the sheriff's mind on other things."

"Yeah," Beau grumbled, "lucky us."

Minnie held back her laughter. Within seconds of seeing Beau and Jenna together, she'd known which way the
wind blew. Now all she needed to do was make sure it
blew them together instead of apart.

"Of course, you being here didn't hurt anything," she
said. "Men pay more attention when a man talks than a
frail, little old woman."

Beau snorted. "You're about as frail as a cornered
bobcat."

She ignored the comment. "Still, it was sure nice
havin' you here to defend the henhouse. Lord only knows
what would've happened if you hadn't convinced the
sheriff that we are a respectable bed and breakfast."

He raised an eyebrow at her. "We are a respectable bed
and breakfast, right, Minnie?"

She flapped a hand. "Of course we are."

"Then why did you send the invitation to Jenna?"
he asked. "Jenna overheard you talking with Moses on
the phone and is now convinced that she's adopted and
the daughter of a hen. She even plans on staying here a
couple more days to prove it." He leaned up, resting his
elbows on his knees. "So is it true?"

Minnie tried to hide her smile. One down and one to
go. "Why else would I send her an invitation?"

"Damn it, Minnie." He got to his feet and started pac-
ing. "You and the townsfolk can't just screw with people's

lives. Jenna was happy in New York with her boyfriend. Now she's all tangled up in this mess."

"A woman who is happy doesn't hop in the tub with another man."

Beau's face turned bright red. "That was just an accident." He pointed a finger at her. "And I'm warning you, if you invited her here for something other than learning about her heritage, I'm going to turn you in to Sheriff Hicks myself."

"Go sell that to someone else, Beauregard. You love me and the hens too much to hand us over to the law. Besides, I'm not going to do anything to harm Jenna. The invitation was sent as a way of helping. Family is important. Something you tend to forget."

"Just make sure you've got the right information on Jenna, is all. She might be assertive, but she's as gullible as the day is long." He walked over to pick up his hat. "Could you call Moses and tell him that Jenna's staying the night and I'll have his truck back to him by tomorrow morning? I'm meeting the guy with the rental car around nine at Josephine's."

"You don't need to rent a car. You're welcome to use any vehicle on the place, including that big van Brant got us to transport guests. Since Sunshine doesn't drive, Baby is as blind as a bat, and Starlet lost her insurance after the last accident, we've been needing a driver."

He paused in the process of putting on his hat. In Brant's clothes, with his silver hair covered, he looked just like his brother. His wounds were almost as deep.

"I won't be back, Minnie," he said. "I have other commitments."

"Don't lie to me, Beauregard," she said. "Your family

might accept your excuses, but I refuse to. You're leaving because you can't face Texas without facing your own mortality."

Beau's mouth, that rarely went without a smile, pressed into a hard, firm line. Minnie wasn't trying to be cruel. But she figured that people had pussyfooted around Beau for long enough.

"I know you went through a lot with your cancer," she continued, "but that doesn't give you the right to ignore your family while you've been off traipsin' around the world. I figured you deserved a break. But two years is a long enough vacation, Beauregard. It's time to come back to your family and your business."

"Thanks for the pep talk, Minnie. But if I've learned anything in the last two years, it's that my family and my business can do quite nicely without me. And as for running from my mortality, aren't we all?" He pulled his hat down on his forehead. "Now if you'll excuse me, I have a date with a hammock and a couple cottonwood trees."

Minnie let him go. Beau wouldn't be swayed by guilt. His family had tried that, sending him family pictures and those cell phone videos. No, Beau needed something stronger to hold him in Texas. Something that would make him forget the cancer he had suffered through and still feared. Something that would bring out the protective nature that was inside all the Cates boys.

After pouring herself a stiff drink of brandy, she picked up the phone and dialed. Moses always answered his cell phone on the second ring. For a man who napped most of his life away, he was twice as alert as most folks. Alert enough to notice who Marcy had been talking to earlier that afternoon. Alert enough to help Minnie carry out the plan that was forming in her mind. A plan that might take care of two hens with one stone.

"I need some help, Moe?" she asked.

He stifled a yawn. "Anything for you, Millicent."

"I need you to spread a little gossip."

"Ain't much for gossip," he said.

"I think you'll enjoy this." Minnie sat back in her chair and smiled. "Texas has a whorehouse in it."

Chapter Sixteen

"I THINK I'VE FIGURED OUT your erectile dysfunction."

The muscles in Beau's neck tightened, as did his grip on the steering wheel of Moses's truck. He tried to take deep, calming Ojai breaths like he'd learned from his yoga teacher in India, but it was getting harder and harder to keep his cool around the woman. Especially when she paid absolutely no attention to his warning about staying the hell away from him. The night before, she had sat next to him at dinner, pressuring him to give the hens a raise. Then she had followed him into the billiard room where she'd distracted him so much by bending over the pool table in her short shorts that she had beaten him two games out of three.

At the end of his patience, Beau had hopped up early this morning with every intention of sneaking out before she woke. But who was waiting for him on the porch the moment he stepped out the door? A bright-eyed and bushy-tailed Jenna, who insisted she needed a ride into town. The only thing that saved his sanity was knowing that he was only hours away from leaving her and Texas far behind.

"I think it stems from your commitment issues," she continued. "You don't have any problem getting things started—like the henhouse, bull riding, and Peggy Sue. It's the act of completion that you can't accomplish."

Beau's gaze snapped over to her. She had ditched the shorts and midriff top for her western wear, which should've been a good thing considering that her mile-long legs and cute little belly button were now covered. But full coverage didn't keep Beau's libido in check. Through his haze of annoyance, his brain was still thinking about whether or not she had a bra on under her plaid shirt and how it would only take a quick yank on the snaps to find out.

Jenna's eyes scrunched up in thought. "I think if you committed yourself to something—saw it through to completion—your little sexual problem would be solved."

"I don't have a little sexual problem," he said through his teeth.

"Okay, a big sexual problem." She cranked down the window, and the wind blew in, playing with the strands of her wheat-colored hair. "At any rate, I think you'll have to deal with your commitment issues before you'll be able to reach—"

"Look," he cut her off before she could completely emasculate him, "could we talk about something else? Anything else."

"Fine. But I think you need to face the subject, instead of avoiding it. Problems don't get solved by ignoring them."

"And I guess you believe that all problems are fixable."

"I haven't run into one yet that isn't," she said. "Although some problems take a little more work and dedication. Two things you seem to know nothing about."

"Maybe I just haven't found something I want to dedicate my time to."

"So you've never been in a serious relationship?"

Beau glanced over to find her watching him intently. He could've told her about Cari Anne, but then he would have to tell her about the cancer that had caused them to break up. And he wasn't about to be on the receiving end of Jenna's pity. Or worse, to become another one of her causes.

"I've learned to never take relationships, or life, too seriously," he said. "Something you should've figured out with Davy. Speaking of which, there's a problem that you didn't solve, your parents accepting Davy."

She lifted a hand and held back her flyaway hair. Beau's gaze dropped to the front of her shirt, and the image of her breasts all naked and water-slick flashed through his mind.

"Well, I'm about to," she said.

He was so caught up in his bathtub fantasy that he lost track of the conversation. "You're about to what?"

"To fix the problem between Davy and my parents." She turned and met his gaze. Her eyes were the same color blue as the May sky outside the window. "I'm going to marry him." She sent him a weak smile. "I should've thought of marriage before. It makes perfect sense. My parents will have to accept Davy when he's part of the family." She paused. "I know what you're thinking. You're thinking that the Scroggs might not even be my real family."

Beau hadn't been thinking that. He'd been thinking about Davy replacing him in the bathtub, and it did not sit well with him.

"Well, I've thought of that too," she continued, completely oblivious to his vexation. "But I've decided that just because the Scroggses adopted me that doesn't make them any less of my family. In fact, it makes me love them even more for opening up their home to the child of a prostitute."

He closed the bathroom door on Davy and Jenna with a resounding bang. If she wanted to marry the nipple-ringed dude, more power to her. Beau had a life to get back to. An exciting life that included women much less annoying than the one sitting next to him.

Ignoring the tight feeling in his chest, Beau pressed down on the accelerator. The sooner he dropped Jenna off, the sooner he'd be back to his happy-go-lucky self. Fortunately, she finally shut up and remained quiet for the rest of the trip, no doubt dreaming of her wedding plans.

When they reached Bramble, Beau pulled up in front of Sutter's Pharmacy where Moses was sitting on the park bench sleeping. Not wanting to wake him, Beau left the keys in the ignition and hopped out. As he looked around for the SUV the rental car company was supposed to have dropped off, he realized that Jenna was still in the truck.

It seemed that Miss Van Damme was having trouble opening her door.

Beau's mood brightened considerably as he walked around to the passenger's side. She had just leaned down to put her shoulder into it when he tugged open the door. She fell out and would've landed on the pavement if he hadn't caught her in his arms.

Today, she smelled like the lilacs that grew in Miss Hattie's garden. It was an intoxicating scent that had him taking a deep breath. Jenna lifted her head and bumped the brim of his hat. In the shadow it cast, her eyes looked an even deeper blue.

"So I guess this is good-bye," she said.

"It would seem that way."

"You headed to Mexico?"

"I haven't made up my mind."

She nodded, then reached up and adjusted his hat. "So take care of yourself, cowboy."

"You too, Blondie," he said, wondering why the words seemed so hard to get out of his throat.

They stared at one another for a few seconds more before she arched an eyebrow. "So are you going to let me go?"

Suddenly, Beau realized that his hands were wrapped around her waist like a kid trying to hold on to a greased pig. He released her and stepped back. A moment later, Jenna had her hat on and was strutting down Main Street.

Beau stood there watching, trying to figure out why he didn't feel as happy as he thought he would. The miserable feeling intensified when she glanced over her shoulder and smiled. He had been mistaken when he thought she had an ordinary smile. There was nothing ordinary about Jenna Jay. Not her smile. Or her wrestling ability. Or those damned legs that seemed to go all the way up to her waist.

"She's a bit of a spitfire, that one."

Beau turned to Moses Tate, who was still slumped on the bench with his hat tipped low. A weathered hand lifted and pushed back the hat, revealing a wrinkled face and piercing eyes.

"Her sister Hope is a spitfire, too," Moses continued. "But Hope has always cared about what people thought of her. Jenna Jay don't give a hoot. She has a mind of her own and won't be bullied by the townsfolk's craziness." He shook his head as his gaze followed Jenna. "With that one, the more you push her in one direction, the more she'll head in the other. Something I don't think her family has figured out yet."

Considering the fact that her family wasn't blood, it made sense that they wouldn't understand her nature. And Beau had to agree that Jenna Jay was one obstinate woman. He watched as she turned the corner by the post office, and a thought struck him. Maybe that explained her interest in a tattooed band member. Maybe dating Davy was just Jenna's way of rebelling against her parents. Of course, it made no difference now. Beau was leaving.

"'Course, it's better to be obstinate than selfish," Moses said. When Beau glanced over, he found the old guy glaring at him. He watched as Moses took a squashed plastic Solo cup from his shirt pocket and spit a stream of tobacco in it.

"And you're pretty dadgum selfish if you're thinkin' about leavin' the henhouse. Especially now with the rumors flyin' about it being a whorehouse."

Beau slammed the truck door. "I don't think there's anything to worry about. Sheriff Hicks seems like a reasonable man, and he's not going to close the house down based on rumors."

Moses studied him for a moment before putting the cup back in his shirt. "And maybe that ain't the only reason you should stay." He looked back up. "Did you know that Doc Mathers has been goin' out to the henhouse on a regular basis?"

"With four women to take care of, three of them over the age of seventy, it makes sense," Beau said.

"He's not going there for Baby, Sunshine, or Starlet."

Beau had lived with a knot of fear in his stomach ever since learning he had cancer. He had grown used to ignoring it. He couldn't now. Not when it felt twice the size.

"Minnie's sick?" he asked.

Moses squinted in the sun that had peeked over the roof of the library. "I don't know for sure. The stubborn woman denies that anything is wrong. But Baby told me that Minnie wanted to go see Doc Mathers a few months back, and the Doc has been makin' regular visits ever since."

"Maybe Doctor Mathers just wants to keep an eye on her."

"Maybe. But I can't hardly see Minnie puttin' up with his visits unless she needed to."

Moses had a point. Minnie didn't put up with people fussing over her. Which might explain why she hadn't mentioned anything to Beau, and why she hadn't pushed very hard for him to stay.

"Have you talked to her daughter or her granddaughter about this?" he asked.

Moses shook his head. "I didn't want to worry them in case it wasn't nothin'."

A man pulled up in an SUV and parked it only a couple spaces down. Beau didn't even acknowledge the arrival of his rental car before he looked back at Moses.

"Where is Dr. Mathers's office?"

A strong scent of antiseptic hit Beau in the face as soon as he stepped in the glass door. Memories of all the other doctors' visits he'd had to endure fogged his mind like a swarm of angry bees, but he swatted them back with images of Minnie's wild hair and wrinkled, grinning face. Still, he needed to take a deep breath and slowly release it before he could walk up to the reception desk. The receptionist was bent over a filing cabinet while she talked on the phone.

"...well, I wasn't fooled for a second. I knew when it reopened that it wasn't a good thing. Before we know it, all our men are gonna be headed out that way, and us women will have to resort to usin' our back massagers—" She glanced up at Beau. He flashed her a smile, and her eyes widened. "Uhh, I-I g-gotta call you back, Cindy Lynn," she stammered. With her gaze still pinned on Beau, it took her four tries before she got the receiver in its cradle.

Since it didn't look like she was going to say anything, Beau took over. "I'm here to see Dr. Mathers."

She blinked. "Huh?"

"Doc Mathers. Is he in?"

Before she could answer, a side door opened, and Kenny Gene stepped out, followed by an older man in a white lab coat. Beau had met the doctor at Shirlene and Billy's wedding. He was a tall, thin man with wire-framed glasses and a shock of snow-white hair that shot up from his head like a rooster's comb.

"I don't think Jenna did any permanent damage, Kenny Gene," he said as he fought back a smile. "But next time, if you don't want to end up being punched, I wouldn't be involved in kidnapping."

"It weren't kidnappin', Doc," Kenny said. "Jenna is well over twenty-one."

The doctor looked confused before he noticed Beau. "I'm sorry. I didn't realize I had another patient waiting."

He stepped forward and held out a hand. "Beauregard Cates, isn't it?"

Beau shook it. "Yes, sir. Nice to see you again."

"Hey, Beau." Kenny Gene thumped Beau on his hurt shoulder, and it took a real effort not to groan in pain. "I thought you'd left town for good. And I was hopin' we'd get a chance to go fishin'." A guilty look entered his eyes. "You ain't sore at me for bringin' you here, are you?"

Beau smiled. "No hard feelings, Kenny. And if I decide to stick around for a few days, I'd love to go fishing."

The door opened, and a woman carrying a baby walked in, prompting Dr. Mathers to move the conversation along.

"Continue to ice it, Kenny, and it should be healed up by next week." He handed a chart to the receptionist.

"I shore hope so, Doc. A dep-u-tee of the law can't be runnin' around lookin' like he got his butt whupped." Kenny Gene tugged his hat on and headed for the door.

"Did Sheriff Winslow finally make Kenny Gene a deputy?" Beau asked as he followed the doctor back to the examining room. Just the sight of the table had sweat breaking out on his forehead.

"I think the sheriff refers to Kenny as his on-call deputy." Dr. Mathers stepped back and waited for Beau to precede him into the room, but Beau couldn't seem to get his feet to cooperate.

"Do you think we could talk in your office, Doc?"

"Of course." The doctor led him down a short hallway to the room at the end. "Please excuse the clutter." He removed some books from a chair. "I don't let the cleaning woman into this room." After Beau was seated, the doctor sat down in the desk chair. "So what can I do for you, Beau—besides give you some painkillers for that sore shoulder?"

Beau wasn't surprised that the doctor had noticed his cringe. The eyes behind the wire-framed glasses might be old, but they were alert. "I'm not here about my shoulder, Doc. I'm here about Minnie."

"Ahhh." The doctor leaned back in the chair and rested his hands over his white coat. "Well, I'm afraid that's patient-doctor privilege."

"So you have been seeing her?"

He hesitated for only a moment before nodding. "I see just about everyone within a good sixty miles. All except for that ornery Moses Tate who thinks modern medicine is nothing but smoke and mirrors."

Beau shrugged. "Seeing how he's lived so long, maybe he has a point."

Dr. Mathers's bushy eyebrows lifted. "Maybe." He got to his feet and was examining Beau's shoulder before he could stop him. "Dislocated it, did you?"

"Twice."

The doctor nodded. "I've seen my share of dislocated shoulders over the years. Some got surgery and some just opted to deal with it. I take you for the dealing type." He reached for a pad and wrote out a prescription. "But if the pain gets worse, take a couple of these." He tore off the paper and handed it to Beau. "As for Minnie, I'm sorry I couldn't tell you more."

"So am I." Beau got to his feet. "I was hoping you could tell me whether it's bad enough that I need to stay. Thanks for the prescription, Doc." He set it back down on the desk. "But like Moses, I'll take my chances." He was halfway down the hall when Dr. Mathers stopped him.

"Beau."

He turned to find the man standing in the doorway of his office, his direct eyes staring over the frames of his glasses. Beau expected to be harassed about his shoulder. Instead, the doctor said only one word.

A word that pierced Beau's heart clear through.

"Stay."

Chapter Seventeen

As soon as Jenna got back to her parents' house, she started digging for evidence that she had been adopted. She went through every drawer in the house, but found nothing to prove Minnie's words. No birth certificate. No adoption papers. She had about given up when she remembered her daddy's lockbox. She hurried into her parents' bedroom and pulled it out from under the bed. It was locked, but fortunately the key dangled from a ring on the handle. She had just fit it into the keyhole when the doorbell rang. Since she was still annoyed with the townsfolk, she decided to ignore it. Too bad the people in Bramble had a tendency to walk right in uninvited.

"So the prodigal daughter has returned home to rip off her loving parents." Shirlene Dalton sashayed into the room with a big smile and a fat pig. "Your mama told me that New York had ruined her little girl, but I didn't believe her until now. If you needed money, honey, all you had to do was ask."

Before Jenna could say a word, the pig trotted over and covered her face in piggy slobber.

"Geez Louise, Sherman!" Jenna tried to push the pig away, but Sherman wasn't having it. He knocked her back to the floor and would've continued his kissing assault if Shirlene hadn't grabbed him by his rhinestone collar and pulled him off.

"Easy there, Piglet. You don't know what kind of germs Jenna brought back from the big city."

Jenna wiped her face off with the back of her hand and scowled up at Shirlene. "Real funny, Shirl." She climbed to her feet. Unable to ignore Sherman's soulful, pleading eyes, she reached down to scratch his soft ears. "Hope have you pig-sitting while she's in Charlotte?"

"Yes," Shirlene said, "but I never mind watching my Sherman. He's more family than pig."

It looked as if Sherman nodded his head in agreement. Jenna wouldn't have been surprised. The pig had more human qualities than most humans.

"So how did you know I was here?" Jenna headed for the kitchen, hoping to keep Shirlene from asking questions about the lockbox. Besides, in her hurry to catch a ride with Beau, she hadn't eaten breakfast and her stomach was as hollow as a wooden leg. Being a healthy eater himself, Sherman beat her to the refrigerator.

"Lucky guess." Shirlene slipped onto a stool at the breakfast bar. "When we found out about the abduction, Billy drove out to Miss Hattie's to see Beau." She smiled brightly. "And I stayed here to welcome home our little Jenna Jay."

"Thanks, Shirlene, but it isn't exactly how I wanted to come home for a visit," Jenna said as she poured a bowl of Cocoa Puffs for Sherman. "And Beau isn't out at the henhouse. He brought me back to town this morning, but doesn't plan on staying."

"I was afraid of that." Shirlene released her breath in a long sigh. "Billy is going to be so disappointed."

Jenna gave Sherman his cereal and poured a bowl for herself. "So why is Beau so against staying here?"

"Probably the same reason you are." When Jenna looked at her, Shirlene shrugged. "I think it has to do with sowing your wild oats. Obviously Beau isn't finished yet. Now the question is, are you?"

Jenna opened the refrigerator and pulled out a half-empty gallon of milk. "My aversion to Bramble has nothing to do with sowing my wild oats and everything to do with my parents not accepting my choices."

"Lord have mercy," Shirlene said. "You can't tell me that you're still involved with that walking tattoo."

"There is nothing wrong with Davy's body art, Shirl. And if anyone should know that, you should. Your brother Colt has more than a few tattoos."

"True," she said. "But along with the tattoos, he's got a paying job. In fact, Desperado Customs has done real well since Colt moved his business here to Bramble. *Orange County Choppers* even came out and did a show with them—the younger son, not his mean ol' daddy."

"Davy has a paying job." Jenna sniffed the milk and wrinkled her nose. "He's a musician, and it's only a matter of time before he makes it big."

It wouldn't have been so bad if just Shirlene had rolled her eyes, but Sherman stopped eating his Cocoa Puffs and rolled his eyes, too.

"Okay, so don't believe me." Jenna poured the milk out in the sink. "But it doesn't matter if Davy makes it big. He's the man I love, and he's the man I'm going to marry. And once I'm married to Davy, my family will have to accept him."

"That might be true in another family, but I'm not so sure about yours, honey. Your mama is as stubborn as Faith, Hope, and you are."

Stubborn? Jenna was anything but stubborn, but Shirlene's knowledge of her family might help Jenna out.

"Do you remember the day I was born, Shirlene?"

If Shirlene was surprised by the topic change, she didn't show it. "Just like it was yesterday. I remember your mama climbing out of Burl's truck with a teeny, tiny pink-blanketed bundle. I think I was more excited than Hope was to get my hands on you. You were no bigger than a minute with the whitest head of downy curls anyone had ever seen. Didn't look anything like Tessa and Dallas looked when they were newborn."

"Do you think I look like a Scroggs now?"

Shirlene laughed. "Certainly not like the scrawny women in your family."

"But you remember my mama being pregnant with me?" she delved a little further.

Shirlene's eyes narrowed. "What are you gettin' at, honey?"

"Nothing. I was just curious about what my mama looked like when she was pregnant."

It only took a second for Shirlene's green eyes to widen. "Are you nesting, Jenna Jay? Is that why you're in such a doggone hurry to get married and steal from your daddy's lockbox?"

"No!" Jenna shook her head. "I wasn't stealing from my daddy's lockbox. And Davy doesn't want children."

Since Shirlene had adopted four children when she couldn't have any children of her own, Jenna figured she would be shocked by the news. Instead, she didn't even blink.

"There's nothing wrong with not wanting children as long as it's agreed upon by both parties," Shirlene said. "You don't want children, Jenna Jay?"

It was hard to answer such a direct question, especially when she wasn't exactly sure. She agreed with Davy that there was no place for a child in their lives right now. But she wasn't so sure she would feel the same way in the future. She just couldn't tell Shirlene that. Not when Hope and Shirlene were best friends, and the information would easily find its way back to her mother. And Jenna didn't want to give her mama any more reasons to object to the wedding.

"I'm too busy for kids," she said.

Shirlene's gaze pinned her for a few uncomfortable seconds before she walked over and picked up Sherman's empty bowl. "Well, speaking of kids, I better get back to mine. Mia's leaving today to work as a counselor at summer camp, and she's not quite packed yet. I also need to call Billy and let him know about Beau. Did Beau mention where he was going?"

Jenna followed her and Sherman to the door. "When we were in Bear's camper, he mentioned Mexico."

Shirlene stopped and arched a perfectly sculpted eyebrow. "I heard about your trip. And I guess if nothing else, it proves how much you love Davy."

"How so?"

"If a woman can still think about another man after two days with Beauregard Cates, then it must be love."

Once Shirlene and Sherman were gone, Jenna went back to the lockbox. But she didn't find anything that pointed to her adoption. Instead, she found three guns, a bunch of old coins, and some very disturbing pictures of her mother naked.

The pictures did give her an idea, and she spent the next two hours munching on a bag of stale Fritos she'd found in the pantry and scouring through family photo albums, looking for a picture of her mother pregnant. She found only four. Three dated way before Jenna was born and one dated after. She had almost given up on finding anything when she stumbled across a large manila envelope of pictures in the very back of a photo album.

The pictures were of two children riding horses, playing in the sprinklers, and eating Popsicles in front of Sutter's Pharmacy. Jenna recognized her mother immediately, but she didn't recognize the other child. She was much taller than Jenna's mother with long blond hair and serious brown eyes.

Jenna went to put the pictures back in the envelope and discovered a folded piece of notebook paper. When she pulled it out, another picture slipped to her lap. It was the same blond-headed child, except grown. The teenage woman stood in front of a rundown house, looking sad... and pregnant.

With a tingle of apprehension tiptoeing up her spine, Jenna carefully unfolded the notebook paper and read the awkwardly scrawled words that looked like they were smudged with tears.

Please watch out for my baby girl... The next word was too smudged to read, but Jenna had no trouble reading the signature. *Love, Olive*

As much as Jenna had wanted proof that there was a reason she was different from the rest of the family, now that she had it, she didn't want to believe it.

She studied the picture. This couldn't be her mama. Her mama was petite and dark-headed with a smile that always made Jenna feel better. This woman was big-boned and dishwater blond with a somber, almost mean, mouth. Obviously, Jenna was just letting her imagination get the best of her. Beau was right. Minnie had been talking about someone else and this letter and picture were all just a coincidence.

Of course, there was only one way to find out.

At three in the afternoon, Josephine's Diner wasn't crowded. In fact, only two people sat at the counter. Both women were talking to Rachel Dean and were so engrossed in their conversation that they didn't even glance up when Jenna stepped through the door.

"...I kid you not," Cindy Lynn said, "Mabel said he walked in as pretty as you please and propositioned her right there in Doc Mathers's office."

Rachel Dean snorted. "Are you tellin' me a good-lookin' man like that has to proposition women? Why, women are beating down his door—" She glanced up. "Jenna Jay?" She hustled around the counter and enveloped Jenna against a soft bosom that smelled like onions and bacon. "Why, we thought you'd gone back to New York City."

"I decided to stay a few days." She pulled back and gave Rachel a stern look. "But that doesn't mean that the folks of Bramble were right in kidnapping me. You can't force people to do things they don't want to do. And I expect you to call Kenny Gene and have him fix every car on my daddy's lot by sundown."

"They're already fixed, honey." Rachel beamed at her, showing off the space in between her front teeth. "He fixed them as soon as you left with Beau." She released

Jenna and headed back behind the counter. "Now what can I get you to eat? You've gotten way too skinny while you've been away."

The delicious scents coming from the kitchen made Jenna realize just how hungry she was, and she walked over and sat down on a stool next to Twyla. She lifted the menu from between a sugar dispenser and a bottle of catsup and was happy to see that it hadn't changed a bit. Chicken fried steak was still surrounded by a rectangle of stars, and you could still order frog legs and chicken gizzards.

"Do you think Josephine will make me some chili and eggs this late in the day?" she asked.

Rachel set a glass of water down in front of her and wiped her hands on her apron. "Of course she will. I'll just go back and let her know you're here."

When she was gone, Cindy Lynn spoke up. "We're all glad you stayed, Jenna. But if Beau didn't take you to Lubbock, where did he take you?"

Jenna closed the menu. "Miss Hattie's."

Twyla sucked in her breath. "You spent the night at the henhouse, Jenna Jay?"

Before Jenna could answer, Twyla started rambling. "Did you see anything naughty? Do the hens run around in that fancy lingerie? Or do they just run around butt nekked?"

"Who cares what the hens wear," Cindy Lynn jumped in. "I'm more interested in the male prostitute." Her thick, mascara-covered lashes batted. "Is it as big as it looks? And do you have to pay to touch it?"

The menu slipped from Jenna's hand as she stared at the women. "What are you talking about? Beau is not a male prostitute. And Miss Hattie's is a bed and breakfast."

Cindy Lynn and Twyla exchanged looks before Twyla spoke. "That's what we thought, too, especially when Brant and Ms. Murphy were runnin' things. But now that they moved back to Dogwood to raise that cute little baby of theirs, those old hens have taken over. And from what Moses heard, they ain't interested in runnin' no bed and breakfast. There's shady business goin' on out at Miss Hattie's. And Beauregard Cates is right smack dab in the middle of it."

"That's absolutely ridiculous," Jenna said. "And whoever started such a rumor has a few screws loose."

Cindy Lynn gasped and made the sign of the cross.

"I don't know what they taught you in that big city, Jenna Jay. But here in Texas, we don't blaspheme men of God."

Chapter Eighteen

MISS HATTIE'S WASN'T QUITE WHAT Pastor Sean Robbins had expected. And he wondered if he hadn't taken a wrong turn until he got close enough to read the large sign about trespassers being prostituted. Some might find the sign funny. Sean just found it brazen and infuriating. Especially when he thought of the poor women who were being taken advantage of. He had hoped that Sheriff Hicks would take care of the situation, but the sheriff had the audacity to imply that Sean had misunderstood the entire episode with Marcy. Of course, Sean had refused to give the sheriff her name, which was probably why the man couldn't do a better investigation.

Sean pulled his Jeep into the circular driveway and got out. Well, the sheriff might not be willing to do anything about the house of ill repute, but he was. He had tossed and turned all night, his mind consumed with thoughts of Marcy Henderson offering her favors. Not just to him, but to other men.

Sean just hoped he wasn't too late.

He climbed the steps of the porch and lifted his hand

to the door knocker that actually resembled a pair of...
His eyes widened, and he pushed the doorbell instead. A
young woman in a formal gown answered the door. She
looked disappointed when she saw Sean, but quickly hid
it behind a bright smile.

"Welcome to Miss Hattie's," she said. "You must be
Mr. Sedberry from California." She didn't wait for a reply
before she ushered him into the house, reciting the history
of Miss Hattie's as she led him toward the stairs.

Sean started to correct her mistake and then realized
that God had just handed him the perfect opportunity
to prove what was taking place in the house. If this girl
found out who he really was, he didn't doubt for a second
that the hens would try to pull the wool over his eyes like
they had with Sheriff Hicks.

The young woman led him to a room on the second
floor. He expected red satin sheets and dim lighting.
Instead, the room was decorated in virginal white and
sunshine. He waited for the young woman to proposition
him, but once she had shown him the room amenities, she
headed for the door.

"Dinner is at six," she said before she turned and sent
him a smile. "And someone will be up very shortly with
the house specialty. I can guarantee that you're going to
love it. All men do."

The door closed with a click, and Sean found himself
alone in the room. A room that, for all its virginal white,
turned out to be more seductive than Sean first thought.
The comforter on the bed was fluffy and inviting. The
lace curtains on the window frilly and feminine. And the
bouquet of lilacs on the nightstand sent out an aroma that
was calming and at the same time arousing.

No wonder Miss Hattie's had done so well in a time when men outnumbered women. The henhouse offered everything a single man's life was missing—everything Sean's life was missing. He had grown up with a mother and two sisters, yet he had forgotten what it felt like to be surrounded by the scent of fresh-cut flowers and baking cookies.

He had just reached for the pretty sachet that was hooked over the knob of the dresser when the door was opened, and Marcy stepped in. A part of him was happy to see her, but the other part was sad to have to finally acknowledge her profession. And there was no denying her profession when she turned and let the fuzzy robe she wore slip off her shoulders to reveal a body that took Sean's breath away.

Desire pooled deep inside of him, threatening to drown every logical thought in his brain and all the spirituality in his soul. He'd had girlfriends in high school and college, but he had never seen them completely naked. Naked and so beautiful that he couldn't speak. All he could think about was touching this woman, gliding his hands over her smooth skin and soft breasts that drooped like heavy fruit from a tree. If this was what Adam had felt when he took the bite of apple and first *saw* Eve, Sean understood why Adam had sinned.

Sean wanted to sin. He wanted to pull this woman down into the soft down of the comforter and sin until he was consumed in the flames of hell. But then he noticed the way her hands nervously clenched at her sides, and the way she couldn't seem to pull her gaze away from the tips of her scarlet-painted toes.

Sean's desire was eclipsed by compassion.

"Starlet mentioned that we had a guest," Marcy said in a voice that showed no indication of her fear. "I don't go in for kinky stuff. And I'd appreciate it if you made it short and sweet." When he didn't say anything, she lifted her eyes.

"Sean?"

The sound of his given name coming from her lips resounded in his heart like the peal of a Sunday church bell. As if his feet had a will of their own, they propelled him across the thick rug. He stopped just a breath away from her, so close that the tips of her breasts almost touched the palm trees on his shirt. The carnal side of him wanted to touch those breasts, to cradle them in his hands and worship them like they deserved to be worshipped. Instead, he kept his hands at his sides and tried to breathe.

"You are so beautiful," he whispered.

She leaned up and kissed him, her lips warm and pliant beneath his. When she pulled back, tears were in her eyes. "You don't have to say sweet things, Preacher Man. I don't need lies to go to bed with you. Just money."

Her words extinguished his desire like a candlesnuffer to a flame. And Sean bent down and picked up her robe. He held it out, but Marcy ignored it.

"I realize that you're probably new at this," she said with a sassy smile. "But I think things will work much better if I leave it off."

He kept his gaze pinned on the painting of lilacs that hung above the brass headboard, trying to ignore the living, breathing work of art that stood before him.

"Put the robe on, Marcy." He swallowed hard. "Please."

The please worked, and she slid her arms in the sleeves. He pulled the edges closed, but discovered that he couldn't resist the small temptation of brushing the back of his knuckles against one soft breast. It was a mistake. His heart almost jumped from his chest, and as he tied the sash, his hands shook worse than Moses Tate's. When he was finished, he stepped away.

"Go pack your things," he said. "You're coming with me."

There was a long pause before her derisive snort. "You plannin' on taking me away from my life of sin, Preacher Man?"

"Yes."

This time she laughed and waltzed over to the bed and flopped down. "Too late. I've already made my bed; now I have to lie in it." She fell back, one shapely leg appearing through the split in her robe. Before he could be tempted anymore, Sean walked over and tossed the edge of the comforter over her.

"It's never too late to change your ways, Marcy," he said. "Mary Magdalene is a perfect example."

"Well, I ain't no Mary Maggie." Marcy leaned up on her elbows, and Sean's gaze dropped to her well-displayed cleavage. She smiled. "And you ain't no Jesus. So we might as well accept that and get to the real reason you came here." She cocked a finger at him. "Don't deny it. I might not know the bible, but I know desire when I see it. And you want me."

It would've been better for all concerned if he lied, but Sean couldn't bring himself to do it.

"Yes, I do. But if everyone gave in to their fleshly desires, we'd be no better than animals. There are few people on the earth as good and Godly as Jesus, but that doesn't mean we should stop trying. I realize your life hasn't been an easy one, and I'm not here to pass judgment. I'm here to offer you another choice. I've spoken to Mayor Sutter, and he's agreed to give you the job of librarian until we can find another person to take it."

Since he had heard the townsfolk talk about how good Marcy was in the library, he expected her to jump at the chance. Instead, she seemed angry. Her eyes darkened, and her lips pressed into a firm line. There was a moment when he thought she would reach out and hurl the vase of lilacs at him. But her anger passed quickly, replaced by the Marcy the town got to see.

Sean preferred her anger.

"Sorry," she swung her legs over the edge of the bed, uncaring that she exposed her body from the waist down, "but I ain't never cared for charity." She got up and walked toward him, her hips swaying provocatively. Stopping in front of him, she ran a finger along the open neck of his Hawaiian shirt. "And what better place for the town slut than a whorehouse."

Sean might've believed her if she hadn't lifted her eyes to him. Eyes that were filled with so much pain that he was forced to look away.

"Good-bye, Preacher Man," she whispered before she slipped out the door.

After Marcy left, Sean stood there for a few moments, praying for guidance. His prayers were interrupted by cackling laughter that sounded like it came straight from hell. The analogy turned out to be close to the truth when he turned to find the scariest woman he'd ever seen sitting in the doorway.

"Now there's a first," the woman said as she powered the wheelchair into the room. "'Course I guess that depends on what you're prayin' for." She held up a plate of cookies. "Cookie?"

Too upset to demonstrate good manners, Sean strode to the door and looked down the hallway in both directions before turning back to the woman. "Where did Marcy go?"

The old woman took a bite of the chocolate chip cookie and slowly chewed it. "I guess that depends on who is askin'."

"Pastor Sean Robbins."

A smile broke across the woman's heavily painted face, and her gaze drifted down his body and back up again. "You sure don't look like a pastor to me. You look more like a Beach Boy." She pointed the half-eaten cookie at him. "I met them once. Their touring bus got a flat tire right down the road from here." She chuckled. "They weren't so happy about being stuck in Texas until the hens changed their mind about wishing all girls were from California."

She finished off the cookie, then brushed her fingers off on her negligee before holding out a hand. "I'm Millicent Ladue, Pastor Robbins. But my friends call me Minnie. I'm the proprietor of this establishment—or what you would refer to as the madam." She cocked an eyebrow. "I'm assuming you're the one who wanted Sheriff Hicks to close us down."

"Wants," Sean corrected her. "What you're doing is wrong, Miss Ladue, and now I have proof. The young woman who answered the door brought me straight up to this room and talked about the house specialty. And not more than moments later, Marcy Henderson was stripping naked and offering me sex for money."

Miss Ladue held up the plate of cookies. "These are the house specialty, Pastor Robbins. And as for Marcy offering you sex—well," her eyes swept over him, "there's nothing like a handsome preacher to warm a wild girl's blood." Her gaze pinned him. "But unless money changed hands, I would say your proof doesn't have a leg to stand on."

As much as it galled Sean, he knew the woman was right. His lust for Marcy had overridden his brain. Now he wouldn't get a second chance to save her. An overwhelming depression settled over him, and he didn't know why. He barely knew Marcy, and she had told him herself that she didn't want to be saved. Yet somehow he felt as if his entire happiness was based on doing this one good deed.

"How much?" The words came out of his mouth without thought.

"Excuse me," Miss Ladue said.

"How much do you charge for a night with a hen? And I'm not talking about one night. I want all her nights."

Miss Ladue cocked her head. "So am I to understand that you want Marcy exclusively?"

Sean knew what she was thinking. He also knew that if word got out, it would be the end of his pastoral duties. And yet, he couldn't bring himself to let Marcy go.

He nodded. "I have thirty thousand saved up, but I can get whatever I need to save Marcy from Miss Hattie's spell."

Miss Ladue smiled. "It does weave a spell, but I don't think it's quite the spell you think it is, Pastor Robbins." She tapped her chin. "Still, you may have stumbled onto something. Yes, I think a pure Lancelot is exactly what our Marcy needs." The smile dropped, and her eyes grew intent. "Of course, there can be no sex—that would be prostitution."

"I'm a pastor, Miss Ladue," he stated. "I'm not interested in Marcy for sex."

After only a moment's hesitation, the old woman spoke. "You're also a man, Mr. Robbins."

Chapter Nineteen

BILLY AND HIS SON JESSE were at the henhouse when Beau returned. As much as he had wanted to talk to Minnie, it was nice to see his big brother. After the first awkward hug, they took up right where they left off. They spent a couple hours in the library talking about family and Beau's travels before moving out to Miss Hattie's lilac garden where they talked business over the leftover chicken and dumplings that Sunshine had served them for lunch.

"So it sounds like you rescued Dalton Oil, big brother," Beau said as he munched on one of Baby's chocolate chip cookies. "Those figures are pretty impressive."

Billy flashed a smile and reached for the glass of iced tea that Sunshine had refilled just minutes earlier. "Damn straight I did." He glanced over at Jesse, who had twisted himself up in the hammock that hung from the huge cottonwood. The kid looked like a cocoon, dangling upside down. "Don't break it, Jesse, or I'll be taking some of that money you like to hoard."

A scowl settled on Jesse's freckled face. But instead of

smarting off like he would've done a couple years back, he carefully unwound himself and tumbled to the ground.

Beau laughed at the kid's antics. At one time, Jesse had been too busy trying to make money to support the ragtag family of orphans he lived with to act like a kid. Beau was happy to see that Billy and Shirlene's love had changed that. Not that the kid didn't still like wheeling and dealing. When Jesse had first arrived at the henhouse, he'd brought one antique after another down from the attic and tried to talk Minnie out of them. Surprisingly, he had ended up with a few. Beau didn't know if it was Jesse's bargaining ability or Minnie's love for the kid.

Maybe a little of both.

The thought of Minnie had him glancing back at the house.

"So what's going on?" Billy asked. "Why do you keep looking back at the house? You got a thing for that young woman who turns bright red every time you walk into the room?"

"Starlet?" Beau shook his head. "Not hardly. She's like a little sister to me. And speaking of little sisters, how is Bri? Last time I talked with her, she sounded a little depressed. Of course, I don't know how she can be depressed when all she has to do all day is spend money. Mama and Daddy have thoroughly spoiled her."

Billy shrugged. "It's hard not to spoil daughters. They're just so dadgum sweet. When Baby Adeline pouts for something, I'd just about give her the moon if I could. And all Mia has to do is look at me with those big, soulful eyes, and I'm toast."

"You goin' soft, Big Bro?" Beau teased.

"Not hardly," Billy said. "I'm still pretty pissed at you

for not coming home sooner. So what's going on? And don't give me that shit about wanting to see the world. I bought that for the first year, but two years is too long to be away from your family. Especially when Jenna Jay told Shirlene that you were about to slink off and not even stop by and see me."

Jenna Jay. The woman was still annoying him a good sixty miles away.

"Yeah, well," Beau hedged. "I just didn't want to disrupt your life."

Billy reached over and thumped him in the back of the head, knocking off his cowboy hat. "I'm your brother, you idiot. You disrupted my life by leaving, not by coming back."

Rubbing his head, Beau reached out to grab the hat off the ground, but before he could, the wind caught it and sent it sailing over a lilac bush. "I hope you know that's Brant's."

"It's about to be your head if you don't stop being an asshole and tell me what's going on," Billy said. "Does this have to do with your cancer?"

Billy didn't know about the test results from Beau's last checkup. Brant was the only one in the family privy to that information. Beau didn't know why he had kept his secret. Maybe because Brant realized that Beau wasn't going to change his mind about going through more treatment and he didn't want to worry the rest of the family. But more than likely it was because Brant was an honorable man who wasn't about to break a promise. Beau was grateful. He had already gotten into a fight with Brant over not wanting to go back for more tests, and he wasn't about to get into one with Billy. Not when Billy hit harder and would have no qualms about dragging Beau straight to the hospital.

Still, Billy was right. Beau had been an asshole for thinking he could leave Texas without seeing his family. And since Jenna was responsible for ratting him out, he figured she owed him an excuse.

"Maybe I left because I wanted to see who I am outside my large, overachieving family," he said. "Here in Texas, I'm just another Cates brother. Out there, I'm my own person."

Billy squinted at him. "What the hell are you talkin' about? Please don't tell me that you've turned into one of those guy-crying dudes who want people to understand their sensitivity. Because if you think I'm going to have a sissy for a brother, you can think again. I'll whup your ass into the middle of next month before I let that happen."

Beau slumped back on his chaise lounge. Obviously, he shouldn't have used Jenna's exact words.

"Whose ass are you gonna whup, Dad?" Jesse came strolling up with his John Deere hat, identical to Billy's, curled above his freckled face. "Mike Miller for starin' at Mom's titties?"

"Watch your mouth, son," Billy said before quickly adding, "Mike Miller was looking at your mother's titties—I mean, breasts?"

"Yeah, but I guess if you're gonna whup his ass, you'll have to whup half the town's. There's not a man in Bramble who don't take a peek—"

Billy held up his hand. "Enough. And if you say 'ass' one more time, yours will be the one stinging." He got to his feet. "Now we better get home before your mother starts to worry. Go settle up with Miss Minnie."

Rising out of the chaise, Beau couldn't help but tease his brother. "You going straight home or are you going to stop by Mike Miller's welding shop?"

"What do you think?" Billy tugged his cap lower. "Nobody gawks at what's mine and gets away with it."

Chuckling, Beau followed Billy and Jesse out. He helped them load the antique sewing machine and coffee grinder that Jesse had finagled from Minnie, and would no doubt sell within the week, into the back of Billy's monster truck. It was a redneck truck if ever there was one, and Beau couldn't help but grin at the blatant bumper stickers plastered on the back.

"I'm surprised Shirlene let you keep it."

Billy slammed the tailgate closed. "She loves this truck almost as much as I do." He winked. "It's great for sneaking away from the kids for a little alone time at Sutter Springs." He walked around to the driver's door, but before he climbed up, he turned to Beau. "I realize you've had a hard time of it. And I don't begrudge you the fun and excitement of traveling around the world. But you can't ignore family, Beau. Shirlene and I are having a barbecue this weekend, and I expect you to be there."

"On one condition." Beau leaned in for a quick hug and a hard thump on the back. "You don't tell the rest of the family I'm here for a few days. I don't need the Cateses converging on Miss Hattie's just yet."

Billy pulled back and studied him for a second before nodding. "Fair enough."

Once Billy's truck had disappeared on the horizon, Beau went in search of Minnie. His brother's visit had kept him from talking with her about the doctor's visits, but now he intended to get to the truth. Unfortunately, he found her napping in her wheelchair in the library. Figuring she could use all the rest she could get, he wandered back out to the garden and climbed in the hammock. The afternoon was hot, and after only a few minutes, he removed his boots and socks and unsnapped his shirt. Dangling one foot to the ground, he set the hammock in motion.

He closed his eyes and breathed deeply of the lilac bushes that surrounded him.

It was good to be home. Good to see his brother and the hens. Good to feel the welcome and love that no stranger can offer. Still, he didn't feel like he belonged. Jenna's words came back to him, and he wondered if she wasn't on to something. Not that he felt like he didn't belong in his family. It was just that he didn't feel as if he belonged anywhere. He felt like an island. One wheel on a cart. One sock without a mate.

One puzzle piece without a puzzle.

His mama had always thrown out puzzles with missing pieces. And maybe that's what he'd done to himself. Thrown himself out of Texas and a family that reminded him of his solitary situation. And what choice did he have? How could he ask a woman to share his life when he didn't know how long his life would last? At one time, he thought it didn't matter. He thought that if you loved someone, any time you had with them was special and worth it.

Cari Anne had proved him wrong. His beautiful college sweetheart's love had only lasted through his first chemo treatment. Of course, Beau hadn't blamed Cari. Who wanted a bald husband with no eyebrows or lashes?

Still, it had hurt. And not even his family rallying

around him had made him feel any better. As much as they tried to be there for him, it wasn't the same. Something inside him died the day Cari Anne left, and he'd become what he was today. A loner without a home.

For some strange reason, the image of Jenna Jay flashed in his mind. Or more like multiple images. Jenna Jay in a short skirt and high heels wobbling down the path in Central Park. Jenna Jay in boxers and a white tank standing by the window in her apartment talking about Texas. Jenna Jay in western wear and a sexy cowboy hat driving Moses' truck. Jenna sitting on his lap in the bathtub with her shirt unsnapped, showing off her pretty little mole above her even prettier rose nipple. He could only imagine what Jenna would do if Davy ended up with cancer. She'd probably single-handedly come up with a cure.

Damn, tenacious woman.

Beau drifted off to sleep thinking about Jenna, so it wasn't surprising that he dreamed about her. Dreamed of lying with her in a bed of lilacs. They weren't naked or even close to having sex. They were just lying there, looking up at the clear blue sky and listening to the sound of birds chirping and bees buzzing. And a heart beating. A slow and steady thump that was calming. But then suddenly, the thumping stopped, and there was nothing but silence. No birds. No bees. Nothing.

Then Jenna lifted her head and her cool fingers slid through his hair, strong and reassuring. It didn't matter that he couldn't hear his heartbeat. All that mattered were the soft lips that brushed his.

Reaching out to cradle her head, Beau deepened the kiss, his tongue slipping into her mouth. She gasped, and his eyes opened. He expected to see eyes as blue as a summer sky above their heads. Instead, they were a deep innocent brown.

Beau jerked back from the kiss and stared into Starlet's flaming face.

"Shit!" He scrambled back so quickly that he flipped off the other side of the hammock and landed in the grass.

"Oh!" Starlet said. "Are you all right? Did you break anything? Do I need to call an ambulance?"

He rolled to his back only to come face to face with Starlet's bosom that spilled over the top of her dress. Most men would've appreciated the nice display. It just made Beau mad at the hens for not making Starlet dress appropriately. He took his anger out on Starlet.

"Would you quit sneaking around, Starlet!" He sat up and tested his sore shoulder.

"I-I'm sorry," she whispered. "I w-was just coming out to see if you wanted some more sweet tea, and when I saw you sleeping, you looked so...beautiful," she swallowed hard, "that I—"

Feeling like the biggest jerk, Beau pressed a finger to her lips. "I'm the one who should be apologizing, Starlet. I didn't mean to yell. You just startled me, is all."

Her eyes turned hopeful. "So you're not mad at me for kissing you?"

"Of course, I'm not mad at you. But I don't think we should do it again."

Her face fell. "Because I'm fat."

If Beau had a nickel for every time a woman brought up her weight, he'd be a lot richer than he was. Fortunately, all the practice had given him a pat answer.

"You're not fat," he said. "And it would be a pretty boring world if people only came in one size. That's what I like about traveling. I get to see women of all different shapes and sizes. And each and every one of them is beautiful in their own way." He flashed a smile. "You're beautiful, Starlet, and don't you let anyone tell you differently."

She no longer looked crestfallen, and he took that as a good sign...until she spoke.

"I love you, Beau," she blurted out. "And I know you want to keep traveling. But I could travel with you and take care of you. And if you don't want me to do that, I'll be waiting right here for you when you get back. Just like I was last time."

"You were waiting for me?"

She nodded and smiled shyly.

Holy shit. What was he supposed to do now? He didn't want to break her heart, but he couldn't let this infatuation with him continue. Not when he had no intention of staying at Miss Hattie's longer than it took to make sure Minnie was okay.

"I can't be your boyfriend, Starlet," he said. She dropped her head to study her hands, and he reached out and tipped up her chin. Her sad eyes broke his heart. But it was either break her heart now or break her heart even worse later. "It's not because I don't think you're beautiful and sweet. It's because..."

"You love Jenna Jay," she whispered.

It was the furthest thing from the truth, but Beau dove on the excuse like a wrangler on a steer.

"Yes," he said. "I love Jenna—"

The back door slammed, and Beau glanced over his shoulder. As if he had conjured the woman up with his words, Jenna Jay came striding down the path, her cowboy hat pulled low and her blond hair whipping in the breeze. He should've felt annoyed. If she hadn't shown up, he could've played the role of smitten suitor much easier. But the funny thing about it was, now that she was here, he felt a little smitten. His heart did a little back flip at the sight of those mile-long legs, the small breasts that jiggled with every arrogant step, and the determined tilt of her stubborn chin as she looked around the garden.

With her hat shading half her face, he couldn't see her eyes. Yet, he knew the exact moment that they settled on him. He flashed a smile, and the words that came out of his mouth didn't feel in the least like a lie.

"Hey, Blondie. I've missed you."

Chapter Twenty

JEALOUSY WAS NOTHING NEW TO JENNA. She had been jealous of her sisters' and brother's ability to get through their homework in under an hour. Jealous that Hope and Tessa could always find jeans that didn't come up to their ankles once they were washed. Jealous that Dallas could bench press a good two hundred pounds more than she could. But she had never been jealous of men. Probably because she hadn't dated all that many, and the ones she had dated no other woman seemed to be interested in. So it took her a moment to identify the green-eyed monster that reared its ugly head.

Once she did, she tried to ignore it and pin on a smile as bright as Beau's. "You and Starlet playin' a little spin the bottle without the bottle?"

As if he'd just remembered Starlet, Beau glanced over at the girl who was looking at Jenna as if she wanted to shove hot coals in her eyes. Or maybe that was what Jenna wanted to do to Starlet. Especially when Beau caressed her cheek before dropping his hand.

"Actually," he rolled to his feet, feet that were long

and bare and made a tingle skitter along the center seam of Jenna's jeans. "We were just talking about you." He ducked underneath the ropes that held the hammock and encircled Jenna's waist, pulling her close to his chest. "I thought you were going to stay in Bramble for a few days, sweetheart, and visit your friends."

With him pressed against her, it was hard to think, much less talk. In just a few hours, she'd forgotten how handsome he was, and virile, and hot—he flashed his bright smile and winked—and arrogant.

Her head cleared as her eyes narrowed. "I realize you love to race around and make all the girls giddy with your sexy smile and your twangy 'sweetheart,' but in case you've forgotten, I'm planning on getting back with Dav—"

Beau's lips silenced her. It wasn't a soft, gentle kiss. More of a hard, thorough, controlling one. It left Jenna as weak as a day-old kitten—the runt of the litter. When he finally released her, she swayed on her feet.

"Damn," Beau breathed.

Jenna might've repeated the word if he hadn't been looking at the empty spot where Starlet had been sitting.

"I don't understand women," Beau said, once the back door had slammed. "How can you love someone you don't even know?"

Jenna released her breath and flopped down in the hammock before her knees gave out. "We don't have to know you. You just have to fit in the illusion we have of the perfect man."

"Are you telling me that Davy is your illusion of a perfect man?"

It was a good question. When had her illusion of the perfect man become a longhaired rocker? Since she couldn't come up with an answer, she ignored the question. "So am I to assume that your little display was to throw Starlet off your scent?"

Beau sat down next to her. "Your timing was perfect, by the way."

"I hate to tell you this, but Starlet isn't going to give up that easily."

"Sort of like someone else I know. So did you call him?" He lay back on the hammock, and his shirt spread open, exposing his hard chest and ripped abs. Starting at the little hollow at his throat, her gaze wandered down his smooth, tanned skin. The man cleavage between his hard pectoral muscles. The angled bones of his rib cage. His corrugated stomach. And the dark slit of his belly button right above the waistband of his jeans.

Perfect.

The word popped into her head, and her brow knotted. Beau cracked open one eye. "So you didn't talk to him?"

"Who?"

He tipped his head up and looked at her as if she'd gone loco. "Davy?"

She shook her head, trying to clear out any confusing, wayward words. "No, not yet. I was too busy looking for clues about my birth mother. Which is one of the reasons I'm here. Why are you here? I thought you were leaving."

He tucked a hand behind his head. "I was, but then Moses told me that Minnie has been seeing Doc Mathers, and I wanted to stay and make sure she was okay."

The information was so contrary to the fun-loving, self-centered Beau that Jenna knew, she didn't know how to reply. She knew that he loved the old woman. She just hadn't known how much.

"I'm sorry," she said. "But it's probably a good thing that you stayed. Especially after what I heard in town this afternoon."

"Let me guess," Beau said. "Rachel Dean has bunions? Twyla is still trying to get Kenny Gene to set a date? Sheriff Winslow is afraid of his wife? And Bear is gay?"

Jenna laughed. "None of the above." Her gaze drifted down to his chest and the small tattoo that peeked out from the edge of his shirt. "Is that Japanese? What does it say?"

Beau opened his eyes. "Life force. Now what did you hear in town?"

It was hard to pull her gaze away from the tattoo. Or maybe it wasn't the tattoo as much as the hard pectoral muscle it was inked on. "Only the name of the man who ratted out Miss Hattie's to Sheriff Hicks."

"Who? I'd like to whup his ass."

"I don't think that's a good idea," she said. "It's Pastor Robbins."

Beau's eyebrows shot up. "Pastor Robbins?"

Jenna nodded and took off her hat to wipe the sweat from her brow. "According to Rachel Dean who heard it from Rye Pickett who heard it from Mayor Sutter who heard it from Moses Tate, Pastor Robbins was propositioned by a hen."

"Jesus H. Christ!" Beau sat up so quickly that it bounced Jenna up and sprawled her over his chest, knocking him back to the hammock. "What hen?" he asked, seemingly unaware of their bodies smashed together.

"I don't know, but I find it hard to believe that the pastor would raise such a ruckus over the older hens doing it." She tried to sit back up. Unfortunately, their combined weight had caused the hammock to dip in the middle, and it was easier said than done.

"So you think it was Starlet?" he asked.

"Who else could it be?"

After only a moment, Beau answered. [ ]
Henderson."

"Marcy Henderson? The Marcy Henderson I grew up with?"

"I guess Minnie hired her to help the hens with some of the house cleaning and cooking," Beau said. "No doubt, she made a pass at the pastor, and he thought it had to do with her working here. If that's the case, it should be easy enough to resolve. The few times I've met Pastor Robbins, he seemed like a reasonable man."

"If it was just him," Jenna said, "I'd say you were right. But the entire town is talking about it. The townsfolk are convinced that there are all kinds of naughty things going on out here." She made another attempt to get off Beau's chest, but his arms came around her and halted her efforts. She glanced up to find him watching her with hot, blue eyes.

"Like what kind of naughty things?"

Just that quick, the tingle returned to the spot between her legs, and her breath caught in her lungs. "Just things."

His eyelashes lowered to half-mast as he studied her mouth. "So why didn't you call Davy? One phone call wouldn't have taken that much time."

It was a struggle to get words out, especially when she didn't know why she hadn't called Davy. And she certainly couldn't think of a reason now. Not with Beau stuck to her like a Velcro tab.

She had always thought that Beau was uncommonly handsome, but up close, with the last rays of the sun slanting over his face, he could only be described as perfect.

From the silver hair that dipped over his forehead to the dark stubble that shadowed his chin, the planes and angles of his face melded together to form a masculine beauty that would make any woman mindless.

"Maybe Moses was right," he said, his voice barely a whisper. "Maybe you don't like people telling you what you want. Maybe you like making up your own mind." He dipped his head until his lips were inches from hers. "So what do you want, Jenna?"

At the moment, she wanted him to kiss her. To press those lips against hers like he had only moments earlier and sweep her into the heated haze that only Beau could generate. Licking her lips, she closed her eyes and leaned closer. But instead of feeling the heat of his mouth, she felt his hands tighten on her waist as he lifted her off him and got to his feet. Without his weight to balance the hammock, it flipped over, spilling her to the ground.

She landed facedown with an *oomph*, and it took a moment before she could catch her breath and roll to her back. Beau stood over her wearing a cocky grin.

"No need to answer now, Blondie." He leaned down to scoop up her cowboy hat. "We've got all night."

Spitting out a clump of grass, Jenna sat up and tried to figure out what had just happened. "I'm not staying the night."

"Of course you're staying." Beau pulled her to her feet and placed her hat on her head, pulling it down until her ears bent. "Where else would my girlfriend stay, but with me?"

Jenna stayed for dinner. Not because of Beau's hare-brained scheme to dissuade Starlet, but because of the picture that was burning a hole in her back pocket. She wanted to check the photo albums in The Jungle Room and see if she could find the same woman. That, and she had a weakness for pot roast, which was what Baby made for dinner.

"I swear," Minnie said, "you two eat more than the entire Texas A&M football team put together. After their bus pulled out, our cupboards were barer than Moses Tate's head." She smiled, slyly. "But it was worth it to take those boys away from The Chicken Ranch."

"About that." Beau finished placing the last slice of cherry pie on his plate—the same piece Jenna had been eyeballing. "It seems that the henhouse is the topic of gossip in Bramble."

"Well, that's nice to hear," Minnie said as she rolled away from the table and took her dirty plate to the sink. The other hens had left the table only moments before to clean up after the guests who had eaten in the dining room. "Gossip is always good for business."

"Not this gossip." Beau cut into his pie and lifted a perfect-sized bite. Jenna couldn't seem to stop herself from grabbing his fork and redirecting the bite to her mouth. He shot her an annoyed look before he continued. "It seems that Pastor Robbins thinks that Miss Hattie's is back in the business of prostitution."

The sound of shattering glass had Jenna almost choking on her pie. She looked up to see Marcy standing in the doorway of the kitchen, a couple broken plates at her feet. If the dropped plates weren't enough to confirm Beau's suspicions, her guilty face was. Although Jenna had to hand it to her; she recovered quickly.

"I guess I tried to handle too many at once," she said

in a belligerent tone. She looked at Beau. "You can take it out of my paycheck."

Jenna jumped up from the table. "Of course he's not going to take it out of your paycheck," she said. "It was an accident. I make those all the time at Herbs and Spices." She leaned down and picked up the larger pieces of broken china.

"I don't need Scroggs's charity," Marcy hissed under her breath as she knelt next to Jenna. "I thought I got that across to your mama years ago."

Jenna didn't realize that her mother had offered Marcy charity. But now that she thought about it, her mother had always had a soft spot for Marcy. She invited her to every one of Hope's birthday parties, even though Marcy never attended. And once Dallas had gotten a hard smack for referring to her as a slut.

"Helping a person clean up china isn't charity," Jenna said. "It's just being polite."

"Well, go be polite with someone else, would ya?" Marcy got up and stomped from the room.

Jenna would've gone after her, if Minnie hadn't stopped her. "Leave her be, Jenna. She's like a feral cat. She'll come around, but not by force."

Beau snorted. "I'm afraid Jenna doesn't know any other way. Besides, Marcy might need a little forcefulness. It seems she's the reason that Pastor Robbins thinks the henhouse is back in the prostitution business."

"You don't say." Minnie looked at the doorway. "Well, I'll be sure to have a word with her about that."

"And I'll talk with Pastor Robbins," Beau said, "and clear things up."

"No." Minnie rolled over to a closet and pulled out

a broom. "I think it would be best if we let Marcy do that. It will be a good lesson for her about cleaning up her own messes." She handed the broom and dustpan to Jenna. "You're stayin' the night, aren't you? I don't like the thought of you driving back in the dark."

"Thanks for the offer, ma'am, but I'm afraid I need to get back to Bramble." Jenna hesitated. "But do you mind if I go down to The Jungle Room? I wanted to get another look at that painting by the artist in Houston, in case I want to buy one for myself."

Minnie's eyes narrowed, but she nodded. "Help yourself. I'd go down with you, but I'm feeling a little tired. So I think I'll call it a night."

A concerned look settled over Beau's features, and he pushed back from the table. "Before you go to bed, I'd like a few words with you, Min."

Minnie didn't look happy about it, but she didn't argue as she rolled out of the kitchen with Beau right behind her.

After rinsing off her dishes, Jenna headed down to The Jungle Room. The photo albums weren't dated, but it only took going through the first two on the top shelf to realize that they were organized chronologically. She skipped the first two shelves and started with the third. She went through hens dressed in poodle skirts, crop pants, and bell-bottoms before she got to the puffed bangs, ruffled skirts, and leg warmers of the eighties. She was almost through two complete eighties albums before she stumbled upon the woman in the picture.

Wanting to be sure it wasn't just the poor lighting, Jenna carried the album over to the zebra couch and switched on the lamp. She pulled the picture out of her pocket and compared the two. Her hair was curlier in the henhouse photo and her smile brighter, but it was the same woman.

She took out the picture and flipped it over. One word stared back at her. Olive. Jenna found more pictures of the woman, and in all of them, she was smiling brightly. No doubt happy that she'd gotten rid of her unwanted child.

Unwanted.

Jenna had always felt like the oddball, but she had never felt unwanted. The Scroggses had loved her and given her everything two parents could possibly give a child. It was funny, but now that her family wasn't her family, she suddenly realized how much she appreciated her parents. Everything they had done for her had been out of love. Even their dislike of a man they didn't think was good enough for their daughter.

Getting to her feet, Jenna walked over to the phone and dialed her mama's cell number. It rang only twice before the voicemail picked up. Not knowing what to say, she placed the phone back in the cradle.

She hesitated for only a moment before she picked it back up and dialed Davy's number. She needed to hear a familiar voice. Needed to know that her life hadn't been completely changed with just one photograph and scribbled note. Unfortunately, the voice that came through the receiver wasn't familiar.

"Hello," a woman said.

"I'm sorry," Jenna said, "I must've dialed the wrong number." Before she could hang up and try again, the woman stopped her.

"Are you calling for Davy? He's in the shower, but if you hold on, I'll get him." There was a muffled sound, the creak of the door, then Davy's muted voice.

"You coming in with me, babe?"

Jenna slammed the phone back in the cradle, then stood there trying to absorb the fact that Davy had found another "babe." It should've hurt more than it did. Or maybe she was already so upset that she couldn't distinguish between the pain of losing her family and the pain of losing her boyfriend.

The tear that dripped down her face took her by surprise. She had never been a crier. Crying was for weak girls who didn't know how to fight for what they wanted. Jenna knew how to fight. She just wasn't sure who, or what, she was fighting for anymore.

Maybe herself.

Chapter Twenty-one

BEAU HAD EXPECTED TO HAVE his conversation with Minnie in the library. Instead, she went straight to her bedroom. It concerned him more than he cared to admit. She had just taken a nap that day, and now she was going to bed early? The Minnie that he remembered didn't nap, nor did she go to bed before midnight.

"I'm calling Dr. Mathers," he said when they reached her room.

"No, you're not." Minnie rolled toward the bathroom. "He's already had to come out here way too much as it is. The pills he gave me for my arthritis are just makin' me a little tired, is all." She went into the bathroom and closed the door behind her.

Beau stared at the door. He knew it wasn't going to be easy to get information out of Minnie. She had always been as tight-lipped about her personal affairs as Doc Mathers was about his patients. Still, Beau wasn't going to leave there until he had some answers. Since the old woman would no doubt take her good sweet time in the bathroom in hopes that he would give up and leave, he walked over to the bed and sat down.

He had been back a couple times since the house had been remodeled, but neither time had he been in Minnie's room. He was glad to see that Brant had made provisions for her handicap. The room was big enough to maneuver her wheelchair around, the clothing bars had been lowered in the closet, and the bed was at just the right height so Minnie could easily get in and out of it from her chair.

His gaze wandered over to the nightstand. Three amber prescription bottles sat on the top, and Beau didn't waste any time picking them up to examine them. Two he didn't recognize, but the last one had his heart thumping in overtime. A wave of nausea washed over him just as the bathroom door opened and Minnie wheeled out. She stopped when she saw him, her eyes intent.

"By the look on your face, I'd say that you recognize that one." She shrugged. "I guess that's what I get for leavin' my medicine out for snoopy folks to look at."

His grip tightened on the bottle. "Cancer?"

"That's what Doc Mathers thinks," she rolled closer. "But I never put much store in doctors." She pulled the bottle from his numb fingers and set it back on the nightstand.

"What kind?" he whispered.

"Breast," she said, "which surprised the heck out of me, considerin' I always thought my lungs would be the ones to succumb to the disease. Lie down, Beauregard, before you pass out."

Since he felt like he was about to do exactly that, he listened. But even when he was completely stretched out and staring up at the ceiling, he didn't feel any better. It was strange, but it was like he was reliving the first time the doctors had told him he had cancer. It was like someone had set a five-hundred-pound barbell on his chest and said, "Okay, now figure out how to live with this." He couldn't breathe. He couldn't move. He couldn't think.

A wrinkled hand reached out and took his, giving it a gentle squeeze.

"I figure you must be thinkin' about your own cancer, which is exactly why I decided to keep mine a secret. You don't need the worry, and neither does Brant. Not when he has just found happiness with my granddaughter, Elizabeth. They don't need something like this taking it away."

Beau wanted to jump up from the bed and yell and scream out his frustration. Instead, he took a couple deep, even breaths and sat up.

"It's going to be okay, Minnie." He squeezed her hand. "Breast cancer has a good success rate. Once you get the surgery—"

"I'm not sure I'm gettin' the surgery." She released his hand.

"What do you mean?"

"I mean, that I'm not sure I want to have my breasts removed. They may be old and wrinkled, but they've served me for over sixty-some-odd years. And I won't just slice them off because some doctor tells me to." She swatted at him. "Now move out of the way so I can lie down."

"Damn it, Minnie!" He came to his feet. "You need to get this done now. The longer you wait, the less your chances of survival."

"I've survived long enough." She maneuvered the chair next to the bed, almost running over Beau's toes, before she dropped down the arm of her chair. "The henhouse is up and running, I've contacted the hens I've needed to, and my daughter and granddaughter are happy. What more can I ask for?" She pulled the covers back and scooted over onto the mattress. Regardless of his anger, Beau quickly moved the chair and helped position her legs under the sheet.

"This isn't just about you, Minnie." He lifted the sheet back over her. "It's about the people who love you. The people who want to see you get better."

Her eyebrows shot up. "You don't say." She fluffed up the pillow behind her head before she lay down and adjusted the covers over her breasts. "Turn off the light when you leave, Beauregard." She closed her eyes and dismissed him.

Beau just stood there, a thousand questions racing through his head. How large was the lump? Had it spread to her lymph nodes? And the most important question: How long did she have if she didn't do the surgery?

A loud snore pulled him from his thoughts. It seemed while he was worrying, Minnie had gone to sleep. As much as he wanted to wake her up and continue the argument, he didn't. It wouldn't do any good. Minnie was as stubborn as the day was long.

He left the room, shutting off the light and closing the door behind him. He walked aimlessly through the house, his mind a mass confusion of thoughts and emotion. As much as he wanted to criticize Minnie for her actions, he couldn't. Hadn't he done exactly the same thing? Hadn't he failed to tell his family about the mass in his lung that the x-ray had found?

Like Minnie, he hadn't wanted to worry them. But now that he was on the other side of cancer, he realized how hurt you felt when people you loved didn't share life-threatening information with you. Beau might have thought that he was saving his family worry, but what he was actually doing was taking away their opportunity to grieve with him. Their opportunity to spend as much time with him as they could in case he died.

Suddenly, Beau realized that cancer wasn't just about the victim. It was also about the people who loved you. The people who wanted you to stay on this earth for as long as you could. No matter how many surgeries it took. Or how many radiation or chemo treatments. Yes, it was your body and you should make the final decision. But that decision could not exclude the people who loved you. Their love gave them the right to weigh in.

Beau didn't think he could feel any worse after hearing about Minnie's cancer, but he did. He felt like a selfish idiot for not understanding what he was doing to his family sooner. And what he was doing to Brant. Minnie had talked about Brant being happy, but how happy could his brother be carrying around the secret that Beau had given him?

Hell, he'd just found out about Minnie and already felt like he had to tell someone or crumble beneath the weight of such a burden. Walking over to the elevator, he punched the down button. The Jungle Room looked unoccupied when he got there. He thought he had missed Jenna until he walked farther into the room and spotted her sitting on the floor with photo albums scattered around her. It was hard to summon up a smile, but he did it.

"I thought you had slipped out without saying goodbye, which isn't very considerate of a girlfriend." She glanced up at him, and his smile fizzled. Her pretty blue eyes held a sadness that reflected the way he felt. It didn't take a rocket scientist to figure out what had happened. "So I guess you found what you were looking for," he said as he moved closer.

She nodded and held up a picture. "My mother was a hen."

Beau took the picture and studied it. The woman had long blond hair like Jenna, but other than that, he didn't see the resemblance.

He handed the picture back. "So what are you going to do?"

"Well, I'm going to find her, of course. If Minnie won't tell me the truth, I'll have to ask my mother—or my adoptive mother. It's funny, I always knew I was different than my brother and sisters, but I never thought I was this different." She swallowed hard, as if trying to fight back tears. It was so like Jenna to think that tears were a weakness.

He held out a hand. "Come here." She hesitated for only a second before she took his hand and allowed him to pull her to her feet and into his arms. Most upset women nestled against his chest like little lost kittens, allowing him to do all the holding, but Jenna gave as good as she got. Her arms encircled his waist, and she hugged him as tightly as he hugged her. The feel of her warm body pressed against his took away some of his fear about Minnie, and he released a sigh.

"It's okay," he whispered against the side of her head. "It doesn't change who you are. You are still Jenna Jay Scroggs." He stroked her back in soothing circles. "And you are still the most annoying woman I've ever met."

A puff of laughter came out of her mouth. "I bet you say that to all the girls."

"Only the ones I really like."

She pulled back and looked at him. "Do you really like me, Beau?"

He had been trying to tease a smile out of her, but looking into her blue eyes, he realized that he'd spoken the truth. He liked Jenna. He liked her dry wit and her sassy tone. He liked her soft heart and the way she refused to give up the fight—any fight. But mostly, he liked the way she fit in his arms.

"Much more than I want to," he whispered right before he kissed her.

Chapter Twenty-two

BEAU'S KISS NOT ONLY EASED the pain Jenna felt at finding out she was adopted. It made her feel something other than sorrow. It made her feel like she belonged. Like she belonged right here in this man's arms.

She gave herself over to his skilled lips. And within seconds, she was lost in his heated mouth. One kiss melted into another, and desire grew thick and heavy. She pressed closer, rubbing up against his fly. He moaned and pulled his lips from hers, trailing kisses down her neck as he scooped her up in his arms.

"Your shoul—der," she said, her voice halting when he sucked on a spot behind her ear.

Without answering, he carried her across the room to a hidden door behind a huge plastic plant. Through the door was a stairwell that led up. Beau took the stairs two at a time, seemingly unconcerned with the extra weight he carried. At the top of the second flight, he turned and headed down a dimly lit corridor to a door that was cracked open. Beau kicked it the rest of the way before carrying Jenna through Miss Hattie's closet to the bedroom.

He stopped by the huge bed that covered one entire wall and released her, allowing her to slip down the planes of his deliciously hard body. The bedside lamp was on, the multicolored lampshade reflecting in his eyes.

"Now would be the time to say no," he said.

It probably would've been the smart thing to do. With all that had happened that night, she was probably working more on emotions than logical thought. Her gaze settled on his mouth. A mouth that held not a trace of a smile. And Beau without a smile just didn't seem right.

She reached out and ran a finger over his bottom lip. "After you impressed me with that trip up two flights of stairs? Not likely."

Beau's lips curved up, and he nipped at her finger. "Saddle up, Blondie, because you're in for a wild ride."

She cocked her head. "Is that a challenge, Beauregard?"

"Damn straight," he whispered right before he pulled her down to the bed.

They barely stopped bouncing before Jenna rolled on top and straddled him. "Well, I do love a challenge." She grabbed the front of his shirt and jerked open the snaps. But before she could even contemplate feasting on all his tanned skin and hard muscle, he rolled her back over.

"No more than I do, sweetheart." He reached for the front of her shirt, but he didn't yank quite as hard as Jenna had. In fact, he took his time, undoing each snap with a gentle tug. He smoothed back the edges, and his eyes turned hot as he looked down at her bare breasts. Lifting a finger, he traced around each one.

"Did I tell you how much I love your underwear?" he said, his voice low and sexy. "Or maybe I should say your lack of underwear." He continued to caress her, his finger brushing first one nipple and then the other, tightening them into hard points of need.

"Beau," she breathed.

His gaze lifted. The heat in his eyes sent another wave of desire rippling through her body, but it was nothing compared to the shock wave that hit her when he dipped his head and pulled her nipple into his hot, wet mouth. He gently sucked, rolling it against his rough tongue, and she literally saw stars—little spots of light danced behind her eyelids. It was like there was a string that ran from her breast to the point between her legs. With every stroke of his tongue and every pull of his lips, the string was yanked a little tighter until Jenna was nothing but a twitching ball of pent-up desire waiting to be released.

Then suddenly, Beau released her breast and climbed off her, leaving only the cool air on her wet nipple. She opened her eyes to see him stripping off his jeans and boxers. She caught a glimpse of his tanned butt before he stood back up and turned to her.

"Holy smokes," she breathed as her gaze settled on Beau's hard length.

He laughed. "I'm going to take that as a compliment." He reached for her boot and pulled it off, followed by her sock.

"It wasn't a compliment as much as an exclamation," she said as she slipped off her shirt and reached for the button of her jeans. "I guess what they say about big feet is true."

He pulled off the other boot and sock before holding up her bare foot. "And how does that work for girls? Big feet, big…"

"Hair." She smirked.

"And you've got your fair share of that, Blondie." With a yank, he pulled off her jeans and suddenly she was as naked as the day she was born. Since Davy was the only man who had ever seen her completely naked, she thought she would be embarrassed. But Beau didn't make her feel embarrassed. His heavy-lidded gaze made her feel beautiful and sexy. "Pretty blond hair that I really want to touch."

Somehow she didn't think he was talking about the hair on her head. This was confirmed when he dropped her jeans and moved closer to the bed, his gaze never leaving the juncture of her thighs. He took her foot in his hand and slowly caressed the instep as he spread her legs.

Okay, so now she was embarrassed. She pulled her foot from his hand, but before she could close her legs, he was resting between them, his face inches from her most private parts.

"And maybe I don't want to touch you as much as taste you," he whispered right before his mouth covered her.

Jenna's eyes slammed shut as heat shot through her. Beau tasted like he kissed, with gentle sips and plenty of tongue. His hands slipped beneath her hips, and he lifted her closer, manipulating her against his mouth. Once he had done a thorough tasting, he settled into a rhythm of tongue flicks that left her mindless.

Her fingers dug into the satin sheets as the pressure built. And built. And built. "Oh Beau," she panted. She lifted her hips and clamped her thighs against his head as her orgasm shattered around her. "Oh Beau!"

Once all the tension drained out of her body and she

sagged back down into the mattress, Beau lifted his head and grinned. "That good, huh?"

If she'd had the strength, she would've rolled her eyes. Instead, all she could do was watch as Beau sat up on the edge of the bed and reached for the nightstand drawer. When he returned, he wasted no time slipping deep inside her still quivering body. He was big, but not too big. The fit felt tight and wonderful.

Beau must've thought so too because he closed his eyes and released a satisfied groan. "Damn."

"That good, huh?" she teased.

His eyes opened, but he didn't smile. "You don't know the half of it, sweetheart."

He kissed her, a thorough kiss that left her almost as breathless as his words. Then he started to move, slow and steady strokes that brought her desire back to the surface. Except he didn't look as if he was enjoying it as much as Jenna was. In fact, he almost looked like he was in pain. His eyes were clamped shut, and his breath hissed from between his lips. It didn't dawn on her what was wrong until he spoke.

"I'm sorry," he gritted out, "but I can't—"

"It's okay." Jenna brushed her fingertips over his face, trying to ease out the tension. "Don't rush it. If you can't come, you can't come. We'll just keep trying until you do."

He stopped moving, and his eyes opened. "What?"

She cradled his jaw in her hands. "There's nothing to be embarrassed about, Beau. Impotency is a problem lots of men have. But I'm not going to give up. Would it help if I used my mouth—or maybe we should try another position? You could get behind me and—"

Beau thrust into her, banging the heavy, wooden

headboard into the wall. He continued to pump as his muscles tightened and his face contorted with pleasure. Jenna wasn't sure what was going on until Beau slumped over her.

"You had an orgasm?" she asked.

He released his breath in a long sigh before he lifted his head. He didn't exactly look happy. "Yes. And you might have gotten another one if you hadn't been so busy trying to save me."

"But you said you couldn't—"

"I was going to say I can't wait. And then you started spouting off about what you were going to do to fix things, and I really couldn't wait."

"So you don't have a problem?"

A smile broke over his face. Not his usual smile, but devilry mixed with a touch of humor. "If it means that we get to try some of the things you mentioned," he leaned down and brushed his lips over hers, "then yes, I've got a problem. A very big problem."

Jenna woke to the disconcerting feeling of being watched. She cracked open her eyes. But instead of seeing the silver-haired cowboy who had rocked her world with numerous mind-blowing orgasms, she saw nothing but rumpled satin sheets.

Yawning, she stretched her hands over her head and rolled to her back, then almost jumped out of her skin when she saw Starlet standing by the open door.

"Holy crap!" Jenna sat straight up. When she realized she was buck-naked, she grabbed the sheet and jerked it over her. Her face burned with embarrassment at being caught red-handed in Beau's bed. Unfortunately, there was no help for it now so she tried to bluff her way through. "Geez, Starlet. You scared the heck out of me."

Starlet looked almost pleased by the information. "Minnie said that you need to get dressed and get out of Miss Hattie's room so I can clean it for the next occupants."

"Oh. Okay." She swung her legs over the edge of the bed and waited for Starlet to leave, but the girl didn't seem to be in any hurry.

Starlet wandered over to the window and looked out. She might be a little overweight, but she was one of the prettiest women Jenna had ever seen. Her hair was curly and rich brown, her nose small and perfect, and her lips plump and full. And her eyes were dark with a seductive tilt to them.

She turned those eyes on Jenna. "Beau said that he loved you. Do you love him?"

The question took Jenna aback, especially when her body was still tingly from Beau's lovemaking. Of course, it hadn't been lovemaking. Love hadn't entered into it. She and Beau had just had sex.

Wonderful, glorious, orgasmic sex.

Jenna's face got even hotter, and Starlet's face fell.

"So you do love him?" She moved away from the window and shook her head. "Of course you love him. Who wouldn't love Beau? He's beautiful, and sweet, and funny. And when he smiles my heart almost—"

"Jumps clean out of your chest," Jenna finished, although she didn't have a clue where the words had come from.

"Exactly." Starlet flopped down on the bed next to Jenna, her shoulders slumped. "So I guess you're going to get married."

Suddenly figuring out how she could make Starlet feel better, Jenna shook her head. "No. I'm afraid that Beau isn't the marrying kind. He's not going to give up his traveling lifestyle for a wife and kids."

Starlet looked up. "He's not?"

"No." Jenna tried to look as forlorn as possible. "In fact, you and I are in the same Beau-lovin' boat."

"Except you had sex with him."

Jenna cleared her throat. "True, but it will only make his leaving that much harder."

It took a while for Starlet to mull this over, and while she did, Jenna studied the busting seams of her teal prom dress. Why would a college-aged woman wear ugly prom dresses every day? Of course, Jenna had known a girl in high school who wore leotards and tights every day to school. But Ester May had wanted to be a ballerina in a bad way, and her parents had flat refused to pay for ballet lessons when Ester was as clumsy—

Jenna looked up at Starlet's face. A beautiful face that some boys might overlook because of a little extra weight.

"I like your dress," Jenna said, startling Starlet out of her thoughts. "I always wanted to go to prom, but no one ever asked me."

Starlet's eyes widened. "They didn't? But you're skinny."

"And a little masculine and competitive," she said. "I think the boys were scared I'd whup their butts if they tried anything."

Starlet laughed, but her humor died quickly. She picked at a hangnail on her thumb. "I got asked to prom. Tommy Milner was the most popular boy in school. I should've known that he was just kidding. Of course, that's what I get for spending five months of my Putt-Putt salary on a dress and shoes."

"So he didn't show up?" Jenna asked, even though she knew the answer.

Starlet surprised her by shaking her head. "No, he showed up. He showed up at midnight with all his drunk friends. But he wasn't there to see me as much as my mama, who had stopped by my Auntie and Uncle Bernard's on her way through town." She smiled. "My mama has always been a favorite with the men. It runs in our blood, you know."

It was about the saddest story Jenna had ever heard, and if Tommy Milner had been there, she would've kicked his ass from one side of Texas to the other—along with Starlet's mama. Of course, now Jenna had a mama just like that.

"I'm sorry." Jenna reached out and took Starlet's hand. "But you can't let things that happen in the past dictate how you live your life. You're a beautiful woman with a kind heart. And one day, a really special man is going to realize that."

"But not Beau." Starlet smiled sadly.

Jenna felt as sad as Starlet looked. "No," she said, "not Beau."

Starlet nodded. "I guess I always knew it. I just have a hard time accepting things." She looked back at Jenna. "I lied before when I said Minnie wanted you out of Miss Hattie's room. I was the one who wanted you out—"

"Well, if it isn't two of my favorite girls." Beau walked in the door, carrying a tray that was piled high with food. Suddenly, Jenna was starving. She just didn't know if it was for the wonderful-smelling breakfast or the sexy-looking cowboy.

Flashing a smile at Starlet that turned her face crimson, Beau set the tray on the nightstand and leaned over to give Jenna a kiss. It was only a mere brush of lips, but it sent a tingle through her body that made her realize she was hungrier for the man than the food.

"Good mornin'," he said.

Jenna felt her face heat and knew she blushed as brightly as Starlet. "Good mornin'."

A door clicked closed, and they both glanced over to see that Starlet had left.

"I guess she's pretty hurt," Beau said as he walked to the door and locked it.

"I think she'll get over it." Jenna reached for a piece of bacon. "I tried to make her see that you're not a happily-ever-after kind of guy."

He hesitated on his way back to the bed, his hands hovering over the snaps of his shirt. For a second, she thought her words had hurt him, but then he tugged open his shirt and continued to the bed.

"I'm glad you realize that." He tossed the shirt in the corner and undid the button of his jeans, slowly sliding down the zipper and exposing a very hard...

Jenna's mouth went dry, and she had trouble swallowing down the bite of bacon she'd just taken. "What are you doing?"

He pushed down the jeans and stepped out of them before climbing in bed. He positioned himself behind her, his long legs spread on either side of her hips. Through the satin of the sheet she could feel every hardened inch of him pressing into her bottom. Leaning over her bare shoulder, he took a bite of the bacon she still held in her hand.

"Why, I'm eating breakfast, of course." He swallowed the bite before nibbling a heated path along her bare shoulder.

Jenna's eyes dropped closed, and the bacon fell forgotten to the floor.

Chapter Twenty-three

"...AND I'M THINKIN' I SHOULD head on out to Miss Hattie's and check it out for myself."

Marcy didn't usually pay any attention to what Kenny Gene said, but today she couldn't help but stop and pretend to look in the window of Duds 'N Such so she could listen in on his and Rye Pickett's conversation.

"But I thought you said that Twyla would have a fit if you went out to the henhouse," Rye said.

"But this is bid-ness," Kenny said. "It's my professional duty as an officer of the law to make sure nothin' shady's goin' on."

"But I thought Sheriff Winslow took away your deputy duties after you gave a ticket to his wife, Myra, for failing to signal on a turn," Rye said. "Besides, even if you were a deputy, Miss Hattie's ain't even in your jurisdiction. And I wouldn't want to mess with Sheriff Hicks. I hear he carries a gun with real bullets."

"Well, he ain't gonna shoot one of his law enforcement buddies," Kenny huffed. "And no matter what Sheriff Winslow says, eventually, I'm going to be a dep-u-tee. In fact, exposin' what's goin' on at Miss Hattie's just might be my ticket in."

If it had been anyone but Kenny Gene talking, Marcy might've been worried. But Kenny couldn't expose a Popsicle from a paper wrapper. Still, it angered her to find out that Beau had been right. Sean had told people about her proposition. And she didn't know if she was more angry or hurt. For some reason, she thought that he would keep things between the two of them. She should've known better. Men had never kept secrets about Marcy.

Another woman might've slunk down the street and hoped they didn't see her. That wasn't Marcy's style. Adjusting her bra, she walked straight toward them. Kenny was so engrossed in talking about the henhouse that he almost didn't notice her.

"Besides," he said, "I got a good excuse for being out at the henhouse. I need to take Beau his backpack that he dropped the night we shanghaied him—Well, hey, Marcy! You still helpin' out at the library?"

She wasn't. Which was something else she held against Sean Robbins. If he hadn't turned it into charity, she would still be able to work there. But she had never taken handouts from the town, and she never would.

"No," she said with a smile and a wink, "you boys should know that I have better things to do with my time." Obviously, Rye and Kenny hadn't heard about her working at Miss Hattie's because they both looked confused.

"You takin' that ceramics class that Darla's teachin'?" Kenny asked. "I hear tell that for twenty-two dollars you'll end up with an entire nativity scene, includin' a pig and an extra baby Jesus just like our live nativity a couple years back."

Marcy remembered the live nativity scene. It was the same night that she locked her sister, Samantha, and Ethan in Lowell's barn together. Now they were happily married with a farm to take care of, a new veterinarian business, and a baby on the way. Which was the main reason Marcy hadn't asked for their help with her financial problem. They had enough to worry about.

Although Sam would be devastated if she ever found out—and if she ever discovered what Marcy was willing to do for the money. She swallowed. Well, that was just something Sam would have to live with. It shouldn't be too hard considering Marcy's history.

"See you later, boys," she said and continued down the street toward the bank.

The inside of The Bank of Bramble was cold compared to the heat of the afternoon. Rubbing her bare arms, Marcy walked over and stood in line behind Wilma Tate, who was wearing a hat with a pathetic-looking bird perched on top. She was leaning so far over the counter that the bird looked like it was pecking her forehead.

"...I'll tell you one thing," she said to the teller, Ruby Lee. "If the good folks of Bramble aren't going to do something about that den of iniquity, I will. The Reverend Jessup says that this country will end up in the hands of heathens if us god-fearing folks don't stand up for what is right."

Ruby Lee counted out Wilma's money. "Isn't Reverend Jessup that television evangelist that swindled those old folks out of their retirement?"

"There was no swindlin' involved," Wilma said. "Reverend Jessup explained everything on a two-hour special—" She glanced behind her, and when she saw Marcy, her mouth puckered up. Marcy steeled herself. If anyone had heard about her working at Miss Hattie's, it would be the biggest gossip in Bramble.

But instead of laying her low with snide comments, she only nodded her bird. "Hello, Marcy. I heard you were back in town."

"Hello, Mrs. Tate," Marcy said. "Your ears didn't deceive you."

The woman snorted before she took her money and left. Marcy waited for the door to close behind her, then stepped up to the counter. "I need a money order, please."

She pulled out the envelope of cash. The money had been a welcome surprise. Minnie had called her into the library just that morning and given it to her, saying it was advance payment from a client. Not wanting to think about what she would have to do for the money, Marcy quickly handed it over to Ruby Lee.

No more than five minutes later, Marcy left the bank and headed for the post office. Too bad she had to go past the First Baptist Church on her way. As she walked beneath the stone steeple with its sky-high cross, she kept her eyes pinned to the sidewalk in front of her. But that didn't keep her stomach from knotting or her throat from feeling all choked up. And it didn't keep the images from popping in her head. Images of Sean standing in the sunlight that streamed in through the lacy curtains. His gaze as it ran over her body. His kiss that had completely disarmed her.

He had desired her. She had been around enough men to know desire when she saw it. But desire was just a product of physical attraction. It meant nothing. She meant nothing. At least, not to Sean. As much as his body wanted her, his mind was only interested in her as a project. As a charity case that needed tending to.

Marcy stiffened her spine. Well, she wasn't a charity case. She was who she was, and no preacher man could change that. She was so wrapped up in getting by the church without passing out that she ran smack dab into Johnny Reardon. His beefy arms came around her waist, knocking her purse from her arm and lifting her clear off her heels.

"Well, if it ain't Miss Marcy Henderson," he drawled. "I waited at Bootlegger's for you most of the night and you never showed up. And if I hadn't wasted my time on you, some other gal could've been gettin' some Johnny-cakes. Now I figure you owe me."

"Put me down." She squirmed to get out of his arms, but he only tightened his grip.

He lowered his gaze to her cleavage that pressed against his chest. "You look like you've gotten a little bigger since—"

His words cut off as an arm clamped around Johnny's neck. An arm partially covered in bright yellow material with hula dancers on it.

"Let her go," Sean said in a commanding voice that had no doubt scared more than a few sinners into repenting. Marcy wasn't scared. She was confused. No one had ever come to her rescue before. Probably because no one ever thought she needed rescuing.

Not even Marcy.

Johnny released Marcy and held up his hands. "Okay, Preach," he spoke in a tight voice. "Me and Marcy were just havin' ourselves a little fun. But if it offends you, we'll find somewhere more private to do—" His face turned a deeper red, and he clawed at the arm around his neck.

"I might not know a lot about the Bible," Marcy said, "but doesn't it say somewhere that you shouldn't kill folks?"

Sean seemed to snap out of whatever daze he was in, and he released Johnny.

Johnny gasped for air and glared at Sean. "I-If you w-weren't a preacher..."

Marcy laughed. "Go on home, Johnny Reardon. You might be as big as a barn, but you've never been able to fight your way out of a paper bag. And everyone in town knows it."

Johnny rubbed his neck. "You sure got uppity since leavin' town, Marcy." He turned and headed down the street.

Once he was gone, Sean's gaze ran over her from the top of her head to the tips of her high heels.

"Are you okay?" he asked.

"I'd be better if you hadn't told the entire town about what happened at Miss Hattie's." She bent down to pick up her purse, wanting to get out of there as quickly as possible.

Sean squatted down next to her, reaching for the items that had fallen out of her purse. "I may have called Sheriff Hicks, but I never used your name, Marcy. And I never will. What happened at Miss Hattie's will remain between us. But that doesn't mean I'm going to stop trying to save you from the spell Minnie has weaved."

Marcy stared at him. "You just don't get it, do you? Minnie didn't corrupt me, Sean. I was cast in my role long before I ever met her." She smiled. "Just like you were cast in yours. And nothing will change that. So stop trying to save me and accept the fact that I'm evil and you're good. And both are needed to make this little planet of ours go round and round."

She jerked her wallet from his hand, not realizing that the money order was beneath it. Sean glanced down at it, and his brow knotted before she grabbed it and stuffed it back in her purse.

As Marcy turned and walked away, part of her longed for him to stop her while the other part knew that he couldn't. If God had a sense of humor, she figured that He was probably laughing His butt off about now.

It seemed that the biggest slut in Bramble had gone and fallen in love with one of His angels.

Sean started to go after her, but something stopped him. Maybe it was the pain in her eyes. Or maybe it was the deep-down knowledge that she was right. They were two different people, with two different paths. He couldn't save her. Only God could do that. All he could do was pray for her.

He turned and headed back to the church. Inside, Mr. Sims was working on the squeak in the door.

"Almost got it fixed," he said.

Sean nodded. "Thank you. I'm sure Danny Bailey will be happy that he can sneak out during Sunday school and no one will be the wiser."

Mr. Sims laughed. "The mail came while you were gone, and I told Tom to put it on your desk."

Sean walked into his office and shut the door. Once seated in his chair, he looked through the mail. A letter caught his eye, and he quickly ripped the envelope open. When he was finished reading through it, he eased back in his chair. It seemed that God had given him his wish. The

California congregation he had applied to had accepted him. He expected to feel nothing but joy. God had given him what he had been praying for. But he didn't feel joyful. He just felt...empty. Like he had unwrapped a box with nothing in it.

"Forgive me, Father, for my ungratefulness," he whispered as he started to bow his head in prayer. A flash had him glancing at his desktop computer. The screen displayed the schedule of hospital visits he needed to make over the next couple weeks. Since he had been sitting back in the chair and hadn't touched his mouse, he wondered how the screen had switched from his screen saver. Wanting to check to see if his computer was broken, he leaned up to click to another page when the name of a hospital caught his attention.

And not a hospital but a rehabilitation facility.

The same rehabilitation facility that had been on the money order that had fallen out of Marcy's purse.

It took a moment for him to remember who had given him the name. Then he tried to remember the conversation he'd had with Marcy's sister, Samantha. Sam had mentioned something about how fortunate they were that Medicaid had paid for the facility for her mother since it was one of the most sought after ones in the country and normally cost thousands of dollars—

The truth hit him like a lightning bolt from heaven.

Marcy.

An angel of mercy disguised in a harlot's body.

Chapter Twenty-four

"YOU SHOULD BE ASHAMED OF YOURSELF, Beauregard Cates," Minnie huffed as Beau pushed her through the corridor of the cancer center in Houston. "Forcin' an old woman to do something against her will. And you," she shot a mean look over at Brant, who was walking right next to Beau, "should be home with your son and wife. Not flyin' that helicopter of yours out to help your little brother with his sinister plot."

"You're lucky that Bobby has a cold and Elizabeth had to stay home," Brant said, "or you'd be getting your butt chewed out about now. What were you thinking not telling us about your cancer?"

"I was thinkin' that it's my body and my life," she snapped. "Obviously, I was wrong."

As worried as he was about Minnie, Beau couldn't help smiling at the woman's feistiness. "Calm down, Minnie," he said. "We're not forcing you to get surgery. We're merely having you talk to a specialist so you can get all the facts before you make your decision."

"I have all the facts," she blustered. "You Cates boys

are nothin' but a bunch of control-freak cowboys who expect all women to do your biddin'."

Beau shot a glance over at Brant. Brant was the somber one of the family, the brother who was all business and rarely smiled. But he flashed a smile now as they answered in unison.

"Pretty much."

Minnie continued to fuss all the way through the hospital corridors. She didn't shut up until they entered Dr. Flanders's office. Then the darn ornery woman refused to speak at all. Beau knew how she felt. Dr. Flanders had been his oncologist, and there was a moment when he first entered the room that he was struck speechless. Fortunately, the feeling left once the doctor started talking about Minnie.

The doctor was optimistic. Since Minnie went for regular mammograms, the cancer had been caught early. And with surgery and treatment, he felt like the odds were in her favor—even with her advanced age.

Although Minnie stared at a spot over his head, the doctor spoke directly to her, occasionally reaching out to pat her hand that rested on the arm of the hospital wheelchair. Beau couldn't remember Dr. Flanders patting his hand, but he did remember his soothing voice and caring demeanor. And Beau suddenly felt guilty for never thanking the doctor. Especially for being so kind to him when he'd been one pain-in-the ass patient.

In Minnie's belligerent face, Beau saw a reflection of himself. It was so much easier to hide your fear behind anger.

Beau reached out and took Minnie's hand, and the doctor smiled as he continued. When he was finished outlining what he would suggest for treatment, he sat back in his chair.

"Of course, the decision is all up to you, Miss Ladue."

Minnie finally looked at the doctor. "I'm not gonna let no wet-behind-the-ears surgeon cut on me." She pulled her hand from Beau's and wheeled her chair back. "And I figure I'm done listenin'."

Dr. Flanders got to his feet and nodded. "Very well, but I was wondering if I might ask you a question before you go, Miss Ladue. Do you remember my grandfather, Colonel Barnes? He spoke about the henhouse often before he passed away—especially a Miss Millicent Ladue who helped him out of his depression when he returned from fighting in Europe during World War II."

Minnie stopped in the middle of turning her wheelchair around. "You're Lester's grandson?"

"Yes, ma'am."

Minnie wheeled back toward the doctor. "Well, why didn't you say so in the first place? So about this surgery, would you take one boob, or two? And can I get me some of those fake ones like the movie stars have? I'm thinkin' Raquel Welch. She looks damned good for her age."

Dr. Flanders laughed. "I'll see what I can do."

A gleam came into Minnie's eyes, and Beau figured the decision had been made.

Once they had scheduled the surgery, they wheeled Minnie down to another floor for some tests. Since Brant and Beau weren't allowed in the room with Minnie, they were shown to a waiting room.

"She is an ornery old cuss," Brant said as he took a chair. He smoothed out the brim of his cowboy hat before resting it on the table next to him. "One I want to keep around for a while."

"Me too." Beau walked over to the magazine table and picked one up. He barely glanced at it before he tossed it back down and moved to the window. He hated hospitals. Hated the expired magazines. Hated the smell. And hated waiting around for news that never turned out to be good.

"You okay?" Brant asked as if reading his mind.

Beau continued to look out the window. "Yeah, I guess I'm just a little scared—or more like scared shitless." He turned around and looked at his brother, who was watching him with their mother's piercing blue eyes. The same color eyes Beau had. "Is this similar to the hell you've been going through since I left?"

When Brant didn't say anything, Beau turned back to the window and ran a hand through his hair. "I'm sorry, Brant. I had no idea what I was asking of you." He released a breath. "No, that's not right. It wasn't that I didn't know. I just didn't care. I was too wrapped up in my own fears and selfish desires to worry about other people. Even the people I love most in the world."

A hand settled on his shoulder.

"After what you'd been through, you had the right to be a little selfish," Brant said.

Beau turned and looked at him. "No one has that kind of right. You and our entire family stood beside me through all this." He waved his hand around. "And I repaid you by running off like a coward with my tail between my legs."

"You're young, Beau," Brant said.

"I am a selfish bastard, Brant. I've been home twice in the last two years, and both times, I left after only a few days. And do you want to know why? Because I was so jealous of what you and Billy have that I couldn't stand to be in the same state with you."

Beau didn't know what he expected from his big brother, but it certainly wasn't a smile. A smile that rivaled any Beau had ever flashed.

"And just what are you grinning about?" Beau asked, suddenly annoyed.

"Because I think my little brother has finally grown up." He thumped Beau twice on the back. "And I'd say it's about time. So when are we going to set up the tests for you?"

Beau took a deep breath and released it. "I figured I'd do it after we get Minnie squared away."

"Like hell." Brant strutted over to the table and picked up his hat. "We're here today so we might as well kill two birds with one stone—no offense."

Beau laughed. "None taken, but just how are you going to get me in without an appointment?"

He smiled slyly. "The same way I got Minnie in so quickly. I'll just mention a certain wing C-Corp helped build." Reaching in his shirt pocket, he pulled out his cell phone and tossed it to Beau. "I called Elizabeth when you and the nurse were getting Minnie into the x-ray room, but while I'm browbeating Doc Flanders, why don't you call the hens and let them know that everything is okay. They looked terrified when you carried a ranting Minnie out of the house this morning. All except for the new girl." Brant's eyes narrowed. "What did you say her name was? Jennifer Jane?"

"Jenna Jay," Beau said. Just the name made him smile.

His smile had Brant lifting an eyebrow. "Do we need to have that talk about bosses fraternizing with employees?"

"Jenna isn't an employee." At least, Minnie hadn't hired her. But that hadn't stopped Jenna from helping out with all the work around the place. She wasn't much of a cook or maid, but she was great at customer service. If a guest had a problem, Jenna was more than happy to help.

Especially if she had to go up against management.

"Then who is she?" Brant asked.

It was a good question. One he didn't have an answer for. If Brant had asked the question two days earlier, Beau would've said that they were just friends. But after spending the last couple nights with her, friendship didn't even come close to describing their relationship. Not only because of the phenomenal sex, but also because of the way Jenna made him feel. Like anything was possible.

The thought made him realize that Minnie's condition wasn't the only reason he was willing to face the return of his cancer. Jenna was also responsible. Most women would be devastated after finding out that they were adopted. Jenna had embraced it and was making the best of the situation. Her determination was not just admirable. It was inspirational.

"She's my life coach," Beau said with a grin.

Brant shook his head before he turned and walked out of the room.

The henhouse phone only rang a few times before it was answered, and Beau wasn't surprised to hear Jenna's voice. He *was* surprised by the way his heart thumped in overtime.

"Miss Hattie's Henhouse. Hen Jenna Jay speakin'. How can I help yew?"

"Well, that depends," he said. "Just what does Hen Jenna Jay have to offer?"

There was a pause before she spoke. "We offer all kinds of things here at the henhouse. Was there somethin' you had in mind, sir?"

"Oh, sweetheart, there's plenty I have in mind," he said. "But I think tonight we'll try out the handcuffs and some of those antique sex toys." He could almost envision her rolling her eyes.

"Really? Well, that sounds like fun. And I promise to go easy on you."

Just like that the tension of the morning was gone, and Beau laughed. "You just can't resist being in charge, can you?"

When she spoke, her voice was barely above a whisper. "You didn't seem to mind last night."

Beau closed his eyes and visualized Jenna straddling him. Nope, he hadn't minded at all.

"So how is Minnie?" she asked.

"I think she's going to go through with the surgery."

"Good, I've been looking up breast cancer online and there's an entire support group of women over sixty-five who have undergone the surgery. I got all the information just in case Minnie wants to contact them."

Beau's smile got even bigger. It was so like her to want to champion the underdogs of the world. "So did you get a chance to call your mama and ask her about Olive?"

"No," she said, "I haven't yet decided if I'm going to tell her that I know. It would only hurt her. And you're right; it doesn't change who I am. Although I do plan on meeting my biological mother."

"You got Minnie to tell you who she is?"

"No. When I showed her the picture, she said I had it all wrong. Of course, she refused to go into detail. She wouldn't even tell me the woman's name. Fortunately, Sunshine didn't have any problem giving it to me. Olive Washburn."

"Washburn? That's almost as bad as Scroggs."

"And just what's wrong with Scroggs?"

"Not a thing," he quickly replied. "So how are you going to find this woman?"

"I just got finished calling Dusty to see if he could find an address for me. Hopefully, he'll have it tomorrow when I meet him for breakfast."

A feeling settled in Beau's stomach. A feeling that had his eyes narrowing and his fists clenching. "Dusty as in Sheriff Hicks?"

"The same," she said. "He wasn't real thrilled about doing it, so it might take a little sweet-talking to get it out of him."

It took everything inside Beau not to push a hole in the waiting room wall. "Firstly, you're not going to breakfast with Sheriff Hicks. And secondly, you're sure as hell not going to sweet-talk him out of anything. You want an address. I'll get you an address."

There was a long pause, and for some reason, Beau thought he heard a giggle.

"Firstly," she said with a definite smile in her voice, "who are you to tell me who I can have breakfast with? And secondly, are you jealous?"

Beau flopped down in a chair and rubbed a hand over his face. Was he jealous? Damn straight, he was jealous. Unfortunately, he didn't have the right to be. Not when his life could easily come tumbling down like a house of cards with just one x-ray. And Jenna didn't deserve to be caught beneath the pile.

Still, he couldn't quite hand her over to Dusty either.

"I was just thinking about Sheriff Hicks, is all," he lied. "You can't expect the man to jeopardize his job for you. I'll be more than happy to get you an address. And we can discuss it over dinner tonight."

"You are jealous." She sounded pretty happy about it. Or just gloating. "And stop being stupid. Dusty is only a friend, and he can get the information a lot easier than you can." She paused. "And yes, I'll have dinner with you tonight. Just like I had dinner with you last night and the night before last. I like having dinner with you."

Her words completely snuffed out his anger and replaced it with a feeling of contentment that Beau hadn't felt in a long time. The feeling concerned him almost as much as his jealousy. Now would be the time to slow things down. To offer up some witty joke or casual comment.

Too bad he wasn't feeling witty or casual.

"I like having dinner with you too, Jenna," he said.

"Are you sure it's the dinner you like or what we do afterwards?"

"Both," he answered truthfully. Sharing a meal with Jenna was almost as much fun as sharing a bed.

"Speaking of afterwards," she said, "Miss Hattie's room is booked this weekend, along with every other room at the henhouse. So unless we want to sleep in the barn, I guess we'll be spending Memorial Day weekend in Bramble."

"Are you inviting me home with you, Miss Scroggs?"

"It would appear that way, Mr. Cates. Although I probably should have my head examined."

Beau smiled. "I don't know about your head, but I'll be happy to examine the rest of your body."

"I'll look forward to it," she said. "Now go take care of Minnie and quit bugging me."

"Good-bye, Blondie."

"Good-bye, Cowboy."

Chapter Twenty-five

THERE WAS NOTHING LIKE MEMORIAL Day weekend in Bramble. It was the official start of summer, and all the townsfolk were in a festive mood. Children sat on street corners and sucked on melting Popsicles, or raced through Confederate Park with squirt guns blasting streams of water. Their parents loaded up on hot dogs and watermelon at the Fresh Mart for their backyard barbeques or weekend camping trips. And the old folks sat on the benches that lined Main Street, gossiping about how hot the summer would get and if there would be rain.

Jenna Jay hesitated on the corner, right beneath the huge flapping flag of the post office, and couldn't quite contain the bubble of happiness that welled up inside her.

Of course, it wasn't just the sight of the townsfolk enjoying a holiday weekend that had her feeling like she wanted to skip down the street, singing "Zip-A-Dee-Doo-Dah." The steamy hot cowboy she'd left sleeping in her bed probably had something to do with it.

She still wasn't sure why she had invited Beau to her house. It would've been easier to leave him at Miss

Hattie's—a clean break, so to speak. Except Jenna wasn't ready to say good-bye. To Beau. The hens. Or Bramble. And standing on the corner, a corner that she had passed thousands of times in her life, she worried that she might not ever be ready.

Which was crazy. Even without Davy, she had a life back in New York. She had a job and friends and causes to champion. Yes, her family was here. And in the last few days, she'd come to realize just how much family meant. But she could be part of their lives without moving back. Just like she would continue her relationship with the hens. And who knew, maybe she would even keep in touch with Beau.

As soon as the thought popped into her head, she realized it wouldn't work. Whatever they had was only for now. Once they went their separate ways, she would never see him again. Never experience the brilliance of his smile. Or the heat of his touch. Or the sweetness of his kisses.

For a moment, she thought about forgetting all about breakfast with Dusty and racing back to the warmth of Beau's arms. But then sanity returned, and she headed down the street toward Josephine's Diner. She had just passed Sutter's Pharmacy and Moses Tate snoozing on the bench when she saw Dusty. He was standing beneath the maple tree in front of the town hall, talking to Sheriff Winslow.

The sight of him had her feeling anxious. Did she really want to know about her mother? No, not her mother. Olive Washburn. Her mother would always be Jenna Scroggs. The woman who had changed her diapers, made her chicken noodle soup when she had a cold, and washed her volleyball uniform before every game. Olive Washburn was just the woman who gave birth to her. A woman she couldn't ignore, but who would never be more than just a gene pool.

"Hey, Jenna Jay," Sheriff Winslow greeted her as she walked up.

"So what are you two crime fighters talking about?" she said. "Are you planning a stakeout to catch those rascally criminals who will be setting off illegal fireworks this summer?"

Dusty only grinned at her little joke, but Sheriff Winslow latched onto it like a trout to a worm.

"That ain't a bad idea, Jenna Jay. I could set up a sting operation—"

"I think that might be biting off more than we can chew, Sam," Dusty cut him off. "Especially when every man in Texas considers himself a pyrotechnic professional."

Sheriff Winslow glanced around. "Well, you might have a point there. Just between us, I can't help but buy me some of them Roman candles. It just wouldn't be a holiday without those fiery colored balls."

There was a slight twitch at the corner of Dusty's mouth. "I won't tell a soul, Sam." He looked over at Jenna, and she could see her reflection in the mirrored lens of his sunglasses. "We were just talking about the henhouse. Sam says he's gotten some more complaints."

"Pastor Robbins again?" she asked.

Sheriff Winslow shook his head. "No. In fact, I haven't heard another word about Miss Hattie's from the pastor. This time, it was Wilma Tate who called me. She was in a tizzy about me allowin' a house of ill repute to start up in Bramble's backyard. Myra says she wrote some letter to that crazy television evangelist and has gotten the Ladies, Club all up in arms. And those women can be pretty cantankerous if they set their minds to it. Especially if they think their men are going to be lured away by a bunch of painted ladies."

"But that's ridiculous," Jenna said. "The henhouse is just a bed and breakfast. And if you were to go out there, you would see for yourself."

Sheriff Winslow's eyes widened. "Uh, I'll have to leave that to young Dusty, here. Myra ain't gonna like me goin' out to Miss Hattie's—whorehouse or not."

"I'll take care of Miss Hattie's, Sam," Dusty said, "but I'd sure appreciate it if you'd try to squelch the gossip here."

Sheriff Winslow pulled off his hat and wiped an arm across his forehead. "That might be easier said than done. There's nothin' like a little gossip to take people's minds off the heat." He tugged his hat on. "Now I better get on back to the jail."

"You got yourself a prisoner?" Dusty asked.

"Nope, but occasionally Kenny Gene gets to foolin' around and locks himself in the jail cell. The time that Myra and I went to visit her folks in Big Springs, he was locked in there for two days before anyone noticed." He shook his head. "That boy has a good heart, but he's about three marbles short of a bag." His eyes lit up. "You wouldn't be needin' a deputy, now would you, Dusty?"

"Thanks, Sam, but I work better alone."

"That's what I was afraid of." Sheriff Winslow turned and headed down the street. Once he was out of hearing, Jenna looked at Dusty and teased.

"Now come on, Sheriff, I think a deputy is exactly what you need."

"Smartbutt doesn't suit you, Miss Scroggs." He swatted the brim of her cowboy hat before he started down the street toward Josephine's Diner. "Nor does investigation work. Just why did you want me to get you information on Olive Washburn? And don't give me that crap that she's your mama's long-lost childhood friend."

"So you found her?" Jenna stumbled, and Dusty reached out and took her elbow.

"Yes, I found her. And if Ms. Washburn really is your mama's childhood friend, it's best if she forgets about her."

She stopped and turned to him. "What do you mean, Dusty? What did you find out?"

He rested his hands on his hips and released his breath. "Olive Washburn has a criminal record that covers half of Texas. She has spent time in jail for prostitution, check forging, and armed robbery."

The cement beneath Jenna's boots seemed to shift, and she suddenly felt overwhelmingly hot and cold all at the same time. "So she's in jail?"

"No." Dusty looked out on the street. "But she should be. Some people are just dyed-in-the-wool criminals, and I'd say that Ms. Washburn is one of them." When Jenna swayed on her feet, he reached out and took her arm. "Are you okay, Jenna?"

"I'm okay," she said, even though she wasn't. The woman who gave birth to her, whose genes ran through Jenna's body, was a criminal.

"Did you find out where she lives?" she asked.

"If she hasn't broken probation, she lives in a trailer just outside of Odessa." He stepped closer and put his arm around her shoulders. "Come on. You look like you're about to drop. Let's get you inside where it's cool."

They had only taken two steps when Dusty suddenly stopped. Jenna glanced up to see Beau blocking their path. He looked like he had just rolled out of bed. His silver hair was mussed and his shirt wrinkled and unsnapped. There wasn't a twitch of a smile on his face.

Jenna should've been mad at the look he was giving Dusty—sort of like a junkyard dog protecting his lot. Or the way he didn't say a word but just pulled her out of Dusty's arms and into his. But instead of putting up a fight and calling him every kind of control freak, she did the strangest thing.

She pressed her face in the toasty warm spot where his shoulder met his neck and took a deep breath.

The trailer was more rundown than Shirlene Dalton's childhood home. Which was saying something. Shirlene had grown up dirt poor on the outskirts of Bramble. But at least Shirlene's trailer didn't look like it was about to collapse at any second. This one listed badly to one side, held up by the pathetic tree that grew in the corner of the lot.

Beau pushed back the weeds with the door of her daddy's pickup, climbed out, and then held it open for Jenna.

"Are you sure you want to do this?" he asked once she was standing so close she could see the tiny specks of gray in his eyes, eyes that were concerned and endearing. "I don't think this is going to turn out so good, Jenna."

"It's not something I want to do. It's something I need to do," she said. "In fact, why don't you stay out here? I just want to talk to her for a minute."

"Not damned likely." He shot her an annoyed look as he slammed the truck door. "I'm not letting you go inside that dilapidated thing alone."

"For a worldly playboy who claims he doesn't want to be tied down with one woman, you've sure gotten clingy." She picked her way through the weeds to the metal crate that served as a front step.

"Clingy? Who are you calling cling—"

"What the fuck do you want?"

They both looked up at the large woman who stood behind what was left of the screen door. Tattoos covered her beefy arms and huge saggy breasts overflowed the tight Spandex tank top. She had jowls similar to a bull-dog's and beady eyes like a rabid ferret. Eyes that stared back at them above a nose that looked as if it had been broken more than a few times. Her hair was platinum blond with a good three inches of darker roots.

Jenna stared at the woman in stunned disbelief. This couldn't be her mother. This woman looked nothing like the picture Jenna carried in her back pocket. This had to be someone else. Obviously, Dusty had made a mistake. She started to turn around with every intention of heading back to her daddy's truck when Beau stepped up and took her hand.

"We're looking for Olive Washburn," he said.

The woman's eyes turned even meaner. "And just who are you?"

Jenna stiffened her spine and spoke. "Jenna Jay Scroggs."

The meanness drained out of the woman's face, leaving her looking stunned and embarrassed. Her reactions confirmed Jenna's worst fears. This large, scary woman with knuckles the size of a pro boxer's was Olive Washburn—her mother.

"Well, I'll be damned," Olive breathed. She stood there for a few seconds staring at Jenna before she held open the screen door. "But I guess I should've figured it out. Your face is a carbon copy."

Jenna stared at Olive's leathery skin and heavy jowls and couldn't help but wonder if this was what she would look like when she got older. It was a terrifying thought, and it took a real effort to pin on a smile as she stepped up on the crate. She achieved the smile, but what she couldn't do was let go of Beau's hand. She tugged him right up with her and through the open door.

The inside of the trailer was worse than the outside. There weren't any weeds, but there were piles upon piles of all kinds of junk. Newspapers and magazines. Open bags of chips and boxes of snack crackers. And more cans of Diet Coke than Jenna had seen in her life.

Olive cleared a pile of clothing off the couch and dumped it on a birdcage with no bird. "Excuse the mess. Could I get y'all somethin' to drink—Snapple or a Diet Coke?"

"No, thank you—" Jenna started, but Beau cut her off.

"A Snapple would sure be appreciated, ma'am." Beau pulled Jenna down on the couch next to him, hooking an arm over her shoulder. "It's hotter than blue blazes out there."

"It ain't any cooler in here." Olive lifted her house-shoed foot to push a large, matted cat out from in front of the refrigerator. The cat hissed at her before streaking under the table. "But it's the best I could do given the fact that people ain't real keen on hirin' an ex-con." She walked back in with the Snapple and Diet Coke.

"So how is your mama doin'?" she asked as she handed Beau his drink. Jenna was kind of taken aback by the question. Taken aback and suddenly sympathetic toward a woman who realized she had no claim on motherhood.

"She's doing well," Jenna said. "They went to Charlotte for the NASCAR races."

"No kiddin'?" She flopped down in a recliner that leaned as badly as the trailer did. "Well, your mama always did know how to have a good time." She popped open the can of Coke and guzzled about half of it down before she looked back at Jenna. "Of course, she always kept it legal. Jenna is a good woman. Even when we was kids, she always followed the rules and never once let me talk her into doing anything wrong. Which was why I asked her..." She swallowed hard and couldn't seem to go on.

Her obvious emotion broke Jenna's heart right in two.

She released Beau's hand and leaned up to touch Olive's knee. "You don't have to say anything. I know all about it. That's why I'm here. I wanted to meet you and let you know that I don't hold anything against you. You did what you thought you had to do."

Olive looked confused for only a second before she nodded. "Well, that's real sweet of you. I can't tell you that I haven't thought about my little baby. 'Course, I never did regret it. Not once. I wasn't mother material. Not the kind of mother my baby deserved, anyway. I was pretty screwed up in my younger days. I might've pulled out of it if I had been smart enough to stay at the henhouse. Instead, I ran off with that no-account gee-tar man and got hooked up with drugs." She took a swig of her drink and burped. "Musicians are nothin' but trouble."

Beau chuckled as Olive leaned back in the recliner. The chair listed so far to one side that Jenna worried she might topple right out of it. "So how is my little Marcy, anyway? She still livin' in Bramble?"

Jenna blinked. "Marcy?"

Olive nodded. "Marcy after my grandma. Of course, I would've liked her last name to be Washburn instead of Henderson, but I guess that ain't how things work."

"Holy shit." Beau breathed the exact words Jenna was thinking. "Your daughter is Marcy Henderson?"

Olive sat up with a thump. "Of course. Who did you think it was?"

"Me," Jenna squeaked.

Olive stared at her for only a second before she tipped her head back and laughed. Laughed so hard that the entire chair shook.

"You scrawny little thing, my daughter?" she gasped. "Why, you don't have tits bigger than a kitten's."

Jenna could've ignored the insult if Beau hadn't joined in with the woman's laughter. She shot him an annoyed look, and he held up his hands.

"I've always had a thing for kittens."

Jenna turned back to Olive. "But what about the note you sent my mother asking her to take care of your baby?"

Olive wiped the laugh tears from the corners of her eyes. "I sent that to your mama after my cousin had agreed to adopt Marcy. I wanted someone else keepin' an eye on things for me. It was a good thing, too. Long after Evelyn stopped wanting anything to do with me, your mama kept sending me letters about how Marcy was doin'. About what a bright child she was—what a good and honest adult." She blinked rapidly and swiped at her eyes. "It does my heart good to know that something so wonderful came from something so bad."

Beau and Jenna exchanged looks. Good and honest weren't exactly words that popped into Jenna's head when she thought about Marcy, but maybe she just hadn't taken a close enough look. She did so now and realized that her mama hadn't been too far off the mark.

"Marcy is a good person," Jenna said. "I hear she spent the last couple years taking care of her mother who had a stroke. And now she volunteers at the library in Bramble and works real hard at a bed and breakfast."

Olive beamed with pride, showing off her missing teeth. "That's my girl."

Chapter Twenty-six

"THERE," MINNIE FINISHED TYING THE ribbon that held back Marcy's hair. "Remember to take it out slowly and then shake your head so your hair falls down around your shoulders all nice and pretty." She cackled her crazy laugh. "Although I don't think it's gonna take much more than you walkin' in the door to seduce your man."

Marcy wished she could be as happy about the planned seduction as Minnie. All she felt was cold and scared half out of her wits. Probably because Minnie had told her very little about the customer who had paid money in advance for Marcy's services.

"How long do I have to stay with him?" she asked, her voice sharper than she intended.

"Only as long as you want." Minnie smoothed back a wayward strand of hair. "This night is about your desires. Your wants and needs."

"And if I want to leave the moment I see him?"

Minnie studied her. "For some reason, I don't think that's going to happen. But if you should, that's your choice. I've never forced a hen to do something they didn't want to, and I never will. Now stand up and let me get a look at you."

Marcy waited for Minnie to back her wheelchair up before she pushed back the vanity chair and stood.

Minnie smiled her approval. "Just like I thought. Virginal white is your color."

Snorting, Marcy slapped at the full skirt of the beautiful white gown. "If he lives within fifty miles, he's not going to be fooled by this get-up. You should've let me wear my own clothes and makeup. At least then, he'd know what he was getting."

"I think he knows exactly what he's getting—a beautiful woman with a heart of gold." The sincerity of Minnie's words had Marcy looking away.

"Yeah, well, I always knew you were blind as a bat." She hesitated for only a moment before adding, "I was real sorry to hear about your cancer." She wondered where the tears came from that burned the back of her eyes. They seemed silly since she'd only known the woman for a couple weeks. She covered the uncharacteristic emotion with her normal belligerence. "I guess it's true what they say: Life is hell and then you die."

"Oh, Marcy," Minnie said, "whoever came up with that *was* as blind as a bat. Life isn't hell; it's a journey. A wonderful, breathtaking journey. Yes, there will be bumps along the way. And more than a few times, you'll find yourself down in a ditch that looks so deep you think you'll never get out. Some folks like to stay in the ditch. They like to moan and groan about how hard life is and blame all their troubles on other people. Little do they know that in the time they spent complainin' they could have been out of the ditch and standing on top of the mountain."

She reached out and took Marcy's hand. "All of us have made mistakes in our lives. All of us have been so angry at what life dealt us that we do things we regret. But that's the wonderful thing about livin'—a mistake you make one second will be in the past the next." Her direct eyes seemed to drill straight through Marcy. "It's this second you have to worry about. This second you need to make the right decision."

"And what if I've been making the wrong decisions for so long that I don't know what the right ones are?" she said.

Minnie squeezed her hand. "You'll know in your heart. All you need to do is listen. Now dry those eyes and go make me and all the hens proud."

Not more than five minutes later, Marcy was standing outside the door to Miss Hattie's room. Her heart pounded like a bass drum, and her palm was slick with sweat when she reached for the pretty crystal doorknob. But before she turned it, she paused.

This second.

Minnie's words came back to her. Marcy only had this second to make the right decision. At one time, she had thought the right decision had been to do whatever she needed to do to get her mother well. And she still wanted to achieve that goal. But suddenly she realized that she couldn't do it by sacrificing herself. Suddenly, she realized that she wasn't expendable just because she'd made some mistakes in her life.

Marcy Henderson mattered. And because she mattered, she needed to make the right decision, not just for her mother, but also for herself.

Twisting the knob, she pulled open the door and

stepped inside. The room was dimly lit. The only light came from pillar candles on the dresser and long tapered candles on the white-clothed table that had been set up in front of the fireplace.

A man stood at the window with his back to Marcy. Unlike the other day, she recognized him immediately. But this time, she wasn't nearly as happy to see him.

"So you finally decided to take me up on my offer?" she said as she closed the door behind her.

Sean turned. Gone were the tropical shirt and baggy shorts. Tonight, he looked like the preacher he was, in black pants and a dress shirt. He looked nervous, his eyes uncertain and wary. Marcy didn't feel nervous. Just sad. She tried to cover it with attitude, but her attitude deserted her.

"So how much did you pay for all this?" she waved a hand around. "Miss Hattie's room doesn't come cheap." She spread out the skirt of her dress before glancing over at the covered dishes on the table. "Especially with add-ons."

He watched her, much as he had done the other day. But this time, his eyes didn't devour her. Instead, they rested on her as if she was some vision he couldn't quite believe.

"You look beautiful," he said.

She ignored the leap of her heart. "It's not really my style." She moved over to the table. "Minnie seems bent on portraying me as the sacrificial virgin."

"And aren't you?" Sean stepped closer, bringing with him the scent of sunshine that always followed him.

For a brief second, her hand halted in midair before she reached down and lifted one of the silver-domed lids.

Marcy stared at the food artfully arranged on the pretty china, but she was too consumed with the man who moved up behind her to know what she was looking at.

"Only an idiot would think that," she whispered.

"No, only an idiot would think that you needed saving." He touched her arm, but she refused to turn around. His hand dropped back to his side. "I'm sorry for making that mistake. I guess I was so blinded by gossip that I couldn't see the truth." When she didn't say anything, he released his breath. "Would you please look at me, Marcy? I'm trying to apologize."

She turned, but refused to look him in the eyes. There was something about his eyes that made her forget who she was—who he was. "There's nothing to apologize for. I'm the one who made the mistake."

"And do you think it was a mistake?" His voice had a desperate edge to it.

Marcy lifted her gaze. "I can't be a prostitute, Sean. Not for you. Not for anyone."

He closed his eyes and tipped his face toward the ceiling, a slight smile curving the corners of his mouth. After a long moment, he opened his eyes and focused on Marcy. "I didn't invite you here to go to bed with me. I invited you here to give you this." He pulled an envelope out of his back pocket and handed it to her. It wasn't sealed, but she couldn't bring herself to open it.

"It's a check for thirty thousand dollars," he said, "made out to your mother's rehabilitation facility. I know it won't cover everything, but I figure it will last for a while."

"I won't take charity." She shoved the envelope back at him. "Or is this a bribe to keep me from telling people what happened between us? Sort of like thirty pieces of silver?"

"Damn it, woman!" He shook the envelope at her. "Would you quit being so pigheaded and accept some help?"

Marcy's eyes widened. "Did you just cuss?"

He looked at her with complete frustration. "Yes, I damn well cussed." Tossing the envelope on the table, he picked up the bottle of wine and took a long swallow before he wiped off his mouth with the back of his hand. "And I've been known to drink from time to time." He grabbed her around the waist and whirled her across the Oriental rug. "And I dance." He stopped suddenly. "And kiss pretty girls." He dipped his head and brushed his lips briefly across Marcy's. "Because as much as you think I'm some kind of an untouchable saint, Marcy, I'm a human being. A human being with needs and desires like any other human being."

His hands tightened on her waist. "What I'm trying to say is that we're not that different," he whispered in a voice so achingly sweet that tears gathered in her eyes. "We both feel pain." He took one of her hands and pressed it to his chest. "We both cry." He kissed the tear that trickled down her cheek. "And we both need love."

His lips moved over hers. She expected them to be as gentle as they'd been before. Instead, they were hot and demanding. He lifted her completely off her feet as he plundered her mouth. When he had kissed her senseless, he lifted his head.

"I'm a flesh and blood man, Marcy Henderson." He smiled, his eyes brimming with tears. "A flesh and blood man who has fallen head over heels in love with you."

For a moment, Marcy was too stunned to do anything

but stare back at him. All her life she had waited for someone to say those words to her, and she just couldn't quite believe her ears.

"You love me?" she said. "But you can't love me. Everyone knows that I'm the biggest—"

He placed a finger over her lips. "Heart in Bramble, Texas. It doesn't matter to me who you were. All that matters to me is who you are. And to me, you are the most beautiful woman I've ever met—inside and out."

"Oh, Sean!" She flung her arms around his neck, and they tumbled back to Miss Hattie's bed.

The desire they'd worked so hard to ignore came bubbling back to the surface, thick and rich and hot. One heated kiss turned into another as they learned the shape and feel of one another's bodies. When Marcy reached for the button on Sean's pants, he stopped her.

"You don't have a clue how much I want you, Miss Henderson," he panted out. "But as fleshly as I'm feeling right now, I think we need to wait."

"Why?" Marcy leaned up and smiled down on him. "I promise I'll still respect you in the morning."

He laughed, a deep, husky laugh that touched her heart and her very soul. "Well, I appreciate that. But as much as I want to make love to you, I have a responsibility to my congregation. And I can't very well tell them to wait until they're married if I can't."

Marcy's smile slipped. "Married? You want to marry me?"

"Did you think that I'd tell you I love you and not want to spend the rest of my life with you?"

"I-I didn't know." She sat up. "But Sean, you can't marry me. It could ruin your career here in Bramble."

"I've already been offered a position in California." He sat up next to her and took her hands. "We could move from Bramble and start fresh. No one in California would know anything about our pasts." He brought her fingers to his mouth and kissed each one. "Or we could stay right here in Bramble and see what happens." He lowered her hand, his expression solemn. "It won't be easy, Marcy. There will be gossip. And I'm afraid most of it will be centered on you. Because of that, I want you to make the decision."

Marcy was stunned. No man had ever asked her opinion, let alone let her make a decision on something this big. A part of her wanted to start fresh in another state that knew nothing about her. But there was another part, a part that she had just discovered, that wanted to see if she could continue to love herself without going anywhere.

It was that part that won out.

"Haven't you heard, Preacher Man? There's no place like home."

"Well?" Minnie asked as Starlet came back into the room. "What happened? Did the saint or the sinner win?"

"It was hard to hear in Miss Hattie's closet," Starlet said as she reached for one of Baby's chocolate chip cookies. "But I'd say that they both won. Although I don't think they'll be using the bed as you'd hoped. When I peeked out, it looked as if they were sitting cross-legged on the bed praying."

Minnie smiled. "And that's even better."

Chapter Twenty-seven

"WELL, WOULD YOU LOOK AT what the cat dragged in," Minnie greeted Jenna and Beau as they walked in the back door of Miss Hattie's. There was a knowing look on her face and a sparkle of happiness in her eyes. "So where have you two been keepin' yourselves?"

Tired of beating around the bush, Jenna cut straight to the chase. "We've been out to see Olive." She shot a glance over at Marcy, who was standing next to Baby at the counter, but Marcy didn't react to the name. She just kept peeling potatoes with her eyes glazed over and a smile pinned on her face.

But the name did get a reaction out of Minnie.

"Marcy," she said, "why don't you show Beau that leaky faucet in the Daring Delilah bathroom and see if he can't do something about it?"

While Marcy rinsed off her hands, Beau leaned in and whispered to Jenna, "Don't let the old gal get the best of you, Blondie." He tagged her on the butt before following Marcy out of the kitchen.

When they were gone, Baby glanced between Jenna

and Minnie, her eyes huge behind her thick glasses. "I think I'll just go get the toolbox." She set down her knife and scurried after Beau and Marcy, her high heels clicking on the linoleum.

Minnie continued playing the game of solitaire that was spread out on the kitchen table. "I figure you've got more than a few things on your mind."

That was an understatement. Ever since talking with Olive, Jenna's mind had felt like an overfilled shopping cart.

"Why did you lie to me?"

Minnie took her time answering, shifting a column of cards and moving a king to the empty slot. "Now, I don't know that I'd call it lying."

"What would you call it?" Jenna sat down in one of the kitchen chairs. "You let me go on believing that I was Olive Washburn's daughter and all along it was Marcy Henderson."

Minnie glanced over at the doorway. "Keep your voice down. I don't want Marcy overhearing you."

"Why not? I think she has a right to know who her mother is."

Minnie snorted. "You're all about what's right and what's wrong, aren't you, Jenna Jay? To you, black is black and white is white. But sometimes there are gray areas. Sometimes the right thing can mean doing something that someone else might think is wrong. For example, some folks might see keeping a secret as lying. I see it as letting things play out the way they should. Marcy Henderson doesn't need to know who her mama is. Not yet, anyway. Not when she's just started to acknowledge her own worth—her own value."

The truth dawned on Jenna, and she pointed a finger at Minnie. "Marcy was who you were talking to Moses about. You invited her to the henhouse, just like you did me."

"Not quite. You got an invitation. Marcy thought she was coming for a job. Although the job she had in mind wasn't exactly the job I had in mind."

Jenna sat back in the chair, her mind feverishly trying to fit everything together. It didn't take long. "So Marcy thought you hired her as a prostitute?" She stared at Minnie in disbelief. "And you let her go on believing that?"

"If I hadn't, she would've gone lookin' for another way to make money." Minnie set an eight of clubs on the nine of diamonds. "In order for me to help her, she needed to stay here." She hesitated with her hand over the cards. "I couldn't figure out a way to keep Olive here long enough to heal from her daddy's abuse. I wasn't about to make the same mistake with Marcy."

"Marcy was abused?"

"Not sexually like her mama, but neglect can be just as damaging," Minnie said. "Daughters will go to great lengths searching for 'daddy love.'"

"No wonder Pastor Robbins thought Miss Hattie's was back in business when Marcy propositioned him," Jenna said. "Marcy thought she *was* a prostitute."

Minnie grinned. "Talk about something wrong turnin' out right. I think that's going to be the best proposition the pastor has ever gotten. Marcy will make a fine pastor's wife."

The news shocked Jenna. "They're getting married?"

"I figure sooner, rather than later." Minnie flipped down another card and cackled. "I don't think the good pastor can hold out much longer." She glanced up. "So how are your weddin' plans coming?"

It took a moment to figure out what the woman was talking about. "There are no wedding plans. Davy has found someone else."

"That surprises me, seein' how he's called here at least fifty times in the last two days lookin' for you."

The information should have made Jenna feel something. Instead, she felt absolutely nothing. Not happy. Sad. Or even curious. While she tried to figure out her lack of emotion, Minnie collected the cards and slipped them back in the box.

"Now if this conversation is done, I think I'll take a little nap."

"Oh no," Jenna got up from the chair. "You haven't answered the most important question. Why did you send me the invitation in the first place when I'm not even a hen?"

Minnie looked up at her. "All women have a little hen in them. But you're right. You weren't chosen by accident. Moses Tate was worried about you being at odds with your folks, and I figured an invitation might get you home. 'Course, I didn't have a clue that the crazy townsfolk would take matters into their own hands."

"You could've explained that once I got here."

"I could have, but I wanted you to stay around a while." Minnie shot her a wide-eyed look. "To make up with your mama, of course. Speakin' of which, have you called her?"

Jenna hadn't tried to call her mother again. Her emotions had been too scrambled over Olive. And now, she wasn't sure what to say. Sorry just didn't seem like enough after a year of silence.

When Jenna didn't answer, Minnie pointed a finger at the doorway. "You can use the phone in the library. It doesn't matter who is right or who is wrong. Good mamas are hard to come by. Something you should've learned when you visited Olive."

Jenna had learned a lot of things from Olive, and one of them was how lucky she was to have a good mama. She'd also learned that crime doesn't pay and tattoos look much better on young, smooth skin than old and wrinkled.

"Olive might've been a good mother," Jenna said, "if she'd had the right kind of love as a child. In fact, I was going to ask you if you could give her another chance at being a hen. I think she's really trying to change her ways."

"No wonder people are so fond of you, Jenna Jay." Minnie smiled. "You are one softhearted woman. And I guess you're right; all hens deserve a second chance."

Jenna's mother picked up on the second ring. It took a while for Jenna to be able to speak. Just hearing her mama's voice caused a flood of emotion to well up in her chest and clog her throat.

"Hey, Mama," she whispered.

"Jenna Jay?" her mother said. "Is that you, honey? What's wrong? Did Delbert hit you? Because if he did—"

"No, Mama," Jenna smiled at her mother's feistiness. "Davy didn't hit me. And I'm fine. I'm just happy to hear your voice, is all. And I'm sorry that I ran off and haven't called."

"Ah, honey." Her mother started to cry. "I'm sorry, too, Jenna Jay. Your daddy and I should never have made you choose between your family and the man you love. That was just wrongheaded. If you want Delbert, we're one-hundred-percent behind you."

It wasn't hard to hear her daddy's voice bellowing in the background. "Speak for yourself, woman. I don't have a problem with tattoos, but those booby rings have got to go before I'm one hun-nerd percent. And tell that little girl of mine if she ever again pulls a stunt like runnin' off to some big city and not tellin' us where she is, I'm gonna whup her butt three shades of Sunday."

"Shush up, Burl," her mother said. "It's time to let bygones be bygones. In fact, I'm thinkin', that after the races, we should head on up to New York City and make up proper like."

Just the thought of her parents in New York City had Jenna smiling. "You won't have to go that far, Mama. I'm in Texas."

"You're in Bramble?" Her mother sounded like she was about to combust with happiness. "Well, why didn't you say so earlier? I'll just talk to your daddy and see if we can't drive home today. I'm sure your sisters will want to come, too. Of course, Dallas isn't with us. The danged college football coach of his is some kind of a slave driver and wouldn't let him take off weight-trainin'."

"That's okay, Mama. I don't want you cutting your vacation short for me. I plan on being here for a couple days, and there will be plenty of time to visit when you get back."

"Well, if you're sure, Jenna."

"I'm sure, Mama. I'll call you tomorrow." She paused. "I love you."

"I love you, too, Jennie Bean."

The nickname had Jenna Jay smiling as she walked

around the desk to hang up the phone. As she replaced the receiver in the cradle, she remembered what Minnie had said about Davy. Now would be a perfect time to call him and find out why he'd been trying to get a hold of her. But before she could lift the phone back up, the door opened and Beau walked in.

"I thought you were supposed to be working on a leaky faucet," she said.

"I think that was just a ploy to get me out of the room. The faucet works fine." He tossed his hat over to the couch. "So did you get all your questions answered?"

"I did."

"And are you satisfied?" He strode toward her. Or more like stalked. His eyes danced with a devilish light. Which made her wonder if he was talking about getting her questions answered by Minnie or something else. His next words proved that it was something else. "Because if you aren't, Miss Hattie's room is now vacant, and I was thinking that after our long, hot afternoon a bath would be just the thing..."

Beau pulled her into his arms and gave her a kiss that skillet-fried her brain.

And Jenna forgot all about phone calls.

Minnie listened at the door of the library and couldn't keep the grin from her face. Things were progressing much better than she had expected. Now that Beau had decided to face his cancer, she didn't think it would be long before he would accept his love for Jenna Jay.

And instead of planning one wedding, the hens would be planning two.

Humming a tune, she wheeled the chair around and

headed back to her bedroom. As she passed the kitchen, a flash caught her eye. She stopped and watched as a cowboy hat bobbed above the window.

By the time she got to the door and opened it, the cowboy was pressed against the side of the house, peeking into Sunshine and Starlet's room.

Pulling her derringer out of the side pocket of her wheelchair, Minnie pointed the small gun at the man's back. "The hens don't take kindly to peepin' toms. Leastways, not unless you've paid for the pleasure."

The cowboy whirled around. When he saw the gun pointed at him, the dark eyes beneath the brim of his hat widened. He looked familiar, but familiar or not, he had no business sneaking around the henhouse.

"Now if I was you," Minnie said with a wave of the gun, "I'd hightail it out of here. Especially since I'm the kind of woman who shoots first and asks questions later." She cocked the gun and that was all it took for the cowboy to take off like the hounds of hell were after him.

Cackling, Minnie put the gun away and was about to close the door when she noticed the black backpack sitting next to the house where the cowboy had been standing. It didn't take her long to reach it. Although it took a little more effort to pick it up. It almost weighed more than Minnie did.

Once it was on her lap, she unzipped it.

Her eyes widened.

It looked like the cowboy was willing to pay for a peek after all.

Chapter Twenty-eight

"So I GUESS THE TATTOOED rocker is history."

Jenna glanced over at Shirlene, who was stretched out on the chaise lounge next to her, sipping a virgin margarita. In her silver sparkly bikini, wide-brimmed hat, and designer sunglasses, Shirlene looked like a voluptuous movie star. Jenna, on the other hand, looked like a skinny boy in the tropical-print bikini she'd borrowed from Mia.

"What makes you say that?" Jenna took a sip of beer and gazed out at the swimming pool. Or not the swimming pool so much as the man in it, who was horsing around with Jesse.

"Maybe because you can't seem to keep your eyes off Beauregard," Shirlene said. "Although I must admit that the man has one fine-lookin' body."

Fine wasn't the word. Beau's body was more than just fine. It was danged breathtaking in the navy swim trunks he'd borrowed from Billy. He lifted Jesse up out of the water, and his biceps and abs flexed as he tossed the hollering boy into the deep end.

Shirlene lifted her sunglasses and looked toward the end of the pool. "'Course, mine is finer."

Jenna followed her gaze to the man in the crumpled straw cowboy hat who stood on the diving board. Billy jumped, and the board twanged and sent him up in the air where he tucked his knees to his muscular chest and executed a perfect cannonball. The loud splash had three-year-old Adeline squealing with delight as the wave sent her whale inner tube bobbing.

"So admit it." Shirlene's green eyes sparkled, and the smile she sent Jenna was smug and contagious. "Cowboys beat out rockers any day of the week."

Jenna laughed. "Fine, but don't tell Beau I said so. He already has an ego the size of Texas."

"Watch me, Mama!" Brody yelled in a deep voice Jenna couldn't believe belonged to a five-year-old. Just like his father, he strutted to the end of the diving board and jumped in. His splash was much smaller than Billy's, but when his head broke the surface, Shirlene and Jenna applauded loudly. Sherman was next on the board and beat out both Brody and Billy. Of course, the pig's orange life vest might've contributed to the wave that almost washed Adeline out of the pool.

Shirlene giggled and let her glasses drop over her eyes as she lay back on the chaise lounge. "Is this heaven, or what?"

Stretching out on her own chaise, Jenna had to once again agree with Shirlene. It did feel like heaven. She didn't know if it was the dry west Texas heat. Or the happy squeals of children at play. Or the deep laughter of Billy and Beau. But she felt more content than she'd felt in a long time. She felt at peace. Like she was right where she belonged.

Too bad Shirlene shattered that peace with her next question.

"So what is going on between you and Beau?"

It was a question that Jenna had been asking herself a lot lately. And she still didn't have an answer. She didn't know what was going on between her and Beau. All she knew was that, whatever it was, she liked it.

She liked falling asleep in his arms at night. And waking up to his smiles in the morning. She liked taking a bath with him in Miss Hattie's tub, or sharing a double-decker ice cream cone with him at the Dairy Treat, or watching a Texas Rangers baseball game snuggled against his side.

She opened her eyes. Beau was standing in the shallow end of the pool pushing Adeline in her whale. His gaze shifted over to her, and even from that distance, she could feel its intensity. Her heart did more than just skip a beat. It thumped so wildly that she wondered if it would jump right out of her chest. She tried to remember if she'd ever felt this way with Davy, but no memory came to mind. She had always been happy to see Davy, but never close to a heart attack.

"You love him."

Jenna's gaze snapped over to find Shirlene studying her. Her expression wasn't exactly happy. Of course, Jenna knew how she felt. Just hearing the words made her feel more than a little sick to her stomach. She took another swallow of beer, but the lukewarm liquid only made the feeling worse.

Figuring she knew what had caused Shirlene's sad expression, Jenna tried to ease her mind. "Don't worry. I knew from the beginning that Beau isn't the marrying kind. We're just having fun. In a few days, I'll go back to New York, and Beau will go back to his playboy lifestyle."

Shirlene rolled to her side and faced Jenna, the brim of her hat arching up like a bonnet. "And is that what you want to happen or is that what you think Beau wants?"

Jenna looked away. "It's what is going to happen, Shirl. Beau's not interested in anything long-term. He told me so himself."

"And maybe there's a reason he feels that way," Shirlene said. "Maybe he just needs the right woman to come along to prove him wrong." She reached out and took Jenna's hand. "But she would have to be a strong woman, Jenna. Someone who can help him face all the demons in his past and some that still might lurk in his future."

Jenna sat up. "What are you talking about, Shirl? What kind of demons does Beau have in his past?"

Shirlene ignored the question. "If you love him, tell him, Jenna. Your love just might bring Beau back—" She released a squeal as Billy's arm snaked around her waist.

No more than a second later, Jenna was being lifted off her chaise lounge. She didn't squeal. Her brother Dallas had done the same thing more times than she could count. So when Beau tried to toss her into the pool, she latched onto the waistband of his swimming trunks and pulled him right in after her.

Beau didn't seem to mind. Once they were both underwater, he turned into an octopus with more hands than Jenna could fight off. By the time she resurfaced, she'd been thoroughly violated.

"You perv!" She tried to kick away from him, but Beau only laughed and tightened his arms. She had just clamped her legs around his waist in a scissor hold when she noticed the gasping and splashing behind her. They both turned to see Shirlene floundering around in the center of the deep end with her floppy hat drooping over her face.

"You're doin' real good, Shirley Girl," Billy cheered her on from the side. "See, all you needed was a little push and you're swimming."

It didn't look like swimming to Jenna, especially when Shirlene didn't seem to be moving. She wasn't drowning exactly, but she sure wasn't swimming.

"I-I'm—going—to—kill—you," she sputtered as she flailed her arms.

Suddenly, Sherman appeared on the diving board. Like a pig on a mission, he sailed into the water right next to Shirlene. But instead of helping, he took her down with him. That set the Cates boys into action. Billy dove in, and Beau released Jenna and swam out. But before they could get there, Shirlene resurfaced like a Las Vegas aquatic show. Her red hair was pulled back from her beautiful face, her bodacious breasts were slick with water, and the sparkle in her bathing suit glittered in the bright overhead sun as she rose from the water astride the orange life-vested pig.

Billy popped up right next to her. After seeing that his wife was safe, he started laughing so hard that it got Jenna to laughing and the kids to shrieking. Shirlene didn't find it so amusing. Her eyes narrowed, and swimmer or not, she dove at her husband.

"You lowdown snake, Billy Cates! I could've drowned."

"Now, Honey Buns." Billy caught her fists and pulled her close. "I would never let that happen to my best girl. Didn't I save you once before from drownin'?"

Before Shirlene could do more than sputter, Brody pointed a finger at Sherman and yelled in his deep voice.

"Hey, look! Sherman's got him a hat."

Everyone turned to look at the pig. And sure enough, Sherman had on a hat. Just not Shirlene's. Instead, two tropical bikini cups curved over his pink ears, the white strings dangling in front of his beady eyes. Jenna recognized the bikini at the same time everyone else did. All eyes turned to her, and she did something she'd never done in her life.

She released a girlie squeal before she dove underwater.

Jenna's embarrassment lasted long after Shirlene had shooed the kids out of the pool and Billy had tossed her a towel. Probably because Jesse couldn't stop looking at her breasts, even after her bathing suit top was back on and covered by one of Billy's t-shirts. And the warning looks she sent him didn't seem to make one speck of difference to the pubescent kid.

"I got me a motorcycle," Jesse said around a big bite of hot dog. "It's a classic Harley. Colt Lomax restored it for me. You know Colt? He's the best motorcycle designer in the world. If you want, I could take you for a ride on it."

"Easy, sport." Beau pulled Jenna's chair away from the table. "This one's taken." He took her hand and pulled her to her feet. "Come on, Blondie, let's go look at the new filly Billy bought."

Once they were away from the house, Jenna turned on him. "I wasn't finished eating, you know."

He grinned. "You're never finished eating. Which is something I find very sexy."

"Sexy?"

"Very." Still retaining her hand, he pulled her inside the stables. Stables that were dark and empty.

"Where are the horses?"

Beau looked around. "They're probably just lying down."

She arched a brow at him. "Horses don't usually lie down, even when they're sleeping."

"No kidding." He tugged her to the end stall. "Then I guess they must be out in the corral. Why don't we wait for them in here where it's nice and cool?" He pushed open the stall door before he scooped her up in his arms and carried her inside. The stall smelled of fresh hay. Hay that had been piled high and covered with a patchwork quilt. Either Shirlene and Billy had a secret getaway or Beau had been a busy little camper while Jenna was putting away two hot dogs, a cheeseburger, and a pint of potato salad.

Since he liked food as much as she did, his effort made her a little more receptive to his plan. Or maybe what made her more receptive were his low-riding swim trunks and the bare skin peeping out of his unsnapped shirt. A shirt he stripped off as soon as he set her down on the quilt.

"I don't know if this is a good idea," she said, unable to keep her eyes off the fine array of muscles. "Not when Jesse is probably hot on our heels."

"Don't worry about the kids." He knelt next to her

and pulled the t-shirt over her head. "That's the one good thing about having brothers. They cover for you." He tossed the t-shirt into the corner and leaned back on his heels, his gaze greedily running over her. "Damn, you look good in a bathing suit." He lifted his hand and traced a finger along the edge of one cup, over her collarbone, and around to the back of her neck. With one tug, the top fell away from her breasts.

Her nipples were already tight from her damp suit. But beneath his hot gaze, they beaded even more. His hands lifted and cradled each one in a warm, firm grip.

"So pretty," he whispered before he dipped his head and captured a nipple. His mouth was much hotter than his hands, his tongue skilled as it teased and caressed.

Beau took his time, giving each breast equal attention. When her nipples were thoroughly wet and so tight it was almost painful, he tugged the bikini tie behind her back and eased her down to the quilt. He kissed his way down her stomach to the edge of her bathing suit bottoms, then slowly pulled the strings on either side.

His breath fell hot against her as he pushed the triangle of material away. She waited in anticipation for his touch. And when it didn't come, she glanced down. He was looking at her, just looking as if she was the most beautiful thing he'd ever seen.

Beau was the most beautiful thing she'd ever seen. His silver hair was messed. His jaw slightly stubbled. And his shoulders smooth and tanned.

His gaze lifted, his eyes locking with hers. But before she could identify the emotion that swirled in the sapphire depths, he lowered his lashes and his hands curved around her hips as he leaned down and kissed her.

The kiss started out light and gentle, but soon became deep and merciless. Beau's tongue and mouth took her hostage with rhythmic flicks that pulled her toward the crest and sinister sips that eased her back down. When he finally released her from the torture, her orgasm was so intense that she completely forgot where she was.

"Oh, Beau," she moaned out her orgasm. "Beau!"

"Shh," he hummed against her. With a gentle kiss, he brought her back to earth.

She opened her eyes to find him smiling down at her.

"I think next time I'm going to have to find a sound-proof room," he said. "You are quite the screamer, Jen."

She felt too happy to be mad over the remark, but that didn't mean she wasn't up for a little revenge. Using one of Dallas's wrestling moves, she quickly had him on his back. With a wicked smile, she peeled off his swimming trunks.

"We'll see who's the screamer."

It turned out that Beau wasn't as vocal as Jenna, but if his low moans were any indication, he enjoyed his oral sex as much as she had. Except he stopped her before he reached climax.

"Enough," he panted.

She moved up his body, kissing his belly button and then the tattoo on his chest. "Don't tell me you prefer hand jobs."

"No." He gave her a kiss that curled her toes before he reached over and pulled a condom out of his shirt pocket. Once he was suited up, he eased her down to the quilt and, with only a slight adjustment, slid deep inside. He paused for a moment, his eyes serious and intense. "When I finally reach nirvana, I want to be touching as much of your body as I can possibly touch."

An ache settled in Jenna's heart, and when Beau started to move, the stretch and pull of each stroke caused the ache to grow until it consumed her entire body. When she climaxed, it wasn't just physical. It was almost spiritual. Like she had moved into a higher realm. Three words popped into her head. Three words that pushed at the back of her throat like floodwaters against a dam. She was still struggling with them when Beau moved to his side and pulled her into his arms.

"Jenna." Her name floated from his lips in a way that made her happy and, at the same time, terrified. He swallowed hard, and she realized that he was as choked up as she was. "I've been thinking," he continued in a voice barely above a whisper. "No one can promise forever. All a man can do is take things one day at a time and hope that he can stay on this earth with the people he loves for as long as he can."

He reached down and tipped up her chin and smiled that wonderful smile that melted her heart. "And you, Blondie, are a person I—"

"Where the hell is he?" a deep voice boomed, causing Beau to drop his hand and sit up. He made a quick grab for Jenna's t-shirt and tossed it to her before he reached for his swim trunks. Jenna barely got her head through the neck as a feminine voice joined in.

"Watch your mouth, Brant," the woman scolded. "And I think we should've waited for Shirlene and Billy before we invaded their home."

"I'm not invading their home, Elizabeth," Brant said.

"Jesse let us in and sent us out here to look for Beau since Billy and Shirlene were busy putting Adeline down for a nap. Besides, I can't wait to give Beau the good news about his test results."

Beau froze in the middle of pulling up his trunks.

"News you shouldn't even have," Elizabeth said. "Beau's the patient, not you, Brant."

There was a masculine snort. "A patient who would've had to wait two more days if I hadn't bullied the damn doctor into giving them to me earlier. This way, he'll have two more days to enjoy the news that he's cancer free." He let out a whoop. "Did you hear that, Beauregard Cates? You're cancer free!"

Jenna's swimming suit bottoms slipped from her hands as she tried to comprehend what she had just heard. It didn't take long for the truth to sink in. Not after her conversation with Shirlene or the way Beau was watching her now—sort of like he was waiting for the bomb to drop. It landed with the impact of Hiroshima. She felt like she did the time she fell off the swing in her parents' backyard. All the air was forced from her lungs and, no matter how hard she tried, she couldn't seem to get it back.

The sound of approaching footsteps snapped her out of her daze, and she scrambled to her feet and quickly pulled on her bikini bottoms just as a black-haired man with eyes as blue as Beau's peeked in at them.

"There you are, Beauregard." His gaze swept over to Jenna, and his eyes widened. "I beg your pardon. I didn't realize Beau was with someone."

"Jenna Jay?" Ms. Murphy moved up next to the man, a cute little dark-haired boy straddling her hip. "Why, I didn't know that you and Beau were . . . friends."

It took everything Jenna had in her to keep the hurt and betrayal from turning her into a sobbing heap. With her head held high, she walked through the stall door Brant held open.

"Obviously, we're not."

Chapter Twenty-nine

BEAU PULLED BILLY'S MONSTER TRUCK into the dirt lot of Jenna Jay's parents' house and almost plowed into the compact car that hadn't been there that morning when he and Jenna had left to go to Billy's. And the car wasn't the only vehicle that hadn't been there that morning. There was now a red Cadillac and a couple of brand-new SUVs parked in the lot. It didn't take a brain surgeon to figure out whom the vehicles belonged to.

It looked as if Jenna's family was back from Charlotte, which was probably what Beau deserved for not going after Jenna right away. But he'd figured that she needed some time to cool off. And he'd needed some time to digest Brant's news. He hadn't been willing to believe it until Brant had popped the disk into Billy's computer and showed him the results of the scans.

Beau's cancer was still in remission.

In remission.

He had been so happy that he had danced around Billy's house, swinging Jesse around and then a giggling Brody. His celebration had been cut short when Billy and

Shirlene had come downstairs after putting baby Adeline to sleep. When Billy had discovered that his brothers had been keeping secrets about Beau's health, all hell had broken loose. The celebration quickly turned into a brotherly brawl that resulted in ripped shirts and numerous broken vases and lamps. Even Brant had hopped into the fray. The brawl ended when Shirlene brought in the garden hose and thoroughly doused all three Cates boys.

Staring at Jenna's house, Beau figured he was in for another fight. Jenna hadn't looked all that happy when she'd left the stables. Of course, his cancer had to be shocking news, and she wouldn't easily forgive him for not telling her about it sooner. But she would forgive him. She had to.

He opened the door of the truck and hopped down. He tried walking slowly and getting his thoughts collected before he knocked on the door, but he couldn't seem to harness the energy that flowed through him like an electrical current. He felt like a kid on the first day of summer vacation. Like a parolee on the other side of the steel bars. Like a man who had his entire life spread out before him.

He had tried to convince himself that he'd been living life to the fullest. But it turned out that, regardless of the wonderful things he'd experienced on his many travels, he hadn't been living at all. Not when death was his constant companion.

Suddenly, he realized that his life started now.

Right here.

With Jenna.

He jogged up the pathway that was lined with lawn ornaments and took the porch steps in one leap. The door was open, and he could hear laughter and conversation coming through the screen door as he pressed the door-bell. After what seemed like forever, a large beefy man appeared on the other side of the screen, his eyes squinting in the porch light.

"Can I help you?"

Beau took off his hat and flashed a smile. "I'm Beauregard Cates. I was—" He jumped back as the man threw open the door.

"Well, get on in here, son." The man grabbed his hand and pulled him into the house before giving it a strong shake that almost sent Beau to his knees. "Burl Scroggs." He gave Beau a jarring thump on the back. "I'm glad to finally meet you. I think we've run into each other a time or two at weddin's and whatnot. But I don't think we've ever been formally introduced. Although I've heard so much about you that I feel like we're old friends."

Beau's happiness tripled at the thought of Jenna telling her daddy about him. It diminished when he realized that Mr. Scroggs had gotten his information from Billy.

"So what are you doin' in Bramble? Last I heard from Billy you were doin' a little bull ridin'. I rode a bull only once in my life, and it pert near made Hope and Faith only children and Jenna a very unhappy wife."

Jenna?

Before Beau could question him, a petite dark-haired woman hurried into the room. "And I'm gonna be a very unhappy wife if you don't get in there and eat your dessert before your ice cream melts." She glanced over at Beau, and his breath caught as he looked into a face almost identical to Jenna's. "And just who is this good-lookin' cowboy?"

"Watch your flirtin', woman," Mr. Scroggs said as he

hooked an arm around her. "Jenna, this here is Beauregard Cates."

"Bubba's brother?" Mrs. Scroggs engulfed him in a hug. "Well, why didn't you say so sooner? Billy has been about the best boss Burl could ask for. Come on in and join us for a piece of cherry pie and ice cream." She took his hat and herded him into the dining room.

Eight or nine adults and children were squeezed in around a table, eating and talking over one another. Beau recognized Slate and Faith Calhoun and their daughter, Daisy. And Colt and Hope and their daughter, Daffodil. But he didn't recognize the dark-haired woman that sat next to Jenna. Or the sleeping baby in Jenna's arms. The sight of the baby cradled against Jenna's shoulder made Beau's heart thump in double time.

"Lookee who stopped by for a visit," Mrs. Scroggs said.

Everyone stopped talking and looked up at Beau. Slate and Colt jumped up to shake his hand, and Faith and Hope each gave him a hug, but the entire time he was greeting them, he couldn't take his eyes off Jenna.

He expected surprise, anger, and maybe a slight amount of joy. Instead, the blue eyes that stared back at him were empty. No surprise. No fire. Not even recognition. She looked right through him as if he didn't even exist. The look drained all the happiness right out of him and left him floundering like a fish out of water.

"I'll just run out to the garage and get another chair," Mr. Scroggs said.

"Don't bother, Daddy." Hope walked around to take the baby from Jenna. "The kids are all tuckered out from the trip and seeing their Aunt Jenna Jay so we better get on home."

"We should get home, too," Slate said as he wrapped an arm around Faith and settled his hand on her rounded stomach. "Little mamas need plenty of rest."

There were hugs all around and promises made for Sunday dinner before the two families headed for the door. As soon as they were gone, Mrs. Scroggs turned to him.

"Are you still single, Beauregard?"

With his eyes pinned on Jenna, he nodded. "Yes, ma'am."

"Well, ain't that nice," Mrs. Scroggs said as she guided him over to the chair next to the dark-haired woman. "This here is my daughter, Tessa, who's as single as a slice of cheese."

Tessa rolled her eyes. "Don't pay any attention to my mama, Mr. Cates. She's just worried that I'm going to end up an old maid. Especially since my baby sister, Jenna Jay, is about to beat me to the punch."

Beau halted midway between standing and sitting. He stared at Jenna, but she refused to look at him.

"It was the darnest thing," Mrs. Scroggs said. "We had no more than walked in the door when Delbert called and proposed to our little Jenna Jay. It was almost like a sign from heaven that God wanted us to stop feudin' and accept Delbert into our family with open arms."

"Not Delbert, Mama," Tessa said. "His name is Davy."

"Oh, right." She shook her head. "Why can't I seem to remember that? Anyway, Beauregard, we were just goin' over the weddin' plans when you showed up. Jennie Bean might want to live in New York City, but she's gonna have her weddin' right here in Bramble." She shot Jenna a warning look. "Or else."

Just the thought of Jenna and Davy getting married—in Bramble or otherwise—had Beau jumping up from his chair.

"Would you excuse me and Jenna Jay for a second? There's something I need to talk with her about." He moved behind Tessa, who seemed to have no problem scooting up her chair to let him by. Jenna wasn't as considerate. When he went to pull out her chair, she hung onto the table.

"I have nothing to say to you," she said through clenched teeth.

"Oh, but I think you do." He jerked harder, and the tablecloth shifted, causing plates to slide and glasses to wobble.

Mrs. Scroggs grabbed for her water glass. "You know our little Jenna Jay, Beau?"

"Yes, ma'am," he said as he unclenched Jenna's hands from the edge of the table. "We met in New York and traveled all the way out to Bramble together in a single bed cab-over—*oomph*!" He groaned when Jenna's elbow connected with his stomach. Ignoring the pain, he made a grab for her arm, but she shoved back the chair and sidestepped out of his reach.

"What in tarnation is goin' on here?" Mr. Scroggs got to his feet. "I will not allow my daughters to be manhandled, Beau. I don't care how much we owe your family."

Jenna stopped and got a smug look on her face. "You tell him, Daddy. And this isn't the first time he's manhandled me. So whup his butt and send him on his way."

"Now, Jenna Jay." Mrs. Scroggs got to her feet with the brightest of smiles. "Is that any way to treat a guest? Of course, your daddy is not going to whup Beauregard's butt. Not when you two have become such good... friends."

"Friends?" Mr. Scroggs looked confused for only a second before a smile almost as bright as his wife's settled on his face. "Why, I wouldn't think of it. You two just go right out on the porch and do all the...talkin' you want. And take your time. All of us were just about to go to bed."

With her parents' permission, Beau didn't hesitate to move around the table and scoop Jenna up in his arms. She didn't fight him. Now her anger seemed to be directed at her parents.

"Fine. Just let him abduct me right in front of your noses. I should've known all it would take was a handsome cowboy to get you to forget that I'm your flesh and blood daughter!"

Beau might've smiled if he wasn't so damned mad. Walking through the living room, he kicked the screen door open and stepped out on the porch. He set her on her feet but kept his hands around her waist.

"Why didn't you tell me that you got back with Davy?" he asked.

She glared back at him, but her anger was soon replaced with the vacant, empty look that made his stomach hurt. "I guess the same reason you didn't tell me you had cancer."

"Those are two different things."

"Are they? Obviously, neither one of us feels close enough to the other to share important information."

"Not fuckin' close enough?" His hands tightened on her waist, and she flinched. He immediately released her but refused to step away. "Not more than three hours ago, we were as close as two people can get, Jenna."

"That's sex, Beau. There's a difference."

"So are you saying it was all about sex for you?"

"Isn't that what you wanted? You told me you didn't want a serious relationship. You just wanted some fun." She turned away from him and moved to the railing. While he'd been inside, the air had changed. It was now humid and thick with the scent of rain.

He ran a hand through his hair. "Okay, so I spouted off a lot of crap about not wanting to get involved in a relationship. But I think you can understand why. I didn't have the right to get close to anyone. Not when I had cancer hanging over my head. Still, I admit that I should've told you. And I was going to tell you today, but then Brant showed up."

Time seemed to slow to a painful stop as he waited for her to speak. When she did, her voice sounded like a stranger's—tight and lifeless. "What kind of cancer?"

"A type of lymphoma," he said.

"Is that why your hair..."

"It came back that way after the chemo."

He could hear her swallow. "But you're okay now?"

"For now."

He wanted to touch her. Instead, they remained where they were—staring out at the storm that moved ever closer. When he couldn't take the silence anymore he spoke. "So you're going to marry Davy?"

A lifetime passed before she answered. "As much as my mother has decided to jump on the marriage bandwagon, I haven't given him an answer."

Beau took her arm and turned her back around. "But you're going to say yes."

"I don't know." She wrapped her arms around her chest as if trying to hold in her heart. "Everything has come at me all at once. You. Davy. Your cancer. I can't think."

His hand tightened. "You don't have to think, Jenna. Just feel. What do you feel?"

"I don't know!" she yelled.

"Well, I know," Beau said as he jerked her closer. "I know exactly how I feel."

"Don't, Beau." In the light that shone through the curtains of the living room, her eyes looked watery and frightened. "Please don't. Not now."

"Don't what? Tell you that I love you? That I need you as much as Davy does, if not more? That I came here tonight to get down on one knee and ask you to marry me?"

"Stop it!" She pulled away from him. "Just stop it. You can't be in love with me. Not when you don't even trust me enough to tell me the truth. I would've told you if I had cancer," she sobbed. "I would've told you so you could've gotten out before you gave your heart."

Behind her, the storm had moved closer, jagged lines of lightning cracking open the darkened skies like an eggshell.

Like his very soul.

He watched as tears trickled down her cheeks. They were the last things he wanted to see. Especially when they were tears of good-bye.

"All right, Jenna." He pushed her away. "I get it. You need a cause you can win. And cancer is an iffy thing at best. Yes, the test results came back clear, but what about next year? Or the year after? So run back to Davy. I don't have any doubt that you'll whip him into shape eventually. And it's better to love a loser than a man who can't even promise to be around on his next birthday. Or yours."

How Beau managed to turn away from those watery

blue eyes, he didn't know. One minute he was standing staring down at her, and the next he was heading across the yard toward Billy's monster truck. The skies opened up before he reached it, soaking his hair and shirt. He had left his hat again, but he didn't care. He welcomed the cold, stinging drops. He tipped his head up and let the deluge soak him for a full five minutes before he reached for the handle of the truck. Once inside, he twisted the key, and the engine rumbled to life. As he started to back out, he switched on the headlights.

They illuminated the entire front of the house.

Including the empty front porch.

Chapter Thirty

"It's the blame-dist thing I've ever seen," Twyla said. "It's just like that bible story about Jesus and that Mary Mag-da-lena. Except we never did try to stone Marcy. Although I wanted to once when she fooled around with my boyfriend Joe. 'Course, I guess she did me a favor. That man loved Jack Daniels more than he would've ever loved me." She pointed a finger at Jenna, who had just leaned over the counter to pour Twyla a cup of coffee. "You remember Joe, don't you, Jenna Jay? You got him hooked up with that AA—or is it AAA? I always get them two confused."

"Alcoholics Anonymous," Jenna said absently as her gaze wandered to the window where Marcy and Pastor Robbins were walking past. The pastor had his arm around Marcy and was looking down at her like she hung the moon. The sight of them pulled up memories of the henhouse, which led to memories of Beau. Of course, everything led to memories of Beau. Vivid, gut-twisting memories that haunted her at night and plagued her during the day.

"Well, I think someone should have a talk with the pastor," Cindy Lynn said. She took a bite of her oatmeal while she eyeballed Darla's blueberry pancakes that Jenna had just set down in front of her. "Obviously, the man doesn't know about Marcy's sordid past. When he finds out what kind of woman she is, he'll forget all about marriage and run for the hills."

Twyla lifted the sugar dispenser and poured a steady stream into her coffee. "I don't know about that. Sordid pasts didn't stop Ed from marryin' you."

"And just what are you sayin', Twyla?" Cindy Lynn snapped. "My sordid past was nothin' compared to Marcy's. Why, I heard that she was workin' at Miss Hattie's."

Turning, Twyla trailed a line of sugar across the counter. "No foolin'? Would that make Beauregard Cates her pimp? Because I would pimp myself out for that man anytime."

Just Beau's name had Jenna's face flushing. To hide her reaction, she turned and placed the carafe back in the coffeemaker.

"It doesn't matter if he's her pimp or not," Cindy continued. "What matters is having a prostitute as our pastor's wife. Why, we'll be the laughingstock of Haskins County."

"As if we haven't been that before." Darla adjusted the wooden hoop that held the pillowcase she was embroidering with the Texas state flag. "But you might be right. The pastor's wife is responsible for taking on all charitable works in the community, and Marcy has never been very charitable—at least not with the womenfolk. Although she's shore done a good job at the library."

"Too bad you're marryin' that tattooed rocker dude,

Jenna Jay." Twyla poured half the container of cream in her cup. "With all the charity you do, you'd make a great pastor's wife."

Jenna wasn't surprised that the townsfolk had heard about Davy's proposal. News traveled fast in a small town, and it had been a week since Davy had proposed to her. And a week since Beau had left her feeling as if her heart had been jerked out of her chest and repeatedly run over by an eighteen-wheeler. The feeling had convinced her that what she had with Davy wasn't enough to marry him.

"I'm not marrying Davy," she said.

"Davy?" Twyla said. "Who's Davy? I was talkin' about you marryin' Delbert."

Before Jenna could tell her that Davy and Delbert were one and the same, the bell over the door jangled, and Rachel Dean hustled in, holding a picket sign that read, *Shoo the Hens Out of Texas*.

"Good Lord." Rachel placed the sign in the umbrella holder of the coatrack. "Wilma Tate caught me just outside of Doc Mathers's, and I thought I was never gonna get away. Seems she's all hell bent on gettin' rid of the henhouse—no doubt because Elmer will be out there first chance he gets. I had to take a sign from her just to get her to shut up."

"She corralled me into helpin' her out, too," Twyla said. "She promised to get a perm and haircut if I'd picket for an hour. Although I'm not about to stand out there in the blazin' sun. The only reason I'm goin' is to take a peek inside."

"Well, I have to admit that I'm a little curious myself." Rachel came around the counter and pulled her apron off the hook. "I shore appreciate you takin' over for me, Jenna Jay, so I could get my bunions looked at."

"Any time, Rachel." She took off her apron.

"So when do you leave for New York?"

"Tomorrow," she said. Jenna didn't know why she suddenly felt so sad. It should be a relief to get away from Bramble and all its memories.

"Well, we'll sure miss you." Rachel pulled her into her arms and gave her a big hug. A hug that left Jenna feeling so emotional that she rushed through her good-byes to the other women and hurried out of Josephine's Diner before she started sobbing like a baby.

Once outside, Jenna headed for her daddy's truck that she'd parked in front of Sutter's Pharmacy. She started to cross the street when she glanced up and saw Marcy unlocking the doors of the library. At least, the woman's face and hair looked like Marcy. The conservative pants and blouse looked more like Ms. Murphy.

For some reason that she couldn't explain, Jenna changed directions.

When she got inside the library, Marcy was already standing behind the desk, checking books back in. A slight smile played around her lips as she hummed a song that sounded suspiciously like "Jesus Loves Me."

"Hi, Marcy."

Marcy's gaze snapped up, and she slapped a hand to her chest. "Shit!" She glanced up at the ceiling before correcting her language. "I mean, shoot, you scared the crap out of me, Jenna Jay."

"Sorry," Jenna said. "I just wanted to stop by and ask how Minnie was doing."

"Minnie or Beau?" She went back to checking in the books. "Don't look so surprised. Even an imbecile can figure out that you two had some kind of falling out.

Especially when the grinning cowboy has turned into The Grinch Who Makes Everyone's Life a Living Hell. If he points out one more speck of dust, I'm going to beat him to death with my Swiffer."

"I'm sure his personality change has nothing to do with me," Jenna said, even though she desperately wanted it to be true. "He's probably just going a little stir crazy being cooped up in the henhouse when he's used to traveling all over the world."

Marcy snorted. "Yeah, I'm sure that's it. Anyway, between him and that convict that they hired to drive the van, I'll be glad to leave the henhouse in another couple weeks."

"Olive Washburn is working there?"

Marcy picked up another book. "I wouldn't exactly call it working. All she does is follow me around like some stray mutt. Although her dry sense of humor has kinda grown on me."

Just the thought of Marcy and Olive being together had Jenna smiling for the first time in days. "So are you moving in with Pastor Robbins?"

Marcy's sigh could only be described as pure frustration. "I wish. No, I'm moving into the apartment over the bank so I can be closer to my new job." She held up a book. "Meet Bramble's new librarian. Mayor Sutter hired me yesterday. Although I think it had more to do with disgruntled volunteers than my qualifications."

"That's not true. Everyone has been talking about what a great job you've been doing."

Instead of being happy with Jenna's words, Marcy's eyes turned sad. "I only wish it would be so easy for them to accept me as Sean's wife."

Jenna reached across the counter and squeezed her hand. "They will. Once you're married, they'll forget all about your past. You'll just be Mrs. Robbins, the pastor's wife that grew up right here in Bramble."

Marcy studied her for a moment before she spoke. "You really are a good person, Jenna Jay. And I'm sorry I've treated you so badly. I guess I was still mad at you."

"Mad at me? For what?"

Setting the book she'd just checked in to the side, Marcy rested her hands on the counter. "Do you remember the time that Theo Brewster called me a slut?"

"It was right before the Thanksgiving parade."

Marcy nodded. "There were lots of folks around, but you were the one who walked your horse right out of the parade line and cornered Theo next to the Fresh Mart. Sitting there astride the horse like some warrior princess, you told him to shut up. That there was nothing wrong with women exploring their sexuality." She laughed. It wasn't the cold, cynical laugh that Jenna remembered. This laugh was warm and genuine.

"And if I remember correctly," Jenna said, "you told me to mind my own damned business."

Marcy's smile faded. "Because I was embarrassed, Jenna Jay. Yeah, Theo called me a slut, but no one would've paid him a speck of attention if you hadn't jumped in. Theo was always calling people names."

Jenna stared at Marcy in disbelief. "But I was just trying to help."

"Look, I get it now," Marcy said. "You were just trying to help when you beat up the kid who called Dudley Owens a pimple puss. Just trying to help when you organized the garage sale to send Jeffrey Miller to fat camp.

But sometimes the underdogs of the world don't want you standing up for them. Sometimes they just want to get through what life dealt them without a bunch of attention. And without their shortcomings being pointed out by a girl who has everything."

"But I didn't have everything. I was an outcast, too."

Marcy shot her a skeptical look. "Because you weren't homecoming queen or a prizewinning hog caller? No, you're right. Instead, you were a tomboy and an amazing athlete who every person in town loves for her soft heart."

This time Marcy reached across and squeezed Jenna's hand. "Don't get me wrong. Occasionally, everyone needs a hero, Jenna. Especially the underdogs. But it works so much better if you treat them as friends instead of as victims."

Marcy's words stayed with Jenna long after she left the library. As she walked down the street, she thought back to all the times she had helped someone. Had she cared about their feelings? Or had she just been more concerned with being the hero? Maybe her need to help people had nothing to do with them and everything to do with hiding her own insecurities and weaknesses.

She was so lost in thought that she stepped out in the street without looking and almost got run over by Wilma Tate's Taurus filled with picket signs. Wilma blared the horn as Jenna raced to get out of her way. She had just gotten safely to the other side when her mama came tearing out of The Feed and Seed.

"Crazy woman!" Her mother shook her fist at Wilma's departing car. "Next time you almost run over my baby girl, you'll find yourself hog tied and cryin' 'Uncle!'" She looked back at Jenna. "Are you okay, Jennie Bean?"

Jenna didn't feel okay. She felt a little disoriented and lost. Which is why she allowed her mother to walk her back inside The Feed and Seed and sit her down in the chair behind the counter.

"Just take a few deep, even breaths," her mother said as she rubbed her back in soothing circles. "A scare like that can take the life right out of you."

Jenna wasn't scared. Just confused.

"Why am I so different, Mama?" The words spilled out with every stroke of her mother's hand. "Why am I dumb and boyish and look nothing like the rest of the people in our family?"

Her mother's hand stilled, and she drew back with a shocked look as if Wilma's car was headed straight for The Feed and Seed's front window. "Why, Jenna Jay Scroggs, what in the world are you talkin' about?"

Jenna waved a hand at her body. "Look at me. I'm nothing like a Scroggs. I'm tall and skinny as a stick with blond hair and enough testosterone to fuel the entire Dallas Cowboys football team."

Her mother stared at her for only a moment more before she broke out in laughter. "Oh, Jennie Bean, you always have made me laugh."

Jenna crossed her arms and glared at her mother. "It's no laughing matter. It's not fun to feel like the odd man out. You can be truthful with me, Mama. Am I the product of a sordid affair?"

This caused her mother to sober, and she pointed a finger at Jenna. "You watch your mouth, young lady. I have never cheated on your daddy in my life. Just who do you think you got your athletic ability from? And your name resides on the Bramble High gymnasium wall right

alongside your daddy's to prove it." She pulled Jenna up
out of the chair with surprising strength and pushed her
all the way to the bathroom in the back. "As for you not
looking like anyone in the family..." She turned Jenna
around to face the mirror over the rust-stained sink. Standing on tiptoe, she pressed her cheek against Jenna's.

Jenna stared into the mirror at the reflection of her
and her mama. At first, all she noticed was the difference
in hair and eye color, but after only a few seconds, she
started to study the features—the high foreheads, the arch
of the eyebrows, the angle and width of the noses, and the
curve of the top lips.

When she reached the stubborn tilt of the identical
chins, Jenna realized that Olive had been right.

Jenna Jay *was* a carbon copy of her mama, right down
to the freckles on her nose.

Her mama lowered down to her boot heels, but continued to look at Jenna in the mirror. "Do these insecurities
have anything to do with breakin' a certain good-lookin'
cowboy's heart?" When Jenna's eyes widened with surprise, her mama smiled. "Me and your daddy might've
done a little eavesdropping after Tessa went to bed."

Jenna turned away from the mirror. "I didn't break
Beau's heart. We barely even know each other." She
started to walk out of the bathroom, but her mother
stopped her.

"Now I know you thought I didn't like Davy because
he was different. And there is probably a little truth to
that. But the real reason I didn't want you with Davy is
because I never thought you were a good match."

"And how do you know what's a good match for me,
Mama?"

Her mother smiled. "Because not only do you look like me, Jennie Bean, you have the same fiery personality. And no milk-toast man who lets us tell him when to go to the bathroom is going to work. We need manly men. Men who admire our strengths and understand our weaknesses. Men who refuse to play second fiddle and demand the truth. Even if the truth is the worst thing you'll ever face."

Tears welled up in Jenna's eyes, and she didn't even try to blink them back. "But I don't know if I can do it, Mama. I don't know if I'm strong enough to watch him die."

"Aww, honey," her mama hugged her close, "I wish I could give you a guarantee. But there are no guarantees in life. We all just have to accept that and do the best we can. But I'll tell you one thing. If I was betting on anyone to come out victorious, it would be you, Jennie Bean. You do love to win."

Suddenly, Beau's words came back to her. *You need a cause you can win.*

There in her mama's arms, everything became crystal clear. Jenna hadn't been mad at Beau for not telling her about his cancer. She was mad because he had offered her something that would take more work than picketing a market for a few hours or putting a couple videos on YouTube. This challenge would be the challenge of a lifetime. And she might not come out the hero. She might just end up a woman with crushed dreams and a broken heart.

Which left only one question to answer.

Was Beau worth it?

Once Jenna had made up her mind, she didn't waste any time saying good-bye to her mama and heading out to the henhouse. She expected to find Beau out back in the hammock, but he wasn't there. Nor was he in any of the rooms on the main level. And what was weirder—neither was anyone else. Not Baby, Sunshine, Starlet, or Minnie. Jenna really started to get worried when she ran upstairs and all the rooms were vacant. There was no luggage or any signs of guests.

She took the stairs from Miss Hattie's closet down to The Jungle Room two at a time. But she slowed on the last flight of stairs when she heard Beau's voice.

"...I think you must have a hearin' problem. I told you Jenna Jay Scroggs means nothing to me."

The words hurt, but Jenna didn't believe them for a second. Beau cared about her. He might not love her, but he would. And right now, she had enough love for both of them. Taking a deep breath, she burst through the door of The Jungle Room, almost knocking over the plastic plant that hid the doorway.

"I love you, Beauregard Cates—"

The simultaneous clicks of guns being cocked had Jenna sliding to a stop in the middle of the dance floor. A dance floor that now held four bound and gagged hens.

And one very annoyed silver-haired cowboy.

Chapter Thirty-one

"DAMN IT, WOMAN." Beau looked up at Jenna from where he knelt on the floor, his face heartbreakingly battered and his eyes frustrated. "Will you ever learn when to keep your mouth shut?"

Jenna wanted to fall to her knees and kiss every bruise on Beau's face. Instead, her gaze narrowed and sought out the man responsible for Beau's condition and the gagged and bound hens. He stood at the bar, a drink in one hand and a cigar in the other. His thin lips curled up in a smile as he waved the cigar at her.

"Welcome, chica. We've been waiting for you."

"Hello, Alejandro." She tried to keep the anger from her voice. "Did you run out of people to bully in New York City?"

Alejandro set down his glass and moved closer, the heels of his expensive dress shoes tapping against the floor. "I never bully. I just persuade."

Jenna glanced around at his gun-toting henchmen who seemed to be everywhere. "With muscle and guns."

Alejandro shrugged. "If I need to." He nodded at

Beau. "This one is more stubborn than most. I was almost starting to believe him when he said he didn't know where you were."

"So what do you want, Alejandro?" she asked. "Don't tell me you came all the way out here because I was trying to convince Miguel to stop being your 'yes boy.'" Her eyes narrowed. "How did you find me?"

Alejandro reached into his suit jacket and pulled out the henhouse invitation. "Miguel remembered delivering this to your house, and it only took a quick search of your apartment to find it." He released his breath in a sigh. "But too bad for you that we didn't find the money you stole from me."

"Money? I don't know what you're talking about."

"So you want to play as stupid as your cowboy," he said. "Very well. I'm talking about the money in the black backpack that Miguel was carrying the night you caught him on the fire escape."

Minnie, who was bound to her wheelchair, tried to say something, but with the piece of tape over her mouth, it came out as nothing more than mumbles. Alejandro ignored her and stepped closer to Jenna. Close enough for Jenna to smell the brandy on his breath.

"The boy seems to think that he and this cowboy got their backpacks mixed up. Which would explain why I have a backpack containing cowboy boots and one silver high heel." He took a puff of the cigar and blew the smoke in her face. "I was worried that being the lily-white do-gooder you are that you would've already turned it in to the police. But my connections tell me that no money has shown up. And with you disappearing so suddenly, I can only come to one conclusion." He smiled. "I guess that amount of money can even tempt a saint. So where is it?"

"Sorry," Jenna said, "but I don't have a clue."

In a flash, Alejandro's hand twisted in her hair and jerked her head back, the glowing end of the cigar inches from her face. "Think real hard."

"Get your fuckin' hands off her!" Beau made a dive at Alejandro's legs. Even on his knees, Beau succeeded in pushing him away from Jenna before he was grabbed up by two of the men. They jerked hard on his bound arms, and Jenna saw him grit his teeth in pain. She made a move to go to his aid, but Alejandro stopped her.

"Don't be foolish, chica. I'm not going to harm any of your friends as long as you don't give me any trouble." His fingers stroked the inside of her arm. "But one sign of resistance, and I'll have your cowboy shot where he stands."

"You wouldn't dare kill a U.S. citizen," she said. "You would never get away with it."

Alejandro laughed. "I'll get away with it." He smiled. "I've gotten away with it before."

For the first time, Jenna was terrified. Not for herself, but for Beau and the hens. Alejandro wasn't going to let anyone go. Even if they had the backpack, he was going to kill them all. And no one would figure out the connection between him and the murders.

But how was she going to stop seven armed men single-handedly?

She was still considering her lack of options when a movement caught the corner of her eye. She glanced over at the huge plastic plant in front of the staircase. Was it her imagination or were there eyes looking out at her? A head popped out. A blond head with bad roots.

Olive!

She was only one woman, but just knowing she was there gave Jenna hope. Olive had probably already called the police; now all Jenna needed was time.

"I have the money," she blurted out, causing everyone to look at her. "If you leave my friends alone, I'll take you to it."

Alejandro smiled his oily smile. "I figured the thought of losing your cowboy might jog your memory. So where is it?"

"I buried it in the barn. I'll have to show you exactly where."

He only hesitated for a moment before he snapped his fingers. "Pacho and Marcus stay here. The rest of you come with me." He pulled her toward the elevator, but when she got close to Beau, she tugged him to a stop.

"Jenna," Beau said through his teeth, "don't do this."

"You were right." Her voice quivered with suppressed tears. "I was too scared to admit my feelings. Too scared to take on a challenge I didn't think I could win. But I'm not scared anymore." She reached out and caressed his bruised face. "I love you, Beauregard Cates."

Before he could say anything, she let Alejandro pull her away.

The elevator ride was over too quickly. And before Jenna knew it, she was outside and headed for the barn. She was just about to slow things down by tripping and faking a sprained ankle when a familiar voice called out her name.

"Jenna Jay Scroggs!"

She glanced behind her to see Wilma Tate hustling around the side of the house wearing a hideous flowered hat and carrying a picket sign that read, DON'T LET HENS ROOST IN TEXAS.

"You should be ashamed of yourself," she said as she huffed up. "Your mama would have a fit if she knew where you were." She pointed a finger in Jenna's face. "And don't think I won't tell her, young lady." She finally noticed the men with Jenna, but since men with guns weren't anything new to Texas, she barely blinked an eyelash.

"I sure appreciate your concern, Mrs. Tate," Jenna said. "But I'm headed home just as soon as I show these gentlemen around."

Wilma's eyes narrowed. "They don't look like no gentlemen to me."

Jenna almost rolled her eyes. The woman waited until her life was in danger before getting a brain.

"They're from New York," Jenna said.

"Well, I don't care if they're from the moon." Wilma gave Alejandro the stink eye, although the drooping flower that brushed her nose ruined the effect. "You had better treat Jenna Jay with the respect she deserves. She ain't one of those nasty hens who goes for all that wicked depravity." She glanced at her watch. "I need to get out front. The Ladies' Club should be here any minute to help me picket." She turned and trotted back the way she'd come, her sign propped over her shoulder and a bee circling her flowered hat.

Once she had disappeared around the corner, Alejandro pulled open the barn door. "If you don't find the money before that women's group gets here, chica, you'll be responsible for a lot of dead ladies."

Beau thought he would never be more scared than when the doctors had told him that he had cancer. He was wrong. Just the thought of Jenna Jay being in the barn with Alejandro and his thugs made the blood in his veins turn to ice and unrelenting fear eat at his insides worse than any disease. Especially when he could do nothing about it. He was trussed up like a Christmas goose and guarded by two men who hadn't taken their eyes or guns off him since their boss had left the room.

And the hens were no help. They had all been tied up and gagged: Sunshine, Baby, and Starlet on the floor and Minnie in her wheelchair. Minnie was looking at Beau now, her eyes darting away and then back to him. Before he could figure out what she was trying to get across, the plastic plant in front of the door shook as if caught in a strong wind.

Both men swung around with guns ready. The taller one closest to Beau spoke in rapid-fire Spanish, and the shorter man moved stealthily toward the plant. When he had almost reached it, it shook again. He jumped back and fired off a couple rounds from his revolver. The sound of the shots resounded off the ceiling of The Jungle Room, and the plant stopped moving.

Beau didn't waste time wondering who had rattled the plant or if they had been shot. With both men's attention diverted, he scooted back against the glass table and tried using a metal leg to saw through the duct tape that bound his hands. While he worked, the shorter man moved closer to the plant and kicked it out of the way.

The taller one spoke again, but this time slow enough for Beau to understand that he wanted his comrade to "check it out." The shorter one didn't seem real keen on the idea, but he obeyed. Moving up against the wall, he slowly peeked around the edge of the door. When nothing happened, he stepped inside the darkened doorway and disappeared from sight.

A few seconds passed before the taller man spoke again.

"Pacho?"

When there was no answer, he glanced nervously back at Beau before waving his gun and speaking in Spanish. Beau caught just enough words to figure out that he wanted Beau to go see what had happened to his friend.

Beau got to his feet. There was a good possibility that Pacho was just checking out the upper rooms, which didn't give Beau a lot of time. He hadn't been able to cut completely through the layers of tape, but he'd cut enough that one good tug should finish the job. But he would have to time it perfectly. If he screwed up, it could cost him his life or one of the hens' lives.

Once on his feet, the man rammed him in the back with his gun, and Beau moved forward. He decided he would wait until he was inside the doorway before he made his move. That way there would be less chance of any bullets finding their way to a hen. As soon as he was over the threshold, he flexed his wrists and pulled. The tape ripped apart. But before he could make his move, a figure came out of the shadows with a frying pan held over its head.

Fortunately, the cast-iron pan didn't come down on Beau's head, but rather the man's hand that held the gun. The gun clattered to the cement floor as the man yelped in pain. His yelps were cut short when the pan came back up and clipped him in the chin, knocking him out cold.

A second later, the light was switched on and Olive stood over the bodies of the two men with a mile-wide grin on her face. "Two down. Five to go."

If there had been time, Beau would've kissed her.

Instead, he jerked the tape off his hands and searched for both of the guns. One he handed to Olive.

"Have you called the sheriff?"

She shook her head. "Can't. They did somethin' to the landline. And I ain't had a cell phone since I wrote those bad checks."

Beau slipped the other gun in the waistband of his jeans. He wanted to stay and help her tie the two men up, but time was ticking. Olive must've read his thoughts.

"Go on and save your sweetheart," she said. "I can handle these two."

"Are you sure?"

Olive shot him an insulted look. "Does a huntin' dog have ticks?"

Beau flashed a grin before he took the stairs two at a time. He came out in the ballroom and ran straight to the front door, figuring it would be best if he moved around the front of the house and approached on the other side of the barn. He jerked open the front door and sprinted out only to come to a skidding stop on the porch.

The brick circular driveway was filled with cars, a huge Winnebago, and a bunch of women with picket signs resting over their shoulders. Marcy Henderson was standing in the midst of them, talking loud enough for all to hear.

"... so you can see that it was all just a misunderstanding. When Pastor Robbins discovered I worked at the henhouse, he mistook my flirtation for something more."

A creak had Beau glancing behind him. Rachel Dean rocked in one of the wicker rockers on the porch, her picket sign propped on the railing.

"Well, I can certainly see how the pastor was confused," she said. "Marcy can flirt the pants right off a man. And I'm glad she's clearing things up. I sure wasn't lookin' forward to mannin' a picket line. My bunions are killin'—"

"You need to get everyone out of here, Rachel." Beau strode past her to the railing at the end of the porch. "Then you need to call Sheriff Hicks and tell him that Jenna has been taken hostage by armed men."

He didn't stop to explain, and fortunately Rachel Dean didn't expect him to. By the time he vaulted the railing and headed around the corner of the house, she was issuing orders like a drill sergeant.

"Put those picket signs down, and everyone get to your cars! Twyla, get me your cell phone!"

When Beau got to the back of the house, he peeked around a lilac bush and found two of Alejandro's thugs guarding the front door of the barn. He ducked back against the house and popped the clip out of the gun to check his ammo. It was half full, more than enough to take out the two men. Still, he wasn't willing to waste bullets if he didn't need to. Not when there was a side door to the barn and enough mesquite that ran along the fence to hide behind.

The door on the side of the barn opened into the tack room. And once Beau made sure the room was empty, he moved over to the door that led into the barn and cracked it open. The barn was dark, the only light coming from the sunlight filtering in through the cracks and knotholes of the wood siding. He couldn't see Jenna and the men, but he could hear her. She was leading Alejandro on a wild-goose chase. One Alejandro was growing weary of.

"I'm starting to think that you're playing me for a fool, chica," Alejandro said.

"Now why would I do that?" Jenna tossed back. "Especially when your henchman is pointing his gun right at me. The money is here. Sal just needs to dig a little deeper."

"You better be right," Alejandro said. "If not, Sal is digging your grave."

Just the thought of Jenna lying dead in the ground had Beau easing out of the tack room. Fortunately, Minnie had yet to clean out all the old antiques from the barn so there were plenty to hide behind. He moved over to the double doors of the barn and peeked out through the crack. Both men were still standing guard, but seemed to be preoccupied with trying to see what was going on in the front of the house. While their attention was diverted, Beau picked up a piece of rope and tied the handles on the backs of the doors together. It wouldn't hold them forever, but hopefully long enough. Once the rope was knotted, he moved toward Jenna's voice.

"...now there's no need to look so skeptical, Alejandro," she said. "Tonight you'll be rollin' in your drug money." Her voice didn't betray the lie. In fact, it didn't hold a tremor of fear. Beau, on the other hand, was scared enough for both of them. Especially when he peeked over the seat of an old wagon and saw the gun pointed straight at Jenna's head. A head that glowed like spun gold in the shafts of sunlight.

Sweat gathered in Beau's palm and felt slick against the steel of the gun. What if he missed? It had been years since he'd shot a gun. What if his aim was off and he hit Jenna? He might've remained frozen forever if Jenna hadn't glanced up. Her gaze locked with his, and in one split second, all of Beau's fears completely disappeared.

Not because of the love he saw in her eyes, but because of the trust.

Coming from a woman like Jenna, who only trusted herself to do things right, it was just the jolt of confidence he needed to lift the gun and take aim. The bullet was true. It hit the man in the arm, causing him to drop the gun. Within seconds, Jenna had it pointed at Alejandro.

"Go ahead. Make my day," she said with enough "Dirty Harry" in her voice to have Alejandro easing his hand away from his coat pocket.

Tension released in Beau's shoulders, and he laughed. "Go ahead and make my day?" he said as he walked out from behind the wagon, his gun aimed at the man in the hole.

Jenna flashed him a smile. The brilliance of it took his breath away. "I've always wanted to say that."

"I bet you have, sweetheart." He glanced back at the barn doors, expecting to see them rattling as the men tried to kick them in. Instead, they were perfectly still. Which made the tension return. Quickly, he waved the gun at the man who stood in the three-foot hole and rattled off some Spanish.

"What did you say?" Jenna asked.

"I either told him to drop the shovel or drop his shorts."

Jenna laughed. "Either one will work."

Beau waited for the man to climb out before pulling his gun from his shoulder holster and shoving him down on the ground. He motioned for the other one to follow. Having roped and tied a few steer in his day, it took him no time at all to bind the men's hands and feet together with some baling wire he found in one of the stalls. Jenna remained with her gun pointed at Alejandro, and Beau had little doubt that she would shoot him if he made one false move. Alejandro seemed of the same mind. He didn't make another attempt to get his gun. Although he didn't look all that scared either.

"This is a waste of time," he said with a smirk on his face. "My men outside aren't going to let you leave here alive."

Beau knew he had a point. The men had no doubt heard the gunshot and were already making plans to shoot as soon as Beau and Jenna stepped out the door. Which meant that they should wait it out in the barn for Sheriff Hicks. Except Sheriff Hicks could be hours away, and Beau had never been good at waiting.

He walked over and twisted Alejandro's arm behind his back before slipping the gun out of his coat pocket. "Which is exactly why you're going to lead the way, El Patron." He shoved him toward the tack room and issued an order to Jenna. "Stay here until I come back for you."

"Oh no." Jenna fell in step next to him. "I'm not letting you waltz into an ambush, Beauregard Cates."

Beau gritted his teeth. "Damn it, Jenna. For once in your life, would you let me be the hero?"

"What do you mean?" she said. "I just did."

Beau glanced over at her. "Are you telling me that you could've taken on three men by yourself without a gun?"

"Of course." She pulled open the tack room door. "Once Sal had dug a hole for himself that he couldn't easily get out of, I was going to offer to help. He would hand me the shovel, which I would then use to dispatch Julio and Stupido here."

"And you think that Sal wouldn't have pulled his gun on you?"

"He would've been hard-pressed to hit me when he was in a deep hole." She opened the side door of the barn and peeked out.

"So you're saying that you didn't need me at all?" Beau grabbed an old towel off the workbench and shoved it in Alejandro's mouth.

Jenna looked back at him. "Not for that."

"Then for what?"

She thought for only a second before she spoke, a smile tipping the corners of her mouth. "I need your smiles like I need sunshine. Your kisses like I need food. Your love like I need air." She shrugged. "I guess I just need you, Beauregard Cates."

There had been only a few times in his life when he had to fight back tears. This was one of them. Before, when she had told him that she loved him, he'd been too scared for her life to enjoy it. Now, his heart felt like a big ol' hot-air balloon. Except this wasn't exactly the right time to let it float away. So instead, he shoved Alejandro out the open door and kept it brief.

"Well, that's nice to know, Blondie."

She didn't look real happy with his reply, but he planned on making things up to her. Something he realized he might not ever get to do when he stepped out the side door of the barn to the staccato clicks of guns cocking.

Beau froze with his gun pressed to Alejandro's head as his gaze scanned over the barrels of at least twenty guns of various shapes and sizes.

Thankfully, the guns weren't being held by members of the Mexican Cartel.

But rather by members of the Bramble Ladies' Club.

A camera flashed, and Beau was surprised to see the tourists Marty and Laurie standing amidst the gun-toting women.

"Not now." Laurie pushed the camera away from Marty's face. "He's not naked!"

Chapter Thirty-two

"I'M GONNA SUCCEED IF IT's the last thing I do." Twyla finished lacing up her purple running shoes before she got to her feet and executed a few lunges. "This time," she clasped her hands together and stretched her arms over her tower of teased hair, "I will come out the victor." She eyeballed the bouquet that sat on the long banquet table beneath the huge cottonwood tree. "Come hail or high water, I'm gonna get my hands on yew. And Kenny Gene won't have a cowboy boot to stand on."

Normally, Twyla's antics would've gotten a smile out of Jenna Jay. Today, she wasn't much in a smiling mood. Not even when a tall, handsome cowboy came up and sat down next to her.

"I'd ask for the pleasure of a dance with the woman who brought down one of the major players in the Mexican Cartel," Dusty said, "but I've never cared much for dancing."

"That's fine with me," Jenna said. "I don't feel much like dancing either." Her gaze moved over to the dance floor that had been set up amidst Miss Hattie's lilac bushes. Most of the folks of Bramble were gliding around on it. But Jenna only had eyes for the silver-haired cowboy who stumbled through a two-step with Shirlene. His head was tipped back, and he was laughing like he was having the time of his life.

Jenna tried to pull her gaze away, but it was a losing battle. As much as she wanted to ignore Beau like he was ignoring her, she couldn't seem to do it. Not during the ceremony where Marcy and Pastor Robbins vowed to love, honor, and cherish. And not during the drawn-out dinner where Beau sat a good five tables away.

"According to the Feds," Dusty continued, "they've been tracking Alejandro for years, trying to get something on him." He flashed his crooked smile. "And all it took was a skinny, blond cowgirl to bring him down."

"I didn't do it alone." Jenna's gaze remained on Beau.

"I'm sure no one will overlook Beau's part in it," Dusty said. "He's a Cates, after all. They never get overlooked. Although I have to admit that the federal agents did do a good job of keeping your names out of the news." He poured some champagne in a fluted glass and handed it to her. "The picture that ended up on those tourists' Facebook page was easily explained as a joke."

"Some joke." Jenna watched as Beau switched partners with Billy for the waltz. Starlet looked as if she'd just won the lottery, which was almost laughable considering Beau's dancing skills. But Jenna didn't laugh. Not when she would've given anything to change places with Starlet. Except Beau hadn't asked her. Or smiled at her. Or looked at her.

"So what's going on with you two?" Dusty asked.

"Nothing."

There was nothing going on between her and Beau. For an entire week and a half, ever since he had rescued her in the barn, there had been no kisses, no sex, not even a brief phone call to her parents' house to see how she was doing. It was like she had fallen off the face of the earth as far as Beau was concerned.

Jenna had been trying to convince herself that Beau's strange behavior had to do with his fear over losing her. Their near brush with death had frightened all the good ol' boy flirting right out of him. But seeing him tonight, flirting with every woman but her, destroyed that theory and forced her to face the truth. Whatever she and Beau had had together was over. She might be head over heels in love with him, but Beau didn't feel the same way. The words of love he'd spoken to her on her parents' front porch were only a result of his excitement over learning he didn't have cancer, and it had only taken some time for him to realize it.

The old Jenna would've fought for Beau's love. But the new Jenna had come to realize that you couldn't force a person to change their feelings. Beau didn't love her, and as hard as it was, she would have to live with that.

No longer feeling like she could continue the charade of enjoying the wedding, she set her glass down and got to her feet.

"Do you think you could take me home? I have a bad headache."

Dusty didn't look as if he believed her. Still, he nodded his head and set his glass down. They had only taken a few steps when Rachel Dean came hustling up.

"You ain't leavin', are you, Jenna Jay?" She spoke so loudly that half the people in attendance turned to look at them, including Beau. His gaze locked with Jenna's for only a second, just long enough to make her knees weak, before it moved over to Rachel. He winked and then turned on a boot heel and walked off the dance floor.

Rachel grabbed Kenny Gene on his way by and shoved him at Jenna. "You can't leave when you haven't danced with Kenny."

"Sorry, Rachel," Kenny said. "I don't have no time for dancin'. I've got to get Francine Monroe pumped up to catch that bouquet before Twyla—"

Rachel tightened her large man hand on Kenny's arm until he flinched in pain. "Dance with Jenna Jay, Kenny."

"Yes, ma'am." Kenny grabbed up Jenna before she could protest and swept her toward the dance floor. Kenny had always been a good dancer, and he twirled and whipped her around so fast that all she could do was follow and pray for the end of the song. It happened sooner than she thought. Mid-lyric, the lead singer of the band cut off, and Mayor Sutter's voice boomed through the speakers.

"All you single women get your catcher's mitts ready. It's time for the bouquet toss!"

Kenny twirled Jenna to a stop, and his eyes filled with terror. "Can you still jump as high as you did in high school, Jenna Jay? Because there's a twenty in it for you, if you can."

Before Jenna could answer, Kenny was being pushed off the dance floor by a herd of crazed, single women. Jenna wished that she was as lucky. When she tried to break through the mob, one woman after another blocked her exit. Most of them were married women who had no business being out on the dance floor in the first place.

"Excuse me, honey." Shirlene stepped in front of her. "I just wanted to get a look-see. No tellin' what Twyla will do this time."

"You're going the wrong way, Jenna Jay." Elizabeth Cates steered her back into the group like she was an unruly child.

"You don't have to catch it," Faith said as she hooked an arm through Jenna's.

"As if Twyla would let that happen." Hope hooked her other arm and helped her twin sister guide Jenna to the front of the pack. They left her standing next to Twyla, who was pulling on a pair of those sticky-bubbled gloves that football receivers wear.

"Stay out of my way, people," Twyla warned. "I'm a woman on a mission."

"No can do, sweetie." Olive Washburn stepped up on the other side of Jenna. The hens had given Olive a make-over, and Jenna had to admit that she looked real nice. Her tattoos barely showed in the long-sleeved beige gown, and she'd dyed her platinum hair the same color brown as her daughter's.

According to Minnie, Marcy still didn't know Olive was her mother, but Jenna figured it would only be a matter of time before she did. Jenna could only hope that Marcy would accept Olive as her mother as easily as the town had accepted Marcy as their new pastor's wife.

"Go on, Mrs. Robbins," Mayor Sutter's voice bellowed through the speakers. "Let it rip."

Marcy stepped onto the dance floor assisted by her husband, who wore a brightly colored Hawaiian shirt and lei. Marcy wore a silk flower lei coupled with her simple white dress, and she looked like a beautiful island princess. Pastor Robbins must've thought so, too, because, even after he released her hand, he watched her with the look of a man thoroughly besotted.

Marcy moved to one end of the dance floor. But before she turned her back to the group of women her gaze shifted to another man who stood on the edge of the crowd. Beau looked like the carefree cowboy he was. His arms were crossed over his chest, and an arrogant smile tipped the corners of his mouth. He winked at Marcy just like he'd winked at Rachel. Normally, his blatant flirting would've made Jenna mad. Now she just felt sad that she would never again be on the receiving end of those winks and smiles.

Without a moment's hesitation, Marcy turned and launched the bouquet over her shoulder. Having no desire whatsoever to catch the flowers, Jenna kept her hands at her sides. She had nothing to worry about. The bouquet sailed up in the air, a good three feet over Jenna's head. Olive and Twyla went up at the same time. And not surprisingly, Twyla beat Olive out. The bouquet was only inches from Twyla's fingertips when it was plucked away by a hand Jenna recognized immediately.

She turned to find her brother Dallas standing behind her, his smile big and contagious.

"You always are right in the middle of things, aren't you, sis?" With the accuracy of an all-American college football player, he threw the bouquet across the garden and right to Beau, who was now staring at her intently. The crowd parted like the Red Sea as he walked toward her. He stopped inches away. So close she could hear his heart beating.

Or was that hers?

He lifted the bouquet. "I think this is supposed to go to the next bride." When she just stood there staring at him, he reached into the silk flowers and pulled out a small box. He flipped it open to reveal a beautiful diamond in a simple setting.

Her gaze lifted to his, and he must've read her confusion.

"I wanted to surprise you, Blondie." He gave her the smile she'd been waiting a week and a half for. "And I've been so happy after hearing that you love and need me that I didn't think I could keep it a secret." He glanced up at Dallas. "And I also wanted to give your brother time to get here." Without a second's hesitation, he handed the bouquet to Dallas and got down on one knee. "Jenna Jay Scroggs, love of my life, woman of my dreams, will you marry me?"

Just that quickly, her depression and heartbreak lifted to be replaced with all-consuming…

Anger.

"Why, you lowdown, good-for-nothing snake!" She socked him so hard in the shoulder that she knocked him down to his butt. "Do you realize what kind of hell I've gone through in the last week?" She jerked the bouquet from Dallas and would've beat Beau about the head with it if Beau hadn't grabbed her wrist and pulled her down on top of him. Something of a wrestling match ensued as the townsfolk circled round and called out encouragement.

Mostly to Beau.

"Don't let her get the scissor hold," Dallas instructed. "She'll kill you with the scissor."

"Keep a good grip on her, son," Mayor Sutter said. "Women like our little Jenna Jay need a firm hand."

"Watch her knee," her mama piped up. "I want me some more grandbabies."

"I wouldn't be worried about grandbabies," Rachel Dean chimed in, "as much as I would be worried about the weddin' night."

Just the thought of not getting her wedding night with Beau had all the fight fizzle right out of Jenna, and Beau easily rolled her over and pinned her hands above her head. They were both breathing hard, their chests pumping in and out as she lifted her gaze to him. In his eyes, she saw an ocean full of love and a sky full of humor. A giggle escaped her mouth, and just that quickly, they both started laughing. Not little chuckles, but the deep, hearty kind of laughter that came from knowing that they had years and years of fighting to look forward to.

Years and years of fighting and laughter and love.

"Yes," Jenna said when she finally caught her breath. "I'll marry you, Beauregard Cates. Love of my life. Man of my dreams."

As Beau kissed Jenna silly, Twyla's voice rang out.

"I was an inch away! Just a doggone inch!"

Epilogue

"WOULD YOU LIKE ME TO scrub your back, Mr. Cates?"

"No, thank you, Mrs. Cates." Beau took the loofa from Jenna's hand and tossed it over his shoulder. It bounced off the edge of Miss Hattie's bear claw tub and landed on the floor right between a white high heel and a crumpled, satin gown.

Readjusting her legs, Jenna leaned down to take a nip of his shoulder before kissing her way up to his ear. "I probably should hang up my weddin' dress. Your sister would have a heart attack if she saw the Verna Wong she helped me pick out lying on the floor in a heap."

"I think it's Vera Wang, sweetheart." Beau slipped his hands along the back of her thighs, causing a wave of desire to skitter through her body. "And it doesn't matter what Bri thinks. Especially when she didn't even show up to see you in the gown."

"Now, you can't blame her for getting sick," Jenna said as she caressed his earlobe with her tongue. "She sounded horrible when she called."

He kissed the spot in between her neck and shoulder,

sipping off the droplets of water. "I just find it suspicious that she's missed all three of her brothers' weddings."

She pulled back and looked into the endearingly handsome face of her husband. "It was the most wonderful wedding day ever, wasn't it?"

He smiled the familiar smile that melted her heart. "The best. And Sutter Springs was the perfect compromise between the hens wanting it at the henhouse and the townsfolk wanting it at the town hall."

"Everyone did seem to enjoy themselves. Mama and Olive rekindled their friendship, and I was glad to see that the town believed Marcy and they no longer think Miss Hattie's is a house of ill repute—well, all except for Wilma Tate. She's still convinced that something shady is going on out here."

"Really?" Beau's eyes sparkled with mischief as one hand slipped over the top of her thigh. "Define 'shady.'" His thumb strummed over a spot that made Jenna's breath hitch. "Would it be this?" Two fingers slipped into her wet heat. "Or maybe this?"

Much later, after Beau had thoroughly proven Wilma Tate right, Jenna cuddled against her husband in Miss Hattie's bed.

"Are you sure you don't want to go on a honeymoon?" Beau asked.

"Positive." Jenna caressed his chest, her finger outlining his tattoo. "There's only one place for this Texas girl. And that's right here with my Texas boy—" Her stomach growled loudly.

Beau pulled back and shot her an incredulous look. "Please don't tell me you're hungry. Not only did you eat your entire plate of food at the reception, you ate half of mine. If anyone should be hungry, it's me."

With all the wedding craziness, Jenna had been waiting for just the right moment to share her secret. Now seemed like the perfect time.

Leaning up, she gave him a quick kiss. "But you're not eating for two."

Jenna expected excitement. What she got was a stunned look and scary silence.

She swallowed hard. "I know it's a little surprising. I was surprised myself when I stopped by Mama's to pick up the bouquets that Darla had made and Mama took one look at me and knew. Still, I didn't believe her motherly ESP until I took the pregnancy test." When he continued to stare at her, she socked him in the arm. "Would you please say something, Beau?"

Reverently, he lifted a hand and covered her stomach. "A baby."

Then with a smile that rivaled any he'd ever given her, he tipped back his head and released a whoop that could be heard all the way to Bramble.

Downstairs, Minnie woke from a sound sleep. She didn't know what had awakened her, but she knew what kept her from going back to sleep—the memory of something she had forgotten in the excitement of Jenna and Beau's wedding. Not to mention her surgery and weeks of chemotherapy. Figuring that she couldn't go to sleep until she'd taken care of the matter, she scooted into her wheelchair and rolled toward the library.

To take her mind off the side effects of her treatment, Starlet had insisted she learn how to use a laptop. And over the last few months, Minnie had gotten pretty efficient at e-mailing the women in her cancer support group and ordering wigs off Amazon. It shouldn't take her long to make the large contribution to the American Cancer Society.

She probably should feel a little guilty. After all, the money wasn't exactly hers. But if she had given it over to the Feds, there was no telling what kind of government shenanigans they would've spent it on. This way, it went for a good cause.

Needing to know exactly how much to donate, Minnie rolled over to the bookcase and pulled out a book by Frances Hodgson Burnett, *The Secret Garden*. There was a click as the panel beneath the bookcase opened to reveal a safe. The safe had been Miss Hattie's and had always been used for important papers, jewelry, and cash. Since Minnie had opened the safe so many times in her life, it didn't take her long to dial the combination.

Having lived almost ninety years, there were very few things in life that surprised Minnie. When she pulled open the door of the safe and looked inside, she added another to the list.

The black backpack was gone.

**Did you miss meeting Slate Calhoun,
the sexy cowboy in Katie Lane's
first Bramble, Texas, novel?**

Turn this page
for an excerpt from

Going Cowboy Crazy.

Chapter Two

SLATE CALHOUN SAT BACK IN THE DARK CORNER and watched the woman in the conservative pants and brown sweater take another sip of her beer as if it was teatime at Buckingham Palace. Hell, she even held her little pinkie out. If that was Hope Scroggs, then he was Prince Charles. And he was no pansy prince.

Still, the resemblance was uncanny.

The impostor swallowed and wrinkled up her cute little nose. A nose that was the exact duplicate of Hope's. And so were the brows that slanted over those big blue eyes and the high cheekbones and that damned full-lipped mouth. A mouth that had fried his brain like a slice of his aunt's green tomatoes splattering in hot bacon grease.

The kiss was the kicker. Slate never forgot a kiss. Never. And the few kisses he'd shared with Hope hadn't come close to the kiss he'd shared with this woman. Hope's kisses had always left him with a strange uncomfortable feeling; like he'd just kissed his sister. It had never left him feeling like he wanted to strip her naked and devour her petite body like a contestant in a pie-eating contest.

But if the woman wasn't Hope, then who the hell was she?

He'd heard of people having doubles—people who weren't related to you but looked a lot like you. He'd even seen a man once who could pass for George W. in just the right lighting. But this woman was way past a double. She was more like an identical twin. And since he'd known Hope's family ever since he was thirteen, he had to rule out the entire twin thing. Hope had two younger sisters and a younger brother. And not one of them was a look-alike whose kisses set your hair on fire.

The woman laughed at something Kenny said, and her head tipped back, her entire face lighting up. He'd seen that laugh before, witnessed it all through high school and off and on for years after. Hell, maybe she *was* Hope. Maybe his lips had played a trick on him. Maybe he was so upset about losing last night's game that he wasn't thinking straight. Or maybe, it being a year since her last visit, he was so happy to see her that he read something in the kiss that wasn't there.

It was possible. He'd been under a lot of stress lately. Football season could do crazy things to a man's mind. Especially football season in West Texas. Which was why he had planned a two-week Mexican vacation after the season was over. Just the thought of soft rolling waves, warm sand, and cool ocean breezes made the tension leave his neck and shoulders.

What it didn't do was change his mind about the woman who sat on top of the bar with her legs crossed— showing off those sexy red high heels. Hope didn't cross her legs like that. And she hated high heels. She also hated going to the beauty salon, which was why her long brown hair was down to her butt. This woman's hair was styled in a short layered cut that made her eyes look twice as big and was highlighted the color of Jack Daniels in a fancy crystal glass.

Of course, Hope had lived in Hollywood for five long years. Maxine Truly had gone to Houston for only two years and had come back with multiple piercings and a tattoo of a butterfly on her ass. So big cities could screw you over. He just didn't believe they could change someone from an outspoken extrovert to an introvert who hadn't spoken a word, or even tried to, in the last hour.

Laryngitis, my ass.

That couldn't be Hope.

But there was only one way to find out.

Pushing up from his chair, he strolled around the tables to the spot where her adoring fan club had gathered. It didn't take much to part the sea of people. Hope might be the hometown sweetheart, but he was the hometown football hero turned high school coach. In Bramble, that was as close as a person could get to being God.

As usual, Kenny Gene was talking to beat the band. Sitting on the bar stool next to her, he was monopolizing the conversation with one of his exaggerated stories.

"...I'm not kiddin', the man blew a hole the size of a six-year-old razorback hog in the side of Deeder's double-wide, then took his time hoppin' back in his truck as if he had all day to do—hey, Slate."

Slate stopped just shy of those pointy-toed shoes and trim little ankles. Slowly, he let his gaze slide up the pressed pants, up the brown sweater that hugged the tiny waist and small breasts, over the stubborn chin and the full mouth that still held a tiny trace of pink glittery gloss, to those sky blue eyes that widened just enough to make him realize he hadn't made a mistake.

The woman before him wasn't Hope.

But he was willing to play along until he found out who she was.

"Kenny, what the heck are you doing letting Hope drink beer?" He pried the bottle from her death grip as he yelled at the bartender. "Manny, bring me a bottle of Hope's favorite and a couple of glasses." He smiled and winked at her. "If we're going to celebrate your home-comin', darlin', then we need to do it right."

"I wanted to order Cuervo, Slate," Kenny defended himself. "But she didn't want it."

"Not want your favorite tequila, Hog?" He leaned closer. "Now why would that be, I wonder?"

Before she could do more than blink, Manny slapped down the bottle of Jose Cuervo and two shot glasses, followed quickly by a salt shaker and a plastic cup of lime wedges. He started to pour the tequila but Slate shook his head.

"Thanks, Manny, but I'll get it." Slate took off his hat and tossed it down. Stepping closer, he sandwiched those prim-and-proper crossed legs between his stomach and the bar as he picked up the bottle and splashed some tequila in each glass—a very little in his and much more in the impostor's. He handed her the salt shaker. "Now you remember how this works, don't you, sweetheart?"

"'Course she knows how it works, Slate," Twyla piped in. "She's been in Hollywood, not on the moon."

Slate didn't turn to acknowledge the statement. He remained pressed against her calf, the toe of her shoe teasing the inseam of his jeans and mere inches from his man jewels. His body acknowledged her close proximity but he ignored the tightening in his crotch and continued to watch those fearful baby blues as they looked at the salt shaker, then back at him.

"Here." He took the shaker from her. "Let me refresh your memory, Hog."

Reaching out, he captured her hand. It was soft and fragile and trembled like a tiny white rabbit caught in a snare. He flipped it over and ran his thumb across the silky satin of her wrist, testing the strum of her pulse. As he bent his head, the scent of peaches wafted up from her skin, filling his lungs with light-headed sweetness and his mind with images of juicy ripe fruit waiting to be plucked.

Easy, boy. Keep your eye on the goal line.

With his gaze pinned to hers, he kissed her wrist, his tongue sweeping along the pulse point until her skin was wet and her pupils dilated. Then he pulled back and salted the damp spot he'd left.

"Now watch, darlin'." He sipped the salt off, downed the shot, then grabbed a lime and sucked out the juice—all without releasing her hand. "Now you try. Lick, slam, suck. It's easy."

She just sat there, her eyes dazed and confused. He knew how she felt; he felt pretty confused himself. His lips still tingled from touching her skin, and his heart had picked up the erratic rhythm of hers.

"Go on, Hope," Kenny prodded. "What's the matter with you? Don't tell me you forgot how to drink in Hollywood?"

That seemed to snap her out of it, and before Slate could blink, she licked off the salt, slammed the shot, and had the lime in her mouth.

A cheer rose up, but it was nothing to what rose up beneath Slate's fly. The sight of those pink-glitter lips sucking the lime dry made his knees weak. And so did the triumphant smile that crinkled the corners of her eyes as she pulled the lime from her mouth. A mouth with full lips like Hope's but with straight even front teeth. Not a slightly crooked incisor in sight.

Relief surged through him. The hard evidence proved he wasn't loco. It also proved his libido wasn't on the fritz. He wasn't hot after one of his closest friends; he was hot after this woman. This woman who was not Hope... unless she'd gotten some dental work done like they used to do on *Extreme Makeover.*

He mentally shook himself. No, she wasn't Hope. And if it took the entire bottle of tequila to get her to 'fess up, so be it.

He poured her another shot and had her salted and ready to go before she could blink those innocent eyes. "Bottoms up."

She complied, demonstrating the lick-slam-suck without a flaw. She grinned broadly when the crowd cheered, but she didn't utter a peep. Not even after the next shot. Damn, maybe she was Hope; she was just as mule-headed. And could hold her liquor just as well—although she did seem a little happier.

"Do a Nasty Shot," Sue Ellen hollered loud enough to rattle the glasses behind the bar.

Slate started to decline, but then figured it might be just the thing to get to the truth. Besides, he'd always been a crowd pleaser.

"You wanna do a Nasty Shot, Hog?" he asked.

She nodded, all sparkly-eyed.

For a second, he wondered if it was a good idea. She'd almost set him on fire the last time she kissed him. Of course, that was when he thought she was his close friend and her enthusiasm had taken him by surprise. Now he knew she was a fraud. A sexy fraud, but a fraud nonetheless. Knowing that, he wouldn't let things get out of control. He would get just aggressive enough to scare her into speaking up.

"Okay." Slate lifted her wrist and kissed it, this time sucking her skin into his mouth and giving it a gentle swirl with his tongue. Her eyes fluttered shut, and her breasts beneath the soft sweater rose and fell with quick little breaths.

The man muscle beneath the worn denim of his jeans flexed.

This was definitely a bad idea.

Unfortunately, with the entire town watching, he couldn't back out.

Lifting his head, Slate cleared his throat. "Remember how this works?" He covered the wet spot with salt. "Same premise, but this time we lick and shoot at the same time. Just leave the sucking part to me. Here." He uncrossed her legs and stepped between them, which prompted a few sly chuckles from the men. "For this, we need to get just a tad bit closer."

Those long dark lashes fluttered, and her thighs tightened around him. Slate's breath lunged somewhere between heaven and hell, and his hand shook as he poured a full shot for her and a little for himself.

"Okay, darlin'." Luckily, he sounded more in control than he felt. "You ready?" He dipped his head and pressed his mouth to her skin.

She hesitated for just a second before she followed. The silky strands of her hair brushed his cheek as her lips opened and her tongue slipped out to gather the salt, only millimeters from his. Even though they didn't touch, an electric current of energy arced between them so powerfully that it caused them both to jerk back. Those big baby blues stared back at him, tiny granules of salt clinging to her bottom lip.

His mind went blank.

"Tequila, Coach," Rossie Owens, who owned the bar, yelled.

Snapping out of it, he straightened and grabbed up the full shot, then downed it in an attempt to beat back the rearing head of his libido. She followed more slowly, her wide, confused eyes pinned on him.

"The lime, Slate," Kenny laughed. "You forgot the lime."

Hell. He jerked up the lime and sucked out the tart juice, not at all sure he was ready to go through with it. But then people started cheering him on, just like they had in high school when they wanted him to throw a touchdown pass. And, just like back then, he complied and reached up to hold her chin between his thumb and forefinger as he lowered his lips to hers.

It wasn't a big deal. Slate had kissed a lot of girls in his life. Including one whose eyes were the deep blue of the ocean as it waits to wash up on a Mexican shore. Except he hadn't noticed that about Hope. Hope's eyes were always just blue. Yet this woman's eyes caused a horde of descriptive images to parade through his mind. All of them vivid... and sappy as hell.

Luckily, when he placed his lips on hers all the images

disappeared. Unluckily, now all he could do was feel. The startled intake of breath. The hesitant tremble. The sweet pillowy warmth.

"Suck!" someone yelled.

Her lips startled open, and moist heat surrounded him. Shit, he was in trouble. He parted his lips, hoping that once he did, she would pull back and start talking. But that's not what happened. Instead, she angled her head and opened her mouth wider, then proceeded to kiss him deep enough to suck every last trace of lime from his mouth, along with every thought in his mind. Except for one: how to get inside her conservative beige pants.

Slate pulled his head back. Get in her pants? Get in *whose* pants? He didn't know who the hell the woman was. And even if he did know, he sure wasn't going to get in her pants in front of the entire town. He liked to please people, but not that much.

Ignoring the moist lips and desire-filled eyes, Slate dropped his hand from her chin and lifted her down from the bar. When he turned around, the room was filled with knowing grins. He thought about explaining things. But if he'd learned anything over the years he'd lived in Bramble, it was that when small-town folks got something in their heads, it was hard to shake it. Even if it was totally wrong. Which was why he didn't even make the effort. He just grabbed his hat off the bar as he slipped a hand to the petite woman's waist and herded her toward the door.

It wasn't as difficult as he thought it would be. Which was just one more reason he knew the woman wasn't Hope. Hope was too damned controlling to let anyone herd her anywhere. Just one of the things he didn't particularly miss.

Once they were outside, Slate guided her a little ways from the door before he pulled her around to face him.

"Okay. Just who the hell are you?"

Her gaze flashed up to his just as Cindy Lynn came out the door.

"Hey, Hope. I was wonderin' if you could come to the homecomin' decoratin' committee meetin' on Monday afternoon. I know decorations aren't your thing, but everybody would love to hear about Hollywood. Have you met Matthew McConaughey yet? One of my cousins on my father's side went to college with him in Austin and—"

"Hey, Cindy." Slate pushed the annoyance down and grinned at the woman who, on more than one occasion, had trouble remembering she was married. "I know you're probably just busting at the seams to talk with Hope about all them movie stars, but I was wondering if you could do that later, seeing as how me and Hope have got some catching up to do."

"I'm sure you do." She smirked as she turned and wiggled back inside.

Realizing Cindy Lynn would be only one of many interruptions, Slate slapped his hat on his head and took the woman's hand. "Come on. We're taking a ride."

She allowed him to pull her along until they reached the truck parked by the door. "This is your truck?"

Slate whirled around and stared at the woman who sounded exactly like Hope—except with a really weird accent. He watched as those blue eyes widened right before her hand flew up to cover her mouth.

The hard evidence of her betrayal caused his temper— that he worked so hard at controlling—to rear its ugly head, and he dropped her hand and jerked open the door of the truck. "Get in."

She swallowed hard and shook her head. "I'd rather not."

"So I guess you'd rather stay here and find out how upset these folks get when I inform them that you've been playing them for fools."

She cast a fearful glance back over her shoulder. "I'm not playing anyone for a fool. I just wanted some answers."

"Good. Because that's exactly what I want." Slate pointed to the long bench seat of the truck. "Get in."

The sun had slipped close to the horizon, the last rays turning the sky—and the streaks in her hair—a deep red. She looked small standing so close to the large truck. Small and vulnerable. The image did what the Mexican daydreams couldn't.

He released his breath. "Look, I'm not going to hurt you, but I'm not going to let you leave without finding out why you're impersonating a close friend of mine. So you can either tell me, or Sheriff Winslow."

It was a lame threat. The only thing Sheriff Winslow was any good at was bringing his patrol car to the games and turning on his siren and flashing lights when the Bulldogs scored a touchdown. But this woman didn't know that. Still, she didn't seem to be in any hurry to follow his orders, either.

"My car is parked over there," she said, pointing. "I'll meet you somewhere."

"Not a chance. I wouldn't trust you as far as little Dusty Ray can spit."

She crossed her arms. "Well, I'm not going anyplace with a complete stranger."

"Funny, but that didn't stop you from almost giving me a tonsillectomy," he said. A blush darkened her pale skin. The shy behavior was so unlike Hope that he almost smiled. Almost. She still needed to do some explaining. "So since we've established that we're well past the stranger stage, it shouldn't be a problem for you to take a ride with me."

"I'm sorry, but I really couldn't go—"

Kenny charged out the door with the rest of the town hot on his heels.

"Hey." He held out a purse, if that's what you could call the huge brown leather bag. "Hope forgot her purse."

Slate's gaze ran over the crowd that circled around. "And I guess everyone needed to come with you to give... Hope her purse."

"We just wanted to see how things were goin'." Tyler Jones, who owned the gas station, stepped up.

"And say good-bye to Hope," Miguel, the postmaster, piped in.

There was a chorus of good-byes along with a multitude of invitations to supper.

Then someone finally yelled what everyone else wanted to. "So what are you gonna do with Hope now, Coach?"

What he wanted to do was climb up in the truck and haul ass out of there. To go home and watch game film— or better yet, pop in a Kenny Chesney CD and peruse the Internet for pictures of Mexican hot spots. Anything to forget he'd ever met the woman, or tasted her skin, or kissed her soft lips, or stared into her blue eyes. Blue eyes that turned misty as she looked at the smiling faces surrounding them.

It was that watery, needy look that was the deciding factor.

"Well, I guess I'm going to do what I should've done years ago." He leaned down and hefted her over one shoulder. She squealed and struggled as the crowd swarmed around them. Then he flipped her up in the seat and climbed in after her.

"What's that?" Ms. Murphy, the librarian, asked as she handed him a red high heel through the open window.

After tossing it to the floor, Slate started the engine. It rumbled so loudly he had to yell to be heard.

"Take her to bed."

The woman next to him released a gasp while poor Ms. Murphy looked like she was about to pass out. Normally, he would've apologized for his bad behavior. But normally he didn't have a beautiful impostor sitting next to him who made him angrier than losing a football game.

He popped the truck into reverse and backed out, trying his damnedest to pull up mental pictures of waving palm trees, brown-skinned beauties, and strong tequila. But they kept being erased by soft white skin, eyes as blue as a late September sky, and the smell of sun-ripened peaches.

The town of Bramble, Texas, watched as the truck rumbled over the curb and then took off down the street with the Stars and Stripes, the Lone Star flag, and Buster's ears flapping in the wind.

"Isn't that the sweetest thang?" Twyla pressed a hand to her chest. "Slate and Hope—high school sweethearts together again."

"It sure is," Kenny Gene said. "'Course, there's no tellin' how long Hope will stay."

"Yep." Rye Pickett spit out a long stream of tobacco juice. "That Hollywood sure has brainwashed her. Hell, she couldn't even remember how to drink."

"Poor Slate," Ms. Murphy tsked. "He'll have his hands full convincing her to stay and settle down."

There were murmurs of agreement before Harley Sutter, the mayor, spoke up. "'Course, we could help him out with that."

Rossie Owens pushed back his cowboy hat. "Well, we sure could."

"Just a little help," Darla piped up. "Just enough to show Hope that all her dreams can be fulfilled right here in Bramble."

"Just enough to let love prevail," Sue Ellen agreed.

"Just enough for weddin' bells to ring," Twyla sighed.

"Yep." Harley nodded as he hitched up his pants. "Just enough."

THE DISH

Where Authors Give You the Inside Scoop

From the desk of Debra Webb

Dear Reader,

I can't believe we've already dug into case five of the Faces of Evil—REVENGE.

Things are heating up here in the South just as they are in REVENGE. The South is known for its storytelling. I can remember sitting on the front porch in an old rocking chair and listening to my grandmother tell stories. She was an amazing storyteller. Most of her tales were ones that had been handed down by friends and family for generations. Many were true, though they had changed through the years as each person who told them added his or her own twist. Others were, I genuinely hope, absolute fiction. It would be scary if some of those old tales were true.

Certain elements were a constant in my grandmother's tales. Secrets and loyalty. You know the adage, "blood is thicker than water." Keeping family secrets can sometimes turn deadly and in her stories it often did. Then there were those dark secrets kept between friends. Those rarely ended well for anyone.

Jess Harris and Dan Burnett know a little something about secrets and I dare say in the next two cases, REVENGE and the one to follow, *Ruthless*, they will understand that not only is blood thicker than water but the blood is where the darkness lurks. In the coming cases Jess will need Dan more than ever. You're also going to meet a new and very interesting character, Buddy Corlew, who's a part of Jess's past.

Enjoy the summer! Long days of gardening or romping on the beach. But spend your nights with Jess and Dan as they explore yet another case in the Faces of Evil. I promise you'll be glad you did.

I hope you'll stop by www.thefacesofevil.com and visit with me. There's a weekly briefing each Friday where I talk about what's going on in my world and with the characters as I write the next story. You can sign up as a person of interest and you might just end up a suspect! We love giving away prizes, too, so do stop by.

Enjoy the story and be sure to look for *Ruthless* next month!

Cheers!

Debra Webb

From the desk of Katie Lane

Dear Reader,

One of the highlights of my childhood was the New Mexico State Fair. Every year, my daddy would give me a whole ten dollars to spend there. Since I learned early on what would happen if you gorged on turkey legs and candy apples before you hopped on the Tilt-a-Whirl, I always went to the midway first. After a couple hours of tummy-tingling thrills, my friends and I would grab some food and head over to the coliseum to watch the cowboys practice for that night's rodeo.

Sitting in the box seats high above the arena, I would imagine that I was a princess and the cowboys were princes performing great feats of agility and strength in order to win my hand in marriage. Of course, I was never interested in the most talented cowboys. My favorites were the ones who got bucked off the broncos or bulls before the buzzer and still jumped to their feet with a smile on their face and a hat-wave to the crowd.

It was in this arena of horse manure and testosterone that a seed was planted. A good forty years later, I'm happy to announce that my rodeo Prince Charming has come to fruition in my newest contemporary romance, FLIRTING WITH TEXAS.

Beauregard Cates is a cowboy with the type of smile and good looks that make most gals hear wedding bells. But after suffering through a life-threatening illness, he has no desire to be tied down and spends most of his time traveling around the world...until he ends up on a runaway Central Park carriage ride with a sassy blonde from Texas.

Jenna Jay Scroggs is a waitress who will go to any length to right the injustices of the world. Yet no matter how busy her life is in New York City, Jenna can't ignore the sweet-talkin', silver-haired cowboy who reminds her of everything she left behind. And when her hometown of Bramble gets involved, Beau and Jenna will soon be forced on a tummy-tingling ride of their own that will lead them right back to Texas and a once-upon-a-time kind of love.

I hope y'all will join me for the ride. (With or without a big ol' turkey leg.)

Much Love,

Katie Jane

♥ ♥ ♥ ♥ ♥ ♥ ♥ ♥ ♥ ♥ ♥ ♥ ♥ ♥

From the desk of Erin Kern

Dear Reader,

A few months ago, my editor put me on assignment to interview Avery Price. Little did I know that Avery would end up being the heroine of my latest book, LOOKING FOR TROUBLE. I got such a kick out of following her journey that led her to Trouble, Wyoming, and into the arms of Noah McDermott, that I jumped at the opportunity to revisit with her. What better way to spend my afternoon than having a heart-to-heart with the woman who started it all?

We settle on the patio of her home in the breathtaking Wyoming foothills. After getting seated, Avery pours me a glass of homemade lemonade.

ME: Thank you so much for taking the time to meet with me. I know how much you value your privacy.

AVERY: *(Takes a sip of lemonade, then sets her drink*

down.) Privacy is overrated. And I should be thanking you for making the drive out here.

ME: It's nice to get out of the city every once in a while. Plus it's beautiful out here. I can see why you chose this place.

AVERY: I'd say it chose me. (*Her lips tilt up in a wry little smile.*) I actually didn't plan on staying here at first. But anonymity is something anyone can find here.

ME: Is that why you left Denver?

AVERY: (*Pauses a moment.*) If I wore a pair of heels that were too high, it got commented on in the society pages. No one cares about that kind of thing here. It's refreshing to be able to be my own person.

ME: That's definitely a tempting way of life. Your family must miss you terribly, though. Are you planning on being an active part in your father's campaign?

AVERY: I'll always support my father no matter what he does, which he's almost always successful at. No matter what happens with the race, he'll always have the support of his children. But I've had my fill of the public eye. That life suits my parents and brother just fine. I think I'll leave the campaigning to them.

ME: That's right. Your brother, Landon Price, is one of the biggest real estate developers in Denver. Are you two close?

AVERY: We grew up pretty sheltered so the two of us were really all the other had. I'd say we're closer than your average brother and sister.

ME: Do you think your brother will be moving up here with you any time soon?

AVERY: *(She chuckles before answering.)* Even though we're very close, my brother and I are very different people. He lives and breathes city life. Plus my parents aren't nearly as concerned with his activities as they are mine.

ME: Meaning?

AVERY: *(Pauses before answering.)* Maybe because he has a different set of genitals? *(Laughs.)* Who knows? For some reason they focus all their energy on me.

ME: Is that the reason you're not active in your father's business? Is this a rebellion?

AVERY: I wouldn't really say it's a rebellion. I made a decision that I thought best suited me. The corporate life isn't for me, anyway. I doubt I'd have anything valuable to offer. My father has enough VPs and advisers.

ME: *(I smile as I take my first sip of lemonade.)* I've got to say, you are a lot more down to earth than I expected. And there are a lot of girls in this country who wished they were in your shoes.

AVERY: *(She lifts a thin shoulder beneath her linen top.)* Everybody always thinks the grass is greener on the other side. Growing up in the public eye isn't for everyone. I've developed thick skin over the years. But I wouldn't change my life for anything.

ME: Well, I certainly appreciate you granting me this interview. Good luck with your father's campaign.

AVERY: Thank you. I'm going to grab a copy of the magazine when the article is printed.

Erin Kern

From the desk of Jami Alden

Dear Reader,

As I look back on the books I've written over the course of my career, I'm struck by two things:

1) I have a very twisted, sinister imagination, if my villains are anything to go by!
2) I love reunion romances.

Now in real life, if you ran into someone who was still hung up on her high school boyfriend and who held on to that person (consciously or not) as the one true love of her life, you might think she had a screw loose. Unless you've ended up with your high school or college sweetheart, most of us grow up and look back at those we dated in our youth—hopefully with fondness but sometimes with less affection. But rarely do we find ourselves pining for that boy we went to senior prom with.

So I wondered, why do I love this premise so much in romance? Well, I think I may have figured it out. In real life, for most of us, those early relationships run their natural course and fizzle out with little more than a whimper and a gasp.

But in romance novels, those relationships that start out with unbridled intensity end with drama and more drama and leave a wagonload of unfinished business for our hero and heroine. It's that lingering intensity, combined with the weight of unfinished business, that draw our hero and heroine together after so many years. So when they finally find themselves back in the same room together, the attraction is as undeniable as gravity.

When I was coming up with the story for GUILTY AS SIN, I found myself fascinated by the history between my hero, Tommy Ibarra, and my heroine, Kate Beckett. Caught up in the giddy turmoil of first love, they were torn apart amid the most excruciating and tragic circumstances I, as a parent, could ever imagine.

And yet, that intensity and unfinished business lingered. So when they're brought back together, there's no force on Earth that can keep them apart. Still, to say their road to true love is a rocky one is a huge understatement. But I hope in the end that you feel as I do. That after everything Tommy and Kate went through, they've more than earned their happily ever after.

Happy Reading!

Jami Alden

Find out more about Forever Romance!

Visit us at
www.hachettebookgroup.com/publishing_forever.aspx

Find us on Facebook
http://www.facebook.com/ForeverRomance

Follow us on Twitter
http://twitter.com/ForeverRomance

NEW AND UPCOMING TITLES

Each month we feature our new titles
and reader favorites.

CONTESTS AND GIVEAWAYS

We give away galleys, autographed copies,
and all kinds of exclusive items.

AUTHOR INFO

You'll find bios, articles, and links to personal websites
for all your favorite authors—and so much more.

GET SOCIAL

Connect with your favorite authors, editors, and
other Forever fans, and share what's important to you.

THE BUZZ

Sign up for our monthly romance newsletter,
and be the first to read all about it.

VISIT US ONLINE AT

WWW.HACHETTEBOOKGROUP.COM

FEATURES:

- OPENBOOK BROWSE AND SEARCH EXCERPTS
- AUDIOBOOK EXCERPTS AND PODCASTS
- AUTHOR ARTICLES AND INTERVIEWS
- BESTSELLER AND PUBLISHING GROUP NEWS
- SIGN UP FOR E-NEWSLETTERS
- AUTHOR APPEARANCES AND TOUR INFORMATION
- SOCIAL MEDIA FEEDS AND WIDGETS
- DOWNLOAD FREE APPS

Bookmark Hachette Book Group
@ www.HachetteBookGroup.com